The POINT BLANK READER series

ALSO BY JAMES SALLIS:

A

JAMES SALLIS
READER

POINTBLANK

Acknowledgements

"Ukulele and the World's Pain" first appeared in Alfred Hitchcock's Magazine, copyright 2002.
"Blue Devils" first appeared in Alfred Hitchcock's Mystery Magazine, copyright 1996.
"Jim and Mary G" first appeared in *Orbit*, copyright 1970.
"Potato Tree" first appeared in The Magazine of Fantasy & Science Fiction, copyright 1986.
"A Few Last Words" first appeared in *Orbit*, copyright 1968.
"The Creation of Bennie Good" first appeared in *Orbit*, copyright 1969.
"Get Along Home" first appeared on the website 3 AM, copyright 2002.
"When Fire Knew My Name" first appeared on the website Fantastic Metropolis, copyright 2002.
"David Goodis: Life in Black and White" first appeared in High Plains Literary Review and in *Difficult Lives*, copyright 1992 and 1993.
"Feverish Country, This" first appeared in the program booklet for Readercon and on the website Fantastic Metropolis, copyright 2000.
"The High Road" first appeared in the Boston Review, copyright 2001.
"Incomparable Paco" first appeared as the introduction to a new edition of Paco Taibo's novel *An Easy Thing* by Poisoned Pen Press, copyright 2002.
"Falling to Earth" first appeared in The Magazine of Fantasy & Science Fiction, copyright 2000.

Death Will Have Your Eyes was originally published by St. Martin's Press, copyright 1997.

The poems first appeared in Confrontation, Grasslimb, *Immortelles*, Kansas Quarterly, Mudlark, Oasis, South Dakota Review, Negative Capability, New Orleans Review. Some have appeared, additionally, in the author's collections *Sorrow's Kitchen* and *Black Night's Gonna Catch Me Here: Selected Poems 1968-2002*.

"Increments" first appeared in Dallas Life, copyright 1983.
"Gently into the Land of the Meateaters" first appeared in Western Humanities Review, copyright 1984.
"Approaching the Page" first appeared on website Web Del Sol, copyright 2003.
"Pushing Envelopes" first appeared in *Gently into the Land of the Meateaters*, copyright 2000.
"Temporary Life" first appeared in Negative Capability, copyright 1991.

Renderings was originally published by Black Heron Press, copyright 1995.

To my readers

Introduction

When I look back, I remember long summer afternoons on the screened-in porch with colorful spun-aluminum tumblers of Kool-Aid or pre-sweetened iced tea and books. Biographies of Houdini and of Shelley, *The Winter of Our Discontent*, loads of Heinlein, *Fires of Spring*, a slick-size science fiction magazine devoted to Stanley Weinbaum, Richard Matheson's *Third from the Sun*, the latest issue of If or F&SF, much of Dickens, all of Thomas Wolfe.

I don't know when, precisely, the decision got made. But move along a very few years, past New Orleans and Tulane dorms where I wrote the first of many bad poems, and find me staring out at the darkness that's been thrown like a hood over neighboring Midwest cornfields as, crouched above a Remington Quietriter given periodically to tossing the heads of keys across the room when struck, I type, nearing the end of my first published story: *He's giving me the eye, so I take it and put it in my wallet right next to the finger someone gave me the day before.* It's well past midnight, all are asleep, and likely as not there's Sonny Boy Williamson playing on the phonograph or, if the radio's on instead, maybe Buffalo Springfield. *Something's happening here, What it is ain't exactly clear.*

Then, I listened to news of Vietnam. Writing this introduction, with much the same horror and shame, daily I am inundated by tales of Bush & Co.'s invasion of Iraq.

Skip a couple years past corn and kazoos and it's a window off Portobello Road in London that I'm looking out. A BBC version of *Inherit the Wind*, Donovan songs and "Mrs. Robinson" play on the transistor radio on my desk, its speaker the size of a British penny. Martin Luther King and Bobby Kennedy go down while I'm there. Often, hearing of new deaths, new deceits, I turn off my desk lamp and sit motionless in the dark, taking what comfort I can from the low, steady hum of the Quietriter's tiny engine.

Next our rented, Charles Addam-like house in Milford, an apartment on 12th in the Village, the dexter half of a duplex up flight after flight of terrace stairs in Brookline, Massachusetts. One morning coming home on the streetcar I buy the Boston Globe and open it to find a review of my first book.

These days, I write for the Globe.

As I say, just when the decision got made, I don't know, but by the time I was 20 or so it had become fairly obvious that I was going to be a writer. It was also fairly obvious that, marked by my taste for fantastic literature, I was not, at least not always, going to be a realist writer. I would face the events of my day, the events that battered at me, body counts, the end of relationships, corrupt administrations, my son's suicide, the overthrow of other nations by subterfuge or brute might, not head-on but slantwise.

Renderings, for instance, the short novel included here. I'm not certain how much its description of a ruined and dying world has directly to do with what was taking place in southeast Asia when I first conceived it, or with my own failing marriage. Quite a lot, I suspect. One critic believes *Renderings*—written in the summer that produced *The Long-Legged Fly* as well as half a dozen strong stories and a goodly clutch of poems—to be central to my work. As for realism: about my house, *Renderings* has become something of a watershed, with me resolutely insist that the story's events actually take place, that it's a science fiction novel, while my wife holds that they occur only in the protagonist's imagination.

As a Southerner, I come from a culture whose coarse grain in my youth remained unground to meal on the great American millstone. I grew up eating pig's tails, salt pork and squirrel with brown gravy; and all about me, civility, the single force that more than any other binds civilization, was bespoke in such gestures as standing when elders or women entered the room. It was a culture that in many ways exalted the individual and the peculiar. My first girlfriend had an uncle, quite mad, shambling about the house and carrying on imaginary conversations in corners. As a child I played exclusively with African-American children, the generations of whose parents had survived by dissembling. Why then should it seem strange that I came to speak slantwise about precisely those things most important to me?

The work herein documents forty years of a man sitting alone in a room. You'll find poems both of mimetic and of fantastic bent, science fiction stories, realist stories, essays on literature, and personal essays, along with two novels in their entirety, one a spy novel, the other (depending upon whether you accept my wife's reading or mine) a fantasy or science fiction novel. The single notable omission is my writing on music, for which there was simply not room. Those interested should seek out the recent University of Nebraska Press edition of *The Guitar Players*.

A friend has suggested that it all comes of not being able to decide what I want to be when I grow up, another from the simple fact that, if you keep moving, they can't get a bead on you. At literary gatherings, asked about influences, I'm as likely to cite science fiction and horror movies of the Fifties as I am James Joyce or Albert Camus. For many, many years, no matter what I wrote at the time, I thought of myself as primarily a poet. In recent years a major portion of my income derives from, and hence larger segments of my writing time are given over to, reviews and criticism. While for a long, long time now, whatever other projects might be underway, there's always been, sitting in the driveway with parts scattered about, the half-built hulk of a novel.

Think of this Reader as a personal storage shed: priceless souvenirs, mysteriously full boxes, and chairs missing a leg, all in a jumble.

Recently, having decided I don't have enough to do with a book or two to write each year and reviews and columns forever on deadline (maybe *this* is what I'll be when I grow up?) I began teaching. Two or three days a week I stand there trying to define for my students just what it is a writer does, and how.

One night after a phone conversation with her parents, I tell them, Karyn mentioned that they'd been to see a stage version of *Little Shop of Horrors*, and that the theater had paid $3000 to rent an Audrey. She went on, but I hardly heard what more she said: I was off the block, head spinning with scene after scene about a store that rents Audreys. ("Hey, Margie, that stalk look okay to you?")

Or I tell them about the morning I saw in the newspaper a reference to someone's diary and sat there for long moments imagining a woman who when young saves up to buy a costly, finely-bound notebook in which to record her life. It goes with her everywhere, city to city, apartment to house to hospital to nursing home, always the first thing she unpacks. Long years after, she dies, and her daughter opens the notebook only to find that her mother has never made a single entry. The pages are blank.

That's what writers do, I say to students. We don't listen to our spouses, because we're too busy making up stories, or trying to overhear the conversation at the next table. We see the word *diary* and a whole life, a whole world, drops into our heads.

I suspect that they want secrets, my students, but this is the only secret I have to give them: You never learn how to do it. You only learn that you can. And you learn that again and again, every time.

James Sallis

STORIES

Ukulele and the World's Pain

Sure, I killed the son of a bitch. I mean, what right did he think he had, bursting out in laughter like that when I took Miss Shelley out of her case? I'm a professional, too. I was getting scale just like him. I've paid my union dues and a lot more dues besides.

It was a good date. Sonny Martin had made a name for himself in country music, and now he was doing what he'd been talking about doing for years, he was cutting a jazz album. I'd played on a couple of Martin sessions before. He liked the freshness of the sound, I guess. And he knew that jazz was my first love, too. One time during a session break, I remember, I think this was on his album *Longneck Love*, we started goofing on "Don't Get Around Much Anymore," just the two of us, and before we knew, everybody else had picked his instrument back up and was playing along.

Playing music's not about making sounds, you know, it's about listening. Everything unfolds out of the first note, that first attack.

Sonny always reminded me a lot of the great George Barnes, just this plain, balding, fat guy with a Barcalounger and two or three cheap suits at home doing his job, only his job happened to be, instead of working as an auto mechanic or Sears salesman, recording country hits. Or in this case, playing great jazz and backup. You half-expected a cigar stump to be sticking out of his mouth there above the Gibson.

By contrast, the guy who thought Miss Shelley was so funny was a real Bubba type with stringy hair, glasses that kept sliding down his nose and getting pushed back up, and run-over white shoes with plastic buckles most of the gold paint had come off of. He played a fair guitar, but you know what? That's not enough. Besides him, there was a drummer who looked vaguely familiar and couldn't have been more than nineteen, the great, loose Morty Epstein on bass, and a pianist who gave the impression of spending more time in concert halls than with the likes of us.

We slammed around on a 12-bar shuffle just to start the thing running and get acquainted, and that went well, with the guitar sliding in these little pulls, bends and stumbling, broken runs way up high—Sonny's guitar was so solid Bubba could float. But towards the end he left off that and, staying high, started strumming on just two or three strings, looking over at me.

Sonny called "Sweet Georgia Brown" and we worked it through a time or two by ear, kind of clanging and clunking along, then Sonny had the guitar player scribble out some quick charts. I got mine and we started running it and a line or two in, looking ahead, I can see it's wrong. So I just played right on past it, grinning at the guitar player the whole time. As we started winding down, Sonny nodded me in for a solo. I took a chorus and it was pretty hot and he signalled for another and that one was steaming, and then we all took off again. I looked over and the piano man's staring at me, shaking his head, fingers going on about their business there below. Looks like he just ate a cat.

Next we worked up a head version of a slow, ballady blues, then put some time in on jamming "Take the A Train" and "Lulu's Back in Town." Again Bubba threw some charts together and again mine was wrong—wildly wrong this time. He did everything but hop keys on me. I don't know, maybe his mother was frightened by some Hawaiian when he was in there in the womb growing that greasy hair and trying on those white shoes.

That's where Miss Shelley and her kin came from—you all know that. But you probably don't know much more. That it emerged around 1877, most likely as a derivative of a four-string folk guitar, the *machada* or *machete*, introduced to the islands by the Portuguese. Or how it hitched a ride back to the U.S. with returning sailors and soldiers. Martin started selling them in 1916; Gibson, Regal, Vega, Harmony and Kay all offered standard to premium models alongside their guitars, banjos and mandolins; National manufactured resonator ukes. Briefly, banjo ukuleles came into favor. Other variations include the somewhat larger taropatch, an eight-string uke of paired strings, and the tiple, whose two outer courses of steel strings are doubled, with an additional third string added to the two inner courses and tuned an octave lower. Mario Maccaferri, the man who designed the great Django Reinhardt's guitar, after losing half a million or so with plastic guitars no one would buy, recouped with sale of some nine million plastic ukes. And the players! The ever-amazing Roy Smeck. Cliff Edwards, known as Ukulele Ike. Or Lyle Ritz. Trained on violin, he was a top studio bass player in the 60s and 70s and turned out three astonishing albums of straightahead jazz ukulele.

We worked through what we had again, then broke for lunch. Morty and I grabbed hot dogs at the taco stand by the park across the street and sat on a bench catching up. The fountain was clogged with food wrappers, leaves and cigarette butts as usual. Kids in swings were shoved screaming towards the sky. Old men sat on benches tossing stale bread at pigeons. Morty's son had just started college all the way up in Iowa, he told me, studying physical chemistry, whatever that was. Better be looking for more gigs, I said. He shook his head. Don't I know it, he said. Don't I know it. I told Morty I had a quick errand that couldn't wait, I'd see him inside.

Well, we got back from lunch break, as you know, everybody but the guitar player, and after we wait a while and drink up a pot of coffee Sonny says: Anybody see Walt out there? But none of us know him, of course, and who'd want to look at that greasy hair while he was eating?

So we—Sonny, I should say—finally called the session off, shut it down. And I do regret that. Some fine music was *this close* to being cut.

Can I tell you one thing before we go?

There's this story about Eric Dolphy. He's called in to overdub on a session. Brings all his instruments along. He listens to the tape and what he does is he adds this single note, on bass clarinet, right at the end. That's it. He collects scale for the session, puts his horn back in the case, and goes home. But what he did there, what that one note was, was Dolphy finding his holy moment, you know? That's what we're all looking for, what we go on looking for, that single holy moment, all our lives.

Blue Devils

All the way up from El Paso, which is where you first start noticing how much *sky* there is, the image stays with me. I've managed to shut it away for a long time, but now, maybe because we're on the spoor, getting close, it comes back. I look up at a cloud the size of Idaho, and there it is. At a mountain rising from the ground like a fist polished smooth: there, too. And in cholla and scrub cactus at the side of the road.

"I could definitely use a beer about now. You could probably do with a break, too. Unless you feel the need to push on, that is."

I look over at him. What he's said is slow to register. The world comes to me these days in a kind of stutter, like the time delay on radio talk shows.

"Maybe we could grab something to go?" I'm dry myself, from looking out at this landscape as much as for any other reason.

He nods once, eyes straight ahead as always. Both hands are loosely on the wheel, left elbow a buttress in the window. At the next exit he swings off into a service plaza larger than many of the Southern towns I grew up in. My father was career military, outspoken enough at the incompetencies and inefficiencies involved that he was repeatedly transferred. I counted once: eleven high schools. Maybe that's why I myself have always had such respect for authority. But it could have gone either way.

He fills up, goes inside to pay, and comes out with a six-pack of Heineken and the Slice I asked for. Back on the road he pops one of the beers and sips at it for the next thirty miles. The rest are tucked away under his legs. The two of us, the Slice, and the beer bottles just about fill the little Miata.

Flies.

The sound of them was what I always remembered, always thought of. Then Sergeant Van Zandt's voice at last penetrating. How many times has he already asked?

You okay, Mr. Gorman?

I nodded, said could I see her.

*Well, generally...*He stopped. Motioned with one hand for attendants to uncover her. A plain, somewhat muscular woman herself not much older than Faith folded back a corner, watching me closely the whole time. I nodded, and she put the cover back in place.

It's Faith, then. It's your daughter, Van Zandt said.

Yes.

"You understand that we can't do anything here," Delany says. I lurch back up into the world as it is. "There's no outstanding warrant, which severely limits the scope of my actions."

I went to him because of his reputation as a bounty hunter.

"So here's what we do. We go in, have a look, poke through the ashes of the campfire. We find something, anything at all, then we ask the locals to step in. You okay with that?"

I nod. I see my daughter's face below me, shimmering in heat that rises off the asphalt. An eye is gone. Ear and scalp are torn away on that side.

Delany pulls out another beer, drops the empty bottle back in the pack.

We're coming into the Chiricahuas, mountains unlike any others I know, ghostly somehow, the whole range eroded by wind, water and time to skull-like stands of stone honeycombed with caves and unlikely passages where Cochise eluded all pursuers.

Farther on, past Tucson, reservation lands lie slumbering to every horizon, cluttered briefly by trailers or tarpaper shacks, rusting automobiles and appliances, propane tanks.

"Unless you want to cancel all that and just blow him away, of course," Delany says.

He was, I was told, the best in the state at finding people—the best, period. That information came almost a year after Faith's death, on my last visit to Van Zandt's cubicle tucked away on the fourth floor behind rows of filing cabinets that looked as though cars had been driven repeatedly into them.

"There's just not much else I can do for you, Mr. Gorman," Van Zandt said. "The case remains open, of course. We don't officially close homicides. And bulletins will stay in circulation—till they're crowded out by new ones, at least. You never know. Sometimes things fall into our lap when we least expect it. Meanwhile, you might want to consider giving this man a call. I'm not telling you this as a cop, of course. I have a daughter myself."

He slid a business card across the desk to me with two crooked fingers, tapped it once with the index, and let go.

"He's a detective. Specializes in finding people, and he's damned good at it. Lots, including some who do the same kind of work, say there's no one better."

I looked down at the card. Buff-colored, almost translucent parchment. And engraved: not thermography. Just SEAN DELANY and a phone number.

Brought up on cheap detective movies and hardboiled novels, despite the card I'd half expected to find Delany in some gin mill with a cigarette hanging out one side of his mouth and a madeover blonde on the other arm, with eyes like bad sunsets and a tie that doubled as napkin. Instead, by way of his answering service and a secretary who called back immediately, I found him at Geronimo's, a mid-city health club. He was finishing up a set of handball, had a thing or two to talk over with the investment counselor who'd been his opponent, and would see me outside in five minutes if that was all right.

We met at his car, a British-green Miata. He had traded sweatshirt and shorts for a full-cut cotton suit like the ones Haspel used to make down in New Orleans and wore a knit, alligatorless shirt beneath. At a mall nearby he ordered felafel from a Greek fast-food stall, and I had three coffees as we talked.

What do you do, Mr. Gorman? he asked at one point.

I'm an architect. I build things.

We talked a while longer, and he agreed to help me.

From the first I've been won over by Delany's quiet-spoken, self-assured, ever-so-civilized manner. But now as we move ever farther from the city— into the scruffy hills and scrubland of West Texas, through ancient, barren New Mexico, and on into Arizona, growth like bright green veins in runnels formed by water washing down mountainsides—I can't help but notice how that's begun changing. Simple things, at first: endings dropped from a word here or there, rougher cadences. Then articles and conjugations drop out, leaving behind a language all nouns, present-tense verbs, prepositions. The man with whom I get out of the car in Tucson seems not at all the one with whom I began the trip back in Fort Worth.

"It doesn't have anything to do with justice or finding the person responsible," Chris said to me a few nights before. We'd met for coffee at a carefully neutral restaurant. She came directly from work; I, now unemployed, from the one-room apartment I'd finally settled into after months of motel rooms. "Don't you see that? That's why I left, why I had to. It's the *world* you want to hurt now, Joe. You want to hear it scream, want to tear something away from it, want to hurt it as much as it's hurt you."

Hurt? No. What I feel is numb. What I feel is nothing. I look out at the world and don't recognize, don't register, what's there. Only with effort, in a kind of forced gulp, will my mind take it in.

"Welcome to Tucson," Delany says.

The city has come surreptitiously up around us and now seems to go on forever, sprawling across this treeless, light-struck landscape. Distinctive mountain ranges stand at each point of the compass. A map names them for me:

Catalina, Santa Rita, Rincon, Tucson. We drive along something called the Speedway past The Bashful Bandit, Empress Theater and Book Store XXX, Weinerschnitzel. Past bars, fast-food emporiums, video shops, used-car lots, hardware and auto-parts stores.

"The Miracle Mile," Delany says. "But most people around here just call it the Armpit." Pickup trucks with bodies rusted wholly through in moldlike patches overtake us, leave us behind. "Place we're looking for's up ahead a little ways."

He pulls into the parking lot of a motel that looks as though it might have been built early in the Fifties when such things were novelties. It's set back off the road half a lot or so. The wooden sign is shaped like a palm tree, with the legend REFRIGERATED AIR and its name, NO-TEL MOTEL, painted on.

"Room fourteen," Delany tells me.

It's on the second tier. Inside, a TV plays loudly: sirens, brakes screaming, metal slamming into metal.

"We're in luck." He knocks.

"Yeah?"

"Maintenance. Sorry to bother you, but we've got a major water leak downstairs. Have to check it out. Take us a minute or two, tops."

"Hang on."

Nothing for a time—Delany and I exchange glances—then the door opens a couple of inches, and a slat of face shows in the crack. Sharp, finlike nose, small mouth, drooping eyelid. Day's growth of beard.

He takes in Delany's clothes.

"Hell, man, you ain't—"

But Delany ducks his shoulder into the door, hard, and keeps going.

The man inside staggers back out of the way as the door slams against the wall. He reaches for the rear pocket of his jeans. Delany is there. Stomps down on his instep and, when he bends forward over the pain, pivots behind him on one foot, grabbing his long hair in a fist. The man's eyes round as Delany's hand tightens.

"Be nice," Delany tells him. "Man needs to talk to you."

I step inside and shut the door.

Wary, expressionless eyes follow me.

Delany pulls a gun out of the man's back pocket and hands it to me.

"Your call," he says, stepping off to the side.

So I shoot him.

Delany lets go of the hair as the man goes down. When he tries to breathe, air whistles out of his chest. He puts a hand gently against himself as if to hold the air in, says *Shit* with an even louder whistle, and is still. I notice there's no difference in the eyes.

"Cops be here in six minutes tops," Delany says.

He's standing by the bedside table looking through things piled up there, magazines, a cheap plastic wallet, stray bills and change, a couple of envelopes.

"But we got us another problem," he tells me.

"Yeah?"

"Wrong bird."

I look at him.

"This wasn't your man." He holds up a folded paper from one of the envelopes. "Gentleman here's freshly laundered, just out of the joint. Been a guest of the state almost three years."

"But how…"

He shrugs. "Information's what you make of it. I thought we had a fit. Sometimes it doesn't work out right. Sometimes it does."

Delany takes the gun from me, wipes it with his handkerchief, and puts it in the dead man's hand. He presses the hand hard against the grip, feeds the forefinger into the trigger guard.

"Thing is," he says, "does it matter?"

And I realize that it doesn't. That it doesn't matter at all. Someone's paid. A life's been taken. That's what matters. Maybe I understood all along, understood without knowing I understood, that this was the best I could hope for. Maybe Delany knew that, too.

We go down the back stairs, get in the Miata, and pull away, north on Oracle to West Miracle Mile, then due west till we jump I-10, hearing sirens build to a scream behind us. I watch the Catalina mountains, the Tucson mountains, all this sky. Everything bright and alive, sharply defined, in the noonday sun. I can go back to building things now.

Later I look up again at the Chiricahuas and think how little we've changed. We huddle together in the vertical caverns of our cities, around our megawatt campfires, and try to fill up the darkness with chants, songs, magic. We understand so little, we're always afraid, and sometimes still, the best we can do is offer up a sacrifice—hoping to drive out whatever blue devils overtake us.

Jim and Mary G

Getting his little coat down off the hook, then his arms into it, not easy because he's so excited and he always turns the wrong way anyhow. And all the
time he's looking up at you with those blue eyes. We go park Papa, he says.
We go see gulls. Straining for the door. The gulls are a favorite; he discovered
them on the boat coming across and can't understand, he keeps looking for
them in the park.

Wrap the muffler around his neck. Yellow, white. (Notice how white the
skin is there, how the veins show through.) They call them scarves here don't
they. Stockingcap—he pulls it down over his eyes, going Haha. He hasn't
learned to laugh yet. Red mittens. Now move the zipper up and he's packed
away. The coat's green corduroy, with black elastic at the neck and cuffs
and a round hood that goes down over the cap. It's November. In England.
Thinking, The last time I'll do this. Is there still snow on the ground, I didn't
look this morning.

Take his hand and go on out of the flat. Letting go at the door because
it takes two hands to work the latch, Mary rattling dishes in the kitchen.
(Good-bye, she says very softly as you shut the door.) He goes around you
and beats you to the front door, waits there with his nose on the glass. The
hall is full of white light. Go on down it to him. The milk's come, two bottles,
with the *Guardian* leaning between them. Move the mat so we can open the
door, We go park Papa, we seegulls. Frosty foggy air coming in. Back for
galoshes, all the little brass-tongue buckles? No the snow's gone. Just some
dirty slush. Careful. Down the steps.

Crunching down the sidewalk ahead of you, disappointed because there's
no snow but looking back, Haha. We go park? The sky is flat and white as a
sheet of paper. Way off, a flock of birds goes whirling across it, circling inside
themselves—black dots, like iron filings with a magnet under the paper. The
block opposite is lined with trees. What kind? The leaves are all rippling together. It looks like green foil. Down the walk.

Asking, Why is everything so still. Why aren't there any cars. Or a mail-
truck. Or milkcart, gliding along with bottles jangling. Where is everyone. It's
ten in the morning, where is everyone.

But there is a car just around the corner, stuck on ice at the side of the road where it parked last night with the wheels spinning Whrrrrrr. Smile, you understand a man's problems. And walk the other way. His mitten keeps coming off in your hand. Haha.

She had broken down only once, at breakfast.

The same as every morning, the child had waked them. Standing in his bed in the next room and bouncing up and down till the springs were banging against the frame. Then he climbed out and came to their door, peeking around the frame, finally doing his tiptoe shyly across the floor in his white wool nightshirt. Up to their bed, where they pretended to be still asleep. Brekpust, Brekpust, he would say, poking at them and tugging the covers, at last climbing onto the bed to bounce up and down between them until they rolled over: Hello. Morninggg. He is proud of his g's. Then, Mary almost broke down, remembering what today was, what they had decided the night before.

She turned her face toward the window (they hadn't been able to afford curtains yet) and he heard her breathe deeply several times. But a moment later she was up—out of bed in her quilted robe and heading for the kitchen, with the child behind her.

He reached and got a cigarette off the trunk they were using as a night table. It had a small wood lamp, a bra, some single cigarettes and a jarlid full of ashes and filters on it. Smoking, listening to water running, pans clatter, cupboards and drawers. Then the sounds stopped and he heard them together in the bathroom: the tap ran for a while, then the toilet flushed and he heard the child's pleased exclamations. They went back into the kitchen and the sounds resumed. Grease crackling, the child chattering about how good he had been. The fridge door opened and shut, opened again, Mary said something. He was trying to help.

He got out of bed and began dressing. How strange that she'd forgotten to take him to the bathroom first thing, she'd never done that before. Helpinggg, from the kitchen by way of explanation, as he walked to the bureau. It was square and ugly, with that shininess peculiar to cheap furniture, and it had been in the flat when they moved in, the only thing left behind. He opened a drawer and took out a shirt. All his shirts were white. Why, she had once asked him, years ago. He didn't know, then or now.

He went into the kitchen with the sweater over his head. "Mail?" Through the wool. Neither of them looked around, so he pulled it the rest of the way on, reaching down inside to tug the shirtcollar out. Then the sleeves.

"A letter from my parents. They're worried they haven't heard from us, they hope we're all right. Daddy's feeling better, why don't we write them."

The child was dragging his highchair across the floor from the corner.

Long ago they had decided he should take care of as many of his own needs as he could—a sense of responsibility, Mary had said—but this morning Jim helped him carry the chair to the table, slid the tray off, lifted him into it and pushed the chair up to the table. When he looked up, Mary turned quickly away, back to the stove.

Eggs, herring, toast and ham. "I thought it would be nice," Mary said. "To have a good breakfast." And that was the time she broke down.

The child had started scooping the food up in his fingers, so she got up again and went across the kitchen to get his spoon. It was heavy silver, with an ivory *K* set into the handle, and it had been her own. She turned and came back across the tile, holding the little spoon in front of her and staring at it. Moma cryinggg, the child said. Moma cryinggg. She ran out of the room. The child turned in his chair to watch her go, then turned back and went on eating with the spoon. The plastic padding squeaked as the child moved inside it. The chair was metal, the padding white with large blue asterisks all over it. They had bought it at a Woolworth's. Twelve and six. Like the bureau, it somehow fit the flat.

A few minutes later Mary came back, poured coffee for both of them and sat down across from him.

"It's best this way," she said. "He won't have to suffer. It's the only answer."

He nodded, staring into the coffee. Then took off his glasses and cleaned them on his shirttail. The child was stirring the eggs and herring together in his bowl. Holding the spoon like a chisel in his hand and going round and round the edge of the bowl.

"Jim..."

He looked up. She seemed to him, then, very tired, very weak.

"We could take him to one of those places. Where they...take care of them...for you."

He shook his head, violently. "No, we've already discussed that, Mary. He wouldn't understand. It will be easier, my way. If I do it myself."

She went to the window and stood there watching it. It filled most of one wall. It was frosted over.

"How would you like to go for a walk after breakfast," he asked the child. He immediately shoved the bowl away and said, "Bafroom first?"

"You or me?" Mary said from the window.

Finally: "You."

He sat alone in the kitchen, thinking. Taps ran, the toilet flushed, he came out full of pride. "We go park," he said. "We go see gulls."

"Maybe." It was this, the lie, which came back to him later; this was what he remembered most vividly. He got up and walked into the hall with the child following him and put his coat on. "Where's his other muffler?"

"In the bureau drawer. The top one."

He got it, then began looking for the stockingcap and mittens. Walking through the rooms, opening drawers. There aren't any seagulls in London. When she brought the cap and mittens to him there was a hole in the top of the cap and he went off looking for the other one. Walking through rooms, again and again into the child's own.

"For God's sake go on," she finally said. "Please stop. O damn Jim, go on." And she turned and ran back into the kitchen.

Soon he heard her moving about. Clearing the table, running water, opening and shutting things. Silverware clicking.

"We go park?"

He began to dress the child. Getting his little coat down off the hook. Wrapping his neck in the muffler. There aren't any seagulls in London. Stockingcap, Haha.

Thinking, This is the last time I'll ever do this.

Now bump, bump, bump. Down the funny stairs.

When he returned, Mary was lying on the bed, still in the quilted robe, watching the ceiling. It seemed very dark, very cold in the room. He sat down beside her in his coat and put his hand on her arm. Cars moved past the window. The people upstairs had their radio on.

"Why did you move the bureau?" he asked after a while.

Without moving her head she looked down toward the foot of the bed. "After you left I was lying here and I noticed a traffic light or something like that out on the street was reflected in it. It was blinking on and off, I must have watched it for an hour. We've been here for weeks and I never saw that before. But once I did, I had to move it."

"You shouldn't be doing heavy work like that."

For a long while she was still, and when she finally moved, it was just to turn her head and look silently into his face.

He nodded, once, very slowly.

"It didn't..."

No.

She smiled, sadly, and still in his coat, he lay down beside her in the small bed. She seemed younger now, rested, herself again. There was warmth in her hand when she took his own and put them together on her stomach.

They lay quietly through the afternoon. Ice was re-forming on the streets; outside, they could hear wheels spinning, engines racing. The hall door opened, there was a jangle of milkbottles, the door closed. Then everything was quiet. The trees across the street drooped under the weight of the ice.

There was a sound in the flat. Very low and steady, like a ticking. He listened for hours before he realized it was the drip of a faucet in the bathroom.

Outside, slowly, obscuring the trees, the night came. And with it, snow. They lay together in the darkness, looking out the frosted window. Occasionally, lights moved across it.

"We'll get rid of his things tomorrow," she said after a while.

Potato Tree

We've found the problem," Dr. Morgan told me.

After a moment I said, "Yes?"

"Basically," he said, "you're crazy as batshit."

He was right, of course, but at ninety dollars an hour I had expected more. I waited. That seemed to be it.

"I see. Well. Is there anything you can do?"

"Oh, yes, a number of things. There are several quite interesting drugs on the market. Years of psychiatry—that might be fun. Shock, megavitamin therapy, behavioral training. Probably a lot of others. I'd have to look it all up."

He swiveled his chair to watch a traffic helicopter swing by outside the window. From his new position he said, "Of course, none of them will help any. You're crazy as batshit and basically you're just going to have to live with it, accept it. Here, I wrote it down for you."

He swiveled back and handed me an index card upon which was printed in large block letters: C A B S. Below, in a painstaking tiny script, were an asterisk and the words "crazy as batshit."

"It shouldn't really be any great bother. I mean, you'll be able to keep on going to dentists, reading cereal boxes, having regular bowel movements, humming old songs—all the important stuff. Just a little bit of an interpretative dysfunction, that's all. You just won't ever know if things are as they seem to you; they could be *quite* different."

He wet a finger and wiped at a smudge on the desktop.

"I, for instance, could well be a wig-maker. A canoeist. We may at this moment be the sole attendants of a missile silo in Kansas. Do you play bridge?"

"No."

"Good. Hate that damned game."

He swiveled again to look out the window.

"Is there anything else you can tell me?" I said after a while. "Any advice, recommendations?"

"Only this," he said. "Go with it, ride it. Enjoy it." He turned back to me. "Most of us live in a much duller world than yours, you know." There was something very like envy in the poor man's voice.

"Thank you, Doctor," I said, rising from my chair and looking for the last time at his wall of diplomas. "You've been a great help."

"It's nothing." He removed his glasses, breathed against them, fumbled in pockets for a handkerchief. "Give me a call now and again to let me know how you're getting along." He looked back at the smudge through clean glasses.

"I'll do that."

I walked a few steps to the door. There was no knob, only a hand protruding from the wood which clasped my own in a handshake. I pulled against it, opening the door.

"Don't forget your diagnosis," the doctor said behind me. I turned. The index card dropped to the floor and scuttled towards me.

The world looked not at all different, unchanged by my illness as it had been by my former health, in short, uncaring. The first elevator was full—all of them wearing the doctor's face, perhaps patients of his—and I waited. Eventually I made it down to the plaza and sat on one of the benches under a potato tree. Some of the hospital patients were having a wheelchair race on the grounds, pursued by grim-faced, limping nurses.

"May I join you for just a moment?"

I looked up into a face of great and radiant beauty, though pale. She collapsed onto the bench beside me.

"Are you all right?"

"Fine. Just give me a moment, I'll be okay. Please."

I spent the moment looking at the oxblood gleam of her boots, at the tug and thrust of sweater, into the depths of her gray eyes. Never had I felt more alone; my loneliness entered me like a bullet.

"Well. I proved they were wrong, at least," she said.

"I'm sorry?"

"The doctors...Listen, forgive me. I don't want to inflict you with my troubles. You must have plenty of your own."

"Not really. I'm crazy, you see: nothing can touch me."

I took out the index card and showed it to her. A potato fell to the ground at our feet. The index card leapt onto it and began to feed.

"How wonderful, to have an *interesting* disease. All *I* have's cancer."

"What kind?"

"The worst kind, of course, but it's still pretty dull."

I put out my hand and she held it, just as the door had earlier. We sat together looking out over the grounds as a light snow began to fall. Beside us the potato tree thrust into the sky as though *it* were a hand intent on tearing out that white down, intent upon opening it. The patients had turned on their nurses and were chasing them about the grounds, laughing joyously as they crunched bones with the wheelchairs. Children sat watching.

"How long do you have?" I said finally.

"Not long. They said I wouldn't even get out of the building, it was so bad."

"*How* long?"

She looked at her watch.

"Ten minutes," she said, floating into my arms.

A Few Last Words

What is the silence
a. As though it had a right to more
—W. S. Merwin

AGAIN:

He was eating stained glass and vomiting rainbows. He looked up and there was the clock moving toward him, grinning, arms raised in a shout of triumph over its head. The clock advanced; he smelled decay; he was strangled to death by the hands of time....He was in a red room. The hands of the clock knocked knocked knocked without entering....And changed again. The hours had faces, worse than the hands. He choked it was all so quiet only the ticking the faces were coming closer closer he gagged screamed once and—

Sat on the edge of the bed. The hall clock was ticking loudly, a sound like dried peas dropping into a pail. This was the third night.

The pumpkin-color moon dangled deep in the third quadrant of the cross-paned window. Periodically clouds would touch the surface and partly fill with color, keeping it whole. Dust and streaks on the window, a tiny bubble of air, blurred its landscape; yellow drapes beside it took on a new hue.

He had watched it for hours (must have been hours). Its only motion was a kind of visual dopplering. It sped out into serene depths, skipped back in a rush to paste itself against the backside of the glass, looking like a spot of wax. Apogee to perigee to apogee, and no pause between. Rapid vacillation, losing his eyes in intermediate distances, making him blink and squint, glimmering in the pale overcast. And other than that it hadn't moved. Abscissa +, ordinate +. Stasis.

This was the third night.

His wife stirred faintly and reached to touch his pillow, eyelids fluttering. Hoover quickly put out his hand and laid it across her fingers. Visibly, she settled back into blankets. In the hall, the clock ticked like a leaking faucet. The moon was in its pelagic phase, going out.

The third night of the dreams. The third night that lying in bed he was overcome by: Presence. In the dark it would grow around him, crowding his eyes open, bunching his breath, constricting—at last driving him from the bed, the room. He would pace the rugs and floors, turn back and away again on the stairs, wondering. He would drink liquor, then coffee, unsure which effect he wanted, uneasy at conclusions—certain only of this sense of cramping, of imposition. In the dark he was ambushed, inhabited, attacked again from within.

His wife turned in bed, whispering against sheets, taking her fingers away.

Hoover lifted his head to the dresser, chinoiserie chair, sculpt lamé valet, to glazed chintz that hid the second, curiously small window. A simple room, sparse, clean, a room with no waste of motion. And a familiar room, intimate and informal as the back of his hand, yet his eyes moving through it now encountered a strangeness, a distortion. He cast his vision about the room, tracing the strangeness back to its source at the window: to pale plastic light that slipped in there and took his furniture away into distances. It occurred to him that he was annoyed by this intrusion, this elusive division of himself from his things. He watched the moon and it stared back, unblinking.

Hoover fixed his chin between his fists, propped elbows on knees, and became a sculpture. His face turned again to see the window, head rolling in his hands, ball-in-socket.

A cave, he thought: that was the effect. Gloom, and moonlight sinking through cracks: pitch and glimmer. A skiagraphy of the near and foreign. Quarantine and communion, solitude and confederation. A cave, shaped in this strange light.

And bruising the light's influence, he walked to the chair and stared down at the suit he'd draped over one arm—looked at the hall clock—ten minutes ago. It was happening faster now....

The suit was pale, stale-olive green and it shined in a stronger light. The coat barely concealed the jutting, saddle-like bones of his hips; his wrists dangled helplessly away from the sleeve ends like bones out of a drumstick—and Cass hated it. Regardless of fit, though, it *felt* right: he was comfortable in it, was himself.

He took the coat from the chair, held it a minute, and put it back. Somehow, tonight, it seemed inappropriate, like the man-shaped valet that no one used. As with the room, the furniture, it had been taken away from him.

He turned and shuffled across the rug to search through the crow-black corner closet behind the creaking, always-open door, discovering a western shirt with a yoke of roses across its breast and trying it on, then jeans, belting them tightly, and boots. The clothes were loose, looser than he remembered, but they felt good, felt right.

Stepping full into light at the door, he shattered strangeness, and looking back saw that the moon was now cockeyed in the corner of the pane.

Ticking of a clock, sound of feet down stairs.

He assassinated death with the cold steel rush of his breathing....

The night was pellucid, a crystal of blackness; hermetic with darkness. He moved within a hollow black crystal and up there was another, an orange separate crystal, bubble in a bubble....And quiet, so quiet so still, only the ticking of his feet, the whisper of breath. He pocketed his hands and wished for the coat he'd left behind.

Hoover turned onto the walk, heels clacking (another death: to silence).

A sepulchral feeling, he thought, to the thin wash of light overlaying this abyss of street. A counterpoint, castrati and bass. Peel away the light and you: Plunge. Downward. Forever.

Another thought....you can tell a lot by the way a person listens to silence.

(Sunday. It was evening all day. Over late coffee and oranges, the old words begin again. The speech too much used, and no doors from this logic of love. We go together like rain and melancholy, blue and morning....)

At the corner, turn; and on down this new abyss. Breath pedaling, stabbing into the air like a silent cough, feet killing quiet—

I am intruding.

Darkness is avenging itself on my back.

(And I, guilty realist, dabbler at verses, saying: There is no sign for isolation but a broken spring, no image for time but a ticking heart, nothing for death hut stillness....)

Light glinted off bare windows. Most of the houses were marooned now in a moat of grass and ascending weed. Driveways and porches and garages all open and empty, dumbly grinning.

(Evening all day. World out the window like a painting slowly turning under glass in a dusty frame. Rain in the sky, but shy about falling. The words: they peak at ten, pace by noon, run out to the end of their taut line....)

The shells have names, had them. Martin, Heslep, Rose. Walking past them now, he remembered times they were lit up like pumpkins, orange-yellow light pouring richly out the windows; cars, cycle-strewn yards, newspapers on steps. The casual intimacy of a person inside looking out, waving.

(And I remember your hair among leaves, your body in breaking dew, moonlight that slipped through trees and windows to put its palm against your face, your waist; bright and shadow fighting there....)

Darkness. It moves aside to let you pass. Closes, impassable, behind you.

(Four times: you came to bed, got up, came back to bed. You turned three times, you threw the pillows off the bed. Michael, never born, who had two months to live, was stirring in you and stirring you awake.

Your hair was on the bed like golden threads. The moon had pushed your face up into the window and hidden your hands in shadow. You were yellow, yellow on the linen bed; and opened your eyes.

—If I weren't afraid, I could leave and never look back.

You say that, sitting in a hollow of bed, knees tucked to your flanneled breasts, arms around yourself.

—Would you follow, would you call me back?

I watch your steps track down the walk to the black, inviting street. And later, when I open the door, you're there, grinning, coming back; coming back to make coffee and wait for morning. And another night, another day, saved from whatever it is that threatens at these times....)

Hoover looked at the streetlight shelled in rainbow and it was ahead, above, behind, remembered. Darkness shouldered itself back in around him. Snow hung in the air, waiting to fall. The dead houses regarded him as he passed, still, unspeaking.

(October, time of winds and high doubt. It comes around us like the shutting of a light: the same thing is happening to others. And the people are going away, the time has come for going away....It all boils up in a man, and overflows. His birthright of freedom, it's the freedom to be left alone, that's what he wants most, just to be left alone, just to draw circles around himself and shut the world out. Every man's an island, why deny it, why tread water. So people let go....)

Hoover picked the moving shape out of the alley and was down in a crouch, whistling, almost before the dog saw him. It raised its nose from the ground and walked bashfully toward him, sideways, tail banging at a drum, whining.

"Folks leave you, fella?" A brown shepherd with a heavy silver-studded collar; he didn't bother to look at the jangling nametags. "Take you home with me then, okay?" The shepherd whimpered its agreement. Hoover rummaging in his pockets.

"Sorry, fella, nothing to give you." Showing empty hands, which the dog filled with licks and nuzzles, snuffling.

"Bribery, eh. Sorry, still no food." He stroked his hand into the dog's pelt, found warmth underneath. It sat looking up at him, waiting, expecting, its tail swishing across pavement.

When he erected himself to full height, the dog jumped away and crouched low, ready to run. Hoover walked toward it and put out a hand to its broad, ridged head.

"It's okay, fellow. Tell you what. Come along with me to see a friend, then I'll take you right home and see about getting you something to eat. Think you can wait?"

They punctured the night together, down the walk, heels clacking, claws ticking. Hoover kept his hand on the dog's head as they walked. The nametags threw bells out into the silence.

"Or maybe he'll have something for you there, come to think of it."

Click, clack, click. Staccato tattooed on the ponderous night. The sky is still ambiguous.

(Remembering a night we sat talking, drinking half-cups of coffee as we watched stars sprinkle and throb and fade, then saw dawn all blood and whispered thunder. I remember how your eyes were, pink like shrimp, pink like the sky when it caught the first slanting rays and held them to its chest. And as morning opened around us we were talking of Thoreau and men who sailed the soul, of ways and reasons to change, the old orders, and of why things break up. Outside our window it was growing between them, people were letting go, were wanting their Waldens, their Innisfrees, their Arcadias, they were falling away from the town like leaves, like scaling paint, by twos, by ones. Even in our house, our hearts, it moves between us. Between us. We feel it turning, feel it touching. But we care, we love, we can't let go....)

Hoover drew up short, listening. The shepherd beside him cocked its ears, trembled happily.

It happens like this...

A drone, far off. Closer. Becomes an engine. Then a swelling of light blocks away. Then a rush and churning and soon two lashing white eyes. Loudest, chased by a dog. A roar and past, racing. A thrown thing. Neil's car....and silence again.

And minutes later, the shepherd's body went limp and its head fell back onto his lap. Hoover took it in his arms and walked out of the road, its head rolling softly along the outside of his elbow. In the streetlight his face glistened where the dog had licked it.

Crossing the walk, kicking open a gate that wind had shut, Hoover surrendered his burden into the lawn. Ten steps away he looked back and saw that the dog's body was hidden in deep grass, secret as any Easter egg.

Three hundred and some-odd steps. Two turns. Five places where cement has split its seams, heaved up, and grass is growing in the cracks. Pacing this map...

(The sea grew tired one day of swinging in harness, ticking in its box of beach. One spark in the flannel sea, possessed of fury, gathering slime like a seeded pearl, thinks of legs and comes onto a rock, lies there in the sun drying. It seeps, it slushes, it creeps, it crawls; it bakes to hardness and walks....All to the end: that I am walking on two feet down this corridor of black steel and my hand is turning like a key at this found door....)

The door collapse-returned. He looked around. A single light cut into the café through a porthole of glass in the kitchen door; powdery twilight caught in the mirror. In the dim alley before him, neon signs circled and fell, rose and blinked across their boxes like tiny traffic signals. Profound, ponderous grayness, like the very stuff of thought....

Decision failed him; he had turned to go when he heard the door and saw light swell.

"Dr. Hoover..."

He turned back.

"Didn't know for sure you were still around." Nervously. "About the last ones, I guess."

Hoover nodded. "Any food, Doug?"

"Just coffee, sorry. Coffee's on, though. Made a pot for myself, plenty left." He stepped behind the counter and knocked the corner off a cube of stacked cups, burn scars on his hands rippling in mirror-bemused light.

"Sugar, cream?" Sliding the cup onto crisp pink formica.

Hoover waved them both off. "Black's the best way."

"Yeah...No one been in here for a week or more. I ain't bothered to keep the stuff out like I ought to."

Hoover sat down by the cup, noticing that Doug had moved back away from the counter. "Like you say, I guess. Last ones."

Doug scratched at his stomach where it depended out over the apron. Large hands going into pockets, rumpling the starched white.

"Reckon I *could* get you a sandwich. Or some toast—then it don't matter if the bread's a little stale."

"Coffee's fine. Don't bother."

"You sure? Wouldn't be any trouble."

Hoover smiled and shook his head. "Forget it, just coffee. But thanks anyway."

Doug looked down at the cup. "Don't mind, I'll have one with you." His penciled monobrow flexed at the middle, pointed down. It was like the one-stroke bird that children are taught to draw; the upper part of a stylized heart. "Get my cup." Over his shoulder: "Be right back."

Light rose as the kitchen door opened; died back down, leaving Hoover alone. He turned his eyes to buff-flecked white tiles; let them carry his attention across the floor, swiveling his chair to keep up. Light picked out tiny blades of gleam on the gold bands that edged formica-and-naugahyde. A few pygmy neons hopscotched high on the walls. The booths were empty as shells, humming with shadow; above them (showing against homogenized paint, rich yellow, creamy tan; sprinkled among windows) were small dark shapes he knew as free-painted anchors.

(All this shut in a small café, sculpt in shades of gray. Change one letter, you have cave again....)

Doug came back (light reached, retreated), poured steaming coffee. He squeezed around the end of the counter and sat two seats away.

"Neil left today."

"Yeah, I saw him up the street on the way here."

"So that's whose car it was. Wasn't sure, heard it going by. Going like a bat out of hell from the sound." He drank, made a face. "Too hot. Wonder what kept him? Said he was going to take off this morning." He blew across the mouth of his cup, as though he might be trying to whistle, instead breathing vapor. He tried another taste. "Will came through, you know...."

Hoover's own cup was sweating, oils were sliding over the surface. It was a tan cup; the lip was chipped. They weren't looking at each other.

"That big cabin up on the cape. His grandfather built it for a place to get away and do his writing, way the hell away from everything. Now it's his."

"I know. My sister called me up last week to say goodbye, told me about it, they thought it was coming through. Wonder when *she's* leaving?"

Doug looked up sharply, then dropped his head. "Thought you knew. She left about three, four days ago." Doug belched, lightly.

"Oh. I guess she went up early to get things ready, he'll meet her there. You know women."

"Yeah. Yeah, that's probably it." He went for more coffee, poured for them both. "Coffee's the last thing I need."

"You too."

"Yeah—lot worse for some, though. Been over a week for me, lost about twenty pounds. Catnap some...Thing you wonder about is, where'd they find a lawyer? For the papers and all. Didn't, maybe, guess it don't make much difference anymore, stuff like that. Anyhow, they're gone."

(And the wall's a wedge. Shove it between two people and they come apart, like all the rest....)

Hoover shrugged his shoulders, putting an elbow on the counter and steepling fingers against his forehead.

"Almost brought a friend, Doug...."

The big man straightened in his chair. His mouth made "Friend?" sit on his lips unspoken.

"But he was indisposed, disposed, at the last minute."

Doug was staring at him strangely.

"A dog. Neil hit it. I was going to see if I could talk you out of some food for it."

"Oh! Yeah, there's some stuff, meat and all I'm just gonna have to throw out anyway. What isn't spoiled already's getting that way fast. Didn't know there were dogs still around, though? Whose is it?"

"There aren't now. I hadn't seen it before. *Was* it: it's dead." Extinct.

"Oh. Yeah, Neil *was* going pretty fast. Dog probably wandered in from someplace else anyway, looking for food after they left him." Gazing into the bottom of his cup, Doug swirled what coffee was left against the grounds, making new patterns, like tiny cinders after a rain. "Always been a cat man myself. Couldn't keep one, though, haven't since I was a kid. Sarah's asthma, you know."

"You do have to be careful. Used to have hay fever myself, fall come around I couldn't breathe. Took an allergy test and they cleared it up."

"Yeah, we tried that. Tried about everything. You oughta see our income tax for the last few years, reads like a medical directory. Sarah got so many holes poked in her, the asthma should have leaked right out. Wasn't any of it seemed to help, though."

"How's Sarah doing? Haven't seen her for quite a while. She's usually running around in here helping you, shooing you back to the kitchen, making you change your apron, talking to customers. Brightens the place up a lot."

Doug tilted the cup to drain an extra ounce of cold coffee off the grounds.

"Not much business lately," he said. "Boy I had working for me just kind of up and left three-four months ago and I never got around to looking for help, no need of it, specially now."

"She's well, though? Doing okay."

Doug put his cup down, rattling it against the saucer.

"Yeah, she's okay. She—" He stood and made his way around the counter. "She went away a while. To get some rest." He dipped under the counter and came up with a huge stainless steel bowl. "Think I'll make another pot. This one's getting stale. Better anyhow if you use the stuff regularly, easier on it, works better—like getting a car out on the road to clean her out."

He started working at the urn, opening valves, sloshing dark coffee down into the bowl. Hoover watched Doug's reflection in the shady mirror and a dimmer image of himself lying out across the smooth formica.

So Doug's wife had gone away too; Sarah had gone to get some rest.... Hoover remembered a song he'd heard at one of the faculty parties: Went to see my Sally Gray, Went to see my Sally Gray, Went to see my Sally Gray, Said my Sally's gone away—only this time Sally Gray had taken everybody else with her....

Doug was chuckling at the urn.

"You know I gotta make twenty cups just to get two for us, I mean that's the least this monster here'll handle. Ask him for forty-fifty cups, he'll give it to you in a minute. But you ask him for two, just two little cups of coffee, and he'll blow his stack, or a gasket or something." He went back to clanging at the urn. "Reckon you can handle ten of 'em?" He started fixing the filter, folding it in half twice, tearing off a tiny piece at one corner. "Hell, there ain't enough people left in town to drink twenty cups of coffee if I was giving it away and they was dying of thirst. Or anywhere around here."

He bowed the filter into a cone between his hands, climbed a chair to install it, then came down and drew a glass of water, putting it in front of Hoover.

"That's for while you wait."

"I need to be going anyway, Doug. Have to get some sleep sooner or later."

Doug reached and retrieved Hoover's cup, staring at the sludge settling against the bottom. "One last cup."

"All right. One more."

One for the road...

Doug bent and rinsed the cup, then got another from the stack and put it on the counter. He stood looking at the clean empty cup, wiping his hands against the apron. He lit a cigarette, nodding to himself, and the glowing red tip echoed one of the skipping neon signs on the wall behind him. He put the package on the counter and smiled, softly.

"You know, you could've sat right here and watched the whole thing happening. I mean, at first there'd be the usual group, but they were...nervous. You know: jumpy. They'd sort of scatter themselves out and every now and then the talk would die down and there'd be this quiet, like everybody was listening for something, waiting for something. Then a lot of them stopped coming, and the rest would sit all around the room, talking across to each other, then just sitting there quiet for a long time by themselves. Wasn't long before the regulars didn't come anymore—and you knew what was going on, you knew they were draining out of town like someone had pulled the plug.

"That was when the others started showing up. They'd come in with funny looks on their faces, all anxious to talk. And when you tried to talk to 'em, they'd be looking behind you and around the room and every once in a while they'd get up and go look out the window. And then they'd leave and you'd never see them again."

Hoover sat with his legs cocked back, toes on the floor, regarding the glass of water (the bubbles had nearly vanished). He nodded: he knew, he understood.

"For a while I got some of the ones that were coming through. I'd be in the back and I'd hear the door and come out, and there'd be this guy standing there, shuffling his feet, looking at the floor. He'd pay and take his coffee over in the corner, then the next time I looked around, he'd be gone—lot of them would just take it with them, to go. Then even that stopped."

(The people: they drip, trickle, run, pour, flood from the cities. They don't look back. And the ones who stay, try to fight it—they feel it growing in them worse than before. Turning in them, touching them, and they care they love they can't let go. But the harder they fight, the worse it is, like going down in quicksand, and the wall's a wedge: shove it between two people and they come apart, like all the rest, like all the rest of the world....)

Doug found something on the counter to watch.

"One time during the War, the ship I was on went down on the other side and a sub picked us up. I still remember how it felt, being in that sub, all the people packed in like sardines, stuffed into spaces between controls and motors. You'd think it would be full of noise, movement. But there was something about being under all that water, being closed in, something about the light —anyway, something that made you feel alone, made you want to whisper. I'd just sit in it and listen. Feel. And pretty soon I'd start wanting them all to really go away, to leave me alone...."

Doug stood looking for a moment out one of the small round windows past Hoover's shoulder.

"Yeah. Yeah, that's the way it is all right." Then his eyes switched back to Hoover's cup. "I better go get that coffee, just take it a minute to perk."

He picked up his cup and walked down the counter toward the kitchen, running his hand along the formica. The door swung back in, wobbled, stopped (light had reached, retreated).

Hoover felt suddenly hollow; empty; squeezed. He looked around. The room was a cave again.

Out in the kitchen, Doug moved among his stainless steel and aluminum. Hoover heard him banging pots on pans, opening doors, sliding things on shelves out of his way. Then the texture of sound changed, sank to quiet, became a silence that stretched and stretched. And seconds later, broke: the back door creaked open and shut with a hiss of air along its spring, clicking shut.

(So now the quicksand's got Doug too, for all his fighting. Now he's gone with the rest, gone with Sally Gray....)

Outside in the alley angling along and behind the café, Doug's Harley Davidson pumped and caught, coughed a couple of times and whined away, one cylinder banging.

Hoover sat looking at the abandoned cup as silence came in to fill his ears. Then he heard the buzzing of electric wires.

The last grasping and their fingers had slipped.

The wedge was driven in, and they'd come apart....

He stood, digging for a dime and finding he'd forgotten to fill his pockets, then walked to the register and punched a key. "No Sale" came up under the glass. There were two nickels and some pennies.

He fed the coins in (ping! ping!), dialed, and waited. The phone rang twice and something came on, breathing into the wires.

"Cass?"

Breathing.

Again: "Cass?" Louder.

Breathing.

"Cass, is that you?"

Silence.

"Who is this? Please. Cass?"

A small, quiet voice. "I'm afraid you have the wrong number."

A click and buzzing...

After a while, he reached up and flipped out the change tray. As the lid slid away, a tarnished gray eye showed there: someone had left a dime behind.

Nine rings. Cass' voice in the lifted phone. Sleepy; low and smooth; pâté, ready for spreading.

"Cass?"

"Is that you, Bob? Where are you?"

"Doug's place. Be right home." The space of breath. "Honey..."

"Yes?"

"Get your bags packed, we're leaving tonight."

"Leaving?" She was coming awake. "Where—"

"I don't know. South maybe, climate's better. But maybe that's what every-one will think—anyway, we'll decide. Just get your things ready, just what you absolutely have to have. We can always pick up things we need in towns. There's a big box in the bottom of the utility closet, some of my stuff, some tools and so on I got together a while back. Put that with the rest—there's some room left in it you can use. I'll be right home. Everything else we'll need is already in the car."

"Bob..."

"Just do it Cass. Please. I'll be right back, to help."

"Bob, are you sure—"

"Yes."

She paused. "I'll be ready."

He hung up and walked into the kitchen, came out again with a ten-pound sack of coffee under one arm. He started over the tiles toward the door, then turned back and picked up the cigarettes lying on the counter. He stood by the door, looking back down the dim alley: stood at the mouth of the cave, looking into distances (he'd seen a stereopticon once; it was much the same effect).

The tiny neons skipped and blinked dumbly in their boxes; the kitchen light glared against the window, fell softly along the mirror. Shadows came in to fill the café; sat at tables, slumped in booths, stood awry on the floor; watching, waiting. At the end of the counter, the blank tan cup silently surrendered.

He turned and switched the knob. Went through the door. Shut it behind him. The click of the lock ran away into the still air and died; he was locked into silence....

Cautiously he assaulted the street's independence, heels ticking parameters for the darkness, the motive, the town. The sky hung low above his head.

(I walk alone. Alone. Men don't run in packs, but they run....Death at the wheel expects his spin. Dark seeps in around the edges, winds rise in the caves of our Aeolian skulls, five fingers reach to take winter into our hearts, the winter of all our hearts)

And they came now in the darkness, they loomed and squatted about him, all the furnished tombs: this dim garden of rock and wood.

(Bars of silence. Score: four bars of silence, end on the seventh. See how they show on my white shirt among the roses. Bars and barristers of silence)

The quick blue spurt of a struck match. A cigarette flames, then glows, moving down the street into darkness.

(There is no sign for isolation but a broken spring, no image for time but a ticking heart, nothing for death but stillness...and the wall, the wedge, is splitting deeper but we'll hold, for a while we'll hold on, you and I)

He stood still in the stillness that flowed around him and listened to the hum of insects calling through the black flannel. As if in answer, clouds came lower.

(At the mouth of caves, turning. We can't see out far, in deep, but the time has come for going away the time has come for becoming....At the mouth of caves, turning, and time now to enter the calm, the old orders. At the mouth of caves. Turning)

He walked on and his heels talked and the night came in to hush him.

He shouted out into the dark, screamed once out into silence—and it entered his heart.

He passed a pearl-gray streetlight, passed a graveyard lawn.

("Sudden and swift and light as that the ties gave, and we learned of finalities besides the grave." Is this how it feels, the instant of desertion—a vague epiphany of epochal stillness, primal quiet?)

Around him, scarcely sounding his echo, stood the shells of houses, like trees awaiting the return of dryads who had lost their way.

(The instant of desertion, the instance of silence)

The cigarette arced into the street and fell there, glowing blankly.

He bent his head and began to hurry.

And with a flourish, the snows began.

The Creation of Bennie Good

"Do you like my foot," putting it on the table. There, between the chipped saucer and candle; you have noticed how carefully I avoid the marmalade, the box of salty butter. "Will you accept it as a token of my affection? For you? It is, as they say, a good foot." Earlier, I have deftly undone the laces with my toes, grasped the sock between piano-key toes and foot and slowly drawn it off, like peeling a willow wand. "The arch is long and graceful, with the springy delicacy of a light man. The toes curl in as though to embrace the foot; the nails are flecked with color. And pink is the color of this foot." Pink, with the bright red crescent at the top of the curve: pimple on one side, in the curve, and dimpled on the other. "I am offering this, should you want it, my dear. It is all I have."

Her attention is arrested by my foot. This is true of most. At parties my friends will group together talking, and glancing occasionally with great expectation towards the corner chair where I sit calm, unmoved, unmoving. As the evening advances, their glances are more frequent and begin to form a rhythm; then finally, beginning as a low moan among the women, gradually swelling up through the groups until it becomes a steady, hard, syncopated shout, and bursting at last out of the crowd, the call comes: *Foot! Foot!* Then slowly I lift it to the level of their eyes and one of them, a woman, the chosen, comes forward out of the group wearing shyness like a belt and starts softly to undo the pale pink shoe, dropping it to the floor, where it lies on its side in the carpet pile. You have seen the way a snake is skinned - first the skin is slit away from the mouth, then rolled gently down along the body: this is how my sock is removed - then thrown to them. A few are unable to stand the pressure and must be sent away. Others on the edge near me remove their own shoes and socks and sit staring sadly at the pale uncovered feet. I tell her all this.

"It's all I have, it's yours." But this one, this Sally, is more moved than the rest. Already the tight black circles around her eyes are smearing, becoming less distinct; eyelids covered in green sequins are flashing like tiny chandeliers. Her little hands are perched on the rim of the cup and soon one will creep out across the ceramic dishes to shyly, lightly touch my foot. She is overwhelmed at the size of the occasion, the depth of my offer.

Perhaps I will make conversation; I've found this sometimes helps, especially in the initial slight embarrassment. I will discuss various projects.

Such as ...

Last year I had a large number of foam-rubber genitalia prepared for me by an advertising firm. These were bright pink and varied in size from two feet to six in length, and from a few inches to several yards in circumference. The order was placed on a Monday after a weekend of planning and sketching; on Thursday the genitalia were ready; and on Friday I set out for Niagara Falls with them packed away in my trunk. When I opened the trunk later, at the hotel, the genitalia expanded - virtually exploded - out into my room, filling it. Some had got tangled together, like fingers

in doughnuts. That evening I fought my way through the foam to go out and walk among the people, talking to many and asking questions. And the next morning, when the sun was gleaming on the water, I walked with my trunk to the top of the Falls and floated my collection of vast foam genitals down towards all the people below: they bobbed and raged on the water.

Or. I will have a simulacra head made of intelligent clay - in my image precisely, though perhaps a touch more worldly, without the elusive pale delicacy of my own features. With great patience I will teach this head to say Yes, and I will keep it in a wooden box, a box of dogwood, on my left shoulder. Whenever I am asked a question requiring response, I will reach up across my chest and open the door to this box. The head will open its eyes, say Yes - and I will shut the door.

I will train crickets to function as metronomes and place one with every violinist in the world, thus restoring natural order to contemporary music.

By lies and deceit I have caused the Atlantic and Pacific Oceans to become jealous of one another; already they are creeping across America towards a confrontation. Frantically I have this morning cabled the Dead Sea, entreating it to intervene. Which it will.

And she listens. Even as lorries load cans in the alley and roll away, scraping long grooves in the bricks on each side, as the photographers shyly cover their lenses with their hands, as the waiters come and go, replacing dishes, bringing fresh flowers in vase after vase, the clack-clack of them in their rubber shoes. She listens.

And I tell her again, does she understand: "I am a ruined man. This is all I have left. And this, I offer to you." We sit for several minutes listening to corks pop off bottle after bottle around us, like children pulling fingers out of puffed cheeks. They have worked a long time for this; we are at last together. When I look at them, they raise their glasses towards us in celebration. Quickly, more bottles are brought in. A serving cart full of jangling green and clear, that hums and glides too slowly in front of the trotting waiter. More corks, soda, bubbles cascade into glasses, cubes of ice pop up like fishheads and the bubbles resemble their eyes. Me straight in the chair with a high head talking. Admiring how she maneuvers the delicate machinery of eggcup and spoon.

When I am finished she calls softly for the table to be cleared. With a wave of her hand, and light winks in the rings. The band stops and all is quiet as the waiters come and depart with full arms. I am finished. The lights go up, a few people stand for a better view.

She sits straight. So straight like a Cezanne cypress, and hardly anyone breathes now as, smiling, she moves back in her chair and adjusts the top of her body. We hear the gentle, crisp sound of her skirts . . .

Finally I lift my head out of my wet hands. There is little energy left, in me.

And now there are cheers, calls of approval, relief. She is smiling. Staring straight into my eyes and nothing moves. The green folds of her skirt are pulled back, arranged around her waist and legs like a monster lettuce, and there on the veined-marble table, square in the center by my own, she has put her foot. Her tiny foot is offered, there.

And on it, the most exquisite black shoe.

Get Along Home

It won't be long.

I nodded.

Sorry to take you away.

No problem. I told you I'd be here.

I always knew you would.

A nurse practitioner stepped into the room. As she did so, lighting came up perceptibly, brightening around our small island of bed, table, chair. Is there anything you need? she asked. Her signing was rapid, assured; until then I'd not been conscious of signing, only that we were speaking, speaking the way it seemed we'd always spoken. I'd slipped back into it so naturally, after all these years.

No, but thank you, Tish said. You're so kind.

And to me, once the nurse had withdrawn: There's so much I have to tell you, to ask you.

I nodded. A pigeon lit on the sill outside. Sad looking bird. It staggered on its way to the window, its beak bent back on itself when it pecked at the window. But a bird nonetheless. Most of the others were extinct. How long since I'd even seen one?

Have you been happy? she asked.

Yes.

And are you now?

Most days, I think.

You always had good answers, love.

The pigeon's eye was an orange jewel. It bobbed its head up and down, side to side in that curious stitch they have, trying to understand. Knew it should be wary, wasn't sure of just what.

Everything.

We never get very far from where we start, do we?

That said, her hand fell back exhausted onto the sheet. The word *breathless* came to me.

It's what they call in sports a broken-field run, I told her. They all know where you're headed, but there's that whole field between here and there. You keep moving, keep dodging. Everything's footwork, evasion, misdirection.

They?

The opposition. The visiting team.

She sat looking out at the pigeon.

I hate to ask this, but....

Seeing where her eyes went, I said: It's all right. I arranged her gown about her, helped her onto the bed pan. Flesh on hips and stomach had collapsed, folding in on itself like a tent being taken down. She seemed almost weightless. Breasts, too, hung limp and deflated. Our selves, our identities, are so linked to sexuality. When we no longer have that, in a sense I suppose we become something else.

Once I had wanted this woman so badly. And once this body, like my own, ached just to be wanted. Where do all those feelings go? Into some ozone layer, maybe, out of sight and mind. Forever building up, protecting us quietly.

She turned her face to the wall, eyes unblinking, as I cleaned her.

I brought this for you, I said afterwards.

She held up the clear disk, turning it side to side, watching me through it.

A game I designed. I worked on it a long time. The producers think it's a sure hit.

Her eyes said: Tell me about it.

A man is on his way home from work. Everything goes wrong. He doesn't have exact change, the subway founders, a trio of terrible musicians comes aboard his car. Finally he exits, and comes up into a part of the city he can't recognize at all. He begins walking. Nothing is familiar. He's surrounded by whores in red boots, guys without bottom halves who cruise the city on plywood rafts atop roller skates, twitchy teens stepping off curbs to meet cars and glancing up every four seconds to rooftops, lawyers who've set up offices on the street like lemonade stands, an Islamic Mormon shepherding his flock of wives down towards the harbor. The goal's to get him home.

I hope it does well for you.

Me too. I've a lot of time invested.

Years ago, she said after a moment, I knew a man who was going to be a painter.

Yes, I said. I knew him too.

She nodded, and her eyes went to the window. The pigeon was gone. Rectangle full of darkening sky.

Maybe you should rest now.

Okay.

There are some things I need to take care of. I'll be back later.

Smiling, she closed her eyes. I was almost to the door when I heard her knock on the bedside table, and turned.

"I thought this would be more interesting," she said. From such long disuse and from the damage done, her voice was a poor engine. She had to repeat what she'd said before I understood. Many years had passed since last I heard it, but the disappointment in her voice was something I knew well.

As I stepped into the hall, the nurse practitioner rose from a molded plastic chair. She held one of those heavily waxed packages of juice with a midget straw. Her name tag was a simple rectangle: Carson.

"Do you have any questions?"

I shook my head.

"You do understand, I hope: It wasn't a decision she made lightly."

"To die, you mean."

"We all die, Mr. Decker."

"Most of us for reason, though."

"She has reasons. Some of them we can understand, a lot we never will. Not that it matters."

"That sounds perilously close to mysticism, Ms. Carson."

"We don't much pretend to science here. We're more like... I don't know...wilderness guides, maybe. Helpmates."

She finished her drink and dropped the package into a reclamation bin. With some surprise I realized that we'd been speaking aloud. I had resurfaced, I was back in the world.

"She never could stand decisions being made for her. You know that better than anyone. And it explains a lot, for those of us who need explanations."

"One could look at it that way. Or as easily consider it little more than another expression of massive ego. Just another performance."

Like the time she'd crawled, naked and without language, out of the ice sculpture of a mammoth that artisans had spent eighteen hours carving. Or the way, years back, back when she spoke, she'd sit on stage and slit her skin with razors while reading aloud from the daily newspaper.

"It won't be long, Mr. Decker. You're leaving?"

I nodded.

"I'll call you, if you'd like."

I thanked her and gave her my number. Like the pigeon, I left. Soon I'd be extinct, too. We all would. Meanwhile the goal was to get me home. I had a good chance of making it.

When Fire Knew My Name

Cold, driving weather like this always brought them out.

It had been there in early morning, a presence, a threat, a promise, and by seven had honed itself to a cleaverlike edge on the strop of wind. From my window on the fifth floor I listened to the schlep-schlep-schlep of that edge on the strop and watched as day congealed and the blade began to slice away at the city.

They emerged on their canes and crutches, in wheelchairs, tottering on artificial and makeshift limbs or balanced like flat-bottomed urns on low carts, pulling themselves along with gloved hands. At these times there is an expression on their faces that's difficult to describe. Pain, yes—but within it, at the core, the thing that pain comes wrapped around, a kind of joyfulness, I think.

Others, those to whom the world belonged, walked with heads down, swaddled in scarves and layers of wool and heavy caps. But the survivors tore open their own shabby coats and raised faces to the sky, threw out their arms to embrace it all: this wind, this blade, this impossible city.

"Don't tell me. The fire brigade's out." Somehow or another, originating in the punch line of a joke, I'm sure, that had become our name for them. Sandra stood in the doorway arch whose frame evoked both Chinese calligraphy and *pi* with sheet and blanket wrapped about her, a human teepee. Her hair, so blond it was almost white, had begun growing back in. It poked out a quarter-inch or so all around and she was convinced she looked like a dandelion. "Shut the shockin' window before your nose falls off."

"Yeah, and I've only got *one* of those."

In college, as was the fad for a couple of years, she'd had an ear removed. Half the people in the city her age were walking around with newly grown ones, but that wasn't Sandra's style. She started something, she stayed with it.

"If I shut the window, it frosts over and I can't see out."

"What—they look different this time?"

But of course they never did. They were as generic and predictable as spring, as the run of our daily lives, the news and entertainment piped in to us, what we said to one another. I shut the window. Wind howled as though in complaint and shook the pane fiercely with both hands.

"Breakfast?"

"I'd planned on fishes, but we're fresh out of loaves."

"The cupboard was bare."

"In a word."

"Not even a bone."

"A few exoskeletons, but I don't think those count."

Sandra and wrappings sank into one of the chairs. "I was dreaming," she told me. "Standing on the street looking up at a billboard." With one hand she sketched its cadence, form and line breaks on air. "We're almost done/ World finished soon/ Thank you for your patience/ B&D Construction.

"I'm standing there and I have this warm feeling in my stomach. I realize that for months, as cold winds blew in across bare plains to the east, I've been coming out each morning to admire new buildings that appear overnight, to be among the first to stroll new plazas, arcades, explore tiny parks. I'm tremendously proud of my city, what it's becoming.

"But there's also, it seems, a problem. When I return to my apartment, six brutally handsome young men in jeans, black T-shirts and low-slung toolbelts are waiting in the hall outside. They have to tear out my floor, they say. Possibly the walls as well. They'll know once they get started. But will I be able to stay here while you work? I ask them. Sure, no problem, the foreman says. Long as you don't need a floor or walls."

Rising, Sandra walked into the kitchen area and, ever the child of Famine parents, came out with a half-loaf of bread fetched from one hiding spot or another. I drew hot water, crumbled in tea leaves, and we fell to.

We'd been together almost four years. I'd gone with friends to HOUSE OF th'OUGHT and wound up sitting beside her. The House was another of those intermittent hot spots thronged with patrons for months when it opened, afterwards all but abandoned. Here great books were read aloud, in shifts, by professional readers. We were never able to agree on what was being read at the time. I remembered *Tristram Shandy*; Sandra insisted that by then Burning Cinder Person, the House's star reader and frequent subject of profiles in local papers during the House's brief heyday, was well into the 19th century.

(*In halflight she turns, murmuring, and I trace the scars along her back, by the shoulder blades. The sky splits open like a wound, and birds cough the sun into morning.*)

"So what's on for today?" she asked.

"Have to deliver my Cowboy tapes to Epoch-Z."

Cowboy's a figure so legendary that many claim he never existed. Supposedly he was the first of the great urban freedom fighters—some say the last as well—and went down in the seige of the markets. But street wisdom has it that Cowboy's still out there. He'd never been photographed except—possibly—for less than sixty seconds of blurry footage I'd caught years ago while filming deconstruction of the Skystop Building. One of the news channels was putting together a documentary on Cowboy. They'd learned of my tapes and offered enough money to keep me afloat, us afloat, for a year.

"What, you can't just shoot it to them? You're going outside? To someone's shockin' *office*?"

I shrugged. "They actually called up, on the phone. 'We may be on the bitter sharp edge, but we're also a little old-fashioned 'round here,' they tell me, 'in our own way.' Before I know it, I'm in a conference call with half a dozen vice presidents ranging in age between eighteen and eighteen-and-a-half. 'We like our people to have faces,' they tell me."

Jack London said to understand totalitarianism, picture a boot heel stamping on a human face—forever. Big business is soft Italian-leather loafers carressing that same face. However long and hard we espouse bohemian, alternative, libertarian, contrary lifestyles, we all live off big business, fleas on a dog. I tried to remember when heads of major corporations had begun showing up for work in pullovers and jeans. Revolution in America? Radical change? The country's very genius is its capacity to absorb anything, absolutely *anything*—to appropriate it, bear it on a flood into the mainstream, vitiate it.

"Anything I can pick up while I'm out?" I asked.

"Ginger would be good, for tonight's curry. Oh, and I guess some vegetables and rice. So there'll *be* a curry? Assuming I ever see you again."

"Think of it as an adventure," I said.

"Think of it as stupid," she said. "Not to mention the possibility of freezing nose, fingers and like wee appendages off."

"*Wee*? Did you say *wee*?" Reaching for a Scottish accent, which came out, inexplicably, Jamaican.

"Don't forget the ginger."

We say it together: "A Redemptionist never forgets."

There on the street away from river's edge, I encountered a more normal population—normal for this quarter of the city, that is. Fully half those out in the bite and slash hobbled along on feet with tendons fatally damaged by the police's standard interrogation technique: if they didn't like your answer, they stood on your foot and heaved you mightily backwards. Meanwhile uptown folk were paying clinics huge sums to have facial muscles injected with botulism. The bacteria paralyze the muscle and, in doing so, erase age lines. When these people talk, their eyebrows don't move but float cloudlike above their mouths, like dialog balloons in cartoons.

I began to penetrate the city's many folds and strata. I've always suspected it to be more laminate than veneer, thin sheets pressed close to form something of apparent substance, nothing, not even inferior materials, at its core.

At the corner of Market and Force, several hundred protestors converged in absolute silence on the plaza before City Hall. Riot police formed a human moat around the complex, beating sticks backhand against shields. The juxtaposition was uncanny. Protestors stood motionless looking across. Police beat at their shields. At some invisible cue the protestors withdrew as silently as they'd come.

At First and Desire, a small park had been set fire by the Children's Army. *We burn the bones they throw us*, a placard read. Children in red armbands stood alongside monitoring, making certain the fires did not spread. The fires were doing anything but, however. They were lowering, folding in upon themselves, benches turning to smolder. One of the children stepped forward into the park and gave a fingers-into-palm, come-to-me sign. *Incoming*, he shouted as half a dozen Molotov cocktails rained from windows of the highrise project skirting the park.

Two blocks up, a crowd had gathered. They shouted encouragement, chanted, raised fists in the air. Leaning against the wall of a nearby credit union was a piece of cardboard cut from a heavy box and laboriously handlettered in cockeyed, backward-leaning block letters.

STREET FITING!

It was already over, though, the crowd dispersing, as I approached. One man lay broken and bleeding, body in the street, head on the curb as though on a pillow. I watched as his eyes went still. The other, the winner, wiped blood from *his* eyes and picked up the hat with the money. Then he walked to the sign, lifted it for a closer look, tucked it underarm. His now. Spoils.

The city I find when I come out into it, the one I'm a part of, is invisible to many. As though the city's gone belly up, as though this gray sky were an overturned stone. These are the forgotten people, the ones who don't matter, those ground down on the city's mill, used up, thrown beneath the wheels. Here there is neither history nor future, only a perpetual present tense of motion, hunger, need and momentary ease, a fire that consumes and goes on consuming, through whose flickering silent tongues sometimes we glimpse the shape, the form, the suggestion, of another reality, another world. A better one? Different, at least. And different is enough.

"Cowboy!" I cried out.

He stood at a street corner, buckskin fringe blowing in the breeze, looking a little confused when I approached him. We were at the dangerous border between uptown and down. Age lines crouched like homesteaders, deepset, at eyes and mouth. I took note of the missing ear.

"What's up?" I said. Like so many others, looking for guidance.

"What's ever up but more of the same? Just they practice new grimaces in the mirror is all, tell us more outrageous lies. *You* feel connected?"

No.

But had I ever?

"We have to keep changing. Dodging under, going over, scrambling. We can't let them get a hold, take us for granted."

"But you..."

Seeing the sudden sadness in his eyes, I understood. He was an icon. He couldn't change.

"Here's my ride," he said, stepping not into the city bus one would have thought he awaited but into an ancient VW bus. "Keep the faith?"

I watched him pull away.

Against the horizon the day still burned into life and burned steadily away, like alcohol, in a blue flame. No heat to any of it. What could a man do?

After a moment I snapped an ear plug off the tab and fit it in as I started walking again along the street, past crews of workers tearing up streets, crews of workers rebuilding them. You never know what you'll get, of course, that's part of the deal, but this was okay. *We'll Meet Again in Glory.* I watched my breath go out in plumes with each step.

Glory was the next town over.

LITERARY ESSAYS

David Goodis: Life in Black and White

There are few stranger stories than that of David Goodis.

In 1950, age 33, following a prolific New York career as pulp writer, following publication of a first novel at age 21 and seven years later his best-known book, *Dark Passage*, on the wake of which (with serialization in *Saturday Evening Post* and purchase as a Bogart-Bacall vehicle) he rode to a six-year contract with Warners, David Goodis returned to hometown Philadelphia where he lived with his parents, a virtual recluse, until their deaths just before his own in 1967.

In California he had rented a sofa in a friend's home for four dollars a month; that was where he lived. He drove the same battered Chrysler convertible most of his adult life, wore old suits till they were threadbare (he did sometimes sew in labels from fashionable clothiers) then dyed them blue and went on wearing them.

He'd stuff the red cellophane from cigarette packages up his nose in restaurants and feign nosebleeds; scream in apparent pain as he went through revolving doors; wear a friend's old bathrobe out into public (one thinks of *Pale Fire*'s poor, mad Kinbote) as "a white Russian, an exiled prince of the blood."

Friends on both coasts recall Goodis frequenting ghetto bars and nightclubs, searching out obese black women who would give him the extreme verbal abuse—and perhaps, from the evidence of his work, more substantial abuses—he craved.

The first sentence of his first novel reads: "After a while it gets so bad that you want to stop the whole business."

So, with the retreat to Philadelphia, began what Geoffrey O'Brien (in his introduction to Black Lizard's reissues of Goodis' novels) refers to as "a voluntary and secretive descent into oblivion," a conclusion bearing within it a new beginning every bit as equivocal and contrived as Goodis' own occasional "happy" endings.

Hemmed-in lives grow the densest, Blaise Cendrars wrote. And there in his parents' home, coursing out some mornings in the old Chrysler, junketing by night into Philadelphia's black heartland, Goodis fixed his gaze on the original-paperback novels coming into their own and began, in book after book, most of them for Gold Medal, three, however, for Lion, a reinvention of the self: a ten-year threnody in which his personal history was transformed, but *just*, into novels about losers, outcasts and derelicts, the unchosen, the discarded. There's no evidence that Goodis had high, or any, artistic goals in mind; he seems simply to have adopted a kind of fiction that would at the same time support him and guarantee anonymity. "Goodis didn't choose pulps," one commentator has written, "they chose him."

With the shift to paperback originals, as though mirroring the failure of Goodis' own ambitions, his books turned exclusively to the underside of the American dream. His protagonists became disgraced, alcoholic airline pilots (*Cassidy's Girl*), artists working as appraisers of stolen goods for burglars (*Black Friday*), once-famous crooners or concert performers reduced by fate and their own innate disabilities to street corner bums or barroom piano players (*Street of No Return* and *Down There*, the latter filmed by Truffaut as *Shoot the Piano Player*).

"In this fashion," O'Brien notes, "David Goodis, great literary artist turned streetcorner hackwriter, could tell his own story and ply his trade at the same time." And tell it he did, mapping out a zone in American fiction specifically his, forging novels instantly recognizable for their charged style as much as for characteristic obsessions.

Yet the more one reads Goodis' books, as O'Brien points out, the more insistent is the hint of something beyond simple preoccupation or reprisal, something like real madness.

"There are not a dozen books here," Mike Wallington remarks of the author's work in an introduction to Zebra Books' anthology of four Goodis novels: "rather, with remarkable imagination and depth, and not a little madness, he has written and rewritten his one book a dozen or so times."

That book tells, from the inside, the story of a man—artist, musician, pilot—fallen from considerable height, a man who has collaborated in his fall and now accepts it, embraces it, blurring the hard edge of his loss with alcohol, masochistic relationships and, finally, a passivity reflecting utter disengagement with life.

O'Brien: "Anyone who spends some time with his books learn to identify their peculiarly intense atmosphere, their outbursts of eloquence, their sense of the world as an abyss for falling into."

Two things about all this are truly extraordinary.

First, those twelve books are an unparalleled example of self-revelation in the context, or guise, of genre fiction, a form not generally thought of as flexible enough for, and indeed rarely bent to, such use.

Second, that such quirky, devil-ridden work could ever have sustained a career as paperback novelist is cause for amazement.

"Nothing so downbeat, so wedded to reiterations of personal and social failure," O'Brien writes, "would be likely to find a mass market publisher at present. The absolutely personal voice of David Goodis seems almost to have escaped by accident. It emanated from the heart of an efficient entertainment industry, startlingly, like the wailing of an outcast."

* * *

There are two well-known photographs of David Goodis.

One shows him in profile, sitting in shirtsleeves and figured tie before a large typewriter, arms out straight and fingers poised as he balances on the edge of his words, the very image of the professional writer.

The other, taken in his room in Philadelphia in 1963, shows him from behind, dark against a light-shot window, in the foreground, on the bed behind him, a book rendered huge by perspective.

* * *

Everything connects in Goodis' world; everything circles back, all streets bear one down to the same dead end. One's past, chopped away like a rotting limb, returns in a chance encounter, a woman's face at the window, an opening door. A man's entire life comes down to a stain on the street, to the wrong choice he had to make, to a few safe, seductively shadowed places.

In *Street of No Return* (1954) three bums, "two-legged shadows," sit on a street corner wondering where their next drink will come from. One of them, called Whitey ("The curved glass showed him a miniature of himself, a little man lost in the emptiness of a drained bottle"), wanders off only to return 166 pages later, having relived much of his life—his success as a pop singer and damning, obsessive love for a prostitute, beatings by police, torture at the hands of racketeers who wrecked his throat—and, turning aside a race riot, having become a momentary, reluctant hero.

> The three of them walked across the street. They sat down on the pavement with their backs against the wall of the flophouse. The pavement was terribly cold and the wet wind from the river came blasting into their faces. But it didn't bother them. They sat there passing the bottle around, and there was nothing that could bother them, nothing at all.

Virtually every Goodis novel is cut to this pattern. The books, and the lives they describe, are closed circuits. Something gives the protagonist's life a nudge, lends it new momentum, and for a time, set in motion, it remains in motion; but then inertia's other side rolls up and the life comes back to rest, to full stop. It's a repose for which the protagonist has paid dearly, giving up everything else, and it well may be all he values now.

"Getting down this far, to rock bottom," Mike Wallington writes, "has meant blotting out pain, learning to forget. The dreadful gloom—the foreboding that hangs like a pall over every page of Goodis—is a fear of remembrance." For Goodis's characters there is no escape, only more fateful traps, more prisons of the mind.

In *Hardboiled America: The Lurid Years of Paperbacks*, O'Brien observes that the hardboiled novel strives, above all, for *presence*, pitching its words so keenly at the edge of the real that the text escapes language altogether and in a sense, in its immediacy, almost becomes action. Yet at the heart of this attempt, he notes, something odd happens. Conceived to deal with action, dialogue, with the dynamic interplay of character, location and time, the hardboiled novel "tends in fact toward a zero state of silence, solitude, and immobility. If we remove the temptresses and gunmen, we are left with a drab room in which a man alone smokes many cigarettes and empties many bottles of Scotch."

This is Goodis' repose, the destination printed on his characters' bus tickets and in their hearts, their only heaven a temporary suspension of hell.

It also highlights Goodis' affinity with the other great nihilists of the genre, James M. Cain and Horace McCoy, and suggests why the French have so adamantly admired and preserved these writers' books.

Cain's novels open on a world in which desire is all there is. His characters' lives flare into brief, bright existence around the stabs of this desire, given substance by it, then fall back into numbness, formlessness. *Force of circumstances driving the protagonists to the commission of a dreadful act*, as Cain himself once summed up his concerns—then endless retreat.

McCoy's characters lack even that desire, those bright segments. Gloria in *They Shoot Horses, Don't They* is (O'Brien) "a serene vampire in love with nothingness," in some ways not a character at all but "a borderline of the human personality, beyond which it cannot be said that there is a person there."

It's not difficult to see how postwar French readers came across books like these with a certain shock of recognition. The lack of meaning in it all, the way events just *happen*—that zero at the center—was very much in the air, simmering into existentialism on Left Bank stoves. In American hardboiled writing, French readers found something both of the intense isolation and anxiety of writers like Gide and Malraux and of the stylistic qualities they so admired (and admire still) in Faulkner, Hemingway, Steinbeck and Caldwell.

The French in fact recognized what no American critic at the time perceived: that stripped-down novels like those of McCoy, Cain or Goodis, trembling on the very edge of the real, all but canceling themselves out in their starkness, were something new, achieving a penetration, a depth, not possible with earlier narrative modes. France's greatest homage to this new fiction, and one of the great modern novels, came in 1942, seven years after publication of *They Shoot Horses*, with Camus' *The Stranger*.

Perry Miller noted this French affinity in *Atlantic Monthly* in 1951, in a landmark article titled "Europe's Faith in American Fiction," remarking Gide's and other European intellectuals' preference for "violent"—romantic—American fiction over the realism of an Edith Wharton or Willa Cather. The vision of these romantics, Miller suggested, matched more closely the European's own vision of America and represented for him, if not the literal, then certainly a more important poetic truth. These novels offered, as Gide said, "a foretaste of Hell"—a violent, terrible place quite beyond redemption, but one at least imbued with vitality.

* * *

I am going to America, Svidrigailov says in *Crime and Punishment* just before shooting himself on a street corner.

And so David Goodis returns to Philadelphia.

* * *

Perhaps it's only the outsider, the sleeper waking in some future world, a Tocqueville, artists like Thoreau or Baudelaire forcing themselves into self-exile, who sees clearly.

There's little doubt of Goodis' outsider status, or that of his characters. And if what he saw beyond that Philadelphia window is tenuous, attenuated, reduced to puppet-theater size by his apartness, his preoccupations and his madness, it is also uniquely intense.

French interest in Goodis has continued. Gallimard kept his books in print even when no English-language editions were available, and in 1984 Editions du Seuil published a book-length study, Philippe Garnier's *Goodis: La Vie en Noir et Blanc*.

Like any biography, Garnier's book is an unrealized quest, part reportage, part detective story. Seeking knowledge of the writer whose books he remembered reading, as a child, in the distinctive black and yellow jackets of Gallimard's *Serie Noire*, shuttling from New York to Hollywood to Philadelphia, Garnier spoke at length with virtually everyone who knew David Goodis. He has pulled together and presents most intriguingly a wealth of documentation, atmosphere, oral history; yet, for it all, at book's end Goodis remains a mystery. Garnier's coda comprises an interview with a black woman with whom Goodis sustained a lengthy relationship in the early Fifties. "The David that she knew," Garnier writes, "was carefree, without armor, without family. And, like the rest, she's convinced that this will-o'-the wisp whom she loved and knew was the 'real David Goodis.' Another one."

Among Garnier's most illuminating encounters is that with Paul Wendkos, a documentary filmmaker who in the mid-1950's collaborated with Goodis on an adaptation of Goodis' novel *The Burglar*; this became Wendkos' first feature film, and the collaborators became friends. Of all the many people who spoke with him about Goodis, Garnier writes, and who were surprised at the interest afforded his books by the French, Wendkos was the only one to give this interest serious thought.

> I wonder if the French didn't find a certain existential melancholy in David's novels, an attitude stripped of all judgement toward people touched by destiny in a way that overcomes them completely, but who nevertheless do not lose their dignity, or certain ethical values, or their capacity to feel things. All this despite what life has done to them. There's something existentialist therein, and with the vogue of this movement just after the War, I wonder if it's not this philosophic dimension, this coloration of David's books, which the French have perceived, or think they perceive....It occurs to me to say that it's a notion totally alien to the American public. His characters never lose their humanity, even if they seem always superficially consumed by despair; they always remain capable of being touched by moral principle, despite their profound disillusion. Surely this is what we find, historically and philosophically, in the French experience following the War. But it's a sensibility all but incomprehensible to Americans, who are forever consumed by optimism....

> I wonder if David didn't write these things completely unconsciously; I am nearly certain that he never thought in such terms. He never spoke of it. I have the impression that for him writing was above all mechanics. A choice of formulas. But despite the formulas, it's inevitable that a writer breathe something of his own personality into even the most commercial projects. I don't know that he ever had the ambition to write "seriously." He didn't talk much, never revealed much of himself, despite a very open, jovial exterior....Still, he was a remarkable human being, very endearing, who wrote like no one else. The fact that French readers have been able to recognize this, to divine in the eccentricities of his books this unique aspect, says a great deal for French culture, I think.

* * *

Intensity is what one finally remembers of Goodis, what remains when the
water of specific situations and vagaries of plot boil away.

In a sense, of course, that intensity is his birthright as paperback novelist.
In keeping with their covers, these books were shamelessly exploitative, going about their business, pursuing their ends, with bullish single-mindedness.
Popular art by definition is reductive; this is how it differs from more serious forms which harbor conflicting signals, proliferate meaning. Located at
ground zero of popular fiction, paperback novels were stripped down about
as far as possible, single-cylinder machines built to deliver one hard, powerful punch. Subtlety and depth weren't allowed to cloud the violent and erotic
visions at their heart, and that very narrowness, that meanness, lifted them
out of this world.

Generally, Goodis' command of the "mechanics" of writing is reliable. In
fact, the craftsmanship he mastered in all those years of turning out fiction
for the pulps was sometimes all that salvaged his books from a morass of
aberrant psychology and obsession. Goodis knew how to get his characters
from room to street, how to carry them along like a good tour guide from
the Slough of Despond to Heartbreak Ridge and back again. He knew how
to load his sentences, how to hit the ground running with his prose and keep
going. And yet, again, there is something beyond that, something more than
craftsmanship, good mechanics, momentum. Again and again Goodis pitches
his narrative at so keen a tone that it seems to tremble on the nerve-thin border of terror and fascination.

O'Brien: "The strength of his novels is the way his characters' emotions
color every dialogue, every fragment of physical description....While at his
worst Goodis merely overwrites, at his best he endows his icy street and
wretched shanties with expressionistic intensity."

In a book like *Nightfall*, O'Brien continues, Goodis creates an atmosphere
in which everything—the pressing heat of a summer night, a metal box of wa-
tercolors crashing to the floor, the winding staircase where words of betrayal
are overheard, the mountains towards which the protagonist flees—is at the
same time symbolic and sharply, profoundly literal.

This, then is the hyperrealism of the edge: of drink, fever, madness. And
indeed, there's a directly hallucinatory quality to such Goodis lines as "The
empty room looked back at him" or "quiet came in and sat down," to Parry's
dialogue with the dead Fellsinger in *Dark Passage* or Vanning's dialogue with
his mirror in *Nightfall*. Or the ending of *Down There* (psychiatrists would
label this *dissociation*):

Then he heard the sound. It was warm and sweet and it came from a piano. That's fine piano, he thought. Who's playing that?

He opened his eyes. He saw his fingers caressing the keyboard.

These are not mere literary gimmicks; they evolve from particular situations and from characters' intense emotional states and serve as shortcuts to expression in the way that synesthesia or a poet's choice of sounds are shortcuts. At his best Goodis could make a few careful sentences, a key image or figure of speech, the colors of a room, do a prodigious amount of work. Here, for instance, is the turning point four pages into *Dark Passage*, when passive, innocent Parry, railroaded into prison, betrayed by his presumed friend Fellsinger, takes back his life.

He was sitting on the edge of his cot. He was looking at the bars of the cell door. Like a snake gliding into a pool a thought glided into his mind. He stood up. He walked to the door and put his hands against the steel bars. They weren't very thick but they were strong. He thought of how strong these bars were, how strong was the steel door at the end of corridor D, how ready was the guard's revolver at the end of corridor E, then the two guards at the end of corridor F, and how high the wall was, and how many machine guns were waiting there along the wall. The snake made a turn and started to glide out of the pool. Then it turned again and it began to expand. It was becoming a very big snake because Parry was thinking of the trucks that brought barrels of cement into that part of the yard.

Sleep was a blackboard and on the blackboard was a chalked plan of the yard. He kept tracing it over and over and when he got it straight he imagined a white X where he was going to be when the truck unloaded the barrels. The X moved when the empty barrels were placed back upon the truck. The X moved slowly and then disappeared into one of the barrels that was already in the truck.

The blackboard was all black. It stayed black until a whistle blew. The motor started. The sound of it pierced the side of the barrel and pierced Parry's brain.

The book's opening paragraphs, moving Parry quickly into prison, into place for the book's *real* beginning, are themselves marvels of compression:

It was a tough break. Parry was innocent. On top of that he was a decent sort of guy who never bothered people and wanted to lead a quiet life. But there was too much on the other side and on his side of it there was practically nothing. The jury decided he was guilty. The judge handed him a life sentence and he was taken to San Quentin.

The trial had been big and even though it involved unimportant people it was in many respects sensational. Parry was thirty-one and he made thirty-five a week as a clerk in an investment security house in San Francisco. He had been unhappily married for sixteen months, according to the prosecution. And, according to the prosecution, a friend of the Parrys came into the small apartment one winter afternoon and found Mrs. Parry on the floor with her head caved in. According to the prosecution, Mrs. Parry was dying and just before she passed away she said Parry had banged her on the head with a heavy glass ash try. The ash tray was resting near the body. Police found Parry's fingerprints on the ash tray.

That was half the story. The other half meant the finish of Parry. He had to admit a few things.

Among the things he has to admit are that he hasn't been getting along with his wife and has been seeing other women (the court ignores his wife's infidelities) and that he didn't go to work that day because of a headache. He then has to explain—and this is what finally does him in—why he is 4-F and not in uniform. (One thinks of Meursault, sentenced to death not because he killed the Arab, but because he failed to cry at his mother's funeral. And one remembers Cain's formula: Force of circumstances driving the protagonists to the commission of a dreadful act.) Even his name signals defeat: he can no longer turn aside or fend off the blows that befall him.

It's not difficult to see from all this why Goodis has been so attractive to filmmakers. The establishing pace of those first paragraphs, the looping tumble of information, that silk-smooth, imminently visual transition from cell to barrel—all this is quite cinematic. The celebrated Parry-Fellsinger dialogue, into which the text moves as smoothly and seamlessly as that snake gliding into a pool, would be more difficult to translate to film.

There was blood all over Fellsinger, blood all over the floor. There were pools of it and ribbons of it. There were blotches of it, big blotches of it near Fellsinger, smaller blotches getting even smaller in progression away from the body. There were flecks of it on the furniture and suggestions of it on a wall....It was dark blood where it clotted in the skull cavities. It was luminous pale blood where it stained the horn of the trumpet that rested beside the body. The horn of the trumpet was slightly dented. The pearl buttons of the trumpet valves were pink from the spray of blood.

Fellsinger was belly down on the floor, but his face was twisted sideways. His eyes were opened wide, the pupils up high with a lot of white underneath. It was as if he was trying to look back. Either he wanted to see how badly he was hurt or he wanted to see who was banging on his skull with the trumpet. He mouth was halfway open and the tip of his tongue flapped over the side of his mouth.

Without sound, Parry said, "Hello, George."

Without sound, Fellsinger said, "Hello, Vince."

"Are you dead, George?"

"Yes, I'm dead."

"Why are you dead, George?"

"I can't tell you, Vince. I wish I could tell you but I can't."

"Who did it, George?"

"I can't tell you, Vince. Look at me. Look what happened to me. Isn't it awful?"

"George, I didn't do it. You know that."

"Of course, Vince. Of course you didn't do it."

"George, you don't really believe I did it."

"I know you didn't do it."

[...]

"They'll say I killed you."

"Yes, Vince. That's what they'll say."

"But I didn't do it, George."

"I know, Vince. I know you didn't do it. I know who did it but I can't tell you because I'm dead."

"George, can I do anything for you?"

"No. You can't do a thing for me. I'm dead. Your friend George Fellsinger is dead."

The stage litters slowly with bodies. Stubbed-out cigarettes in an ash tray by the bed become a family that grows through the night. A man and woman sit together in a small circle of light while, outside, the city moves neon-and-steel fingers against an ever-darkening sky.

* * *

The *vita*.

Born in 1917, Philadelphia. Followed in 1919 by a younger brother, Jerome, who dies at age three of meningitis, then, in 1923, by Herbert. Attends Cooke Junior High and Simon Gratz High School, puts in a year at the University of Indiana, then attends Temple University, 1937-38, while beginning to turn out freelance journalism and stories for pulps. Works in public relations locally and, with publication of first novel in 1938, (*Retreat from Oblivion*, Dutton), moves to New York. Here, he writes voluminously for the pulps—as much as 10,000 words a day, better than 5 million words in as many years—and for radio.

Published the year before Chandler's *The Big Sleep*, that first novel is a Hemingwaylike tale of romance and infidelity set against a backdrop of wars in China and Spain. Further "serious" literary efforts for the most part are rejected. But for *Horror Stories*, *Western Tales* and *Dime Mystery Magazine* Goodis produces dozens of stories, a flood of them, also writing whole issues of aviation magazines like *Battle Birds* and *Daredevil Aces* for Popular Publications. He is a regular contributor, as well, to such radio serials as *Hap Harrigan of the Airwaves*, *House of Mystery* and *Superman*.

In 1942 Goodis is in Los Angeles working for several weeks on a treatment of *Destination Unknown* for Universal. He meets and marries mysterious Elaine, who leaves him the following year after their return to New York. There is no record of divorce.

Through 1945 Goodis continues churning out stories for the pulps and for radio, becoming associate producer, in fact, for *Hap Harrigan*. In 1946 he sells *Dark Passage* to Warner Brothers and steps into a six-year contract with that studio, his contract stipulating that half the year will be spent on stories and novels, the remainder on film work. The following year sees the opening of *The Unfaithful* with a script by Goodis and of *Dark Passage*, both huge successes, along with publication of *Behold This Woman* and *Nightfall*.

Goodis' career as screenwriter by this time—and this is truly strange in light of his dramatic gifts, his craftsmanship and the peremptorily cinematic qualities of his writing—is curiously stillborn. He works at various for-hire projects, on an adaptation of Chandler's *The Lady in the Lake*, on an original screenplay which later becomes his last hardcover novel, with Jerry Wald on an epic film concerning the entry of civilization into the atomic age, none of these produced.

Then 1950.

To his credit now are four books. The year of retreat brings a final hardcover, the revamped screenplay *Of Missing Persons*; and the year after, the first paperback original for Gold Medal, *Cassidy's Girl*.

* * *

Probably the most popular of Goodis' paperbacks, *Cassidy's Girl* is a study in failures great and small, written (as O'Brien observes) "in a vein of tortured lyricism all his own, whose very excesses seemed uniquely appropriate to the subject matter." Similarly, Wallington notes that no writer before or since has had so thoroughgoing an obsession with "the shadows cast by the victim, the failure, the drop-out, the has-been"—and *Cassidy's Girl* is where it all first came together, where Goodis got the recipe right for this stew he'd be brewing up the rest of his life.

There is, first, an environment of grinding poverty. Goodis' people dream *up* to cheap chiffoniers and real-veneer furniture. Poverty is just another manifest of how very near the edge—the edge of everything—they are.

There is then, like a jewel dropped into its setting, or perhaps more fittingly like a beer glass put back in the same stained ring, a sensitive and largely inarticulate protagonist unaware of his self-destructive drive.

And finally, two women as the horns of his dilemma, one of them hard-drinking and –talking, earthy, obese, possessive, and the other frail, waiflike, a thing composed of pale, ungraspable dreams, an alcoholic.

> The fourth member of the party was someone Cassidy had never seen before. A small, fragile, pale woman. She looked to be somewhere in her late twenties. Cassidy saw her plainness, her mildness. Something kind and sweet. Something sanitary. And yet, as he watched her, as he saw the way she raised her glass, he knew instantly she was an alcoholic.
>
> It showed. He could always tell. They gave themselves away in hundreds of little gestures.
>
> ...
>
> She sat there with an empty glass in front of her. She was looking at the glass as though it were the pages of a book and she were reading a story.
>
> ...
>
> In the middle of the street they fell again and Cassidy managed to grab her before her head hit the cobblestones. Some light from a street lamp drifted onto her face and he saw that she was expressionless. The look in her eyes was the lost dead look far beyond caring, beyond the inclination to care.
>
> He struggled with her, and again they were on their feet. They moved in a path that had no direction, moving off to the side, then back again, circling and retreating and advancing and finally arriving at the other side of the street and leaning heavily against the street lamp.
>
> As they rested there the damp air coming from the river revived them

a little and they were able to look at each other with recognition.

"What I need," Cassidy said, "is just one more drink."

The dead look left her eyes. "Let's buy a drink."

"We'll go back to Lundy's," he said, "and we'll have another drink."

But then suddenly she shivered and he felt the tender frail body quivering against him, sensed the frenzy of her attempt to keep from falling once more. He held her upright and said, "I'm with you, Doris. It's all right."

The protagonist here is James Cassidy, ex-gridiron star, ex-war hero, ex-airline pilot and in many ways ex-human being, a man around whom disaster hangs "like a magnetic, almost seductive aura" (O'Brien). Wrongly held accountable for an airline crash that killed 78 passengers and from which he alone of the crew survived, Cassidy has embarked on a long decline. Now he is married, to blowsy, brawling Mildred, and when not with her tearing up the apartment, or at Lundy's drinking, he drives a bus.

> The important thing was, he had the bus. It wasn't as big as a four-engined plane, but it was a rolling machine, and it had wheels. And he was at the controls. That was the thing that mattered. That was what he needed. More than anything. He knew he had lost the ability to control Cassidy, and certainly he would never be able to control Mildred, but there was one thing left in this world that he could and would control. The one thing that was real, that had meaning and stability and purpose. The thing that allowed him to grip a wheel and shift gears and come as close as he would ever come to the dimly remembered days of piloting a liner in the sky. It was only an old, battered, broken-down bus, but it was a damn good bus. It was a wonderful bus. Because it would do what he wanted it to do. Because once again J. Cassidy was in the driver's seat.

He's not in the driver's seat, of course, and will never be. The polar tug of those women betokens divisions within himself. And like most alcoholics, he's able to perceive the world only as a reflection of his own thwarted will. There's a moment near the book's end when Cassidy, caught in the clockwork of an incongruous "happy ending," approaches this realization.

> Now he was able to understand the utter futility of his attempt to rescue Doris. There was no possibility of rescue. She didn't want to be rescued. His efforts to drag her away from the liquor had been based on a false premise, and his motive, now that he could see it objectively,

had been more selfish than noble. His pity for Doris had been the reflection of pity that he felt for himself. His need for Doris had been the
need to find something worthwhile and gallant within himself.

Cassidy's Girl proved extremely popular with readers, becoming one of
twelve books published in Gold Medal's first six years to have documented
sales in advance of a million copies. (Others include Vin Packer's *Spring Fire*,
John D. MacDonald's *The Damned* and Gil Brewer's *13 French Street*.)

Its hollow resolution is something *Cassidy's Girl* shares with several other
novels. *Of Tender Sin*'s impotent alcoholic finds redemption by way of psychological revelation and the wisdom of an old black on Skid Row; the py-
romaniac of *Fire in the Flesh* quenches his urge first in cheap wine, then by
Freudian insight. "Many of Goodis' novels follow a similar psychoanalytic
pattern," O'Brien notes. "The thrust of his books is usually toward release,
redemption, resolution of conflict, and there are even some theoretically
'happy' endings; but whatever salvation Goodis as author may cook up for
his characters, it never adds up to more than literary wishful thinking. The
despair does not go away." And the final works, he adds, are suffused with a
depression that creeps into the very rhythm of the sentences.

There is little question that Goodis, like Cassidy in the passage above, was
projecting his own conflicts, displacing his own summary failures onto his
characters. In a sense his novels are a long apology; one, *The Blonde on the
Street Corner*, set in the Thirties and relating a writer's destruction by an alcoholic older woman and confrontation with his own sexuality, comes close
to autobiography, one suspects.

In a paragraph from the first page of *Cassidy's Girl*, O'Brien perceives
Goodis' own face and credo:

> Aside from the pay, it was emotionally important for Cassidy to do
> this type of work. Keeping his eyes on the road and his mind on the
> wheel was a protective fence holding him back from internal as well as
> external catastrophe.

Isn't this Goodis speaking directly, O'Brien asks—not about driving a bus,
but about his own writing? It's not for plot or style that we read Goodis'
books, O'Brien says, but for precisely this sense of impending inner catastrophe, this all but unbearable intensity that handles the description of a street
lamp or the spill of yellow light through barroom windows, even language
itself, with something like hysteria.

"Goodis certainly had no great gift for physical description, and was no
good at describing how something works. His plots were devoid of ingenuity.

His characters were always the same few, repeated obsessionally from book to book. But he did have that anguish, the anguish of his characters' distance from reality. His hero is a frightened, lonely, unworldly, often alcoholic man. He smokes cigarette after cigarette. He walks the streets and never meets a friend. He sits alone in a hotel room staring out the window, or he throws himself into meaningless work and tries to shut out the rest of the world."

Goodis' best books create a unique poetry of solitude and fear, O'Brien writes, and even his lesser, lackluster works often come to life in sudden patches of vivid feeling.

"They read like the improvisations of someone compelled to keep writing, to keep the words, the pages, coming toward him. He writes knowing that he must fill the page, finish the episode, continue as far as the next episode, the next book. His central image is always that of the wounded man, his strength gone, pulling himself forward, yet sensing at the same time that he won't make it, that it will all have been in vain."

* * *

What to make, finally, of Elaine, this silent, powerful force in David Goodis' life?

Elaine and he were married less than a year, yet several of David's friends believed him deeply, perhaps fatally, scarred by the relationship. Did the demanding devouring females of his novels feed and grow, if indeed they didn't originate—for how can we say, after all, if Goodis was attracted to her as a type, or in fact learned his predilections from her—from memories of Elaine?

Goodis' cousin remembers Elaine as red-haired, attractive and sexy, but not really well-proportioned, definitely not the mannequin type. She had large breasts and "a glorious posterior," he recalls, and always wore very tight clothes.

Goodis often spoke of Elaine to his friend Jane Fried in later years.

"I think it was 1942 or '43 that they were married," she told Garnier. "David said that she wasn't at all the kind of woman he'd expected to marry him. He described her as a 'Jewish princess,' very conventional, hard to please, very chic. I don't know that she was, but she did have that style. Anyhow, it was a complete fiasco. She threw him over pretty quickly; I'm sure she found him too odd, not mature or suave enough for her. She left for New York. He'd go there from time to time to attempt reconciliation. She worked in a fashionable clothing shop and was mortified when he showed up like that to badger her, dressed the way he always was....And David would do it purposely, make himself even more shabby and wretched-looking, and he'd plant himself by the shop-window or the door."

Los Angeles friend Marvin Yolin remembers specific behavior later used by Goodis in a scene in *Behold This Woman*.

"Apparently he was completely overcome by her, and had a terrible time of it. She was red-headed and had large breasts which David adored. When they lived in New York she would wake him in the middle of the night and say: 'You want to see them, you want to see my breasts?' And he would say yes. Then she'd send him off to find her an ice cream, in the middle of the night this is, and of course he'd be gone a long time before getting back. He'd come in with the ice cream then and she'd call him names, curse him for waking her up. He told me that she had rendered him physically and mentally deranged, and even though he was finally able to talk to me about it, and with humor, I'm persuaded that all this had marked him for life."

* * *

Excepting the hybrid *Of Missing Persons* published in 1950 just as Goodis began his career as paperback novelist, the last hardcover—following *Retreat from Oblivion* in 1938, *Dark Passage* in 1946, and *Nightfall*, published earlier the same year, 1947—was *Behold This Woman*, a curious book in many ways.

"He was barely 30," O'Brien says of Goodis, "but his career had already peaked," noting also that *Behold This Woman*, "a masochist's dream" which could not have done much for his reputation, was the writer's first mining of his own erotic obsessions.

The novel's portrait of a devouring, evil woman, of course, may look back to Goodis' time with Elaine, or at any rate to what he made of that time in his mind, and it *is* unrelieved, often rather ludicrous stuff (O'Brien calls the woman's climactic murder "a three-page barrage of mangled flesh"), but the badness of the book—the embarrassment of it, in every sense—goes far deeper.

Philippe Garnier addresses just that badness in his biography of Goodis, in a chapter given largely to discussion of the milieu of original paperbacks. *Behold This Woman*, he says, seems almost written for the romance market.

It's the novelistic equivalent of soap opera, and certainly nearer the novels of Cain and "fairy tales for adults" than the world we generally associate with Goodis, that of the gutter and the hopelessly lost. Daydreams are the source of such novels, which describe extraordinary situations, and a special luxury, denied the reader. For Goodis, grand lover of catalogs, such a genre, always written by those with faces pressed to shop windows and showcases, held laughable allure. Since luxury was alien to him, he reduced everything to the *paraphernalia* of luxury, to its trappings.

Goodis' foppish protagonist, numbering among his preferences blue Oxford broadcloth and Montana Saddle cologne, is "a veritable walking catalog." His counterpart Clara is the kind of woman who sucks all day on chocolates, treats herself to opals and gems, and has a color, complete with outfits and bath salts, for each day of the week. And when he writes of the generous charms of this dominatrix, Garnier notes, Goodis' prose becomes as inflated, unworldly and salacious as any Victorian pornographer's.

> One isn't able to help noticing the sardonic and malicious under-currents of this curious novel. The tone is extravagant, the details frankly ridiculous, the story absurd and silly. And still, this book perhaps finally tells us more about the man Goodis than all his novels in the *Serie Noire*. The amount of nonsense in this book is amazing: characters never cease colliding in the most fortuitous and forced circumstances....And of course, characters are regularly knocked down, for Goodis, even in this novel for housewives, didn't surrender his taste for pugilistic fantasy.
>
> One wonders how such a novel could ever be accepted and published.

The answer lies in Goodis' relative celebrity; he had, after all, major movie sales and serialization in *Saturday Evening Post* behind him. But the book is really a harbinger of the paperback originals, in which he would be left alone to do pretty much as he pleased. Knox Burger, who took over as editor at Gold Medal, remembers Goodis as being always ill at ease—especially when asked for revisions in a manuscript, something which apparently had not happened before. Burger describes Goodis as timid and socially inept, comparing him to other, more favored Gold Medal writers such as John D. McDonald and Jim Thompson:

> In my opinion Goodis wasn't in the same league. When I knew him, I think he was trying to do more serious work. He had a lot of ambition, but not the skill, the talent, to pull it off. He was never able to build up much suspense or intrigue because his plots were quite feeble.
>
> In the time of my predecessor Dick Carroll, Goodis was writing his "skid row" novels for Gold Medal. I think those were also an effort towards regeneration. But he wasn't creative enough by then. The well was dry.

* * *

Goodis returns to Philadelphia, to 6305 North 11th Street, which will mean to us always now that photograph, its darknesses and aversions. Hemmed-in lives grow the densest. And we recall Garnier remarking: Because he himself lived in a sketch all blacks and greys, he exulted in *Behold This Woman*, "It was marvelous to live in a world of colors...."

There in his parents' home, dramatic and Goodis-like though this would be, Goodis' life does not end. He moves into the bosom, the center, of his family, making arrangements for the future of schizophrenic brother Herbert, caring for his father, then, following his father's death in 1963, becoming anchor and support for his mother. He goes out to restaurants with old friends like Jane Fried, who gave Garnier a wonderful account of Goodis' last years; meets Truffaut in New York for the 1962 premiere of *Shoot the Piano Player*; travels briefly to Jamaica and Barbados; continues prowling black nightclubs and carrying on affairs, perhaps imaginary ones, perhaps not, with black women, speaking of this continually with friends, concealing it from family.

There are further novels: *Street of the Lost* and *Of Tender Sin* (1952); *The Burglar* and *Moon in the Gutter* (1953); *The Blonde on the Street Corner* and *Street of No Return* (1954); *The Wounded and the Slain* (1955, incorporating scenes from his trip to Jamaica); *Down There* (1956); *Fire in the Flesh* (1957); *Night Squad* (1961).

Each morning Goodis retires to his room and works, breaking off for lunch and a nap, then working on late into the afternoon. His mother, who prepares lunch each day, guards her son's time, telling all who call: "David's working." He himself never talks about his work other than to remark "I really must finish this thing for Fawcett" or "I've had a rough time of it today."

With his father's death it all starts to fall apart for Goodis, this one sheltered place he had, this safe harbor. And with his mother's, three years later, he seems utterly lost. He seldom works now. In 1965, obsessed with the belief that the producers of *The Fugitive* have stolen the idea from *Dark Passage*, he brings legal action. In 1966, he admits himself to a psychiatric hospital. On January 7, 1967, at 11:30 P.M., at Albert Einstein Medical Center, age 49, David Goodis dies.

A final Goodis novel, *Somebody's Done For*, is published by Avon under its Banner imprint the year of his death. At that time nothing else is in print in the U.S. Not for twenty years, until 1987 when Black Lizard begins its reissues with *Black Friday, Shoot the Piano Player* and *Nightfall*, will another Goodis book surface.

"*Feverish Country, This*"
(Gerald Kersh)

In *I Got References*, the collection of stories, sketches and autobiographical snippets that Paul Duncan says may be the closest we'll ever come as readers to sitting down for a chat with its author, Gerald Kersh writes of his devil-take-the-hindmost childhood. "I achieved notoriety on account of my destructive tendencies. Once, when a tramcar fell over near Acton, I was seized and chastised, as it were absent-mindedly, as soon as the crash was heard."

This shows, I think, something both of the man's intense egoism and of his native skill as raconteur. In many ways Kersh continued all his life to be the bad boy of literature. Born early into the new century, some eight years before (as Virginia Woolf has it) human nature changed utterly, he rode in on the last hurrahs of several grand British literary traditions, freelancing articles and sketches to the Daily Mirror and London Evening Standard in Fleet Street, publishing short stories in the many newspapers and magazines for which they were then a mainstay.

This was the heyday of the short story, in fact, and high-circulation, high-profile magazines like Collier's and the Saturday Evening Post and their counterparts in the UK could provide a fine living. Demand, both there and at lower-paying markets such as John O'London's Weekly or the pulps that specialized in various forms of romance and adventure, was high; many writers specialized, turning out stories by the dozen and little else. Modernism might have been busily kicking over the traces elsewhere, but here standards remained deeply rooted in nineteenth-century notions of popular literature and the well-made story. Nor, again as in 19th-century writing, had "unnatural" elements been purged, as shortly they would be, in favor of a thoroughgoing realism. Magazines offered up heady blends of exoticism, sea adventures, Wellsian science fiction and moral tales, ghost stories, crime stories.

Here in the States, it's mostly for his stories, of which he wrote several hundred, that Kersh is remembered when he is known at all. Many of these, though generally given his distinctive stamp, were staple fare for magazine writers of the time: ventriloquist's dummy stories ("The Extraordinarily Horrible Dummy"), Siamese twins stories ("The Sympathetic Souse"), cursed-jewel stories ("Seed of Destruction"), circus- or carnival-folk stories ("The

Queen of Pig Island"), stories of possession ("The Eye" and, again, "The Extraordinarily Horrible Dummy"). These might in fact more properly be called tales. The majority have elements of the fantastic; if not of the fantastic, then of the grotesque. Many are built around some central gimmick—what if one Siamese twin were a drunk, the other a teetotaler, for instance—and have a trick or reverse ending, some final revelation that snaps the tale into new focus.

They share, too, another strategy common to older work. Many are framed, i.e., presented to the reader as true stories garnered from obscure documents (the last days of Ambrose Bierce in "The Oxoxoco Bottle"), come upon in journals (a Japanese man thrown back in time by detonation of the bomb over Hiroshima in "The Brighton Monster"), or overheard from others (the truly nightmarish creatures of "Men Without Bones"). Kersh from time to time even steps directly into the doorway of the story, presenting himself under his own name as interlocutor. This convention has the dual purpose of lending formal credibility to a story's events and, by placing fantastical or highly-charged events at a remove, of softening and safening them—taming the story's savage heart.

History, the shadow of great events, also looms over Kersh's stories—Hiroshima in "The Brighton Monster," the Cold War in "Prophet Without Honor," the Balkans in "Reflections in a Tablespoon," slavery in "Fantasy of a Hunted Man"—perhaps as another way of cranking up wattage, raising the game's stakes. Kersh was, after all, competing vigorously and continuously with hundreds of others for the reader's (and editor's) attention.

As a short story writer Kersh largely belongs to that group of writers Anthony Burgess characterized as making literature from the intrusion of fantasy or horror into a real world closely observed. Their tales more often suggest fable or a sort of grand guignol than the plodding naturalism of much modern work, Burgess notes. They are likely to ransack traditions but not to belong, themselves, to any tradition. And while themselves quite "literary," they play no part in the development of literature: even the most comprehensive histories of English-language literature have no room at the inn for the likes of Saki, John Collier, Mervyn Peake, or Gerald Kersh. This is a type of writer rarely seen today—a type already fading during Kersh's time.

If Kersh's approach at times could be indirect or sidling ("I had this curious story from a gentlemen in the Paradise Bar..."), his engagement with the material was not. One early critic termed his stories "frontal assaults." Not uncommonly do we come upon such arresting descriptions as that of the wasted, drunken beauty whose eyes have become like "a couple of cockroaches desperately swimming in two saucers of boiled rhubarb," or of the divan whose springs protrude "like the entrails of a disembowelled horse."

Nor are Kersh's people often of the nicest sort; he himself spoke of them as having been "quarried" rather than born.

Yet Burgess proclaimed Sam Yudenow from *Fowler's End* a comic character on the order of Falstaff. In *The Thousand Deaths of Mr. Small*, another reviewer asserted, Kersh had created " a character capable of standing on its own feet beside Wilkins Micawber." Harry Fabian of *Night and the City* intrigues us still, sixty years after he first swam into our ken, as do the va-et-vients and divagations of Busto's rooming-house in *The Song of a Flea*. And if at first we read for the outrageous stories and sometimes still more outrageous characters, we reread (and Kersh readers one and all, I have found, are veteran rereaders) for quite different reasons: marvelous evocations of down-and-out London; discursions that springboard off some passing observation and continue on marvelously for page after page, pushing all else for the moment aside; startling felicities of language that seem to appear fullblown from nowhere, as though the sentences themselves had burst into flame.

Harlan Ellison, in his introduction to *Nightshades and Damnations*, offered up a few notes from Kersh's Greatest Hits.

> We hang about the necks of our tomorrows like hungry harlots about the necks of penniless sailors.

> A storm broke, and at every clap of thunder the whole black sky splintered like a window struck by a bullet—starred and cracked in ten thousand directions letting in flashes of dazzling light...

> ...there are men whom one hates until a certain moment when one sees, through a chink in their armor, the writhing of something nailed down and in torment.

Harlan and I alike admire Kersh's description of a man so characterless as to be all but nonexistent, whose tie is "patterned with dots like confetti trodden into the dust" and whose "oddment of limp brownish mustache resembled a cigarette-butt, disintegrating shred by shred in a tea-saucer."

Kersh is a master of metaphor in a manner rare among novelists, lashing whole chapters, the creation of entire characters and vibrant scenes, to the scaffolding of what are essentially extended metaphors. Here, for example, is his stunning portrait of a married couple in Fowler's End, that sinkhole purlieu of London you find by "going northward, step by step, into the neighborhoods that most strongly repel you."

He was a quick, hideously ugly little man, cold and viscous about the hands, with a gecko's knack of sticking to plane surfaces. Once, when I went into his shop to buy a handkerchief, Godbolt, telling me that he didn't have much call for that kind of thing nowadays but thought he had a few in stock, went to get one from a high shelf. It may have been the effect of the fog but I will swear I saw him run up the wall. He had a black-cotton fly of a wife who was always buzzing at him from a distance; she never came within less than five feet of him—for fear, presumably, that he might thrust out a glutinous green tongue and catch her. He was always watching her out of the corners of his horny-lidded, protruberant eyes.

I've slipped here, you'll note, from speaking of Kersh as a short-story writer to speaking of him as a novelist. There's a considerable divorce between the two, and for all his facility as a story writer, for all his touches of the grotesque and fantastic therein, it's in the novel, and as a realist, that his specific genius found full force and strength. Stories often seem to have been taken up rather light-heartedly, perhaps chiefly as a means to pay rent or provide passage for yet another relocation, turned out quickly, one suspects, and sent off virtually as the last page emerged from the typewriter. The novels he appears to have taken more seriously. Again, it is 19th-century models, Kipling early on, Dickens a bit later, to which they invite comparison.

While publication of his third novel, *Night and the City*, in 1938 brought major attention, it was as a war novelist that Kersh first began earning significant money from his writing and became well known. In these novels he showed a naturalist, almost taxidermic slant quite in contrast to the exoticism and fantastic elements of his short stories.

1942 *They Died With Their Boots Clean*
1942 *The Nine Lives of Bill Nelson*
1943 *The Dead Look On*
1943 *A Brain and Ten Fingers*
1944 *Faces in a Dusty Picture*

Of the last a reviewer for the Times Literary Supplement noted: "Once more Mr Kersh's specialty is the plain, coarse, lively, everyday speeches of the troops, and again there is much to admire in the vigour and skill of his dialogue and in the assurance with which he draws from it an impression of English character or of English idiosyncracies." Telling dialogue, the manner in which Kersh caught up the usages and rhythms of those about him and in recreating them used them to illuminate caste, milieu and character, was forever his greatest strength. For Kersh, it's not character, but the way in which one uses language, that is fate.

Like birds that never stray over a mile past their birth tree, some writers pass their entire professional lives working the same territory, circling central themes again and again, grinding the meal down ever finer. Others, generally not to their benefit in this ever-increasingly specialized world (for most publishers, booksellers and readers want to be able to say just what kind of sausage it is they are buying), are all over the place. Beginning with *Night and the City*, a mystery novel in the American vein unlike any other written before, and with a firm reputation for war books, Kersh went on to turn out *Prelude to a Certain Midnight*, a mystery novel unlike any other written before *or* since, before going on to produce intense psychological portraits (*The Thousand Deaths of Mr. Small*), masculine fiction in the Hemingway mold (*The Weak and the Strong*), Huxleyian satire (*An Ape, a Dog and a Serpent*), pulp science fiction (*The Great Wash*, in the U.S. *The Secret Masters*), an outstanding historical novel about Saul's conversion (*The Implacable Hunter*), and demotic, Dickensian comedies (*Fowler's End*).

"I'm sorry, sir, it's just not done that way," British bureaucrats and clerks will tell you when you fail to follow form. And so publishers must have said something of the sort to Gerald Kersh; certainly reviewers said it of him. A general, progressive shrinking of literary boundaries was taking place at the time, a kind of degentrification of the profession. The writer could no longer hope to have it all, to be all things to all men, to write across borders; he was expected to settle down at home and cultivate his garden. He must, to start with, for instance, be either a serious writer or a commercial one.

Kersh, like many of us since, failed to see or admit the distinction.

But surely one did not sit down to write a mystery novel and instead stock it with such darting, solid characters as, in a kind of gentle mutiny, to take over the book entirely? *And* (as if that were not enough) why on earth or in heaven should one choose to employ with great care all the traditional forms of the genre to the express purpose of calling into question the very meaning and significances of that genre? (Care for a game of tennis? But first, let's have these nets down...)

Observed from afar, Kersh's career indeed might be seen as one long careen from genre to genre, each shelter in turn blown over by high winds. I've used the word facility above. And I wonder if that, with the changing role of the writer, is not another key on the chain.

Someone said of singer George Jones that it all came too easy to him, that distinctive sound, the phrasing, song interpretation. What others had to work to develop and achieve, he had at his fingertips. Something of the same might be said of Gerald Kersh. Kersh had from the first a terrible facility. He could do anything, it seemed: bring characters to life with one quick phrase, open up their hearts to our view with what they said or avoided saying to one another, show the pettiness, cruelty and wayward kindness aswarm in the anthills of each of us. He could write beautifully, in ways that all but stopped the reader's breath. And he could write knowingly—he was, after all, a soldier—of true ugliness, real horror, of despair that has no past, no future.

Kersh was also a writer of great energy and ambition. Paul Duncan tells us that he often worked night and day with only a couple of hours of sleep, and that eventually this took its toll in regular collapses. One suspects that as time went on Kersh may have leaned a bit heavily on both that energy and on his native facility, expecting them to carry him. "Abundant energy," "exhuberance," "imaginative intensity," "pounding creative energy"—these are the sort of phrases one encounters again in contemporary reviews of Kersh's work, just as one encounters, invariably, mention of his prolificacy. And in fact critical opinion seems rather early on to have cast itself and hardened about those notions.

"Just why is Mr. Kersh such an infuriating writer?" the Sunday Times asked upon publication of Kersh's collection *Men Without Bones*.

> Because...we have all been charmed or surprised or shocked at one time or another...by Mr Kersh's energy and expertness; but with each book there has been less of the writer whose promise we hallooed and more of the casually professional huckster of trinkets and tricks....There was a time when he looked to have the chance of becoming a Kipling or a Huxley; all we have now is a kind of poor man's Orson Welles of the short story.

Phrases such as "ingenuous and tortuous brilliance" or "a brilliant mess" appear ever more frequently. Anthony Boucher spoke for many, critics as well as readers, in his review of Kersh's effort at a science fiction thriller (*The Secret Masters*):

> The relatively quiet but incisive and suspenseful opening portions of the book are first-rate Kersh, richly peopled with the odd bit roles he sketches so well and written with style and individuality. The large scale melodrama which develops later is as banal and dated as it is overwritten and incredible.

One of the most thoughtful assessments, speaking to Kersh's many strengths as to his weaknesses, came via the Times Literary Supplement upon publication of *The Song of a Flea* in 1948.

Mr. Kersh is at once the delight and despair of his admirers. He is their delight because he is one of the comparatively few living novelists in this country who write with energy and originality and whose ideas are not drawn from a residuum of novels that have been written before; he is their despair because the lack of restraint which makes him such a welcome relief in one direction leads him to all sorts of imperfections in another.

Anthony Burgess, however, rather famously in his 1961 review of *The Implacable Hunter*, took to task the sad and arbitrary state of Kersh's reputation.

> Too many critics affect to mourn a dead talent in Gerald Kersh, a gift that died with his boots clean; there has been a tendency to ignore or disparage his later work, patronise, sigh, and pretend to nostalgia for the tremendous Nelson.
> I can't see why. I read *Fowler's End* in darkest Borneo, at a time when it was hard to laugh, and considered it to be one of the best comic novels of the century, with Sam Yudenow as superb a creation (almost) as Falstaff.
> Many total and partial rereadings have strengthened this conviction. We may adjudge Mr. Kersh, after reading *The Implacable Hunter*, to be now at the height of his powers.

It's impossible to say to what degree Kersh's difficulties in later years were in fact precipitated by changing literary tides, to what degree by editorial preconceptions regarding his work and resistance to it on the part of American publishers, to what degree by his egoism and stubborn insistence upon doing things his way. We know, at any rate, from Paul's biographical sketch, that Kersh had a hard time of it.

Some artists thrive on instability. Hemingway, it was said, required a new woman for each new novel. Others set themselves intricate emotional traps in order to fuel their work. Kersh, instability seems slowly, though progressively, to have undone. To the ever-present fault lines and uncertainties of the freelance life, to market changes and a general decline in the professional's position within publishing, have to be adduced, first, Kersh's failure of health, then a horrendously debilitating marriage, his spendthrift nature, a long series of financial setbacks and unrecoupable losses. It was not that Kersh ever stopped writing. *Fowler's End* came out in 1957, when his problems were well underway, *The Implacable Hunter* in 1961. New stories tumbled from him. But fewer and fewer choices remained open. Profligate with his talents from the first, now he sensed their squander. With books such as *The Great Wash* and *A Long Cool Day in Hell* he was casting about for firm ground, any firm ground.

For me, "The Queen of Pig Island" will always be a central story in Kersh's work. This tale of Lalouette, born without arms and legs, and of Gargantua the Horror who cares for her and of Tick and Tack the Tiny Twins, all of them shipwrecked on an island, manages to compress into just over a dozen pages everything that our civilization and our being human entails. "The Queen of Pig Island" is about love, about treachery, about what society is in its deepest heart and about what men choose to be in theirs. I wonder sometimes if in his final months Gerald Kersh might not have thought back to this story, thought again of Lalouette stranded there so far from the civilization she loved, Lalouette who on that island witnessed the worst and best of which her fellow men were capable, Lalouette arduously, painstakingly scratching on paper with the pencil held in her teeth, working to make a record, to get it all down in the last minutes before, forsaken and utterly alone, she dies.

High Road

The Selected Stories of Patricia Highsmith

A writer is a distinctive kind of loner—psychologically apart, yet committed to communication. This conflict seems particularly true of writers who simultaneously court and challenge genre conventions, people like Theodore Sturgeon, Chester Himes, Iain Sinclair, Jonathan Carroll, Jack O'Connell; often they struggle with self and with reader's expectations as much as with the material to hand. There's a gravity forever working to draw down both work and worker. Each new day, each new novel or essay, each new paragraph and page, requires renewed conviction—a new act of self-persuasion that this is worth doing, that what one does, matters. No surprise then that writers so often prove such a stubborn, contrary lot.

Few more stubborn, contrary or self-assuming writers than Patricia Highsmith. Making no concessions to market forces—perhaps, like other highly individualist, idiosyncratic writers, she found herself unable to do so—she pursued a career unparalleled among contemporaries, baffling readers and critics, many of whom finally threw up their hands. Here in the States, when known at all she was known as a mystery writer. Her books fell from and returned to print in odd cycles, as though editors, recognizing her importance, could not quite leave her alone yet were so disquieted by the work, so intimately troubled by it, that, having initiated conversation, they turned and fled.

In Europe, where she spent much of her productive life, and where, as with Gallimard's La Série Noire, genre writing is more likely to be embraced than scorned, Highsmith won wide recognition as simply a novelist, even though, as with many expatriates, America remained her compelling subject.

American literature, of course, bears a heavy heritage of pulpdom, and for the most part prefers lines between low and high cultures solidly drawn. With *Strangers on a Train* and subsequent meta-mysteries, Highsmith tapped into genre energies, but she also inflamed bare-rubbed spots of the American soul others had agreed to leave alone. Her art records a bursting of the blisters that develop when shoes of seem (the salesman measured and assured you they were perfect) don't fit the feet that be. She pushed things to the very borders of expectation, civility, civilization and reason—even of humanity. The Roman playwright Terence wrote that "nothing human is alien to me." Much that's human is alien to Highsmith. And if America's tale has always best been told by outsiders, by the frontiersmen, Tocquevilles, and Thoreaus among us, by artists who ritually by sheer force of will turn themselves into outsiders, then Highsmith made herself, or found within herself, the perfect outsider.

Half a century before the term came into general usage, Highsmith's work was deeply transgressive, transgressive not only of received wisdom, proscribed behavior, and social attitudes, but also of conventional notions of fiction. She makes little concession to supposed axioms of character development, proper motivation, the necessary shape of a story. Narrative lines may diverge sharply on the third or fourth page, or in the second paragraph. A story's end is likely to find us with recomplication in resolution's place. Characters act, even kill, arbitrarily and without reason, as in *Strangers on a Train*, while others for similar lack of reason fail to do the simple, obvious things (such as going to the police or withdrawing) that would save them. One wonders if she may not in fact be the ultimate realist. Her characters refuse to fulfill our expectations. They dodge and duck, shimmy, signify, dive and resurface, trailing behind them like an insect's egg case all the complications, swellings, self-contradictions, paper cuts, codiciles, boils, blisters, burdens, and sudden turns of our lives.

"She is a writer who has created a world of her own—a world claustrophobic and irrational," Graham Greene noted in his introduction to 1970's *The Snail-Watcher*, reprinted here. A world without moral endings, as Greene says, dark, and lit by sudden flares of violent action. "Nothing is certain when we have crossed this frontier."

Nothing indeed. Everything in Patricia Highsmith's world is fluid, runny, hard to hold onto. Touch it and it breaks up, rolls sluggishly away in pieces, like mercury. The malleability of identity itself proves a constant theme. Tom Ripley, who not altogether coincidentally deals in art forgeries, is the primary example, of course. David Kelsey in *This Sweet Sickness* creates quite literally a house of lies, a kind of stillborn cocoon in which he swaddles himself. Highsmith's characters step between lives, move from fantasy to dailyness and back without so much as wiping their shoes at the threshold. Just as Whitman brought out edition after edition of *Leaves of Grass* in more or less continuous revision, so does America, this great anthology, continually reinvent itself—and so do American lives.

Always the shape of the life looms like a beggar in the doorway, or mad cousins shut away in Southern attics, behind the work.

Patricia Highsmith was born January 9, 1921, in Fort Worth, Texas, to Jay Bernard Plangman, of German descent, and Mary Coates, of English-Scots descent. Shortly after her birth, the parents separated and divorced; Patricia was raised by her Texas grandmother until the age of six, at which time she joined her mother and stepfather, both commercial artists, in New York. She did not meet her father until age 12 and apparently felt no connection to him. Following a series of separations, her stepfather, Stanley Highsmith, and her mother would eventually divorce, though not until after Patricia had graduated from Barnard College and returned to live with them in their Greenwich Village apartment. She wrote scripts for comic books to support herself, turning to more serious literature evenings and weekends.

A story written while at Barnard, "The Heroine," was published in *Harper's Bazaar* and reprinted in *O. Henry Prize Stories of 1946*. Then in 1948, with the sponsorship of Truman Capote, she attended Yaddo, where she wrote *Strangers on a Train*, published in 1950, after six rejections, by Harper and Brothers. Down the hall from Patricia at Yaddo was Chester Himes. Alfred Hitchcock filmed the novel in 1951. Though later reclothed by Czenzi Ormonde, the original script of *Strangers* was written by Raymond Chandler, who, interestingly enough, in a letter to Hitchcock and in these excerpts from his own working notes, remarked the story's implausibility:

> It's darn near impossible to write, because consider what you have to put over: A perfectly decent young man (Guy) agrees to murder a man he doesn't know, has never seen, in order to keep a maniac from giving himself away and from tormenting the nice young man....We are flirting with the ludicrous. If it is not written and played exactly right, it will be absurd.

During the Fifties and Sixties, while chiefly based in New York, Highsmith traveled to and lived in Europe, Mexico and the American Southwest. Tacit assertion of independence of thought came with publication, in 1952, of a lesbian novel, *The Price of Salt*. Brought out under the pseudonymn Claire Morgan, Highsmith's second novel was reissued under her own name only in 1991. In 1963 she moved to Europe for good, first settling in England, then France, finally, for the last thirteen years of her life, Switzerland.

Highsmith never had much that was good to say of her parents. Asked in a 1980 interview why she didn't love her mother, Highsmith replied, "First, because she made my childhood a little hell. Second, because she herself never loved anyone, neither my father, my stepfather, nor me." The same interviewer asked her if she, with a reputation as a reclusive, had ever attempted to live with someone. "Indeed, but it was catastrophic....So, the pleasures of family life, no, thanks."

In her work there are few successful couples or families. Far more common is the sort of desperate isolation à deux demonstrated by Vic and Melinda Van Allen in *Deep Water*. Attractions occur only in tandem, it seems, with repulsion. The stronger character fully subsumes the weaker. Couples seldom reproduce (the Van Allens are an exception), and parents are as absent as children. Highsmith's characters exist as islands, afloat and apart. Tom Ripley is never happier than when shut away from humankind in his train compartment. Highsmith was herself a recluse, living for much of her life alone in an isolated house near Locarno on the Swiss-Italian border. Tom and Heloise in the later Ripley novels do have a workable marriage, true. And Highsmith's lesbian novels—the marriage of Therese and Carol in *The Price of Salt*, and the extended family of her last, *Small g: A Summer Idyll*—offer visions of successful alternatives. But for the most part there is a horror of relationships and, especially, of family.

"Old Folks at Home" may be the ultimate horror-of-family story. Looking to be good people and hoping in some vague way to fulfill themselves, its upper-middle-class couple adopts, not a child, but an elderly man and wife formerly ensconced in a nursing facility. Gradually they come to realize they've forfeited their lives. In order to work, they're forced to move to a rented office; soon thereafter their house, everything they own, goes up in fire as a result of the old folks' smoking in bed. Through it all, though, sinking like stones, they retain their good will. "We'll make it," they tell themselves again and again.

When in "The Kite," a rare story including a child, one parent says to another, "As long as he hasn't been—you know," meaning not masturbation, as we're set up to anticipate, but a visit to his sister's grave, we learn something of the real family values at work: illusion, the status quo, the silent agreements, must be maintained at whatever cost. It's not flying too close to the sun that brings Daedalus down, not heat at all, but the bone-chill of pretense.

Of a long-past era when short stories were thought as urgent in their own way as novels, or at very least proper employment for the imaginative writer, Highsmith published seven collections, beginning with *Eleven* (1970) and ending with *Tales of Natural and Unnatural Catastrophes* (1987), all but the last, posthumous volume brought out in the UK by William Heinemann. W.W. Norton, which is also reissuing many of the novels, brings together in The Selected Stories representations from five of the collections : *The Animal-Lover's Book of Beastly Murder* (1975), *Little Tales of Misogyny* (1977), *Slowly, Slowly in the Wind* (1979), *The Black House* (1981) and *Mermaids on the Golf Course* (1985).

In what is thus far the only book-length study of Highsmith's work, Russell Harrison has likened the early stories to those of Carson McCullers. They are indeed of similar impress. Several collections, such as *The Animal-Lover's*

Book of Beastly Murders and *Little Tales of Misogyny*, congeal about some central conceit. Interestingly, the stories demonstrate far greater variety in subject matter, theme and voice than the novels. They're filled with surprises, sharply drawn intriguing characters, brilliantly realized scenes. One turns the page eager to see what comes next—between as much as within stories. Quite possibly this fine collection, along with Norton's reissues of her novels, will win Highsmith the recognition she deserves. Certainly it should gain her a new cadre of readers.

Still, these stories haven't a great deal in common, Harrison points out, with the mainstream American short story, and strike many chords familiar from the novels: evocations of states of extreme anxiety, displacement of a privileged class, the malleability of history and of identity itself, eruptions of violence, cataclysmic interpenetrations of one world into another.

That last may be the key theme for Highsmith.

When at the end of one story here, having just been pulled, as by a drain, into the occasion of another's death, a man stands imagining his own, we understand not only the importance of imagination to Highsmith and her characters, we understand also that something has begun within this man, and where it will lead. "He stared down a long while, and imagined his body toppling over and over, striking the water with not much of a splash, sinking....But he hadn't even the courage or the despair as yet for suicide. One day, however, he would, he knew. One day when the planes of cowardice and courage met at the proper angle." Does anything better define our ambitions and failures, our much-vaunted freedom and all our much-cherished choices, than that final phrase?

Again and again characters force or insinuate themselves into another's life, altering it beyond recognition. Like black holes, they draw everything, even the very light of those other lives, into them. Tom Ripley's irruption into Dickie Greenleaf's life and gradual assumption of it in the initial Ripley book is the best-known example. But there are many others, Charles Anthony Bruno's annexation of Guy Haines' life in *Strangers on a Train* among them. In *This Sweet Sickness*, David Kelsey will not let ex-girlfriend Annabelle be. He purchases a house and furnishes it just as he knows she would like, then lies abed while masturbating with the thought that "His house had the virtue of never being lonely. He felt Annabelle's presence in every room."

Often it seems as though for Highsmith, for her characters, virtually any connectedness is fraught. Entanglements draw one down. Personal boundaries fallen, others will follow: social, spiritual. Physical contact becomes ontological horror. Ever the observer, ever apart, the recluse looks on, fascinated, appalled.

This basic theme of interpenetration resounds throughout Highsmith's novels and stories alike. And while they may first appear so, such intrusions are no simple co-opting or appropriation. Guy Haines is complicit in Bruno's scheme; Dickie Greenleaf becomes, at least for a time, half the equation that is Tom Ripley. As Francis Wyndham notes in an essay in *Lesbian and Bisexual Fiction Writers*, Highsmith's

> peculiar brand of horror comes less from the inevitability of disaster, than from the ease with which it might have been avoided. The evil of her agents is answered by the impotence of her patients—this is not the attraction of opposites, but in some subtle way the call of like to like. When they finally clash in the climactic catastrophe, the reader's sense of satisfaction may derive from sources as dark as those which motivate Patricia Highsmith's destroyers and their fascinated victims.

More than one critic deems the theme of interpenetration an essential masking, and locates the subtext of all Highsmith's work in homosexual suppression and discovery. Certainly there's that—as there is, also everywhere, Highsmith's most un-American emphasis on class. No doubt she's a master of misdirection, pointing one way, happening another. This is, after all, what artists do. Nor must we demand that artists be fully aware of these displacements. Often they're out there working without a map, making the plough down sillion shine, *gee-* and *haw*-ing by intuition, instinct, crochet, quirk.

With the years, Highsmith became ever more like Tom Ripley shut away from humankind in his train compartment, ever more apart. Wilfullness—stubbornness, contrariness—turned slowly, one suspects, towards true misanthropy; independence of thought to a kind of intellectual fascism. A curious double vision overtook her. Everywhere she looked now were victims. She cared greatly for none of them but could not leave the trailing, pale stories of their lives alone. She had written almost exclusively of victims, it seemed, people whose lives had been annexed, inhabited. Had *everyone's* life been taken over?

Nowhere is Highsmith's misanthropy more apparent than in *Little Tales of Misogyny*, a series of savage vignettes and character sketches with titles such as "The Female Novelist," "The Middle-Class Housewife," "The Fully Licensed Whore, or, The Wife," "The Breeder," "The Perfectionist."

One begins: "A young man asked a father for his daughter's hand, and received it in a box—her left hand."

Another: "There are lots of girls like Mildred, homeless yet never without a roof—most of the time the ceiling of a hotel room, sometimes that of bachelor digs, of a yacht's cabin if they're lucky, a tent, or a caravan. Such girls are bed-objects, the kind of thing one acquires like a hot water bottle, a traveling iron, an electric shoe-shiner, any little luxury of life."

And, from "Oona, the Jolly Cave Woman": "She was a bit hairy, one front tooth missing, but her sex appeal was apparent at a distance of two hundred yards or more, like an odor, which perhaps it was. She was round, round-bellied, round-shouldered, round-hipped, and always smiling, always jolly. That was why men liked her."

The stories of *The Animal-Lovers Book of Beastly Murder* by contrast show great compassion, though not for humanity. "Chorus Girl's Absolutely Final Performance," told from the point of view of an elephant, gives us in nine pages the whole arc of that elephant's captive life. Also extraordinarily touching is "Djemal's Revenge," with a camel as protagonist. This story is a marvel of setting and atmosphere as well as of headlong narrative motion. Other tales feature a cockroach (again, in first-person), a monkey, hamsters, ferrets, goats, cats, a horse and a wonderful truffle-hunting pig named Samson.

Compassion persists, even turns humanward, in *Slowly, Slowly in the Wind*, which appeared in 1979, two years after *Little Tales*, four years after *The Animal-Lover's Book*. Stories such as "The Network" and "Broken Glass" feature aged, lonely people with few ties remaining, sequestered and barricaded in their apartments in cities—in a society—changed beyond recognition. It's as though their lives had been lifted from the shelf, drained of all that's vital, and the shell replaced. All the old certainties are gone, there's minority threat all about, and everywhere, like black smoke from factories, an unfocused fear and dread. Highsmith's novels of the decade, *A Dog's Ransom* (1972) and *Edith's Diary* (1977), essay similar embranchments, particularly the latter, which concerns itself rather directly with media manipulation, active feminism, the civil rights movement and anti-colonialism, as in this passage.

7/Nov./54. In New York people say politics don't interest them. "What can I do about it anyway?" This is the attitude government powers in America want to foster and do. News is brief, filtered and slanted. The Guatemalan "uprising" would have been far more interesting if social conditions there had been described and if United Fruit Company's activities had been exposed—by radio and TV. Discussion clubs should be set up all over America to talk about forces *behind* things. We have been brainwashed for decades (since 1917) to hate Communism. *Readers Digest* has never failed to print one article per issue about the inefficiency of anything socialized, such as medicine.

That Highsmith's shadowy tales bear political intonations should come as no surprise. This is, after all, the woman who dedicated her 1983 novel *People Who Knock on the Door*

> To the courage of the Palestinian people and their leaders in the struggle to regain a part of their homeland.
> This book has nothing to do with their problem.

and *Ripley Under Water*, eight years later,

> To the dead and the dying among the Intifadah and the Kurds, to those who fight aggression in whatever land, and stand up not only to be counted but to be shot.

Also from *Slowly, Slowly*, and continuing Highsmith's investigation of the ever-deepening chasm between rich and poor which she touched on in stories like "Broken Glass" and "The Network," is a rare divagation into apocalyptic science fiction, "Please Don't Shoot the Trees." Elsie and family live in great privilege in a protected enclave safely tucked away from "the cesspools" of the cities. All is ease and good thoughts; even the children travel to school by helicopter. But forces far more ancient than mankind's relentless tucking-away and smoothing-out are at work. That obliviousness we call peace of mind, we purchase finally at great price.

> It was right, Elsie felt, right to go like this, conquered by the trees and by nature... Now the wind whistled in her ears, and she was falling at great speed. A land mass, big as a continent, it seemed, big as she could see, was dropping—slowly for land but fast for her—into the dark blue waters.

Over time the stories, as do the novels, grow denser, layered, increasingly inhabited by darker, more obscure motives and by subtler forms of subterfuge and supplantation. Accordingly they become harder to pin down, to define, and ever more troubling at various subterranean levels.

Stories from "The Black House" are a bleak lot. It's here that "Old Folks at Home" appears, with its adoption of an elderly couple bringing ruin to the adoptive couple's life. Others like "The Kite" and "Under a Dark Angel's Eye" are as deeply disturbing. But the standout is "The Terrors of Basket-Weaving," a masterpiece quite possibly on the order of Henry James's "The Beast in the Jungle." Discovering an uncanny, wholly unconscious skill while repairing a basket found on the beach, a modern urban woman begins to feel simultaneously aligned in spirit with the entire history and character of her race and somehow at a remove from her daily life. She's in equal measure frightened and entranced. "I feel—as if a lot of other people were inside me besides myself. And I feel lost because of that," she tells her husband. But her feelings and her confusion are far more complex than she can relate. In some curious way she glimpsed transcendence, and, in finally burning the basket, has refused it. It's much that feeling we have in the moment great music ends, just before the noise of the world rushes back in and overtakes us.

> Three weeks after the burning of the basket, her crazy idea of being a "walking human race" or some such lingered. She would continue to listen to Mozart and Bartok...and she would continue to pretend that her life counted for something, that she was part of the stream or evolution of the human race, though she felt now that she had spurned that position or small function by burning the basket. For a week, she realized, she had grasped something, and then she had deliberately thrown it away....And in fact could she even put any more into words? No. So she had to stop thinking about it. Yes.

With its sharp sense of alienation from the ordinary, its ambiguity of motive and emotion, its questions of identity and dark interiority, "The Terrors of Basket-Weaving" seems an ideal vehicle for many of Highsmith's concerns. Here again there's an interpenetration of lives that appears to redeem our common humanity, but in the end cleaves us from it. For Highsmith, one suspects, this may be the ultimate horror, boundaries of self utterly lost. The protagonist's tremulous, penumbral state of mind gets captured marvelously in a story as complex, unsettling, and finally as unsortable, as her own emotions.

Curiously, each of the stories from *Mermaids on the Golf Course* in some way deals with families. "A Clock Ticks at Christmas" chronicles the dissolution of a marriage from a couple's differences in attitude towards possessions and inability to cross class barriers. In "Where the Action Is," a freelance photographer still living with his parents happens onto the shot of a lifetime, a young woman fleeing from her supposed rapist—a photograph that makes his career and bends the lies that are his life into a new, ever-hardening form."Chris's Last Party" touches on the extended family of young creative people taken under wing by an older mentor. In "The Button" a man filled with bitterness towards his Downs-syndrome son and empty of feelings for his wife kills a man, throttling him as he has often imagined throttling his son, and finds release therein: "He had killed a man in revenge for Bertie. He had superiority, in a sense, one-upmanship. He must never forget that. He could face the years ahead with that."

These stories are also, in Grace Paley's phrase, about enormous changes at the last moment. They deal in one way or another with people whose well-set lives have been breached, their boundaries disrupted, and who are now retrenching.

The protagonist of the title story, "Mermaids on the Golf Course," happened to be on the grandstand nearby at a St. Patrick's Day parade and instinctively threw himself in front of the President when snipers opened fire. Now he is recovering, but everything in and about his life has changed. Nothing is as it was, nothing is as it seems, and he cannot get a hold on any of it. Like "Please Don't Shoot the Trees" a rare excursion into the literature of the fantastic, "Not in This Life, Maybe the Next" recounts the appearance in a lonely woman's life of a gnomelike creature no one else can see, an appearance that first begins refilling, then empties, that life. In "The Romantic," following the death of her long cared-for mother, a woman dresses in her best, most fetching clothes and sits in fashionable lounges pretending to wait for rendezvous, creating for herself an external life to match the internal. Actual dates only serve to persuade her that her life of mind and imagination far surpasses that of the real. She need not be (as Rilke put it) distracted by expectation. *I prefer my own dates.*

So did Patricia Highsmith. She might dress up to date Mysteries, head downtown to hang out with *noir*, smile at Literature quaffing Merlot at the next table. But she always preferred the life of her own imagination, her own dates. She always knew that was the only place she could rightfully live and work.

Incomparable Paco

(Paco Taibo)

Great writers by definition are outriders, raiders, sweeping down from wilderness territories to disturb the peace, overturn the status quo and question everything we know to be true—then gone. Like deranged cousins shut away in the houses of loving families, they are a great bother, an embarrassment, open secrets trembling always at the very edge of violence, out there just beyond the light of these campfires we call civilization.

No one quite knows what to do with Paco Taibo. Even in his homeland of Mexico, he says, he's an invisible writer – by which he means unapproved, subversive, and in which he takes obvious pleasure. Meanwhile a disarming arsenal of books continues to tumble from his pen: literary novels, revisionist history, collections of journalism, fictionalized biographies, political essays, detective stories.

It's for the last that he may be best known to readers on this side of the Rio Grande, for whom his work poses, I think, a particular problem.

The detective novel *An Easy Thing*, published in 1990 by prestigious Viking Press whose editors could hardly have failed to be aware of its radical subtext, introduced Paco's work here. Viking followed up a year later with *The Shadow of the Shadow*, an extraordinary novel celebrating the streetcar workers' strike in 1922 Mexico City. Neither novel earned much of a foothold on publishing's glass mountain, and Paco soon hopscotched over to The Mysterious Press. Most recently as, one by one, earlier books fell out of print, he's been published, when published at all, by specialty presses such as El Paso's Cinco Puntos, who in 2000 brought out *Just Passing Through*. That novel's fanciful portrait of real-life labor organizer Sebastian San Vicente was an early sketch for *Shadow* and bears every mark of Paco's style: the folding of historical figures into fiction, the persistent, stubborn blurring of boundaries, a tone that trods consistently some unmarked path between the highroad of stridency and the lowlands of melancholy.

It's not only Paco's prolificacy, the variety and very volume of his work, that confuses us. What are we to make of this constant shuttling back and forth from fact to fiction, history to present life, this summa of revolutionary instinct he seems intent upon providing us, Che Guevara rubbing shoulders with Doc Holliday, Mau-Mau with the Musketeers? Is this man a detective-story writer, an avant-garde novelist, the voice of our collective unconscious, a simple contrarian, some half-crazed libertarian Oliver Stone-type, eyes fixed myopically on a handful of moments in history?

U.S. readers in particular, whose knowledge even of their own radical labor movement has been expunged, are unlikely to know much of the general ideas and passions and of the historical movements, specifically Hispanic and Mexican, central to Paco's work. Using the vocabulary available to us, we connect narrative dots, forcing Paco's attitudes and apostrophes to conform, Procrustes-like, to the closest analog we have, the shape of American leftism, unable to perceive it for the radically different thing it is: anarchism. Anarchism, of course, has a long tradition abroad. But we here in the States have never doubted that every other country at its inmost, secret heart wants nothing more than to be just like us. We would make of them all – think that, given the chance, they would make of themselves – little Americas. Further fundamental differences between "American" quiddities and those from which Paco issues, quickly fall into place.

Unlike the realist American novel, perfectly formed loaves of white bread leavened with irony, the Latin American novel has always been quixotic, playful, self-conscious: a heady mix of coarse grains thrown together on the griddle.

What Paco does, it seems to me, is restore the balance between fabulation and objective social realism. Refusing to dispense with the representational, he refuses also to lash its materials to the mast of likelihood and verisimilitude. Grittily realistic depictions of Mexico City come stepping from the doorways of pure invention. If he wants to have Stan Laurel witness Pancho Villa's assassination or show Leon Trotsky, exiled in Mexico, laboring over authorship of thrillers (*Four Hands*); if he wants to gather an army of fictive heroes including Sherlock Holmes and the Hound of the Baskervilles, the Earp brothers and Doc Holliday, the Musketeers, the Mau-Mau and the Light Brigade around a victim of the 1968 student-led Mexican uprising (*Calling All Heroes*); if he wants to dovetail Leonardo da Vinci's invention of the bicycle with the theft of a kidney from a Texas female basketball player and usher onstage as investigator a doppelganger of himself or of Hector Belascoarán Shayne (*Leonardo's Bicycle*); if he wants to kill off Shayne and in the next book (*No Happy Ending, Return to the Same City*) resurrect him ... well, then, he does.

Whatever the story requires.

Paco on Shayne's resurrection: "His appearance in these pages is...an act of magic....irrational and disrespectful toward the occupation of writing a mystery series....the story told here belongs to the terrain of absolute fiction, although Mexico is the same and belongs to the terrain of surprising reality."

Story is all, then. And so Paco goes on pulling real rabbits from imaginary hats.

Initially, he says, he turned to crime fiction from a desire to escape the experimentalism then rampant, to find his way back to storytelling. Like many others (Roger Simon or Stephen Greenleaf in the States, the amazing Jean-Patrick Manchette in France, somewhat later Columbia's Santiago Gamboa), Paco realized that the crime novel gives space and opportunity to address contemporary society as does no other venue, to recreate the actual textures and presence of street life and social levels about him, the flux of assumption and disinformation that keeps the social order afloat, the rifts between reality and appearance that both individual and society must negotiate again and again.

One further spur. Someone told Paco it was impossible to write a crime novel set in Mexico because the crime novel was by its very nature an Anglo genre. Given that, what choice did he have but to write one? Or a dozen?

Again and again here, I've struck out such formalities as *Taibo* and *the author* in favor of, simply, *Paco*. In the cloisters and hallways of my soul I see him striding towards me in T-shirt and leather jacket, Marlboro in one hand, Coke in the other. Uncomfortable at the table of privilege where, attending an international literary conference, he was seated, Paco has escaped. Paco's flown, Paco's once again out and about where he belongs, where all writers belong, at one of the world's small, crowded, unkempt tables.

Reading, he tells the four or five of us sitting there, is the most subversive activity in life. Open any true book and you begin to see the world through somebody else's eyes. Nothing is more redeeming than that—or more dangerous.

He believes, too, in the right to myths, the necessity of them. Speaking about Che and other heroes, even small heroes like Hector Belascoarán Shayne, helps us reclaim other rights: our right to romanticism, to adventure, to the sense that our lives are not shallow but infinitely deep, connected to history and to "all those who have no rights, those who suffer abuse their whole lives, people on the margins, the disinherited, the lepers, the poor, the least of the least."

There's the rabbit and the hat, then. And here's Paco Taibo, writer, magician, small hero. The most important postman of all: the one who delivers you to yourself.

Falling to Earth

(Walter Tevis)

In 1968, freshly repatriated to New York from London where I had edited *New Worlds*, I was consulted by a paperback publisher who wanted to create a science fiction list. Wanting also to remain within the tradition, he planned to spend as little money as possible to accomplish this, so in his office one afternoon we spoke of books that might have been overlooked and readily available. I went back to my apartment, sat down at the table where I worked, and with no hesitation wrote: #1. *The Man Who Fell to Earth*. Published as a paperback original five years earlier (I told the publisher at our meeting the next day), this book had been little noticed and was out of print. It was also, I told him, among the finest science fiction novels ever written.

Each work of art, every book, is a doomed balancing act, the creation of a fulcrum by which the world momentarily may be lifted and brought to rest, tottering. From the textures of daily life and the formlessness of individual lives, the writer or painter attempts to model the world entire—in Baudelaire's words, to rescue from the quotidian frenzy one clear look at truth's enduring face. Near-sighted and far-sighted eyes acting in concert, with luck, to bring the whole thing into focus.

Science fiction and fantasy, the literature of the fantastic, may be uniquely suited to such double vision. Not only has it embraced an agenda abandoned by much other fiction—to place a framework around man's place in the universe—but also its very forms lead easily to mystery, fabulation and parable, the play of archetypes. For that reason, many of us who began writing in the Sixties believed with Michel Butor that science fiction, speculative fiction, might provide a contemporary mythology, pulling together all of literature's grand old themes while also revealing profoundly new ones.

We also believed that the civil rights for which we struggled, those now being bled away from us, would thereafter prove inalienable. And that rock music wasn't some commodity to be packaged by businessman and sold by the yard, but a force to change the world.

These were a few of the fictions we lived by.

And the fictions we live by were exactly what Walter Tevis wrote about.

Two images:

A man walks in the streets of a small town in early morning. Everything he sees about him, everything he encounters, is strange, unfamiliar, frightening. Trying not to think about what he is soon to do, he sits on the bench outside a small store called The Jewel Box to rest. Minutes later, he sees his first human being.

Legs straight out with khaki trousers flapping, metallic brain joyful in its rush towards what it has so long ached for, Robert Spofforth falls at last from the top of the Empire State Building; falls lovingly, mankind's most beautiful toy, towards the ruined streets of Manhattan below, to embrace them.

The first is from the initial page of *The Man Who Fell to Earth*, at the beginning of Thomas Jerome Newton's long and painful apostasy, the second (with its echoes both of *King Kong* and of Hester Prynne on the scaffold at the start and end of *The Scarlet Letter*) from the final page of *Mockingbird*, where robot Spofforth at last achieves his lifelong ambition.

The power of Tevis's *The Man Who Fell to Earth*, *Mockingbird* and *The Steps of the Sun*, what I have to call their greatness, rests in the many levels on which they may be read: their many-sidedness, the simultaneous balances they achieve, their appetite for not only the visible, palpable world but *all* the worlds we dwell in. They are at once fables, parables, social satire, contemporary myth, and genre science fiction—adventure stories of a kind. They are also simultaneously, as is much of our greatest literature, comic and tragic. Pitting the individual in opposition to society, they are romances; chronicling the individual finding or failing to find place in society, they are novels. Like most great work, *Gulliver's Travels*, or *Don Quixote*, they're uniquely of their time and of all times.

The Man Who Fell to Earth, on its surface, is the tale of an alien who comes to earth to save his own civilization and, through adversity, through inaction, through loss of faith ("I want to....But not enough"), fails. Just beneath the surface it might be read as a parable of the Fifties and of the Cold War. Beneath that as an evocation of existential loneliness, a Christian fable, a parable of the artist. Above all, perhaps, as the wisest, truest representation of alcoholism ever written.

Mockingbird collapses the whole of mankind's perverse, self-destructive, indomitable history, cruelty and kindness alike, into its black-humor narrative of a robot's death wish.

It was as parables, "more or less what I do in science fiction," that Tevis himself thought of his books. *The Man Who Fell to Earth* was "very disguised autobiography" of his forced relocation as a child from San Francisco, "the city of light," to rural Kentucky, of his dire childhood illness, most of all (as *Mockingbird* was "about my coming *out* of alcoholism") about his becoming alcoholic. Yet—and this is their specific, indefinable genius—the novels function perfectly as science fiction.

Tevis didn't think of himself as a science fiction writer. He read and loved science fiction as a teenager, he had published stories in genre magazines, but his first, hugely successful novel, published four years before *Man*, the one that made him as a writer, was *The Hustler*. And when he came to it, he wrote science fiction (here, again, his specific, indefinable genius) as though he were inventing it, as though it had not been written before. Tevis wrote, as Jonathan Lethem notes in his introduction for the current Del Rey reissue of *Mockingbird*, "with a sort of beautiful literary amnesia...refusing genre," drawing novels of character and fable from the tired, much-used forms, turning the worn glove inside out to reveal again the all too human hand within.

Briefly then, the facts, the life, from which this autobiographical fiction gathered.

Tevis was born February 28, 1928, in San Francisco. When he was ten, his family went off to live with the father's sister in Kentucky, leaving Walter, who had contracted rheumatic fever, behind in a hospital. He remained there, wholly alone, for a year before joining the family. He attended school, feeling always the outsider, in Kentucky, and, following service in World War II (two years as a carpenter's mate), went on to the University of Kentucky, where he earned his bachelor's and master's in English. He then embarked on a teaching career, first at various Kentucky high schools, later, from 1966 to 1978, at Ohio University.

Published to great acclaim in 1959, *The Hustler* became a film classic in 1961. *The Man Who Fell to Earth*, rejected by Harper's, was published as a paperback original by Gold Medal in 1963. In conversation with Daniel Keyes, Tevis claimed that this rejection led to his lengthy writing block; editor Pat LoBrutto, who worked with Tevis on *Mockingbird* and subsequent books, doesn't think Tevis made so much of it. At any rate, Tevis had become a confirmed drinker ("It's about my becoming an alcoholic. I sobered up to write it," he said of *Man*), and for the thirteen years he taught in Ohio, he wrote little or nothing.

Tevis also told Keyes that he'd always dreamed "of being a New York writer, of being in the center of the literary scene," and in 1978, three years after he quit drinking, Tevis moved to the city. *Mockingbird* came out in 1980, his story collection *Far From Home* the following year, both *The Steps of the Sun* and *The Queen's Gambit* in 1983. *The Color of Money*, a sequel to *The Hustler* written for quick money, also came out in these last years. Paul Newman bought the property, commissioning a screenplay from Tevis; for the 1986 film, however, both screenplay *and* novel were junked.

By his own admission, Tevis still had problems writing. He'd also begun confronting autobiographical materials more directly, in a kind of self-dredging that doesn't always imply salvage, and that can prove as wrenching to the reader as to writer. In stories of the period we often see Tevis peering out at us from within.

> Whiskey had left him unable to answer the telephone or open the door, in Michigan. That had been two years ago. Whiskey had left him sitting behind closed suburban blinds at two in the afternoon, reading the J.C. Penny catalog and waiting for Gwen to come home from work. Well. He had been free ofwhiskey for a year and a half now. First the hospital, then A.A.; now New York and Janet.

He'd continue this transmutation of life in *Mockingbird*, his parable of coming out of alcoholism, and in *The Steps of the Sun*, whose early passages rehearse his own childhood of pain, illness and alienation (and which is, overall, a parable of adolescence). The darkening cities and expended populations of the first, the impoverished, pre-ice age earth of the latter—these are the landscape of their author's own post-alcoholic mind: worlds to be retrieved, reconstructed, reinvented, reborn.

Though sales for *Mockingbird* were disappointing, in subsequent years the book has been much praised, taking its place alongside *Man* as a classic. Thus far *Steps* hasn't elicited as much attention as the others even though, as André- Francois Ruaud points out in a rare essay on Tevis for France's *Bifrost* magazine, it's among the most original and successful science fiction novels of the 80's. It is also Tevis' first wholly optimistic book. In its successor, *Queen's Gambit*, he turned again from the fantastic to the realistic mode, offering in its stone-brilliant story of a driven, alcoholic female chess champion who achieves redemption (much as *Mockingbird* paired with *Man*) a positive retelling of *The Hustler*.

Walter Tevis died of cancer in 1984, the year after his last two, redemptive books were published, age 56. He had experienced, observed, brought to others and to himself great pain, terrible abjurations; his books gave it all up, took our hands to lead us through the backwash. And yet, like his protagonists, he had borne up under it all, survived, endured.

"It is very bad for people to find substitutes for living their lives," he said in what may have been his last interview, wondering if this might not be his abiding theme. Even if late in life, he said, he had found great joy in it: "I'm really pleased that the grass is green. I didn't used to be."

Through it all, out of it all, blows this dark, strangely comforting wind, this threnody of loss. It is, for many reasons, a small body of work, and one of rare unity.

Einstein remarked that in his life he'd had only one or two ideas. Many fine writers are like that, I believe, making a lifetime's agenda of drawing out the universe implicit in those ideas. So the strands that run and interweave in Tevis's work: alcoholism, the artist (pool player, chess player) in whom ambition and wound pull like twin suns, the adolescent's eternal alienation, prisons of self and society, bleak futures, Christ figures, redemption.

Again and again Tevis mounted voyages to the alien, inhospitable planet of self, to bring back odd rocks, strange growths, colors not seen in our nature. Again and again he seized metaphors and wrung their necks, making them give up secrets others had not obtained, could not obtain. There he stood balanced, about to fall. He was, as Lethem writes, "a master manipulator of archetypes, an artist capable of delving into the zeitgeist while nevertheless remaining on his own pure search for himself." His work is unique, with that element of infinite rereadability Nabokov held the hallmark of great literature. Like his characters, though passed through perilous times, disregard and rejection, waking with the day-after, too-late taste of booze, stale smoke and failure upon them, Tevis's work will endure.

NOVEL
Death Will Have Your Eyes

Verrà la morte e avrà i tuoi occhi.

Death will come,
and will have your eyes.

—Cesare Pavese

I.

The man kept opening his mouth, wanting something from me, but it was a language I didn't know. Not Mandarin. Not Thai or Vietnamese. Only sounds. His voice rose and fell in pitch. Shouting, demanding. I shook my head, the sour, foul smell of my own body washing up over me in waves, tongue so swollen I could not talk, could not respond. Soon the pain would start again. And I would rise, hover near the ceiling looking down. Watching. Apart.

I woke suddenly, rushing to exchange the currency of dreams for coin I could spend. Morning light fell dazzlingly through the skylight onto the futon. Those wide shadows were not bars or slats in a cage—only the leaves of plants in hanging baskets up there. That sound was only the phone.

Nothing else in the room. No windows. The futon, a painted bamboo screen against one wall, an expanse of blond wood floor—tongue and groove I'd put in myself. About as close as the real world gets to the ordered simplicity of oriental drawings.

No one else, either. Only Gabrielle and myself.

She slept crosswise on the futon, my head cradled in her lap. Trying to get away from the light, I turned over. "O yes, *please*," she said. But obviously the phone was not going to quit ringing, so I snaked along the bed to answer it. Gabrielle grabbed me as I went by and held on.

I listened for a moment and hung up. "Wrong number," I told her. "*I've got your number*," she said, head moving to replace her hand, but I stopped her, wrapping black hair around both my hands and pulling her up into a slow, easy kiss.

"I'm going for a run," I said. "Get the sludge out. Want to come along?"

"At *six* in the bleedin' *mornin*'?"

With Gabby you never knew what accent you might get. Her features came mostly from an Irish mother and patrician Mexican father, but her extended family was pure goulash. Dad left when she was three, and she and her mother spent years shuttling from household to household, family to family, country to country. This early morning, the accent was British, a better choice than most, I suppose, for gradations of polite outrage.

"Okay, but don't say I didn't ask. So go back to sleep now, my little peasant."

"Pheasant?"

"Peasant. Half an hour, tops, even with a head wind. I'll bring breakfast."

"And here I thought you *were* breakfast."

"Miss, have you considered taking up a hobby?"

"No time for it."

"That was my point."

She shrugged. "One stays with what one's good at. Run along now," and was asleep again before I got shorts and shoes on.

I stood watching her a moment, her compact brown body against light blue sheets, breasts just a little too heavy, rib cage set high, then went into the bathroom. Turned on the radio there. It was Mozart, a serenade performed on "original" instruments with which the musicians struggled valiantly to bring them into tune. Thousands upon thousands of dollars, thousands upon thousands of hours, had been devoted to this bogus authenticity, these elaborate counterfeits. I washed my face and brushed my teeth, then stood at the window looking out till the piece was over. One doesn't hang up on Mozart.

There were few others in the park that early: a handful of runners and dog-walkers, one young mother who looked remarkably like Shirley Temple pushing a pram, another trodding along with three children, all of them androgynous and none over five years old, at her heels, street people starting off on their day's boundless odyssey. Birds and squirrels worried at yesterday's leavings, perhaps hoping their investigations would help them understand these huge, dangerous beings that lived in their midst.

I swung around the park's perimeter in an easy jog, following an asphalt bike path, and stopped at a pay phone on the far side, the kind of old-fashioned booth you rarely see anymore. There I dialed a number I still knew all too well. It was picked up on the first ring.

"Age has slowed you, perhaps."

"As you must realize, I was in no hurry to return this call. At first, I was not even sure that I wanted to respond at all. And after eight years—"

"Actually, it just slipped over the edge into nine."

"—I believed it likely that whatever business you think you have with me could wait a few more minutes."

"Perhaps. However, your plane departs at ten or thereabouts. American, flight 817. You are Dr. John Collins, a dentist on vacation."

"Sir."

Silence.

"It has been, as you say, nine years. I have a career, a new life, commitments."

Silence still.

"I am no longer in your employ."

A still longer silence. Then finally: "It will be good to see you again, David."

I hung up and ran back the way I'd come, pushing myself now. A light breeze was coming up, and full sunlight struck the artificial lake at a slant, tossing off sheets of glare. Birds and squirrels didn't seem any closer to understanding us. Neither did I.

They were waiting by the benches about halfway around, in a space partially screened by trees. You wouldn't be able to see much, here, either from the street or adjacent apartments. So some thought had gone into it, at least.

One was in jeans, black sweatshirt and British Knights, twentyish, a broad, pale-complected man with bad skin. His head kept tic-ing convulsively towards his right shoulder, crossing and recrossing the same minute, almost imperceptible arc. The other was maybe ten years older, wearing what had once been an expensive suit, with a chambray dress shirt frayed to white at the cuff and loose threads at the collar, and a knit tie with the knot tugged down to his breastbone. Lank brown hair tucked behind his ears.

"Your money, sir?" the younger one said, stepping in front of me. "Don't mean to hurt you. This can all be over with in half a minute, you want."

Chest heaving, heart throwing itself again and again against rib cage, I sank onto one of the benches. A placard alongside documented this as *Station Nine (9)*. Pictographs indicated that I was to restretch muscles and tendons, check my pulse against my own personal MHR, perform ten to twenty deep knee bends.

"...Minute," I said. Then, catching my breath: "I don't carry money when I'm running, boys. Better pick another pigeon."

"Done *got* our pigeon." The older one. He raked straying hair behind one ear with the open fingers of his hand. Ran his nose quickly along that coat sleeve. It was slick already from prior crossings. "Just got to fry it up now. Drumsticks."

I glanced briefly at him, and when I did, the younger one made his move.

With amateurs, it's always easier when there's more than one. Then you can use them effectively against each another, the same way you use an attacker's own momentum against him in classic judo. That's the physical part. But they also get overconfident: safety in numbers and all that. And even those who know something about what they're doing can get sloppy or, hesitating to check on the other one, let down their guard for that essential brief second.

With these guys I swiveled into a basic high-low, unwinding like a spring, low and moving inexorably rightward to take out the younger one with a sideways blow to the knee as I spun past, then on past the older one, coming in high and behind as he was looking down to see what happened to his partner, watching him crumple from an open-handed blow just below the third cervical vertebra as I went past.

I followed the arc out to its natural stop and straightened, concerned. You never lose the reflexes, but the edge fades on you. You lose the exact touch, where imperceptible gradations can mean the difference between stunning an adversary and permanently damaging him. I was afraid I might have come down a little too hard.

But apparently not. If anything, from my concern over going in too hard and fast—when I shouldn't have been thinking at all, simply reacting—I'd held back. The older guy had already climbed to his feet and was staggering towards me with a hunting knife he'd tugged out of his boot.

I felt all consciousness of self melt away, felt myself dissolving into motion, reflex, reaction.

The knife clattered onto cement and he lay in a grassy patch beside a bench, elbow shattered, face draining of color.

"Please," he said. "Oh shit. *Please.*"

I stood there a moment. Yesterday, even an hour ago, what had just happened would not have. I'd have handed over whatever money I had, talked to them. Or simply run. And yesterday, even an hour ago, once it *had* happened, I would have called the police and awaited them. I'd spent years trying to turn myself off, shut the systems down, before I was finally successful. And now the switch had been thrown again: deep within myself, whether or not I wished it, whether or not I accepted it, I was again active, and on standing orders.

So I left the muggers there, knowing they were people with complicated histories and frustrated needs like my own and probably didn't deserve what had happened to them, and went home to Gabrielle.

She stumbled into the kitchen just as I was finishing breakfast, wearing one of my t-shirts, which hit her mid-thigh, and white socks that had started off at the knee and now were bulky anklets. She took the cup of tea I handed her, looked at my face and said, "What's wrong, Dave? Something has happened."

"Sit down." I slid a plate of buttered rye toast, fruit and cheese in front of her. Ceramic plate, thrown on a wheel near Tucson, signed by the artist, all brilliant blues and deep greens. I sat opposite her with my own tea, in a mug from the same set.

"This is going to be difficult."

"Yeah, looks that way. But we've been through a lot together. And we've always handled it."

"Nothing like this, G, believe me."

I looked at the window, wondering how the birds and squirrels were doing, then at her face. So familiar, so filled with meaning for me. So open to me now.

"Everything you know about me, everything you think you know, is false."

"No," she said.

"Yes. I have to tell you that much, have to insist on it. But for good reason I can't tell you more, not now. Now I have to ask you to do something for me, to do it immediately and without question."

After a moment she nodded.

"I want you to pack whatever you absolutely must have and I want you to go away. Not back to your apartment, but somewhere—anywhere—else. Preferably out of the city. I don't want to know where you are. In a week, a month, whenever I can, *if* I can, I'll come and find you."

"It would be easier if I knew why, Dave."

"Yes. It would."

"But I don't *have* to know."

She was away maybe ten minutes and came back into the kitchen with a huge over-the-shoulder bag and one small suitcase. I sat at the table and drank my tea, looked out the window. Heard sirens nearby, then, as though just an echo, others far away. Watched an ambulance pull up at a brownstone down the street, lights sweeping.

"Well," she said.

"You're an extraordinary woman, Gabrielle. I love you, you know."

"Yes. You do."

And she was gone.

Outside, several million lives went on as though nothing had happened.

After a while I walked through the archway into the studio. Began capping tubes and cans of paint, turning off burners and hotplates under pots of wax, soft metals, glue. It would be a long time before I came back here, if I came back at all.

At one end of the long room, by the windows, sat the piece I'd been working on, a forbidding mass of mixed materials—burlap, clay, metals, wood, paper—from which a shape struggled to release itself. You could feel the physicality, the sheer exertion, the intensity, of that struggle. I threw a tarp over it and as the tarp descended, the sculpture's form, what I'd been seeking, what I'd been trying to uncover for so long, came to me all at once: suddenly I could see it.

2.

Awake in a motel room at two in the morning, thinking of Gabrielle.

I'd flown straight through to St. Louis, then by connecting flight to Memphis, where at debarkation a message, and this room, awaited Dr. Collins. Ate dinner, something called a "patty melt" held in place on the plate by barricades of french fries smelling of fish, at a Denny's two blocks away, since there was nothing else close by; came back to the room with a Styrofoam cup of coffee and watched half a cable movie about a Pole who'd winnowed his way into the KGB. Then I pulled a book out of my bag but, distracted by memory as much as by the present, finally gave that up as well.

My room was on the second floor, with a sweeping view of the approach: parking lot, street, strip of bars and second-string businesses opposite. The motel itself backed up flush against another building. Once (and still, I supposed) we had hundreds of such safe rooms spread about the continental U.S. and most of Western Europe. Its stairs were cement and steel. They rumbled like distant thunder or a muted percussion section, bass drums, kettles, gongs, whenever someone mounted them.

At this hour only an occasional truck passed outside, but the smell of auto exhaust lingered, so many olfactory ghosts. Behind that, a verdant smell, compounded of pecan and magnolia trees, stretches of bright green grass, honeysuckle, mildew, mold: Delta land was rich land. Still further back, at some level, sensory awareness of the river itself. The bottom two inches of my window were permanently ajar, the aluminum frame immovable. Smells, sound and moonlight spilled over its rim into my room. Including, once, the hoot of an owl adrift in this city at the border of its homeland.

For many years, longer than I wanted to think about, I had lived on the edge, at the verge. I was good at what I did: fast when fast was needed, slow when that seemed to promise better results, always efficient, often surprising in my solutions both to the original problem and those inevitably developing from it. But then one day in Salvador as I stood watching a red Fiat burn, I realized that it was over for me—as though I'd stepped through an unseen door, looked up and found the world transformed in ways I could not fathom, or had blundered over borders into a foreign country where familiar words meant inexplicable things.

Not that I stopped believing in what I was doing. I'm not sure I *ever* believed in what I was doing; it was simply what I did, what I was programmed to do, the way I defined myself and negotiated my days. But it occurred to me there in Salvador that I was becoming what I did—that there was little else, little more, to me. And once I'd paused, even for that moment, I could never get back in step, never remember how the centipede walked.

So I climbed down off the edge I'd blunted with others' blood and my own.

And I'd spent the past eight years turning myself into a human being. Learning to care, to feel, to trust, to let go. At first it had been all form, just going through the motions, and I often felt like some alien creature painstakingly learning to pass, to give a good imitation of humanity. But in time, as it will, form became content.

Now I was reentering the old life—briefly, true, but already it began to feel familiar—and in many ways it was as though that eight years had never been. Except....

Except that Gabrielle had been a big part of my transformation. Except that I carried Gabrielle, carried my feelings for her and memories of our years together, within me now, and always would. Maybe none of us finally is anything more than the residue of those he's known and loved.

Blaise's cratered face came back to me: "You must not *think*. Cast away everything, David, let it go, let your *spine* become brain. The body has an intelligence of its own, far older than your mind's."

Blaise had trained me, trained us all. Taught us to stay alive. And if ever I had loved anyone in that prior life, I had loved him. Leaving the agency, leaving that life, I felt that I had to leave Blaise as well: one of the few regrets I allowed myself, but it was a profound one.

In my years as a soldier (for that's what we always called ourselves, among ourselves) I lived without personal identity, slipping in and out of roles and temporary lives as easily, and as readily, as others change clothing. I had been many people, known many people, taken part in many dramas and not a few (albeit unintentional) comedies. One thing I knew absolutely was that the stories we live by are as real as anything else is. As long as we do live by them. Even when we *know* they're lies.

Towards morning I dreamed that Gabrielle was above me, moving steadily upon me, head thrown back and black hair catching light from the window. Then something changed and my hands, reaching up, touched not flesh, but canvas, steel, the rough grain of wood. I opened my eyes again in the dark and saw it there over me. Half-formed, unalive, its weight ever increasing, it continued to move upon me: the sculpture I'd left behind, unfinished, at the studio.

3.

Towards dawn another thing happened as well.

The old training, the reflexes, were flooding back all at once, and I don't know what cue alerted me, some minutely perceptible shift in the volume of sound outside, a muted footfall or mere sense of presence, but I was awake, *waiting* for the sound, before the sound came.

The sound was my door being tried.

There was a pause, a silence, then the lisp of a flexible pick entering the door lock. Senses at full alert, I could almost feel the tension as again the knob was turned hard right, till it stopped, and held there. The pick raked its way slowly, methodically, along the lock's pin-tumblers.

It had happened a few times before when I was concentrating like this, and it happened now: I was outside *my* self, in another self. I watched my hands (except they weren't mine) working at the lock, felt a trickle of sweat down the middle of my back, became aware of the weight of a folded paper in the side pocket of my coat.

For a moment it rippled back from there. I sat in a large rented room off a hall so narrow that people had to turn sideways to pass one another. The room smelled of canned meats and beef stew, stale coffee, the bathroom four doors away. Bed- and living room furniture were jumbled together indiscriminately. A stack of newspapers squatted under a low window looking out onto a wall, with a sliver of morning light showing at the top.

Then the ripples spread. I was nineteen and terrified, running beneath a thick canopy of green. Minutes ago there had been a riot of birdsong; now the only sounds were my boots slapping into puddles and sucking their way back out, the staccato gabble of those pursuing me in the distance, my own thudding heart.

And, again, my heart pounding: but now when I reached out, my hand fell not against vines and undergrowth, but onto the waist of a slim, dark woman in white shorts and sandals. She stirred in her sleep.

Then, like a thread suddenly unraveling, giving way, it was all gone. I was back in my own body and mind. Back with the old training, the old reflexes.

By the time he got the door unlocked, I was out of bed and in a dark juncture of shelf and wall. By the time he crossed to the bed, pausing twice to listen closely, I was aping his own footsteps. And by the time he realized no one was there, and turned, I was behind him.

"The weather tomorrow will be fair," I said, "with temperatures in the mid-sixties and a light southeasterly wind, brisker towards evening."

He started to speak, then simply shook his head. He was thirtyish, with flat grey eyes, blond hair, a tan poplin suit. He wasn't new at this. He'd been at one end or another of it many times before.

"It would be terrible to miss such a day," I said. "We have so few of them."

A lengthy silence as his eyes caught my own, and held. Then: "The seasons do go on."

"Yes," I said.

Another long silence.

"I do not know you."

I shook my head. "Nor I, you. It can stay that way."

"Yes. Sometimes that is the best choice." He looked briefly about the room. "It seems the client neglected to provide me with information necessary to executing the assignment."

"There's not a lot of professionalism left."

"He failed to tell me what you were. I would have to say that such bad faith voids the contract. You would agree?"

"I would." But this man's utter humorlessness, those gray eyes round and flat and hard as lentils, still frightened me.

"Good," he said. He watched light sweep quickly along the wall, snag in a corner and momentarily brighten there, then fade, as a car passed outside. "I was to kill you, you know."

I nodded.

"Would I have been able to do that?" He remained staring at the wall, as though awaiting the next car.

I held out a hand, palm up. "You didn't." And shrugged. "Maybe the only things that *can* be, are those that *are*."

"But we will never know." Philosophy at five in the morning with the man who came to take you down: we lead a rich life, out here on the edge.

He looked back at me.

"Only once before have I come to kill a man and turned away from it."

"Then I'm glad I could be here to share this moment with you."

After a moment he said: "A joke."

I nodded.

He nodded back. "I was sixteen. I went into my father's room, where he was, as most nights, drunk and sleeping. I had brought along a knife from the kitchen, the sharpest one I could find. For a long time I stood with the knife poised above his chest, looking down at him, slowly coming to understand that I did not have to kill him now, that it was enough just to know how easily I could have. That was the last time I saw him."

He still had not moved. His eyes remained on mine.

"His grave is covered with kudzu now. You know about kudzu? Amazing stuff. Brought over from Japan to help control erosion, then it started taking over everything. Climbs radio towers, covers entire hills a foot or two deep. People have to go out every day and chop it back from their yards."

Lights again went by outside, but barely showed on the wall. He started towards the door and I went along.

"The man you will be wanting to see is Howard the Horse. He will not be wanting to see you."

"And where would I start looking?"

"You would probably start looking at a greasy spoon on Ervay and North Main." He pronounced it *greezy*. "You would probably stop looking there, too."

"A joke."

Nothing. Not a blink, not even a shrug.

"Mindy's Diner. Corner table, rear. Guy wears a jockey cap year round, day and night. Looks to be the same cap going on ten years now."

"Thanks."

"Think of it as professional courtesy."

"I owe you."

"No. No one owes me."

We walked to the door together. I opened it for him.

"Enjoy the fine weather tomorrow," I said.

He looked back. After a moment he said, "You too."

4.

MACARONI CHEESE
RED BEENS & RICE
MUSTARD GREENS COOKED WITH SALT PORK

BEETS
MASH POTATOS
GREEN BEENS (CHOOSE TWO)

The blackboard hung on a side wall, eraser dangling from it by a foot or so of heavy string, menu chalked on in scraggly printed letters.

Those of us who are close to forty, our fathers used to take us to places like Mindy's on rare nights mom was at work or for some other reason not home. That was back before fast-food spots sprang up four to every streetcorner; going in there reminded me how much things have changed, and how little we notice it.

There were two or three career coffee drinkers artfully arranged at the counter, lime-green formica printed with those sketchy boomerang shapes you saw everywhere in the Fifties; a couple of kids sitting together in a booth sopping up grease out of waxed-paper wrappers with their hamburgers; a scatter of older folk with one or another of the day's $4.95 specials, drink and roll included.

I could just make out a steamy corner of the kitchen through the gunport-like window behind the counter. From time to time heads ducked down to peer out, or disembodied hands and arms slid out plates heaped with food. At least two radios were playing back there.

Howard the Horse was, indeed, at his accustomed table, jockey cap every-thing I'd been led to expect. I was reasonably sure it had started out yellow. Howard himself had started out lanky, gaunt. Ichabod Crane was still in there somewhere, sunk in Nero Wolfe's body, waiting. As I approached, he tore open two packets of sugar and dumped them into a glass of milk. Then he slowly drank it all, watching me over the rim of the glass as I sat across from him. The sugar had turned to sludge at the bottom. He kept the glass tilted till the sludge had snailed down the side into his mouth. Then he put the glass on the table with his hand still on it and watched me some more.

"How old are you?" he said.

I told him.

He snorted. A little milk came out of one nostril.

"Young." Though I wasn't.

He shook his head and dabbed at the milk, almost daintily, with a shirt-sleeve. "Used to be young myself. Long ago, in a land far away: you know? I can almost remember it, sometimes. Now I got your basic sugar diabetes, your basic ulcers, your basic high blood. Bad hearts in my family, on both sides, as far back as anyone can remember. When it rains, I can't breathe. When it's dry, I can't breathe. Few days I *can* breathe, my ankles start swelling up like snakebites." He pushed the glass away. "So what can I do for you?"

"Sounds like I better ask fast, before you keel over on me."

"Maybe you should at that, boy. Not the kind for keeling over, though. Most likely just stay propped up here and looking pretty much like I always do. Could even be some time before anyone noticed a difference, come to think of it."

He held up a hand. The waitress must have been watching for his sign and poured him another glass from a plastic jug under the counter. She brought it over and asked if I wanted anything. I thanked her and said no. He reached for two more sugars.

"So you don't want food or a cup of coffee, what *do* you want?"

"I have trouble sleeping."

"I remember that too, being able to sleep. Almost as good as eating whatever you want. Sleep till noon, pull the covers up over your head and sleep till it started getting dark again. Now I know every crack in my ceiling like I know my shoe size. But a man your age, there's no excuse for *you* having trouble like that. Get yourself a woman, son. Or a hot bath. A bottle."

"Whatever works."

"You got it. Good old all-American pragmatism."

"I think the reason I can't sleep is because I have this dream there's someone in the room with me, Howard."

He didn't say anything, but he knew. He dumped in his sugars, drank his milk.

"In voodoo lore," I went on, "spirits take over the bodies of mortal men, inhabit them and use them to their own purposes. Those bodies are called their horses. Is that why they call *you* horse, Howard?"

He put the empty glass down. "You're the one calling himself Collins."

I nodded.

Problems were developing between supply and demand. Several times the waitress, a wiry redhead somewhere between thirty and fifty, wearing pressed jeans and a *Who? Me?* sweatshirt, had shouted back into the kitchen following up on orders and been ignored. Now she picked up a dirty plate from the counter and sailed it frisbeelike through the window. It broke against the wall with a hollow snap.

"'m I gonna have to come back there like I did last week? Huh? You boys want t' talk about each other's mothers or take knives to each other, I could care less, but you better do it on your own damn time, you hear me?"

Two streams of rapid-fire Spanish from the kitchen: suggestions as physiologically incorrect as they were politically so.

"Yeah, whatever. Could be fun," the waitress said. "But right now, either I see my orders on this window in two minutes or you're both out of here. *Comprendre*, gentlemen? And shut off that music."

The music didn't get shut off, but it did get turned down. Two or three plates of food thumped onto the ledge.

"Has a real way with words, Linda has," Howard said. "Charm the buzz off a bee."

He turned back to me.

"I'm a postman, nothing more," he said. "You do understand that?"

"I can accept it. And rain or shine is up to you, postman. I'll have to ask for a return address."

"I can give you a name. I don't know how much good it'll do you." He told me. "Think you might get me another glass of milk before you leave? I usually limit myself to two, but—" With a quick dip of head and hand he shooed away whatever might have followed that *but*.

I went over to the counter, brought the milk back to him, set it down. He sat holding glass and sugar packets, nodding his thanks.

"I been doing this a long time," he said. "I know a few people, people around a long time like me, and I talked to some of them."

I waited.

"You been away a while. My friends knew you. But these boys that wanted the package mailed, they're kind of new hands at all this. Guess they must of thought you were too."

"But you went ahead and sent your man around anyway."

He shrugged. "How else these boys gonna learn? No one teaches 'em anything anymore. Don't be too hard on 'em."

He poured in sugar.

"Besides, like I told you: I'm just a postman."

He drank, waited for the sludge, put the glass down and thanked me again.

"Take care," he said. "There aren't many of us left."

No one knows why the dinosaurs vanished. With our kind, it's a lot simpler.

5.

In the cabin window, against the city's pinpoint lights, what Neruda called "the diminutive fires of the planet," I saw: a forty-year-old man rushing headlong from everything that had sustained him, rushing towards the things that almost destroyed him. But within those things, in large part, were the seeds of what he'd become, what he was, what he couldn't (however he tried) leave behind.

Following my designated assassin's departure, I'd gone back to bed, later had a leisurely midmorning breakfast, then in early afternoon paid my visit to Harry. Two hours still remained before my flight, and I had passed them in a bar by the departure gate drinking Perrier. The same people were milling around who'd been milling around years ago when I spent a lot of time in airports.

I was on my way to Dallas. The message left for me in Memphis had directed me there, to DayRest Motel in Oak Cliff where, as I sank slowly through southwestern skies, I would become Jorge Sanchez and (the message had no need to tell me this part) await further instructions. The address that Howard the Horse gave me also belonged to Dallas.

Just before takeoff a young woman had slipped into the seat beside me, and we spent much of the early part of the flight talking. She was twenty-six, Indian, traveling from New York City, where she lived and worked as a CPA, to attend her husband's graduation from engineering school at SMU. It was an arranged marriage; married a year, they had spent one long initial week and six evenly spaced weekends together. She kept telling me how nervous she was. Now, after a few pages of something gargantuan by Michener and a brief plunge into what appeared to be a prayer or inspirational book of some kind, she'd fallen asleep. Cities scrolled by below us.

And I was thinking about Gabrielle again. I'd been alone a long time. For a year or more after quitting, I sat in my rented room and read things I'd always wanted to read and a lot of other things I'd never even known existed. I ate in anonymous lunchrooms and delis, usually with a book propped before me, and talked to almost no one. I walked in the streets and parks for hours at a time, watching people closely, all the different ways they linked themselves or kept apart. And I spent whole days in galleries and museums, slowly coming to realize that my future, whatever future I had, was bound up with these places, with what they stood for. At one point, I remember, every wall of my room was papered with prints and reproductions torn from books bought cheaply in second-hand stores near the college: Cezanne, Delvaux, Redon, Renoir, Dali, Rothko, all of it in a dazzling, undifferentiated jumble. This was some time before my first makeshift studio and longer still before my first real piece, but studio and piece were there already, nascent, in the half-life I was living. A future had begun coalescing even as I moved blindly (and trying to learn to see) towards it, and in one of the museums on a dim, low November day, I met Gabrielle.

She worked there as a part-time guide, just as she worked as a substitute teacher, as an occasional waitress, as a spear carrier for the opera, as a ballet or tennis tutor. All were ways of staying safely out of the mainstream, of remaining (she liked to say) at the center of her own life and (she'd add, laughing) not ever getting *too* bored.

A major Matisse show was in progress, and Matisse, the way he repealed not just perspective but depth itself, the way he handled large forms and pools of pure color, had recently become important to me. I wound up sitting much of the afternoon in a room full of work from the *Jazz* period. Individuals straggled through. A guard circulated erratically. Tour groups eddied in and out. Then just after the museum's closing was announced, someone came and sat beside me.

"You really like these, don't you?"

I nodded and looked at her.

"Especially these two." She pointed. I nodded. She pointed again. "I couldn't help noticing. When I came through with my tours." She held out her hand. "My name's Gabrielle. Tell me: do you usually have dinner after a tough day of museum-going?"

"Usually."

"Early, I bet."

"Early."

"And alone?"

"Almost always."

"But not tonight."

"I hope not." We stood and walked together towards the door. "My name's David," I told her.

"Come with Gabrielle, David."

Late that night I had returned to a cozy, safe room suddenly gone bare and cold. I stood for what seemed hours looking out at a blood-red moon, at trucks being loaded from the docks across the street for early-morning hauls. I was thinking that I'd just received, without warning, fanfare or expectation, an invitation to rejoin the human race, RSVP. Towards dawn I picked up Pavese.

6.

Two days later I was sitting in Johnsson's office saying, "No, sir."

It was not something he was used to hearing. He dealt with it by waiting to see if I was through, then, when I added nothing more, simply went on talking.

"No, sir," I said again, interrupting him, something he was even *less* used to. It's conceivable that no one had ever interrupted him before. "I will not pull down Luc Planchat for you. Or for anyone else."

He waited again. A bird on the window ledge outside peered fiercely in at us. I thought how birdlike Johnsson himself was. Heavy brow, dark recession of eyes, the stillness in them.

"Yet it appears," he said, "that this must be done."

"According to information you have received, yes. But in the first place, that information remains circumstantial. And secondly, since your own agency has no specific intelligence function, most of that information was piped in from another agency—"

He nodded.

"—one with which you have had disputes in the past—"

No nod this time.

"—and is therefore suspect."

"Perhaps so. One takes nothing at face value, of course."

"Including your own veracity in reporting this information to me."

"There is that, yes. Do you believe I would lie to you, David?"

"Freely. Outrageously. The good reporter looks at his scattered facts, then starts cobbling them into shoes that will fit. There's always an agenda: political, aesthetic, personal. Connect the dots. Constellations."

"You're right, of course. I would do whatever I thought necessary to get done what I thought must be. And so, in another time, would you have."

"It *was* another time, sir." After a moment I added: "If Planchat needs taking out, they should be the ones to do it."

"Ah: *should*. A most dangerous word."

He moved for the first time since we'd begun talking, taking his hands from the chair arms and folding long fingers together on his lap. I thought again of the feet of predatory birds. There was no desk in the room, only chairs with various tables alongside, many of them antiques picked up at flea markets, estate and garage sales. Johnsson hated desks. Hated people who sat behind them. Hated cages.

"Removal, you understand, is no longer a part of their agency's charter."

"And it is of yours."

"As it has always been."

Something suspiciously like a smile darted across his face and was gone.

"They created Planchat," I said. "And then they decided—or someone decided, at whatever level—that the model was obsolete."

"Perhaps more an anachronism than obsolete: *their* thinking, of course, not my own. A killing machine, David. The finest, certainly the most artful, ever devised."

"Yes. And if the machine needs unplugging, it's their responsibility."

"Absolutely. No one would argue that. It *is* their responsibility. But it's also our job: what we do."

"It's not what *I* do, sir."

He looked at me for several moments.

"Very well," he said. "I suppose it is possible that eight years can change a man, perhaps even past the point of recognition."

"Or in that time, the man can change himself."

"By his own bootstraps, yes. I understand that you're an artist now. Critics write of the 'contained violence' and gentleness of your—do you call them statues?"

"*Pieces*, usually. Or just *work*. Most of them aren't sculpture in any classical sense."

He nodded. Anyone not watching closely would have missed it.

"The word *poise* is often used. Meaning, I take it, a kind of rare and comely balance."

"By some."

"Of course: by some."

Neither of us spoke for a time then. Out on the ledge the bird's audition continued. Darkening clouds nudged at the sky. Finally, as imperceptibly as, earlier, he had nodded, he shook his head.

"Be cautious about settling for memory, David. It's far too thin a gruel for the like of us to live on."

I said nothing.

"I suppose that you may have changed in fundamental ways, after all. And I cannot say, finally, that I am sorry for that. I suppose it's time for you to go back to your Gabrielle now, back to your work, your 'pieces.' Thank you for coming."

I stood and held out my hand. After a moment his own left his lap and falteringly searched mine out.

"Forgive me," he said. "I forget, and you could not have known. But for several years now I have been quite blind."

I told him that I was sorry, and to take care.

"David..." he said when I was almost to the door. "A single favor."

"Yes, sir."

"An old friend has many times asked after you. Go and see him. It will not take you long."

"Blaise."

He nodded.

"You will find him here."

He held out a card. I walked back across the room and took it from him. His hand lingered there after it was gone.

7.

Two days past, on a hillside in Oak Cliff, the motelroom TV won't work, bringing in only dim gray forms and phantoms behind a wash of dots, and the real world outside my window, awash with gray drizzle, is little more defined.

Jorge Sanchez lies on his bed in paint- and plaster-spattered jeans and sweatshirt waiting. Occasionally there is lightning far off, or a climb of carlights up the wall. The couple next door (possibly a threesome) has left off its lovemaking, and someone over there's drawing a bath now. The whining glide of a steel guitar reaches out from a radio nearby.

A knock at the door, then: "Pizza."

"Sanchez?" she says when I open the door. In her mid-twenties and in sweats, with a face that still could go either way: towards beauty and character, towards plainness, a kind of vacancy. Her nose is peeling from recent sunburn. Hair tucked into a long-billed baseball cap. "Comes to eleven ninety-seven."

I hand over a ten and a five and tell her to keep it.

"Have a good stay," she tells me in return. Her car is an ancient VW beetle, once beige, in other incarnations green and canary yellow. There's a sign on top, *Free Delivery*, that's almost as big as the car itself. In a good wind you could use it to sail the thing.

Under the pizza there are two waxed envelopes.

The first one contains a dossier on Luc Planchat. I know a lot of this, up till about ten years ago, and go through it hurriedly. There's a gap then for most of that ten years until, six months ago, entries resume.

Planchat had been the pride of a new program established in one of those backwashes we learn to live with, hawkish after several years of a kindler, gentler leadership. Someone with sufficient political clout had decided the only answer to terrorism was an elite killer corps and went about calling in sufficient favors to make it happen. Planchat was first car off the assembly line, the prototype, a real dazzler. He was also a loner. And became ever more so as his fellow grads started checking out to brute craziness: some suddenly proclaiming themselves free agents (as though they were, after all, only football players), many either on their own or with a little help from their friends back at the factory heading out in search of what Rabelais called *le grand peut-être*.

The ensuing backwash was liberal, of course. When word came down that his program was deactivated, Planchat declined further government service and, in time-honored tradition, fostered out to a new identity.

Of three program graduates still undocumented (agency code meaning *not dead*), that accounted for two, Planchat and myself. Meanwhile "out in the world somewhere" (as an old blues song has it), whereabouts unknown, identity unknown—if indeed he were still alive—there might be another. No one could be sure.

No one had an explanation, either, for Planchat's sudden resurfacing. All these years he'd quietly gone about his placebo life of employment, possessions, payments, polls, appointments. Then *something* brought him crashing back out of the closet.

Twenty-three weeks ago two security guards were found dead at Compso, a high-tech electronics manufacturer and research facility in upstate New York. Both had been dispatched instantly, expertly: the first with a single blow, the second by severing the spinal cord through a narrow incision at the base of his neck. There were some blinds and red herrings thrown up, but whatever was missing, *really* missing, didn't show up on any of the company's various inventories.

Four days later a military installation was hit; and in following weeks bodies turned up in hotel rooms, places of business, parks and storage facilities, warehouses, even once a library. There was nothing definite to tie Planchat to any of this, but his name came up in one of those *sotto voce* conversations between our best jockey and his computer, and the more it was looked into, the more it started looking like a match.

For one thing, Planchat wasn't where he was supposed to be, and hadn't been there for a while—about six months.

He may as well have dropped off the edge of the earth, floated away in a balloon, gone to Tahiti to live among natives. Or been collected by extraterrestrials. The few spores that existed were being tracked. Several calls had been traced to a phonebooth in Dallas. That's why I'd been routed through here on my way in. To connect, if a connection existed. If the arc was there.

Rain hasn't abated. I put the dossier down and look again out the window. The world remains obscure. An occasional car scales the curved back of the hill like a momentary moon.

In that rented room of mine, the second month after I'd quit maybe, or the third, I got up one morning and, sitting still naked on the side of the bed, with frost plating the window outside and my own breath spilling out from me in spumes as a portable heater filled the room with the smell of raw alcohol, began a journal.

At first I simply transcribed my day: what I read and saw, where I went, stray thoughts, observations. Before long, though, I found the journal pulling away from the day's details and passtimes.

Memory was strong then; I sank back into it. Scenes of my childhood, friends, family, the way spaghetti or milk and oatmeal cookies had tasted when I was a kid, the first time I kissed a girl (Trudy Mayfield, Friday after school, February 1962), stories about a bibliographic worm in *Boy's Life*, my mother's face. It all came back in a flood.

Cedar Hill, I wrote. A two-story white frame house at the end of the block, with a scraggly weeping willow out front. We never locked doors, didn't even have keys for them as far as I know. Ate at a gray formica table in the kitchen; the dining room stayed closed off except for holidays. A '52 Dodge with green plastic shades for the wing windows and windshield, and fluid drive. *Pecans*. They were everywhere, forever rolling and cracking open underfoot. Wasps in thick bushes that skirted the house. *Honeysuckle*.

But soon I learned that, precise and detailed as my memories were, they were also in some incomprehensible way complete. Once I had gone over a period in my mind, it was set; if I returned to it, there'd be nothing more, just those same memories. There was no depth.

There were also curious gaps. I could visualize my mother's face exactly, curve of cheek into chin, the winglike sweep of eyebrows, but I couldn't, for all my efforts, recall how she smelled, or the touch of her skin. And Trudy Mayfield's name was just that: a name. I had no image of her face, no further memories of her sitting beside me in a classroom or over sloppy joes in the school cafeteria.

Shortly after these realizations, I put the journal away. Best not to think about it, I told myself. I had a present, a life that gradually was taking on form, and *that* was what was important. Not the past, not history, not the stumbles and snags of a faulty memory.

I go into the bathroom, tear the weightless plastic cup out of its paper cocoon, fill it from the tap, and drink. When I come back, the couple (three-some?) next door has again taken up the challenge.

The second envelope contains a copy of the police report on the death of one Raymond Hicks, discovered by his common-law wife early that morning in their home on Colorado. The only mark on Mr. Hicks was a small incision beneath his nipple by way of which, with some flexible knifelike object and what the ME called "astonishing surgical skill," the ventricles of his heart had been pared away like quarters of an apple.

Rain streams on the window. Momentarily I feel like some ancient aquatic being, sequestered from evolution's progress in the depths of its cave and forgotten. When a truck's lights break suddenly against the rain there, I'm startled.

Raymond Hicks was the name Howard the Horse had given me back in Memphis.

8.

It's good to see you.

"How long...?"

Three years.

"What happened?"

Beats me. Woke up one day and turned over to say good morning to who-ever was there and I couldn't. Now I write on this blackboard, like some kid. Nothing wrong physically, the doctors say. Hell, Dave, I'm sixty-two: there's a LOT wrong physically.

"So at this advanced age you've become a writer."

Ha. It ain't funny, I guess. But then if it ain't funny, what the hell is it?

"Life."

Yeah, life. Joke without a punch line. So how you been?

"Good, Blaise. It was rough at first."

Letting go, you mean.

"Yes."

It was hard taking hold at first, too. You forget?

"No, I haven't forgotten. Anything. Including the fact that I wouldn't be here now, probably wouldn't have returned from my second assignment and certainly not from my tenth, if it hadn't been for you."

So you're welcome. YOU have someone to tell good morning?

"Yes. Her name's Gabrielle."

Good. That's important. You never did before. Maybe someday I'll get a chance to meet her. You can take us both to dinner.

"I'd like that."

You'd like it a lot more after a few years of the oatmeal soup here.

"I hope you're kidding."

With croutons. Just a guess, of course. Can't tell a thing by looking at it, even less from tasting it. You ever get around to reading that Frenchman I told you about?

"Cendrars—your namesake. Some of it. What I could find in translation. Amazing stuff."

Amazing life. What are YOU doing these days?

"I'm an artist, Blaise."

Always were. Saw it in you from the first. Told Johnsson that.

"A different kind of artist."

Different, huh? Everybody's hard behind change these days. Like there's always been something wrong with us and we just noticed it so now we're going to do something about it. People and things all changing so fast you can't hold on to any of them anymore.

"I never could."

Yeah. I guess maybe none of us could.

"Are you doing okay?"

I'm not doing at all—that's the problem. But yeah, I have what I need. Johnsson and the others, they see to that. He bring you in because of Luc?

"Yes, sir."

Thought he would. You still THAT kind of artist too?

"You mean, am I going to pull Luc down for him?"

It wouldn't be for him.

"Should I?"

You never asked me before what you should or shouldn't do.

"A dangerous word."

?

"Johnsson called *should* 'a most dangerous word.'"

He's right. But if you take out all the shoulds, what's left that's worth anything?

"I have to go, Blaise. Take care."

You too. Come again.

"I will. And next time I won't wait so long."

I may not wait at all. HA.

9.

I'm certain I am dreaming, and am watching, I think, within the dream, a play.

Scattered about the stage are folding screens, all of them sheer and lit from behind, some plain linen or rice paper, others painted with landscapes, domestic scenes, still lifes, vegetation. As actors speak and move about

onstage, they pass behind these screens, sometimes pausing there, other times moving quickly through, and reemerge. Whenever an actor goes behind a screen (beyond a country hillside, behind a table and chairs or a vase with flowers, among the silhouettes of a crowded street) the actor abruptly, unpredictably changes: how he moves, how he responds, what he says—veering off even in mid-phrase. A comic line suddenly gleams with menace, dialogue curdles to diatribe, an actor's kindly query concerning another's affairs becomes, for the split second he passes behind one of the screens, a fierce, mad monologue. When the actor reemerges then, just as suddenly, the play comes back to keel.

I look down and find I am holding a program. On its front is printed the play's title: *Dailyness*. On its back is a peel-off sticker reading *Hello My Name Is*.

Applause starts up around me. An actor reemerges from one of the screens and the play, whose end he had signaled with a final, summary line while there, resumes.

10.

"Yes, David."

I looked past the window at a group of young people emerging from Wendy's. They wore the general uniform of the day—jeans or baggy trousers, various combinations of T-shirts, denim jackets and oversize sweaters—and were laughing before the jokes got told.

"I just had an interesting conversation on the subject of change."

He had picked up the phone on the first ring. Now he waited a moment and said, "I see. Philosophical discussion, like memories, in time of inactivity can prove somewhat comforting, I suppose."

"Or, again like those memories, disturbing."

"Of course."

The young people, who'd gone out of frame to the right, reappeared in the window imaginatively arranged on the seats of a convertible. They were still laughing. On the wall by the phone someone had written in purple marker: WE NO WHO YOU R.

"I'll need a complete file," I said. "Not the one everybody else sees. Your own."

"Certainly, David. For whatever good it may do you. Which I suspect will be very little, by the way. But I'll have Lawrence run off a disk for you. Your preference as to format? ASCII, perhaps?"

"Paper."

"Very well. Paper, then. Those thrilling days of yesteryear. What else?"

"Clothes. All I have are jeans, sweatshirts, running shoes. Those won't do, not for this."

"Of course. Your measurements would be approximately as before, I assume."

"Close enough."

"Cohen is still with us. I believe he should be able to assemble what's required in short order. Suits for daytime and evening, I would think. Assorted sportswear. Formal?"

"Not for the moment."

"Very well. Shall I have Miss Sidney contact you about travel bookings, then?"

"I'll be driving."

"Driving. I see. Well: as you wish. Have you a preference as to automobile? Fiats are no longer readily available, you understand."

"Anything small and manageable, unflashy. With more power than it looks to have."

"I'll have such a car at your hotel within the hour. Keys will be at the front desk. You will find suitable clothing, an array of it, within the car. And should you need anything more, anything at all, simply call me. You'll be put through instantly."

"Thank you."

There was a low humming in the wires behind our voices, like the voices of all those who came before us.

"I need to know if there's a timetable to this," I said.

"*Our* calendar's open. Intrinsically there may be. We don't know where all this is pointing, of course."

"If anywhere."

A brief pause? "Of course."

"One stipulation."

"Yes?"

"I don't want anyone flying up my butt on this one, sir."

"Department policy—"

"I know department policy, sir, the ones you broadcast and the ones your agents actually follow. I'm telling you that I go out alone, completely alone, or I don't go out at all. And that if I should happen to find someone behind me, I'll assume he doesn't belong there. Once I decide that, he won't *be* there."

"Understood."

"There's one more thing."

"Yes."

"I want a book sent. Poems by Cesare Pavese."

"To Gabrielle."

"Yes. I can't give you an address. I don't want to know, and I don't want anyone *else* to know. No direct contact or inquiry, nothing at all that might be traced. But the agency can find her and get the book to her discreetly. She'll know who sent it."

"Of course she will. David."

"Yes, sir."

"It's good to have you back. I know that Blaise was pleased to see you again after all this time. Thank you for going to see him."

"It accomplished what you wanted, at least."

"Nine years ago I would not have had to do that." Someone spoke. He turned away momentarily to answer, turned back. "But then, nine years ago it would not have worked."

Assume there is purpose, connection, because you must start somewhere.

Assume the features we obtain connecting these dots, these aleatory islands, are those of Luc Planchat, though in fact they may not be.

Assume that a line drawn through the coordinates of my motelroom visit in Memphis and the death of Raymond Hicks in Dallas necessarily intersects other events past and future, bearing them all towards pattern, *completion*, *closure*.

Things of the world try to connect. Prodigal rain issues from a sky into which trees rise like pleading hands. Days bear us lightly across the face of the world as every year the ground pulls harder, recalling like a spurned lover, ever more fixedly, how much it wants us.

Across that same grid (as on the screens of my dream) fall the contours of my own history and future, here congruent, there fugitive, the configuration of *my* face a Venn diagram overlaying *his*, Planchat's.

He knows. The Memphis motelroom visit and Hicks' death signaled that. And while I have little knowledge of the past ten years, of what Luc has become, how he thinks and what might be important to him, I know intimately the rise and fall of far deeper sensibilities.

Essentially (*au fond*, as Blaise might have said) we're the same.

I have only to wait.

12.

Once in France I waited three days in a blind alley among decaying trash, battling rats and ravaged, ravenous birds for a certain man to walk past, as sooner or later he *had* to walk by, that alley's mouth. I lived on stale bread and a foot-long sausage I'd carried in with me. It rained fitfully, and I collected what water I could for drinking. On the fourth day, near sunset, all my preparations began to gather into a single, sudden thrust—then instinctively, for reasons I still don't know, stopped—as the man for whom I'd waited stepped into sight. I crossed the border back into Germany that same night. And months later, far from there and assigned to matters wholly unrelated, discovered that our information had been, in one small detail, wrong. Had I pulled my target down that day, it would have proved a terrible mistake.

13.

In many ways, of course, the clothing available to me determined my role, and though it filled only two smallish leather bags, I should now be able, with middling imagination and care, to graze at whatever social level I required. Cohen was something of a genius in that regard, author of one slim, esoteric book, *Dress: Code and Language*, that brought him to the agency's attention. I often wonder if his fellow academics ever noticed he was gone and thought to question what might have happened to him.

The car was an excellent choice as well, a mid-Seventies 240Z in workabout condition that might just as easily be (considering my age) a leftover from college days or a vintage piece in the throes of restoration. There were patches of primer and the whole thing was an odd bluish-gray that looked as much like undercoat as paint; wheels were mismatched; the passenger door hung askew.

Saying good-bye once again to Baltimore, I threw both suitcases and my own cloth bookbag in the back of the Datsun and started out of town along the Loop in no particular direction with no destination in mind. Away from Baltimore, Washington and this whole stretch of tucked-in coast. And most of all just *moving*. Two things about moving targets. First, they're harder to hit. Second: they get noticed a hell of a lot quicker.

I stopped at a service plaza, bought maps of the northwest states and Florida and paid with a fifty-dollar bill, even putting the faintest, indefinable trace of an East-Europe accent in my voice to be sure I'd be remembered. Reflexes come back fast. Red herrings, feints. The mutability of it all.

I was wearing jeans, leather deck shoes and a cotton sweater without a shirt, sleeves pushed up to my elbows. I'd purposefully not shaved that morning. There was a sedate black watch on my wrist, a calfskin trifold wallet in my left rear pocket.

I had curved slowly inland from coastal routes, and highways here coursed through unbroken stands of trees, oak and maple, birch, elm, with little indication of the towns and communities one knew lay beyond. Only a monotonous cadence of exit signs with icons for GAS, FOOD, DIESEL, RESTROOMS, and every few miles the mast of a gas-station sign rising out of the trees. As though the six-lane interstate had materialized here to allow visitors from other places, possibly from other worlds or times, to experience what this country once was like everywhere: its rawness and awesome scale; how empty it had been, and at the same time how filled. Yet these thickets of growth were Potemkin blinds. Depart the interstate, and you found they shortly gave way to sprawling settlements of Texacos, Exxons, Kwik Stops, McDonalds.

The hills themselves seemed every bit as redundant as the exits, swelling up gradually, monotonously, under prow, then settling in a languid curve towards the next.

An hour or so outside D.C., I topped one of those

hills into the most astonishing sunset I've ever seen. Somehow I'd taken a turn out of real life into a movie, a travel brochure, a romantic novel. I pulled to the side of the road and sat with the motor off, watching. When the last firestruck tendrils darkened to slate and let go, I felt a sense of personal longing and loss, a bristling sadness.

Deep into Virginia, wonder of wonders, I found an FM station that followed some classic Louis Armstrong/Bessie Smith with a Ravel piano concerto and an *a cappella* quartet version of Neil Young's *After the Gold Rush*.

Once, a deer staggered into the wash of my headlights, turned and sprang away.

Other eyes glittered from the growth at road's edge.

Bodies of raccoons, dogs, opossum, a lone porcupine, lay at roadside.

Around ten I stopped to eat. A special section of the cafe (with a phone in each booth) was reserved expressly for truckers whose rigs circled the gravel-and-asphalt parking lot like wagons in old Westerns. Rack upon rack of bright postcards, novelty items, NoDoz, eyeglass cleaner, lighters and pocket knives bearing the Confederate flag. Tattooed arms and huge bellies in black T-shirts crowded around a rack of Books on Tape: Louis L'Amour, Stephen King, techno-thrillers. Little doubt I was in the heartland of America.

An LED banner-box set over the rear counter scrolled by news headlines, aphorisms and self-improvement for the benefit of the truckers as they ate. The Word for the Day was *eschatology*.

My barley-and-beef soup was good, the cornbread even better. Afterwards I had a piece of pecan pie and dawdled over two cups of coffee trying to decide whether to drive on or crash for the night at the motel (*Rooms Scientifically Cooled*) across the street.

"Passing through, honey?" the waitress said when she brought more coffee. I'm fairly sure I had never in my life been called honey before this. She was thirtyish, virtually blonde, with features you'd forget once you looked away. A woman who had made a sudden stop on the way to pretty, who would never quite get over how close she'd been. A white plastic rectangle over one high breast read *Alicia*.

I nodded.

"Well, should you have a taste for a cocktail or two, there's this little place just down the road, Lou's, you can't beat." She gestured across at the motel. "And you won't do better than the Island anywhere within ninety miles of here if you need a place to sleep. If you're of a mind, that is. My husband— ex-husband I should say, really—runs it like a cruise ship. I should know, I put in my share of sixteen- and eighteen-hour days over there. Anything else I can get you?"

I told her no, and thanks.

"You change your mind, we're open all night. I'll be here to twelve, my-self."

Alicia waited a moment, put down the check and walked away.

Lou's was everything I could have hoped for, though I almost missed it on my first pass since the neon sign overhead read *Blue Corral*. But a wooden one in the window said *Lou's*, and that was also painted above the front door in the same DayGlo green.

Basically it was a feeding trough: bar running down the middle of a long shotgun room, with slots for livestock, or in this case stools, on either side. Pool tables floated in their islands of light off in the darkness to one side, a dance floor lined with stacked plastic chairs loomed to the other.

I took a stool near the door beside a cowboy who looked like something from a wax museum and asked for a beer. Out in darkness on the dance-floor side, a guitarist and bass player tuned by harmonics. A dancing couple, the man forty or more and wearing slacks with white shirt and tie, his partner maybe half his age and wearing considerably less than half a T-shirt and jeans, periodically orbited into the bar's dim light and back out into blackness.

I drank my beer and asked for another. The cowboy was drinking coffee with bourbon in it. He had a little squeeze bottle of honey in his pocket and was putting some of that into the cup too.

After a while, having made the round of drinkers, the bartender came back over and stood across from me. He was as quietly animated and as flushed with color as the cowboy was waxlike.

"Lou," he said, sticking his hand across the bar.

I took it. "Dave."

"Good to have you. Haven't seen you in here before, I don't think."

"Haven't had the chance."

He nodded. "Quiet night. There's usually a good group in here, though, most nights. Come in here either to drink and be left alone, or else to dance. Either way, mostly they don't get to minding somebody else's business."

I told him I knew what he meant.

"Not like some places. You want a shot with that beer, maybe? Be on the house, you understand, first-time customer and all."

"Thanks, but I'll stick with beer. I'm not much of a drinker. Just unwinding a little. You know."

"On the road."

I nodded, and he nodded back. Two good old boys who knew what a man had to go through.

There was a loud thump from out of the darkness, then a voice:

"All right, you rebels, cowboys, horsewomen, Jaycees, JD's and all others within the sound of my voice." A pause, an adjustment. "Keep those cards and letters comin' in. And if you have a request, so do we: keep it to yourself."

Lights came up slowly onstage. A portly youngish man stood there with a high-slung hollowbody electric. He wore preppy clothes—sweater, broadcloth shirt, tan chinos—and a cowboy hat. Behind him in shadow, as though they belonged to one another, shadow and musician, the bass player half-sat on a barstool, ragged out in honestly worn jeans with a sateen tour jacket, hair to his shoulders, a single long earring.

There was a sudden, machinegunlike burst of hot jazz guitar.

"Okay, Justin, we're ready if you are. All saddled up up here. Let's *ride*, man."

The cowboy on the stool beside me looked at me for the first time.

"Boy's your basic asshole," he said, "but if there's a better guitar player in four states I ain't seen him."

He got up, ambled onstage, strapped on a bright red electric mandolin.

"Keep it country," he said, "just keep it country," and the band broke into an uptempo version of *Faded Love* heavy on tremolo and sevenths. They worked without a drummer, and with that particular bass player, with the guitarist somehow laying in brick-solid rhythm chords and skirting all around the melody at the same time, they didn't have much need for one.

Faded Love gave way to *Sweet Georgia Brown* and that to a breakneck *Jolie Blonde*. Then a catch-all of current hits with the guitarist singing while the mandolin player stitched bluesy licks and fills all through his lyrics.

Sometime during the second set and third beer, the barstool beside me stopped being empty.

"Okay if I join you?" Alicia said. "Guess you changed your mind huh? God, I love these guys. Bourbon and water, Lou."

She had changed into black jeans, pink hightop canvas shoes, a voluminous man's cardigan (sleeves rolled into doughnuts) over a lowcut cotton top. What appeared to be an authentic Indian arrowhead hung from a rawhide thong and pointed down into her cleavage.

Foucault's pendulum. Use it to deduce and demonstrate the earth's rotation.

"We haven't really met," she said, "but I'm Alicia. You're staying at the Island, too, I bet. Business trip, or pleasure?"

"Business, mostly."

"You ever mix the two?"

I shrugged, and the gesture hung between us there in the air like a ghost struggling to keep its form, like a diminutive fire. She smiled and took a healthy swig of her drink, then a measured one. Accustomed to pacing out a night's drinking.

"Well," she said. "You like country music?"

I nodded.

"You don't look like you would. Not the type, you know? And so much of it's just junk anyhow. I'm gonna get drunk till I get over you. Kick me again, that's the only time we touch. But then in the middle of it all there'll be this one line, or this few seconds of music, that's just absolutely right, that says what *you* need to say in ways you never can."

We had a couple more drinks and sat there talking. Alicia was twenty-eight, legally married but living on her own for about two years now, in furnished apartments mostly, sometimes with a dog, God she loved dogs, but the dogs, like the men, never lasted. They all ran away or turned mean.

We agreed on one last drink, and towards the end of it she said: "Guess you must be pretty tired huh, being on the road and all. Prob'ly just going to go on back to your room and turn in."

I told her that I was.

"Yeah. Well, me too, I guess."

We said good-bye and I walked out into the parking lot, leaving the start of a new set and *Milkcow Blues* behind. An older man in a bowling shirt leaned against the wall puking. A jet whistled past overhead. The neon *Blue Corral* sign flickered once and became *Blue Cor al*. Lost at sea.

Not long after, there was a knock at my motelroom door. I opened it. She was carrying her sweater.

"This is absolutely your last chance," Alicia said. She looked beyond me into the room and smiled: "Or mine."

14.

Outside a town named Stonebrook I pulled off the interstate, stopped at a U-Halt convenience store and at the pay phone there dialed a number that shuttled me through several blind relays and redirects before ringing.

The phone was picked up without greeting.

"Sir," I said, "perhaps you remember Marek Obtulowicz. Also used the name Lev Aaronson. We worked together in Gdansk, then again for a stretch in Santiago."

"Yes. Went to ground some years back. In Budapest, if I remember. We were never able to confirm."

"I've been thinking about something he often said, an old Russian proverb: Do not call in a wolf when dogs attack you."

He waited a moment. "I see. This is the reason you have called on a secure field line, against every policy and all standard practice."

"Yes."

"Then let me offer in return something my father read to me when I was a child. It is from Karl Kraus, I believe. 'To be sure, the dog is loyal. But why, on that account, should we take him as an example? He is loyal to men, not to other dogs.' Is there anything else?"

"No, sir."

"Stay in touch, David."

And the connection was gone.

I stood watching a bluebottle fly throw itself again and again at the window, buzzing furiously. The sill was lined with the dessicating husks of its predecessors.

15.

The road gives us release, reaffirms the discontinuity of our lives, whispers to us that we are after all free, that (around this curve, when we reach the next town, if we can only make it to California) things will change. Twain and Kerouac both knew the great American novel would have to be a book of the road. So did James Fenimore Cooper, before there *were* roads.

When I left the agency, I sank almost my whole severance pay into a car. Since the agency took care of our needs, I'd never been in a position to accumulate things—clothing, automobile, house, apartment—and that car became virtually all I had. It was perforce, for several months, where I lived: a late-Fifties Buick with auxiliary gas tank and custom sound, backseat scooped out to make room for sleeping and cargo. And in it I drove from Memphis to Dallas to Akron to Seattle, often reaching my destination only to turn around and start back or veer off towards yet another fanciful destination, spending nights at the side of wayward country roads or in motels that sprang up sudden and solitary as cactus along Oklahoma highways. And always in those months, music was playing: big bands, Bessie Smith, Bix, Trane, Eric Dolphy. Being on the road, and music, were all that made sense to me for a while.

And so I drove southward now, and westward, thinking of Alicia across from me at the diner that morning. I had the radio tuned to a comedy hour. Jokes about wives, dogs, kids, bosses, kumquats, kangaroos. All equally alien to me. An absolutely impenetrable five minutes of doubletalk on contemporary relationships from "The Professor of Desire."

"You ever be back through here?" Alicia had said, watching me over her coffee cup.

I shook my head.

"Yeah. Well, I didn't think you would be. No way. But that's all right."

The waitress brought our breakfasts and asked Alicia if she worked today. Off, she answered, but I have to pull the night-owl tomorrow.

"There's something in you," Alicia said when she was gone, "something you keep hidden. Dangerous, maybe. And maybe that's why I wanted to know you. But it wouldn't matter how well or how long I knew you, would it? That something would always stay hidden."

"There's something hidden in all of us."

"Dangerous things?"

"For many of us, anyway. Even if we don't recognize them, or know they're there."

We finished our breakfast and coffee and said good-bye outside by the car. There's never a lot you can say at times like that, apartness spreading like a stain between you, sky dumping its endless spaces over your head.

Alicia had touched my arm, very softly, and gone back into the diner.

My reveries were interrupted (again!) by rude reality, this time in the form of a battered gray Chevy. It dropped onto me outside a town called Carl's Bay, dogged me past the town's dozen or so roadside buildings, and finally announced intentions as we passed a city-limits sign and started into a long curve that quickly bore the town out of sight.

The Chevy came up fast on the inside. I saw only the driver. It wasn't Planchat, of course, or anyone I knew; it wouldn't be. But obviously there wasn't enough road for both of us. Out of town by sundown and all that.

The obligatory car chase was taking place rather early on in the movie.

There are several ways you can handle this sort of thing. Probably the best is just to ignore it, and that's what I did for some time, the Chevy's driver growing ever more reckless and erratic, like a bull throwing itself repeatedly at the same stretch of steel fence.

He came up alongside and made as though to swerve into me. Dropped back till I could barely see him, then all at once closed the distance and shot around. Pulled off to the roadside and waited, rocking the car on its rear wheels, as I went by.

Another response is to bail out, just refuse to play, and when I thought the time was right, the stew just about ready for serving, *that*'s what I did.

I braked, neither fast nor slow, and came to a stop in the road.

The Chevy's driver zipped on by, braked hard with an eye on the rearview mirror, then tried a fancy turn and almost lost it. The Chevy sat facing me about thirty yards down the road.

I waved.

Then I floored the little Datsun, feeling everything it had cut in, and headed straight for him.

I was outweighed by at least a ton and would have wound up crushed against his grill like a bug, but reflex won out. I watched him haul the Chevy hard right and, in the rearview, saw him try to bring it back around and fail. It went over on its side, then heavily onto its back in the roadside ditch.

Saw it start to, saw it had to, saw it happen, as Archibald Macleish wrote.

Everything was very still.

This is where the audience whoops it up for the good guy, I told myself.

But there weren't any cheers or applause. Only more road waiting to unwind, most of a day left to unwind it, and god knows what waiting ahead.

I slowed again and drove on.

It was the Sixties, a woman said on the radio, and I decided to drop out, *really* drop out. I went down to Sears and bought me a sleeping bag, a camp stove, some heavy boots. Gave everything else away to friends. Then I hitched out to the middle of Montana with everything I owned stuffed into a backpack. Found this neat cave. Moved in. Lived there four days in absolute, wonderful solitude; and on the fifth day the bear came back.

16.

I once read a story by this guy named Harlan Ellison ending: That night it rained, everywhere in the known universe. I was never too sure what the ending meant in terms of Ellison's story, but anyone who sits alone in a motel room for hours, watching rain wash the world away, begins to understand. Knows what it *feels* like.

I'd lost the Chevy and later in the day, with appreciably more finesse and less violence, another car, a recent Buick; but I had little doubt the stalking continued. He was (they were) out there somewhere in all that water, in what remained of the world, what hadn't been washed away, waiting.

A coded call from another phone booth, though not on a secure field line this time, had brought information at best equivocal: no further incidents involving Planchat, no further sign of him. Presumably I was the distraction from whatever program he'd previously been pursuing. And presumably it was Planchat, or his soldiers, dogging me: *I* was the program now. Just as I wanted.

I'd driven into Helena (Pop. 11,972, all nice people, it said so right there on the sign) in a downpour. There were two motels, one at either end of town, the Sleep Inn and The Deluxe, and I chose the latter, then went back out to sea for provisions.

After me, the deluge? Well, it sure *seemed* to be after me.

I sat on the swayback bed eating canned ham, water crackers and longhorn cheese and watching reruns of old TV shows about humble crises within happy families. Each was resolved when a character decided to do what he or she had known all along to be the right thing. There weren't a lot of families left, happy or otherwise, among the people I knew. And very few people seemed to know what was the right thing to do.

I shifted the dial over to FM music and drew a bath so hot my skin reddened. I soaked in it till the water grew cold, through sets of Buddy Holly, the Beatles and the Talking Heads, then came out and lay on the bed. It was seven-thirty. Lots of night left to fill. No letup in the rain.

Back a few months before I met Gabrielle, for a short while, there had been someone else, a young woman named Carol whom I met in a used bookstore. She was in line ahead of me with a stack of science fiction and biographies and needed forty-two cents. We had coffee at the lunch counter of a drug-store nearby. I followed her home.

Carol lived about as close to the ground as anyone I'd known, in the beach-like expanse of an unreconstructed second-floor commercial loft relieved only by five or six folding chairs, upended crates, an exercise mat she used as a bed, a scatter of bright cotton rugs. Walls were hung with photographs of the city's many baffles and dead ends, and of its denizens. Often there would be a dozen or more versions of the same subject, a battered face, an alleyway opening onto dark sky, each so like the others that only with close examination could I discern subtle shifts in angle or focus, in lighting, in contrast.

Carol had put on water for more coffee and a Tom Waits album. Listening to "Tom Traubert's Blues" there beside her in what was more akin to the waiting room of a train station than a place where someone actually lived, so aware of her, so taken by a woman's softness and scent after so long, buzzed with the coffee we'd already drunk, I was overcome by Waits' music, by the way he became what he sang. By the all but unendurable pain in his voice and the petty, doomed heroism of his people.

We listened to a lot of Waits that summer. It was a world I knew all too well, a world of bars and bleak mornings, of forfeits and endless beginnings-over that never took. A world Carol was courting.

To create his music, to give that world voice, Waits had transformed himself as unmercifully as did *castrati* or Rimbaud, burrowing ever deeper into the city dweller's brutish, subterranean, neon-struck life. And so, for similar reason, did Carol. I never knew whether art or access to that world was her primary motivation: if the photographs were intended somehow to earn her entry, or if perhaps she had come to believe her assumption into that world essential to continuing, to perfecting, her art. At any rate, she followed in Waits' wake, turning away from privilege, family, comfort and safety to live in poverty and to spend her nights roaming the city's black heart, her days slogging down hard coffee and (as she said again and again of her work) *trying to get it right.*

I don't know if she ever got it right. But that world, or some other, did finally open and let her fully in: one morning she didn't come back to the loft, and I never saw her again. In a way, I think, I'd been expecting it. But for a long time I went on looking down into the street half-thinking she would be there; for a long time I listened for the sound of her feet on steel stairs. I waited, there in the loft that later became my own studio. And now, far away from there, I remember.

17.

Dawn was rosy-fingered, just like in Homer. But did someone want it bloody?

Waking every hour or so from old habit, I had been aware of the rain's slow passing. By five, when I came fully awake, it was over. By six I was on the road.

I drove for a couple of hours before stopping for toast and tea at a cafe, Sam's, in the middle, possibly on the edge, of nowhere. Nowhere consisted of Sam's, a gas station and a dancehall. The gas station and the dancehall weren't open.

Oddly enough, Sam's was almost filled.

Or maybe that wasn't so odd, considering the choices available.

I sat over my tea—a generic bag of English Breakfast loosely packed with leaves as dry and brittle as insect legs, all they had—and listened to splinters of conversation, trying to reconstruct in my mind something of the lives around me.

I was, I supposed, in the very heartland of America now, among people whose values, families and bottom-line way of life I had been protecting in all my years, in all my actions, with the agency. A quarrelsome dictator removed here, a cooperative military junta supplied with weapons there, an assassination or two. Eyes-only information passed along, overthrows, "tactical support." All so that (nominally, at least) these people could go on about their lives of Budweiser, proms, sitcoms, Saturday-night football and Sunday church. They'd never know about most of it, of course, and if they did, would never understand. One of the reasons—just one—that I felt so terribly apart from them.

I was still in that contemplative frame of mind thirty or forty miles down the road when the holes appeared in my windshield.

There was no sound or real sense of impact, only two sudden holes about the diameter of pencils, spaced an inch or so apart, slightly to my right. I looked down at foam protruding from the seat just above my shoulder where one of the loads had entered. It looked like a small flower.

I pulled off into a patch of sunlight and killed the engine, not so much looking or listening for anything in particular as simply *opening* myself: becoming a receptacle for whatever sensation might fall in.

Why had I had no indications at all, no premonition?

A raucous flight of birds overhead. An approaching semi. The purr of other engines far off.

Nothing that shouldn't be here, as far as I could see or sense.

No Hollywood glint of steel in the trees or hills.

Ten minutes passed.

I was reaching down to turn the key when two more holes appeared in the windshield, this time to my left, again an inch or so apart.

Two flowers in the seat beside me.

Basically, if someone wants to kill you, if he's any good at it at all—if, say, he's an expert marksman, as this guy seems to be—and especially with current technology, there's not a lot you can do about it.

I got out and stood by the car, breathing deeply, feeling muscles let go. It's a trick you learn, at first. Then it becomes a reflexive response.

Nothing....

Sunlight and silence.

Against the horizon a frail-looking biplane skimmed the top of remnant clouds.

Of course, if he *doesn't* want to kill you, you may have to wonder why he's making such a show of trying to.

I got back in the Datsun and started the engine. Switched the radio on and sat there. *Sympathy for the Devil*: *bamboula* drums, shouts. Called *hocketing* back in Senegambia.

A hawk dived from a nearby treetop and swept low over the Datsun, banking.

No new holes or flowers.

18.

I stopped at the next town and made a great pretense of looking for an old college friend. Asked after him at a diner and gas station, made several phonecalls, kept going back to the car to rummage through the glove compartment and my book bag. Even cruised streets for a while at 20 mph, slowing still further to rubberneck infrequent signs at corners.

As illusionist Howard Thurston used to tell his assistants: If you don't know what's going on, boy, just smile and point the other way.

Soldiers and dinosaurs like myself wouldn't be so easily misdirected, of course, but I wasn't certain just who I was dealing with, not yet, and this could be one way of finding out. Besides, confusion never goes to waste. And it gets to be almost instinctive after a while. All part of the game, chords to play choruses over, steps of the ritual dance we locked ourselves into again and again.

"C'mon, m'am," I said at the local post office. "Give a guy some help here, all right? We go *way* back. Jimmie—with an *i-e*, not a *y*. Never James: Jim. Last name sounded English. You know? I mean, I can see his face like it was yesterday. Parkingham? Markham?"

"The postal service is not a public information system, sir." Visions of long, untroubled breaks, lunches replete with fried-shrimp po-boys, and a fine, secure retirement filled her head.

"I know that, m'am. And I know you guys do one hell of a job. Women too, of course. But hey, this is the first chance I've had to look him up in almost twenty years. It ain't like I'm calling in from home to ask you something. I'm standing right here, and I just drove over four hundred miles, and tomorrow I gotta drive at least that again. Just don't tell me I'm gonna have to go all the way back to Portland without ever seeing my old buddy after all this, okay? Just don't tell me that."

I stared off (fiercely? forlornly?) towards the window. Some double-winged insect the size of a hummingbird butted away at it.

"Hey, hold on a minute. *Berkeley.* That's it! We all used to call him Bish. Esse es percipi, the eraser, what eraser? and all that. How could I have forgotten?"

"I'm happy for you, sir. Have a safe and pleasant journey home."

"C'mon, m'am. Miss? Jimmie Berkeley. How hard is it? I'm begging you. Bail me out here, huh? Whatta we have, if we don't have our memories?"

And wouldn't you know, with all the other towns I might have pulled into, with the name itself (or so I thought) pure invention, just riding way out there on the edge of a blue note, there actually would *be* a Jimmie Berkeley in Marvell, North Carolina.

"I really should call my supervisor—"

"Please. Please do. Absolutely. In your place I'd do the same."

"—but I can't see the harm in it."

"Maybe you should call him anyway? For appearance's sake. Cover your bases. Your ass."

"And things haven't been going at all well for Jimmie this past few years. It should do him good to see an old friend, talk over better times."

Johnsson's *should*. That dangerous word again.

"He's living out at the old Swensen place. Caretaking.

Not that there's any care to take, or much left to take care of. What do you call it? A sinecure?"

She sketched lightly on the back of an old envelope as she went on.

"The mailing address is route one, box nine. But the way you get there is to take Cherry, that's the main street out front," as a bold line crossed the bottom of her improvised page, "on up to Loman's Lane and turn right once you pass the Nazarene church." A square with a cross inside it. "Then you go on four, five miles. Till you come to an old boarded-up Spur station. That'll be on your right. The road to the left's the one you want, the gravel one." Thinner lines now. "Half a mile more, over the creek, first house you come to. First one you'll *see*, anyhow. Out behind the big house, where old Swensen lived, there's a cottage, probably used to be a carriage house or slave's quarters. That's Jimmie's place." An X.

Remaining in character, I thanked her effusively, all the time thinking *Damn, damn, damn*, and *What webs we weave*.

But like a good athlete, now I had to follow through.

I had to go out there, shoot the basket, fumble, trip, foul and withdraw.

So I did.

Jimmie climbed down off a tractor overgrown with vines at the edge of trees as I came up the drive. The ruts coming in were bad enough, but these were worse. I lumbered over them, the low-slung Datsun bottoming out again and again, hood heaving up and crashing back down like a ship in heavy sea. I hit the brake and rocked to a stop. Jimmie stood by the big house waiting.

Okay. I'd indulge in a few moments' small talk and tell him sorry, obviously I have the wrong person. Wrong town, maybe. Completion, closure. Then back the Z up, U-turn and get the hell out of there.

But I saw in his eyes, or thought I saw, some trace of recognition. And something about his face, something in the pace and cadence of his words, was familiar.

"Can I help you, sir?" he said, keeping a distance.

"I...I seem to have lost my way. Can you tell me how to get back to the interstate?"

"Well, I reckon you're lost all right. Leastways the *highway* is." He laughed. "But you just turn around and go on back down the way you came a few miles, and when you fetch up against the creek, you turn left. Don't you cross the creek, now, just turn *at* it. Mile or two farther along, you'll see your highway."

"Got it. Thanks."

He stepped closer to the car.

"I know you?"

"Don't see how."

"Not from these parts, then?"

"No."

"And I been here my whole life. But I do know you. We've met up before." He shook his head and shrugged. "In some other life, maybe. Who knows about these things? You okay now on finding your highway?"

I said yes, thanked him again and sailed back down the ruts.

Who indeed knows?

As I'd told the postal clerk, before this man I thought I was making up out of whole cloth took on flesh and spoke to me: What do we have if we don't have our memories?

What I believed pure invention had become *more*, seemed in fact to have made its way to the surface from some clandestine well of memory.

What if memory itself, in turn—his, my own—were only invention?

19.

For the next hundred miles a Ford Escort moved up to number one on the charts.

Talk about protective coloration. A Ford *Escort*?

It picked me up not long after Carl's Bay and the unseen sniper. A Dodge van had come around some miles back, so for a while it was a toss up, both with a bullet, as they say, but then the van turned off and never came back, meaning either that it didn't figure at all, or that it was running a classic A-B tail and had passed me on to the Ford.

So that's the song we were dancing to.

I drove along thinking of those first weeks in the Buick following my retirement, the endless miles of highway I covered and recovered, all the open road I had felt beginning to unfurl in my mind and life, Brubeck and Bird and Sidney Bechet unwinding on the tape player the whole time. That stuff wasn't readily available then; I'd paid dearly to have collectors dub it for me from their stashes of old records and acetates.

I thought of men long since dead, of a woman's face in Chile, of part of a child I found beside the road one morning in Salvador. I remembered what it felt like when someone died there beside you, how your own body became in that instant instantly more real, more alive.

I wondered what use a soldier with a conscience could possibly be, and if indeed I had one (but I was here, wasn't I?), and what conscience was.

No more trustworthy, no less unreconstructed, perhaps, than was memory?

Just after lunch the Escort ceded favor to a Mazda pickup that paced me at such a calm distance I became certain I was this time in the presence of a pro. Mazda sat uncomplaining in a vacant lot the whole while I stretched a steakhouse dinner to almost two hours. When I left, it came along quietly. And when I went to ground, it pulled into the parking lot between tourist cabin number nine and the sole exit.

Fair enough.

`He knew the moves without having to work them out, instinctively. I was no longer dealing with amateurs.

The cabins were pure Fifties postcard: fake frontier, as though some Titan's idiot child had been given a set of Lincoln logs for Christmas and turned loose, complete with brown plastic chimneys and slab doors painted to look like four planks with crossties. Inside, it was even worse. You could barely turn around in there without bumping into *something*; it was packed full with a green Naugahyde sofa and chair, a bed whose headboard put one in mind of tombstones, matching blond dresser and bureau, a corner desk shelled with aqua Formica that after many years of bondage and struggle had almost succeeded in emancipating itself from its support brackets.

I used the cabin's phone and my own calling card to send a telegram to a deadfall address: *Xanadu tomorrow stop*. More confusion and background noise.

I left open the canvas curtain with its frontier scenes—wagon wheels, lariats, a chuck wagon—and turned on the TV to a Special Report about recent mass murders in Utah. Canted newsreel footage of the suspect, of abandoned back yards and one-time schoolrooms, of a town square, a storm-laden sky. Interviews with a psychologist specializing in (caps? italics?) the criminal mind and with, unaccountably, a "television consultant." (A *what?*) Having become instantly, momentarily, an actor, each spoke his lines with heavy sadness and certitude. Apparently it occurred to no one that, inasmuch as explanations and answers *did* exist, they were complex ones, and might only be found in the suspensions of true discourse or of art, certainly not in homilies, slogans, threadbare aphorisms.

Strike another blow, I thought inanely, for American No-how.

The newscast was followed by a poorly-dubbed Japanese mystery, *Ransom*, that nevertheless immediately swept me up and carried me off, more from the intensity of the lead character's features and the stark, angular black and white of the film itself—like something out of his own mind—than for any facility of plot or technique.

A three-time murderer (though none of them in passion), Osho is released from prison during war with the understanding that, in return for his freedom, he will kill again: this time a most peculiar patriot, an old, once great soldier now leading his people away from confrontation and towards negotiation. Osho instead flees, settling in an obscure mountain village where he becomes protector for a young, mildly retarded woman with whom he falls slowly in love, and for her family. Raiders—refugees from various war zones, deserted soldiers—periodically come upon the village by chance only to be dispatched, violently, by Osho. There are brief flashbacks to beatings he received from his father as a child; to (at the beginning of this same war) the imposition of martial law and subsequent confiscation of his home village's sole source of income, its fishing boats; to the single boat he and a friend carried into the hills and the officer they struck and happened to kill when he came upon them there; to the man whose throat he slit years later in a barroom brawl over a woman whose name he never knew or asked; to the face of a man he almost killed, but from whom he drew back at the last moment, in prison. By film's end, despite all he has done, despite his final, passionate killing, one feels a great compassion, a spilling tenderness, for Osho. In the movie's last frames, half a dozen policemen in plainclothes climb slowly up the mountain to put him to death for defaulting on his bargain. The country is at peace.

I walked to the window, half-expecting the Mazda's driver to be in the window opposite looking back, the same film coming to its end on the screen behind him.

But there was only blackness out there, blackness shot through from time to time with the lash of passing lights, broken by the dull thunder of trucks on the interstate a mile away.

And behind, there was only more news, more detective shows and sitcoms, endless advertising, an interminable hour of sophomoric British comedy in tuxedos and drag.

I slept well, dreaming of the countryside of southern France, its small *caves* and restaurants, its *patés*, oversized bottles of local wine, cassoulets, greens and rolling green hills. I was a leaf carried along by wind. Wind whispered softly to me and would never grow tired. *Ma feuille*, the wind said, *ma petite feuille, ma jolie feuille....*

In the morning, no less surprised than I might have been upon receiving, by return post, a reply to a message in a bottle, or to words whispered into the darkness, I received a response to my telegram.

"Mr. Anderson?" the desk clerk said when I picked up the phone. He was probably also owner, maintenance man and half the housekeeping staff. "I'm sorry about disturbing you at such an early hour, but I have a telegram here for you."

"Yes?"

"You want me to read it?"

"Please."

"Oh. Okay. Let's see...it says: *I await you*. And there's something else here, a name maybe. *K-U-B-L-A*? That's it. Be checking out this morning, will you?"

"Yes. Thanks again."

"Oh no: thank *you*."

Ten minutes later, the Mazda pulled out behind me. We drove up the street like a very small circus and stopped at a truckstop for breakfast. Plenty of parking in front. This time he came in, sat at the counter, and ordered cof- fee.

20.

I ate breakfast slowly and, afterwards, carried a second cup of coffee over to the counter and sat beside him. He was on his third or fourth, with milk and with sweetener from sky-blue packages. Where we were, you could see stacks of glasses in wire racks against the kitchen wall, a tottering tray of napkins rolled, burritolike, around silverware, a badly encrusted waffle iron.

"Come here often?"

A lot younger than I would have thought—but aren't they all?—and good-looking in some indefinably continental way; functionally dressed in loose jeans, sweater, ski jacket, running shoes. I wasn't the only one who thought him good-looking. The waitress spent an inordinate amount of time seeing to his coffee.

"Capricorn," he said. "And no, I don't want to dance."

We sat there a while. Truckers came in, made calls over coffee and burgers, and left. Travelers whose children could be seen looming into the windows of vans outside like sharks in aquariums materialized at the counter and voyaged back out with cartons of food in hand.

"So what do we do next?" I said. "You supposed to smother me with a jelly doughnut?"

"Thought maybe I'd just persuade you to order the chili. That ought to do it."

"Or I could jot down my itinerary, we'd meet a couple of times a day for meals. Save you a lot of trouble. Easier for everybody, in the long run."

"Hmmmm," he said, and got more coffee from the waitress. Can't let a good customer take two sips without a refill. He nodded to her and smiled.

"We could even consider carpooling," I said. "I can't remember if there's an energy crisis right now, but if not, one's bound to be along shortly."

He shook his head, half an inch in either direction, once. "Don't think so. I've seen the way you drive."

"There's that. But you do have to look at the big picture."

He looked into his coffee instead and suggested a walk.

I paid, waited as he spoke with the waitress, then we went out together into a chill, sunny morning. Sunlight on everything, just lying there, trying to get warm.

We walked down the main stretch a block or two, then onto a side street that barely managed to harbor six buildings and a building-sized, overgrown parking lot before surrendering to the chaos of kudzu and what people hereabouts called *woods*. I'd had similar feelings once on a brief assignment in Midland-Odessa, Texas: this sense that three paces out from the city I'd step abruptly off the continental shelf, into quicksand and nothingness

— as though aliens had carved the city from its environs and deposited it here.

"Do you remember a morning in the fall of '68, on Cyprus?" my companion said after a time.

A woman's face floated into my mind. The smell of lemon trees, kerosene.

"I do. But there's no way *you* could."

He went on. "Because of your presence, because of what you did, or caused to happen, there—I don't know the details of this, and you yourself may or may not recall them—a woman selected to die instead was reunited with her children."

Oh, yes: I remembered.

"Years later, far from those islands, in a far different life, in a different world, that woman again found love and remarried. Her husband was a Russian émigré, a childless widower who had long believed his life over, his family name never to be forwarded, his fortunes at an end.

"Dmitri was at first astonished, then grateful, to find love and family so late in his course. Gratitude did not come easy to him, you understand. He had clawed his way up from the rudest dock work. It was difficult for him to credit fortune, chance, destiny—to credit *anything* but his own determination and labor—for what happened in his life. And because that recognition, that gratitude, came with such difficulty, it was taken most seriously. Taken *to his heart*, as he himself might say. It became one of the central facts of his life.

"In time that gratitude extended itself to the person he knew to be responsible for his wife's survival. And so, declaring someday that person would be properly thanked, Dmitri turned his considerable resources towards discovering the man's identity."

My companion paused, watching an Amish buggy make its plodding way along the road's shoulder.

"It was, as I'm sure you know, a for*mid*able task."

Stressed on the second syllable, as the British do.

"I'd think so." Hope so.

"One fraught with false trails, laden with dead ends, blinds, misdirections. And impossible to say, finally, whether it was dogged persistence, money— vast sums of it, pirate chests full of it—or simple luck that's carried me at last to this long-desired end."

"This is the end, then? Here?"

"The Russian, Dmitri, died many years ago—as good a man as will ever see this world. His wife, the woman you knew as Cybelle, followed shortly after.

"In thanking you now, I discharge both my father's gratitude and the vow I made to him.

"*Spaseba*," he said, holding out his hand. "I am Michael. And now, I suppose, finally, I can get on with my life."

Thinking of his obvious professionalism, I said:

"But surely this *is* your life."

"No. I'm an engineer, a shipbuilder, actually. Not that I've had much chance to practice that profession."

We had come back around to the truckstop.

"For all his efforts and dedication, the old Russian was never able to discover your identity. In fact he learned almost nothing. What else was there for me, then, but to become, myself, what we knew you to be? If you wish to find wolves, *become* a wolf.

"This is what I did. I trained and had myself sent out as a field agent and before long in that clandestine, circumspect world I began encountering certain...stories, I suppose you would say. You may or may not know: a kind of myth, a hollowness, exists in the place you once occupied. As in Voznesensky's poem for Robert Lowell:

"You were ensconced, shrouded, in that space. But then it began to seem as though the space might be no longer vacant, the hollowness filling. Rumbles of far-off thunder made their way to me. Rumors, unexplained occurrences, movements on the horizon. All of which led me inexorably to this assignment. To you. And thereby to the end of one career."

We stood near a huge plate-glass door plastered over with travel stickers. Our breath pedaled out into the chill morning air. A middle-aged couple on a Gold Wing pulled up at the curb and sat with engine idling, studying separate maps, he in half-moon reading glasses, she holding the map out away from her, squinting.

"I had assumed it was *my* career that was supposed to end," I said. "And my life."

"So, apparently, had others." Michael looked into the cafe. The waitress looked back at him from behind the counter. They both smiled.

"I must tell you: I am not at all certain that I recognize the game pieces in use here, or that I know their proper moves. And the board itself seems a most peculiar, oddly-shaped one. I hope that you will take particular caution, my friend."

He held out his hand and we shook.

"How very strange to call you that: friend. You have been central to my life for much of it. Yet I've not met you until this day. And now will have no reason to see you again."

"Unless you come simply *as* a friend."

I stood for a moment watching through a tiny map of Texas on the door as he reentered the cafe and sat at the counter. A cup of coffee was put before him. The waitress, apparently, was on break; she came and sat beside him.

21.

For the remainder of that day and much of the next—presumably until someone got around to discovering Michael's apostasy—I was a solo act. Sailing
free and alone on the interstate and through adjunct towns, at peace with
myself and surroundings.

Then about three in the afternoon, roughly alongside a stretch of fiberglass
hot tubs turned on edge like huge jigsaw pieces and another service-road
store selling "chainsaw art" (totemlike figures of bears and other wildlife
liberated waist- or haunch-up from tree trunks), with acquisition of a sporty
little white job and a mooselike Pontiac—countertenor, bass—I became a
trio.

They took the Datsun out an hour or so later.

There wasn't a lot I could do. We'd cat-and-moused for thirty miles or
more on the straightaway before nosing into a cluster of tight, contradictory
curves. The Pontiac had lugged up hard on my outside then, holding me in
the curves and crowding close against me while the sportscar, a Fiat, nipped
and nibbled at the inside like a good cow dog.

It was all timed perfectly, almost balletic. And when finally I did leave the
road—more or less electively, as it happened, taking what I decided might
well be my last chance—for a moment, just before the rear wheels lost purchase, I thought I'd done it, thought I might actually have pulled it off.

The Datsun hit the far bank and paused, listing for an interminable moment during which several Latin American nations changed their names, political ideology and rulers at least once, then, very rapidly, gaining speed all
the while, began rolling.

After six it all seemed academic and I quit counting.

So I started rolling, myself: out of the tight ball I'd tucked myself into and
out of the car in a single ongoing motion. Then let momentum carry me onto
my feet and sprinted between billboards for steak houses, motels and wrecker
services into nearby trees.

I was on a limb high overhead when they finally talked themselves into
coming in after me. I could see their cars pulled into a gap-toothed V back at
roadside. There were only the two drivers, one a middle-aged, crewcut man
in crisp white shirt, tie and windbreaker, the other in Yuppie Lumberjack

and baseball cap. The older one had a shotgun. The younger one probably thought his red shirt was weapon enough.

I stayed up there a long while, letting them wear themselves down and lose what edge they had.

Then the kid stepped around a tree into my elbow and went down. His head lay propped against roots. Blood poured from his nose and pooled at his collar, soaking into the shirt, darkening it to maroon. He snored.

The older one was considerably more trouble, and for a time I was afraid I'd moved on him too hard. But eventually light seeped back into the dull grey eyes he levelled at me.

I nodded to him.

After a moment he said: "Correct me if I'm wrong. But I suppose if I move—if I can, that is—you'll shoot me."

"With what?"

I was sitting, knees up, against a tree. I spread my hands.

"Okay if I sit up? Again: if I can."

I nodded.

He came up slowly, hands flat against legs, breathing deeply, forcing the pain back. Put it in the pantry, use it later.

"Adrian?" he said.

"Asleep."

"Temporarily, or otherwise?"

"Give him half an hour."

He looked off towards the highway, blinked up at the sun through the canopy of leaves. A squirrel was fussing up there somewhere.

"Right, then."

He lifted his left hand and probed at its wrist, experimentally, dispassionately, with the fingers of the other.

"Third time now I've broken the sucker. So...."

He looked at me again. Eyes flat and round as lentils.

"So?" I said.

"So what's the deal?"

"How about we play History? I'm the big bad Russians and you're Julius Rosenberg. Tell me some secrets."

"Yeah, well, I know how that one ended."

"This one doesn't have to."

There was a sudden exodus of birds from trees around us. Moments later, half a block long, a truck heaved into view on the service road, cab black and gleaming, bright cars lashed to scaffolding behind, distinct as paints in a paintbox.

"Cigarettes in my shirt," he said. "All right if I get them?"

"Sure."

He lit one and sat smoking, watching the truck swing back on to the interstate. I thought of camels lumbering among dunes half a world away. Of erector sets, carnival rides, the Eiffel Tower. My sculpture.

"Can't help you much. There's this man—an agent, I guess you'd have to call him. No pun intended. Everything comes through him. Someone needs a job done, he gets in touch, and the man sets terms, strikes the bargain. I call in later, a couple of times a day when I'm not already working, otherwise it might be two or three before I get a chance, and he tells me go here or there. Be in Dallas at five, Akron tomorrow morning, this is what you have to do there. Tickets are always waiting for me. Motel rooms. Cash. Everything about it ultra clean, professional. Smooth. So I can't give you a name. That's why it's all set up the way it is."

He shook his head. "The rest is silence," he said.

But it wasn't.

Adrian's breathing signaled trouble. We both heard the laboring heaves, listened and caught the gasp, realized at the same moment that his breathing had stopped.

And suddenly were there, together, at the tree.

Grabbing ankles, I pulled the boy down flat and thumped at his chest, twice, hard, with a fist. Then quickly measured three fingers up from the xiphoid, locked fingers and began rocking, elbows stiff.

"One thousand, two thousand...."

His companion pinched nostrils shut and blew his own breath into Adrian's mouth.

"Three thousand, four thousand, five...."

Breath.

"One thousand, two...."

Breath.

"One thousand...."

Breath.

Nothing.

After ten or twelve minutes, on *change*, we traded places. I watched him there above the boy rock back and forth with locked fingers and stiff elbows, counting; and every fifth compression I blew my own breath forcibly into Adrian's still mouth. It remained still. Our sweat fell onto him.

We shifted places, shifted again.

Until finally, exhausted, we gave up. Adrian's pupils had been dilated for some time.

"What the hell happened?" my co-rescuer said.

"No way to know," I said. "I'm sorry."

"Yeah. Well." He lit a cigarette and fell back against the roots, breathing hard, looking up at sky. "It's all pretty frail, what holds us here."

"You got kids?" he said after a while.

I shook my head.

"Wife?"

No.

"Not many of us do. Boy there's the closest I was ever gonna come. Twenty-one years old. Would of been twenty-two next month. You even remember what it was like, being that young?"

Not really.

"Me either."

He struggled to his feet and to the Pontiac, fished a bottle of Stoly out of the glove compartment and brought it back.

"Join me?" he said.

We passed the bottle back and forth a few times.

"I don't get out much," he said. "You know how it is, working all the time, never knowing where you might wake up tomorrow morning. Then I *do* get out, and I look at all these people with their suits and their station wagons and the next thirty years of their life stamped out like it's on the back of a coin, and I have to wonder what makes them go on.

"Has to be family, I figure. And I guess Adrian there was pretty much *my* last chance for family."

I handed the bottle across.

He took a small, careful sip and passed it back to me.

I finished it off. Held the bottle close to me. Birds sang again. We sat there a while without talking.

"Come on," he said. "Help me get the boy into the car and I'll give you a lift to the next town. Get on with our lives, as they say."

As if we had them: lives.

22.

Not that, before this, it hadn't been "real" to me.

It was real: I'd seen too many bodies, too many cities gnawed at by flame, too many blank faces and shut-down lives, for it to be anything less. But until that moment my own two lives—the old one, which had embraced these things, which was defined by them, and the new, which at first denied them, later and at best strove somehow to understand them, to incorporate them, to absorb them—had not come together.

Like an eye exam where letters right and left loom wrenchingly out of focus, then suddenly swim towards one another and lock together.

Irony, some would say, is the voice of our time, a time perhaps more given to image, to form, than to substance. And it's difficult to imagine any more ironic image than two veteran killers squatting there at roadside trying to resuscitate a younger, unseasoned version of themselves.

A fever in my bones, Pavese might have said.

It began, truly began, there.

Images swam in my mind. But they swam beneath a dark membrane. I could make out only the faintest outlines of their forms as momentarily they tugged upward, tugged against that surface, then rebounded into the depths.

Premonitions? Memories? Occult understandings? Trying to escape, to break out—whatever they were.

As do we all.

Given paper and crayon, the ape draws, laboriously, precisely, only the bars of its cage, again and again.

23.

Adrian's mentor dropped me at a phone booth on the edge of the next town. Johnsson answered on the second ring:

"Again, David, I must ask that you stop calling on secure lines."

"You had no way of knowing who this would be."

"Chances were quite good. One develops a feel for that sort of thing, you may recall."

"I need a priority-one check."

"Actually, David, that's the only kind we do in these days of computerized files. But go ahead."

I told him about my conversation in the cafe, no more than I had to.

"Michael. The last name may be Danyovich. Father, Dmitri. Mother was Cyprus-born, name unknown, though at one time in her life she used Cybelle."

I described Michael as only a trained observer can (albeit a long unpracticed one) and told Johnsson that I'd stand by. I started to give him the number but he said he had no need of it: that the technology was a bit further along these days. I opened the phone booth door for air and watched traffic ease itself along the two-lane street. Within ten minutes, Johnsson rang back.

"Of several names," he began without preamble, "I find that of Michael Kandinsky—sometimes Michel, or Mikhail—most often used. He matches your description and, as far as we can trace things, the background you sketched. A fairly new player, it would seem. And an extremely cautious one. Almost no tabs to pull."

"Affiliation?"

"Freelance, like most of the East Europeans these days. They— Hold on."

Absolute silence on the line, with every twenty seconds the high-pitched bleep of the sweeper.

"David, the computer's latched onto something else. It's scrolling up now....

"Apparently some years ago, still in his teens, your young man found himself in trouble while on holiday in Turkey. Smoked a couple of joints with his girlfriend and a few of the wrong people, it seems. Spent a most unfortunate week in prison there before his father located and, handing over generous sums of *baksheesh*, retrieved him. The girlfriend was never heard from again. Inquiries were made through channels, officials denied any knowledge, the usual folderol."

"Not all that unusual a story, as I recall."

"No. But a year or so later, three guards at that same prison were found flayed and hung upside down on poles just outside the gates. Caused a bit of a stir, even for those times."

"Could it be coincidence?"

"It *could* be, as you well know, anything. A familial grudge, a military power struggle, depletion of the ozone layer. I myself am no strong believer in coincidence, however."

"He's insane."

"Perhaps. Remarkably motivated, certainly. The young man returned from that Turkish prison and, with his father's virtually unlimited funds, went back to school with a vengeance—though his major had changed.

"Over the following years we can track a stream of mercenaries, martial-arts teachers, munitions and surveillance experts, athletic trainers, gentlemen in our own line of work both active and retired, even a terrorist or two, to and from various locations about the world. We would never have been able to discern a pattern, before this; the activities appeared random. With Michael as fulcrum, however, tracing everything back to him, the pattern emerges."

"He turned himself into one of us."

"So it would seem."

"But why? Surely not all that, simply for revenge?"

"Actually, the incident with the guards seems to have been more or less incidental. Something of an advanced training mission, perhaps: who knows?"

I knew, of course—if what Michael had told me were in fact true.

"After that incident," Johnsson went on, "we keep losing the spore. Michael becomes in effect virtually invisible, surfacing here or there at will and—again—apparently at random, then quickly resubmerging. There are glimpses of him in Santiago, some intimation of a lengthy assignment in Rio, a possible walk-on in Puerto Rico."

"Where does Planchat fit into all this? Assuming that he does."

"Only two roles are possible, David."

"Hunter or hunted, you mean."

"Quite."

"There might be another."

He waited. I heard, twice, the bleep of the sweeper. "Mentor," I said. "He might have been one of Michael's teachers."

Three, four, five bleeps went by.

"Yes," Johnsson said. "Unlikely. But possible."

Three more.

"There has been no further indication of Planchat's presence. Were we the sort of men who make assumptions, we might assume him to be out of the picture."

"You think Michael brought him down, then?"

"Of course we are *not* that sort."

"Or that it's all been Michael, all along?"

That it was Michael I'd been hunting from the first—or allowing to hunt me—made no sense. But then, not much else did, either.

"That is a possibility," Johnsson said. "One there had been no reason to consider before this."

"So what do we do?"

"There may be little left that we *can* do just now. Your instinct, obviously, is that Michael should not be brought down?"

"At this time: yes. What I *feel* is that Michael's truly out of the picture now. But if not, then he's so deeply imbedded that, once we gouge him out of it, there's no picture left."

"In which case...."

"I will continue as before."

"Yes. That is almost certainly best."

Two bleeps. Three.

"So very much activity," Johnsson said, "and to so little apparent purpose. Every light in town is on. And still we are able to see so little."

Or in his case (I remembered suddenly) nothing.

"One thing further, David."

"Yes?"

"Your friend. Gabrielle. It seems that everything is getting gathered up in this tangle. Perhaps you'd best attend to her safety?"

24.

I walked up the street to Norma's Cafe and went in, remembering the beginning of *The Postman Always Rings Twice*. At Norma's, food seemed to be pretty much an afterthought. Instead of dishes there were mostly beercans. The *spécialité de la maison* was Bud Light.

I asked for coffee and got something reasonably close. On the counter nearby, a glass bell preserved half a cake passed down, from Norma to Norma, by untold generations of the cafe's owners. Lift the bell away and the cake would crumble to dust.

I sat sipping at my coffee. Two elderly men played checkers at a rickety back table. Neither one made a move the whole time I sat there. But every minute or two, again and again, from one side of the board or the other a hand would reach out, pause over pieces, and withdraw.

After a while, most of the Cherokee nation came over and sat beside me.

He was at least six-six, easily three-fifty without the boots and beltbuckle that would add another twenty pounds or so. He wore a baseball cap, baggy fatigues with a lot of feathers hanging off. I was pretty sure the stool had groaned when he settled onto it.

He sat smiling at me. Two sips of coffee went by, never to be seen again.

"You remember how it was, man? You do. I can tell. How they'd hunker down out there by the fires for hours while bugs crawled all over your rice and boiled grass and in the corner you always tried to get to before you had to shit. Nothing on their faces, man. Absolutely nothing. That's what I remember. Faces smooth and blank as stones in a river bed. And they'd rock a little on their heels out there by the fires. Looking like birds. Even sounded like them. And finally you'd just give up and eat the slop, bugs and all."

He shrugged. Planes flying overhead may have encountered turbulence.

"Fuck that shit. That's what I say. Just fuck it. Am I right?"

I told him he was.

"Fuckin' *A*," he said, and drank a few more beers while I had a sip of coffee.

"We're Asians too, man—you know that? Fuckin' *walked* here's what we did. Everything was still connected back then. And we could of walked anywhere, you know? But *this* is where we wound up, this was our country.

Then you U-rope-peons heard about the buffalo and came over here thinkin' you could have yourself cheap steaks for dinner ever' day and fucked it all up. Just like you fucked up Nam."

Everything in the cafe got very quiet. I could hear the flame popping beneath the grill.

"You ain't listening, man. And I thought you knew what I was *saying* to you here. Thought maybe you might even care a little. It could happen. But fuckitall: you're just like the rest."

He had another beer to prepare himself for what had to be done. Then he turned to do it—but I wasn't there. So he kept on turning, to where I stood behind him. Still on the stool, he threw an off-balance right that, inches away as I moved, slammed air against my eardrum and left it ringing.

I rolled in a slow circle around the punch, coming back in just as it peaked, adding my own momentum to his. He went along, then somersaulted away from me, unfolded, and slid four or five feet across the floor flat on his back. He would have slid further, but the cafe's tables were bolted down, and the second one stopped him.

"All *right*!" he said, and there was a general exodus towards the far wall as he got up.

It lasted longer than it should have. Finally I did manage to drop him without getting hurt myself or, more importantly, without having to kill or seriously maim my opponent, but it wasn't easy. And it took a while.

After the second tumble, he climbed back to his feet and left brute force, all he'd ever needed for civilian life, there on the floor.

He'd been well and thoroughly trained, and had grafted that training on to what was probably from the first a strong natural aptitude. As I watched now, trying to get a handle on what he was likely to do, he was either weightless and gliding, or he was solid stone. Nothing in between. And the edge came back to him then. I could see the difference behind his eyes, in the way he began moving. As though sharks had swum into the goldfish tank.

I'd go in for feints, just enough to get him moving, then roll away, out of reach.

Like a lot of fighters trained by the armed forces, he was strictly a full-out man: all offense and attack, every movement revved up till the metal screamed, every blow delivered like a bomb.

So I dogged it, made him keep coming after me. Got in close enough for him to strike and rolled off it when he did, looking to be much more affected than I was. I even stumbled once or twice. And then when he came in the last time, low, to shut me down, I wheeled around him and went back off the wall with both legs, adding my own weight and momentum to his, and rode him head-first into the stainless steel lunch counter.

The waiter set another coffee down in front of me.

"That happen very often?" I asked him.

"Never more'n a couple times a day. 'Cept Saturdays, of course. Indian's flat crazy."

"Nam was a bitch."

"Probably so. But Lee there was flat crazy '*fore* he went."

"Is there anyone we should call to see after him? A wife, maybe?"

"Lee done killed one wife and run at least two others off. But I expect someone'll be along shortly."

He nodded at my cup.

"Better hurry and finish your coffee," he said.

25.

Heavy in the hindquarters, with his small, sharp face, J.B. Pickett reminded me of a rodent standing erect. He was stooped, head bent down and forward, and his hands moved all the time. His skin was the color of flour sacks, hair brown and lifeless. He was, he told me, "the law" around here. He was also the Indian's half-brother.

"You can flat fight, that's for sure. Ain't nobody stomped Lee in a good long time." He poured coffee for both of us, into ceramic mugs, and handed one to me. His said *Roy*. Mine said *Dale*. "Reckon the last one who did was me."

We sat at what served for his desk, an old pine table with gouges and grooves polished smooth as marble and saturated with half a century's oils and cleaners. School libraries used to have these tables. Now they have particle board. Hot air poured in through an open, screenless window. So did endless streams of unhappy insects.

The law blew across his cup, blinked at the steam when it rolled back in. Every inch polite, professional and proper, but I couldn't shake the feeling that on a slow day he might sign up for lessons at the Arthur Murray Studio for the chance to step on toes.

"Just passing through, I guess."

I nodded.

"Headin' anywhere in particular?"

The first three words ran together in a long slur. The last one's syllables were ticked off in cadence, *par-ti-cu-lar*, like a banker counting out bills.

"Not really. New Orleans, eventually."

I hadn't known that until I said it, but realized it was true.

"*Coming* from anywhere in particular, then?"

"Last stop was Boston."

"Boston. I was up that way once."

He tugged a styrofoam cooler from under the desk, nudged the top aside and took out a pint carton of Half-n-Half. Held it towards me and, when I shook my head, dumped some in his coffee.

"You have a car, Mr. Edwards?"

He replaced carton in cooler, cooler beneath desk.

"I've been hitching several days now. I'd hoped I might find new transportation around here, though. Something inexpensive and more or less dependable. If anything like that exists."

"I 'spect you'd be likely to find something, if you were to look. You have a job, Mr. Edwards?"

"Self-employed."

"You prove that?"

"Do I need to?"

"Might." He leaned forward, chair springs groaning. "Let me tell you what came to me. You want some more coffee?"

I held the cup up to indicate that plenty remained.

"Came to me that, first, you don't look much like your standard hitcher, if you know what I mean. And that you knew just a little too much about what you were doing in there up against Lee. Came to me that you might be a person someone was looking for, and if so, that I ought to know about that. You able to follow my thinking?"

I nodded. I was following it all too well.

He leaned back in the chair again, springs sighing with relief.

"I was able to lift the better part of three good prints off that cup of coffee you had over to Norma's. Friend of mine who works up in the capitol, I had him run those prints for me. Have any notion what he might have turned up?"

I drank some coffee. Waited.

"Well, his computer kicked the prints and I.D. right out, no problem: *David Edwards*. Along with a dossier it pulled in from various linkages on the data system. But my friend wasn't satisfied with what he got. Said it was too easy, too quick and clean, that he got more than he asked for. That made him suspicious. And the more he thought about it, the more it bothered him. So *he* called in a favor—these guys all know one another, I gather—and piggy-backed on a system that's tied into some pretty obscure, and exclusive, data banks. Privileged, my friend put it. Shielded."

Without asking, he got up and poured more coffee into my cup. Then refilled his own and put the glass carafe on the desk alongside. His chair wheezed like a laryngitic accordion as he settled back into it.

"A strange thing happened, Mr. Edwards. Whatever data banks my friend accessed—credit, military, census—he got back the same thing. *Exactly* the same thing. Said it reminded him of obituaries waiting in newspaper files. Three or four tight paragraphs set as though in cement, scattered facts giving no notion of a real life behind those names, places, dates. And he'd never had anything like that happen before. Never."

He held out the carafe to me and, when I declined, emptied the rest into his own cup.

"My friend has an awesome curiosity. Not for the information itself, you understand—actually he cares little at all for that—but for the getting of it. Says it's the only thing he's ever been good at. And so he dug in, blind as a mole, buried like a dung beetle, burrowing the contemporary world's *real* subterrain."

He drank coffee for a while, smiling across at me.

"Eventually, my friend tells me, he managed to find a few cracks, get his foot in a door or two. But then, almost as though his presence somehow had been detected, those doors slammed shut, all at the same instant. And he was left with only a glimpse, the barest intimations of something, a dissolving shape."

He looked into his cup, moved it in slow circles.

"How old are you, Mr. Edwards? What: late thirties? Forty?"

I picked an age at random. "Thirty-nine."

"Yet, up until nine years ago, your life's a fortune cookie."

I inclined my head slightly, asking that he go on, inviting further information, by my own silence.

"I don't suppose there's a number I should call, anything like that?"

I shook my head.

"So," he said. "The horns of the moment's dilemma."

He looked towards the window. A wasp flew in, circled the room quickly and fled back outside.

"Obviously you'll provide me no information. Yet on the other hand I am enjoined, by my profession and by my charge to this community, to insist upon the answers I cannot have."

He leaned closer to me, arms flat on the table.

"Mr. Edwards. Are you willing, or able, at least to tell me what you're doing here?"

"I haven't misrepresented myself in any way, sheriff, nor do I have reason to do so. I truly am just passing through. There's no more to it than that."

"And if I should release you now, you would continue that passage?"

'I nodded.

"Your presence here has nothing to do with Lee Raincrow?"

"Nothing."

He looked into my face. A kind of information beyond words, small tides of recognition, passed between us.

"Buy you a drink," he said shortly, rising. "Said you had need of a car, I believe?"

I nodded.

He nodded back. "Reckon I might know where you could locate one."

26.

It was in a town called Cross, standing before an acrylic painting of a melting, chromatic city, that I became someone else.

It had happened before—once already this time out, in fact, with my to-be assassin in Memphis. I'd find myself in peril, nerve-ends singing, and suddenly everything out there would *change*, the world would shimmer, go away for a moment, come back transformed. But it had never before happened when I wasn't in clear, direct danger. And never before with such intensity.

I'd been reading signs for fifty miles or more, GREATER SOUTHEAST ART SHOW, rocking along in my VW bug the color of perpetual bruise (someone had painted a dark blue car maroon, badly), so when I finally got to Cross, subject of the signs, host to GSAS, I thought *why not?* and pulled into the parking lot of a Rodeway Inn festooned with plastic red, blue and gold banners.

Everyone in Cross was already there. Most of them seemed to be milling about the parking lot drinking beer. The rest were clustered around tables hurriedly pulled together in the coffee shop. A high-school class and I pretty much had free run of the ballroom, where the artwork was on display.

It was largely what I might have expected: landscapes, a few still lives, primitive portraits and rustic collage, some art-school pieces. Lots of flowers, trees and animals. Still, overall quality of technique was high. The edge wears just a little finer each year, it seems. And the quantity of work was truly astonishing. Had *everyone* turned into an artist of some sort?

The car, incidentally, was Lee Raincrow's. Lee had lost his license a while back, permanently this time, and (I was assured) would have no further need of the VW. I gave Pickett six hundred for it and figured if I got a mile per dollar out of it I'd still be ahead.

I had made a quick round of the ballroom and come back for a moment to the acrylic, getting set to leave, when it happened.

I have no idea how long it lasted. But I know it had been going on for some time when my own consciousness started filtering back in: dull clouds shot with light, bright threads, bright segments.

The painting was no longer there before me. I stood looking down through a rainswept window at the street. Someone stood behind me, almost touching.

"You're apart from me tonight," she said, and I turned to look at her. Hair cut short, boyish. Crimson lipstick and a T-shirt that fell to mid-thigh. "In some other kingdom?"

"I don't mean to be," I said as she moved into the embrace that waited for and fit her precisely. The heat of her skin sliding against my own.

The connection did not end there, not for a while.

Slowly I surfaced, at once a part of their coupling and divorced from it, observer, intruder, and when at last it was over, their bodies falling wordlessly beside one another on the bed *there*, the painting before me once again *here*, I must have felt much the same sense of loss and quiet sadness as they. It bore up like a wave beneath me, bringing thoughts of Gabrielle, of my recent and more distant past, of the solitude enclosing us all.

Fragmentary impressions, scraps of others' memories and others' thoughts, still clung to me: what had washed up on my shores.

27.

So I drove out of the Rodeway Inn parking lot, out of Cross, with a biography forming, like images swimming up in a developing tray, ghostly at first, gradually, almost imperceptibly more substantial.

That biography, those memories, thus far were *only* images, images unaccompanied by words or understanding, images without referent. It was like being in a country whose language you know not at all. Or like being inside someone else's dream.

"I" was from farmland. A skittering impression of jade-green hills and deep blue sky, the smell of damp hay, manure, compost, pollen, decay. Nights rimmed about with the sound of locust and crickets.

Then the sudden descent of cities, still photography giving way to cinema, everything speeding up, wheeling by, shooting away. A procession of women, university years, fine meals and wine in out-of-the-way, *recherché* cafes, hollow-eyed men peering out from dark doorways and from beneath bridges.

And beneath it all, a terrible undertow of despair, an emptiness whose rim "I" often approached though "I" never looked fully in.

There was, with each woman, each bright moment, a strong sense of place as well. Hotels rooms mostly, the occasional *pension*, park or public square. Once a monastery of cloistered stone corridors damp with condensation.

So: "I" travelled often, "I" liked women and music and plain, freshly-prepared foods. "I" preferred coffee so black and thick that Balzac would have passed it up. "I" swam whenever possible in icy waters. "I" was a man of discipline and exacting, though personal, principle.

And "I" circled like a hawk *my* erratic flight south, this fool's voyage, this floundering, freewheeling march from sea to dark sea.

28.

It broke every rule, of course. But that, in a way, is what the agency's all about.

In flight training, for combat situations where you find yourself momentarily confused and unable to make split-second decisions, it's drilled into you over and over just to *do something*, anything, to start a sequence of events. And that pretty much defines us. We're the agency that *does something*.

I remember one time in the Sixties some government body or another informed Johnsson that henceforth he would, *could*, send none of us into Central or South America without that body's express consent. Johnsson immediately posted every man in the agency to Panama. We all passed a pleasant three-week vacation there, filling Panama City's hotels, while back home they went about trying to untangle threads, blame, careers, feet, tongues.

The phone was ringing as I tossed luggage and book bag onto the bed in cabin six of The Cambridge Arms in Piltdown, Alabama. I picked it up, listened a moment and went back out, past the motel's corner office and down the street to a pay phone.

"Yes?"

"This is the rabbit returning Alice's call."

Neither of us spoke as computers swept the line.

"I'm afraid Alice has just stepped out."

I waited five minutes and called back. Anyone breaking into the line now would be shunted over to a recorded conversation.

"In the Bible in your room, second drawer of the bedside table, when you return," Johnsson said without preamble, "there will be a....document, that against all regulation and simple good sense I've caused to be forwarded on to you—only, I would add, because of the circumstances under which it arrived here, circumstances indicating that the document has a certain urgency, both to its sender and, I assume, to its recipient."

"Yes, sir."

"I will tell you also that the document appears to be truly blind. That we have been unable to trace its origin and route and thereby assume that no one else would be able to do so."

I waited. There was more, or he would have hung up. I listened to crackles in the wires, tiny electronic fires flaring up, drained away.

"Often those close to us know far more about us that we think, David. More than we wish them to know. That is, I suppose, in its own quiet way a danger. But it can also be a comfort."

This time he broke the connection. I caught a snatch of recorded conversation before that line, too, was released. Something about mountains and the timberline.

In the drawer alongside a long-out-of-date telephone directory and yellowing hotel stationery inexplicably bearing the crest of the old Fontainebleu in New Orleans, I found the Bible. Gideon checked out and left it not doubt. And in the divide between New and Old Testaments, a blue, unmarked envelope.

The letter began, as Johnsson had, without preamble.

> All the things I might ordinarily say, I leave to the silence between us; but there are things even that silence will not bear.
>
> You are altogether an extraordinary man, Dave. Gentle and strong, principled, supple—in many ways the most complete person I've ever known. And I do know that you have given yourself to me as never before with anyone else. But there has always been something else as well, a closed-up room inside you, an attic where long ago you put things away, whatever those things were, and never went back.
>
> Often at night I would lie beside you, especially when we were first together, feeling the pain that you did not, would not, allow yourself to feel. With time that faded, as everything does; but it has become as much a part of me now as it is of you.
>
> It doesn't matter how I discovered what little I actually know of your past. It was not knowledge I sought; but knowledge that came to me unbidden. Perhaps if we see one another again, if from that uncertain, unreal place we call the future, you return to me (and I must hold close to me the very real chance that you will not), this will become important, but it isn't now.
>
> What *is* important is that you understand how I feel about you, about my life and your place in it. We never talked about such things much, or needed to. Maybe now we do. *I* do.
>
> It's a warm, strangely undark night and I'm sitting outside on an old wood porch with wind in my hair (I cut it a few days ago) remember-

ing your face that first day at the museum. Sometimes I think the only use the past has is to break our hearts. That memory makes me so happy, David—and so sad at the same time. :Your face, and the sky so blue past the windows, and Matisse's circling dancers. The way every-thing *fit*, then.

It's becoming difficult to maintain belief that the world will ever right itself again, that somewhere there's a road leading back to that very small place, that clearing, we shared for a while.

I've been reading Pavese, yes. There's so much feeling in these poems, such a terrible, unforgiving sadness—and so much life. Real people walking everywhere inside them, carrying from place to place the ones they love.

I think that Pavese loved women as you love us. I see that his images of death—always wed to sensuous detail, the smell of rich earth, caress of wind bringing rain, curve of a woman's hip against the sky—are like your own, in your work. And I have to wonder exactly what your message may have been in sending this book.

I will be here, David, if you choose to return, and can. I won't be wait-ing, I'm not able to go on doing that, but I will be here.

There was no signature. Something within me, something that *was* me, had gone suddenly heavy, become a black sun pulling everything into it: matter, energy, even light.

Dearest Gabrielle, I wonder too what my message may have been.

I wonder how one ever learns to sort through and make sense of the mes-sages, signs, signals, meanings coming down all the time on our heads, weigh-ing on us, piling up about us. While we go on trying to guide these frail crafts, our lives, into harbors we never see yet fiercely believe, have to believe, are there.

Low in the water and listing from the burden of memories, I sat in The Cambridge Inn, Piltdown, Alabama, looking out on a small confederate cem-etery and, beyond, a bright ribbon of interstate.

29.

Piltdown, an exacting replica of Oxford, England, had been created in the late forties by a man named Neal Lafferty who conjured it up out of whole cloth, *creatio ex nihilo*, a monument to man's indomitable will to be, well, indomitable.

Brought to you by the same people who at enormous, repetitive effort and expense filled in swampland never meant for human habitation and called it New Orleans.

Lafferty had stepped off the boat from Ireland poor as potatoes a couple generations before and within six years gone from helping build houses at a dollar a day to buying them up cheaply with his savings when the region's economy plummeted and, much later, reselling dear. When an air force base came to Piltdown, Lafferty's construction company got the housing contract and doubled the town's size with an eastward warren of dozens of identical little frame houses, row after row of them, like carrots in a garden.

The base lasted twelve years before peacetime shut it down, leaving the little houses a ghost town. Many of them were vandalized, others (host for migrant workers, vagabonds, late-night teenage parties) burned; they all were crumbling. Eventually Negroes moved in and claimed the houses by squatter's rights, plugging holes with tarpaper, scrap lumber and old tin signs.

Lafferty then turned his attentions westward, where he built, to scale, a perfect replica of central Oxford, this by municipal decree some years later *becoming* Piltdown, leaving the old town hall, shops, post office and churches abandoned there at the edge of things like a shed skin, like so many cast-off shells.

No one knew why Lafferty had undertaken this massive and costly project, or why he might have chosen as model, of all places, Oxford; and he went to his death bed without saying, with (when in Lafferty's last hours the town's mayor asked) a tight smile on his lips. One local legend had it that, from his hatred of the English, Lafferty had planned, after constructing it, to set torch to the town, but that upon seeing it completed, looking upon the beauty of it, as its creator, he could not bring himself to do so.

Some of this I knew from heresay, Piltdown being a huge tourist draw. The rest I learned from brochures in by motel room and from an hour or two spent with afternoon talkers at the motel bar.

Motel bars at three in the afternoon are bleak, desolate places, deserts for souls turning to stone, where even the light seems somehow *wrong*. This one, after a late-lunchtime rush and a few stragglers-cum-historians, emptied out all at once, leaving only myself, a young blond barkeep wearing a muscle shirt and dwelling in some California of the mind, and, at a table by the crackle-glass front window, the dark lady Shakespeare wrote his sonnets for.

She was reading a newspaper. Every few minutes she'd take a bite out of a sandwich in a serving basket on the table, replace it, and refold the paper to another section. There were also a plastic insulated pitcher of coffee and matching mug.

I drank another beer and watched as she finished sandwich, coffee and paper simultaneously. Then she lifted her head, shook back her hair and looked around. Our eyes met. She smiled.

That hair was so black it seemed to soak up light from the window and leave the rest of the room in shades of grey. Her skin was dark, too—Creole blood, most likely—her eyes a startling blue. She wore a loose-cut white linen suite, pale pink cotton shirt, darker pink tie.

I walked over and introduced myself. Her name was Jeanne—like Baudelaire's dark lady. We moved to a booth and ordered drinks, beer, white wine, from Mr. California.

"Are you staying at the hotel?" she asked.

I said that I was, and returned the question.

"Sort of," she said with a half-second frown. Over her shoulder I watched, on a neon sign, a rainbow of crystal-clear vodka glittering with bright colors arc again and again over the head of a Russian footsoldier who looked remarkably like Maurice Chevalier. "I work here. Again: sort of."

She peered at me, a single huge eye, through the lens of her wine.

"I sing in the club. I'm on the circuit: here one week, at some other lounge, maybe over in Jackson or Memphis, next week."

"Like it?"

"Beats cutting hair or checking groceries," she said. Then: "I love it. I really do. But the afternoons will simply kill you."

"Some people's lives are *all* afternoons."

She looked at me for a time without saying anything. The vodka rainbow arced over the Russian's head, arced again, a visible heartbeat.

"I don't think I knew that," she said finally. "But you're absolutely right."

She reached over and rested her hand lightly, momentarily, against my own. Her nailed were cut short; there was clear polish on them.

"I have to get ready for happy hour. Will you come with me?"

I paid, and we walked out into an assault of sunlight, along a corridor formed by the overhand of the motel's second floor, and around back, where first Dumpsters, then volcanic asphalt, then a stand of oak and evergreen took over.

At her room I waited as she showered. The TV was on with the volume turned low, something old, everything charcoal and silver; she told me she kept it on all the time, for company. I held the beer she'd brought me from a closet-sized kitchenette and sat looking around at a toppled stack of books by the bed, fantasy novels mostly; cast-off clothes on the floor in a corner by the bathroom, her guitar case patched with duct tape. It all reminded me uncomfortably of my own life, not so much misspent as somehow misplaced.

Shortly she came out of the bathroom, hair still wet, nipples erect. She held out a hand and I gave her the beer. She drank and handed it back.

"Do you have time to come along? It's only for a couple of hours. We could get dinner or something then, before I start my regular gig at nine. If you want to, that is."

When I said *yes, of course*, it was clear to us both that something far deeper had been decided. Signs again. Hidden meanings, messages. She bent down and kissed me, breasts swaying. One bore a scar, like a twined worm, from nipple to armpit.

She went to the closet and pulled on black jeans, a black sweatshirt and oversize Kelly-green denim shirt. Picked up her guitar case.

"I take requests," she said.

30.

Deep in the night I woke thinking of Gabrielle.

"Are you okay?" Jeanne said beside me.

"I'm sorry. Restless, I suppose. I didn't mean to wake you."

"It's all right. I don't sleep much anyway."

She got beers from the kitchenette and brought them back to bed. Periodically lights, some dim, others vivid, swept across the back of the room's heavy drapes, as though another world were trying to break through into this one. Traffic was a far-off rumble, like the sea.

She drank, and rolled the cool bottle along the side of her breast, where the scar was.

The room was lit indirectly by the TV screen faced away from us; the flicker of scene changes plucked at the periphery of our vision. Its volume was full off now.

"Are you married?" she said. "Or have you been?"

I shook my head, put my hand on her narrow waist. She covered it with her own.

"Neither have I. I'm thirty-one, and there's so very much I haven't done. I've only seen this one little cluttered corner of the world. I haven't made much effort to understand things, that always seemed far beyond my reach, or to become a better human being in any way that matters. Just tread water mostly, tried to stay afloat. I've never loved anyone, or been loved."

"You're an excellent musician, Jeanne. There's tremendous feeling in what you do, every chord or run, the pitch of your voice. And understanding of a sort, too, even if it's intuitive, instinctive, rather than intelligible."

"But that always came easy, like breathing. Or like the way I look: I didn't have much to do with either. I'm attractive, I can play guitar passably and sing. Pretty thin for a biography, and not much of an epitaph. There's one last beer. Split it?"

"I'll go, this time."

We sat quietly drinking, passing the bottle back and forth, and after a while she said, "Two years ago they removed a tumor from my breast. I went to my doctor for a checkup and wound up that same afternoon on the operating table. It was the size of a marble, they said, and benign. There was nothing more to worry about. They'd caught it in time."

After a moment she went on.

"I think sometimes we know things we *can't* know, things that don't make daylight sense, or any sense at all. And we realize how absurd it is for us to believe them. But, still, we know, we just *know*."

She took my hand in her own and traced the curve of the pale, fine scar along her breast with my finger. The nipple stiffened.

"You're the first man I've been with since then. Somehow despite whatever they told me, I always knew that when I had a man again, when I finally made love again, the cancer would come back."

She handed me the last of the beer.

"I know how ridiculous this sounds, how crazy it must seem to you. And please don't be frightened. But I can feel it already, like a flower slowly blooming, opening dark petals, inside me.

"Will you make love to me again, David?"

31.

We had breakfast and parted. Jeanne had shopping to do, she said, and would be leaving that afternoon for Gulfport and the Holiday Inn there. I sat for a while by the pool. It was nine o'clock, cloudy, and a little like one of those science fiction movies where a few survivors are clinging to the wreckage, living out their days in the dry husk of civilization.

Around front, a chartered Greyhound pulled in. I watched through gaps in the weathered wood fence as twenty or so tourists debarked. All Orientals, but a curious mix: Koreans, Thai, a couple of Cambodians, scattered Vietnamese, mainland Chinese in both western and traditional dress. They waited silently in file as the driver went into the motel office and came back out. He stepped along the line, passing keys out.

I didn't think Jeanne's fantasy (if, finally, it *were* fantasy) much stranger than others I've known. We all create such fictions out of the stuff of our lives, small myths, private lies, that help us go on, help us remain human, reassure us that we understand our own tiny fragment of the world. But most of us don't share these myths with strangers. Most of us don't share them at all. And we believe them while knowing at the same time that they *are* fictions.

Maybe that's all my vision of contemplative life, of a life devoted to trying to understand, to the pursuit of balance and beauty, came down to. A private lie, a myth no longer relevant or useful. After all, here I indisputably was. And it was neither balance nor beauty I pursued. The old game, as Holmes said, once again afoot.

I spent the rest of the day afoot as well, treading the streets of Piltdown, in and out of bake shops and butcher's and haberdasher's and milliner's, from time to time looking off towards the Alabama horizon almost expecting to see thatched-roof cottages there at the town's edge.

Or men with scythes, perhaps, dark against the sun.

32.

I finally drove, through Montgomery and Mobile, alongside Biloxi and Gulf-port and over the rim of Lake Pontchartrain, into New Orleans, arriving there after many hours and one terrible meal tasting indiscriminately of salt, stagnant oil and flour, amazed that Lee Raincrow's decrepit VW had made it here, at three in the morning.

I took the Orleans/Vieux Carre exit off I-10, cut across to Ramparts and down to Esplanade and parked there, in front of a two-story Greek Revival mansion chopped up into half a dozen or so apartments and painted lime green. I walked back up into the Quarter and wandered its narrow streets for a while to unwind. Sidewalks worn smooth and concave like old stone stairs and canting abruptly towards street or stoop. Corner groceries crammed with everything from headache remedies to fifths of Glenlivet to sandwich counters serving up po-boys and muffulettas. Balconies drenched in ferns. Wrought iron railings, fences and gates behind which you sometimes catch a glimpse of cool, secret inner courtyards. New Orleans is one of the few places in the States that always feels much the same, year after year—whatever facades they slap up on these century-old buildings, however they jam the streets full of T-shirt and poster shops, massage parlors, fast-food bistros done up in Art Deco or lavender and chrome.

I walked slowly over to Decatur and ambled by the French Market: sharp scent of spices, the deeper earth-smell of rotting fruit and vegetable. Had coffee and beignets at the Café du Monde. Sat by the river watching ships and lights and the long curved spine of the bridge across to the Westbank.

I thought how strange it was to pass directly from Piltdown's antique Oxford to this other ancient place. Something like taking off a coat, turning around and putting it back on. Only in America, as they say.

I thought about assignments and missions and fool's errands.

I though about those things hard, and for a long time.

Then I walked back to the car, drove uptown to what once had been The Fontainebleu and was not called Fountain Bay (and by the time of my next visit would have become Bayou Plaza), and took a room.

All along Tulane, motels, restaurants and office buildings were boarded up, abandoned. A thrift store had moved into the huge grocer's across Carrollton.

Several partially demolished service stations had become used-car lots with six or seven cars, and a proprietor in a folding lawn chair, on them.

"Length of stay?" the desk clerk inquired.

"Undetermined," I told her.

I was given number 12 in The Annex, a string of cabana-like rooms surrounding the pool inside the motel's larger structure. It was like those old cartoons where a Chaplinesque little man sticks to his rights and remains in his modest house while skyscrapers bloom and sway all about him. It was also like moving to another, uninhabited country. No one else seemed to be booked into The Annex, the city's sounds penetrated hardly at all, and only the sighting of an occasional plane through the rift overhead assured me of the existence of a city, civilization, other living beings more or less like myself.

I hauled in luggage and book bag, showered, and lay on the bed product-testing TV, cable and remote tuner.

Of viable channels, four were showing movies (two mysteries, one horror, one martial arts), another couple were given over to such classics of American culture as *I Love Lucy*, *Mister Ed* and *My Favorite Martian*, one was all news and public information, three were soaps, and the rest ranged from talk shows with impossibly earnest moderators, to British comedies and Japanese cartoons, to documentaries on the opening of the Panama Canal, prison rodeos and the Harlem Renaissance.

I picked up the phone, called the desk and asked to be connected to room service. After some initial stammering I was put on hold and listened to a lovely rendition of (I think) *Autumn Leaves*. Then the music shut off abruptly, as though it had fallen through a trap door, and a voice asked if it could help me. I said it could and that I'd like two beers. There was a pause but, mercifully, no more elevator music. Some conversation off-stage, or off-mike, as it were. Okay, two beers, the voice finally said. Where do they come? Twelve, I told him. I didn't add: The Annex. By this time I considered the whole thing a bold experiment.

Nevertheless, five minutes later a fiftyish man in jeans and T-shirt showed up at my door with two Millers, a napkin and a chilled glass on a tray. The Easter Bunny wouldn't have been any bigger surprise. I tipped him seriously, poured and, propped with pillows, settled back on the bed, leaving the TV's volume off, watching from some far-off place the rush of images across its screen.

I thought back to all my years in and out of the country, in a kind of exile really, when I was able to look back on the States for long periods of time as an outsider, gathering my knowledge of its affairs from French and Spanish-language newspapers, local (wherever local happened to be) radio and television, rumor, armed-service broadcasts, and the BBC. I'd known a different

America then. Maybe it *was* a different America.

Assignments and missions and fool's errands.

Lights were on all over town, Johnsson had said.

No more Cold War, no Big Bad Bear. When society has no further need of the warriors it has created, do *they* perhaps come to be perceived as a threat? Does that society come to believe that it must reject them, isolate them, find some way to set them against one another?

Were there others still at my back?

I'd seen no signs of such purposeful companionship since that young man's death. Johnsson had seemed to think it was all over, my dance card filled. Yet he had also voiced concern for Gabrielle's safety.

1. Maybe Michael was just who and what he claimed, and it *was* all over.

2. Maybe Planchat (as Johnsson believed) was dead and out of the picture.

3. Maybe one, or two, or ten other soldiers were even now snuffling across Lake Pontchartrain into New Orleans, hot on my trail.

4. Maybe they were sent out, assigned, only to shadow me, to see where I, or whoever else was dogging me, or whoever I in turn was dogging, would lead them.

5. Maybe, like my shadow self back in that Memphis motel room, they were assassins-in-waiting.

6. Maybe none of the above.

7. Maybe all of the above.

33.

The agency's language school was as unorthodox, as given to getting things done by whatever necessary means, as the agency itself. When I went through, for many years afterwards in the flesh, and forever in spirit, the school consisted of Rima Obtulowicz. Like Cohen with his theories of clothing, in another of those odd dislocations common to the era, Rima had been recruited from academia. Born of a Polish father and Russian mother, she'd once been the highest-paid translator in Moscow. In the early seventies she tired of walking her tightrope and, on holiday at a conference in Rome, requested entry to the U.S. Major American universities leapt from the water. She chose Princeton, and a couple of years later the agency chose her.

With Chomsky, and flying in the face of standard American adherence to Sapir-Whorf, Rima believed language to be encoded genetically within us. And so there were no formal classes: no memorization of vocabulary, no conjugation drills, no lengthy diagrams or descriptions of grammar. Instead, Rima showed foreign-language films and advertisements, tuned in to European broadcasts via satellite linkages, strode among us speaking full tilt in various languages, often switching from one to another in mid-sentence.

And she gave us poetry.

Pavese, for instance, when we "studied" (lived in) Italian. Rilke and Gunter Grass for German. Mandelstam. Li Po. Neruda.

But, first of all: Apollinaire.

She was especially fond of Apollinaire, whose mother was Polish, father a mystery. He had revolutionized French poetry, hauling it by its bootstraps into the modern era. He had gone off to was and come back with a steel plate in his head. Trepanning, they called it: opening a window in the poet's pear-shaped skull to relieve pressure.

Rima would chant these poems again and again until, though we had little if any idea of their meaning, their sounds had become a part of us, mingled somehow with our own heartbeats, with our breath. And finally, suddenly, we'd reach a point where we knew, or at least *felt*, what the poems were about: what was happening in them, what they had to tell us. One moment the poem was there, an object, a sound, a cadence outside you; the next, it was within, curtains pulling back at window after window along the street. A whole new world.

With me, I'll never forget, it was a poem called "Cors de chasse."

Notre histoire est noble et tragique

Passons passons puisque tout passe
Je me retournerai souvent

Rima had spent the morning in a discussion of current affairs in Europe, in French, of course, returning every few minutes to the poem, chanting it several times, going back to current affairs. On the ninth or tenth repetition, realizing that I knew what the poem said—and that now I could follow, as well, *most* of what she was saying—I looked up. It was an amazing moment; there have been few like it in my life.

Memory is a hunting horn
It dies along the wind

Rima was watching me closely. She smiled, nodded, and went on with her teaching.

La vie, she'd always say, breaking the back of syntax and common usage, *c'est toujours entre*. Life is always *in between*. Life was what happened while you were waiting around for *other* things to happen. Life was what sprang up in the places you never thought to look. *In between*.

Like the things we learn, truly learn, I know now, from the few true teachers we have in our lives.

34.

I slept till late afternoon, woke thinking of Gabrielle, then, more an anamnesis, an unfolding, than simple memory, recalled the dream.

Seeking a wise man reputed to live here, I moved ever deeper, through narrow, branching tunnels, into a cave. The cave's entrance was at the edge of a golf course encircled by ancient oaks whose limbs spidered out as much as twenty feet; some from sheer weight had gone back to ground, as though to root there anew. Vague impressions of a city skyline, of grey stone buildings, of a bell tower looming above trees, trailed behind me as I entered the cave, leaving light behind.

Descending, I passed though discrete strata of sound as well: traffic noise from streets bordering the park, the spin and whirr of bikes and rollerblades and the measured footfall of runners, the call of ducks and geese from the central lagoon.

Orderly blocks of writing in some unknown language, looking to be a mixture of cuneiform and script, covered the walls of one passageway. Touched, it came off on my hand, like newsprint or transfer tattoos.

Once, entering a chamber, I saw what I was certain was the cave's inhabitant, the wise man, moving towards another tunnel to elude me—but it was only a rock formation, an excrescence of salts.

I could hear my own blood rushing in my ears, as though heavy winds blew through the cave, as though all about me things were being said that I couldn't make out.

Around another bend I came upon a mass that blocked my way: a root system, I realized, all but filling the chamber, pursuing its own life down here, a life little concerned with that of the tree above. Dark, formless birds perched on its knuckles and knees.

I made my way past them and weaved through toothlike crystalline formations above and below. Then emerged from one of the cave's many throats into another open space where, suddenly, light struck with the force of a physical blow and, reeling, half-blind, I found myself again outside, standing at the base of one of the massive oaks.

I looked up. High on its trunk a small brass plaque bore, both in Latin and in English, the tree's genus and species. The plaque was badly weathered and tarnished; a glare of sunlight further obscured it to the point that I was unable to make it out. I woke still trying.

But I knew those plaques and implacable oaks, knew where I had been in the dream.

New Orleans.

Audubon Park.

Back in Sheriff Pickett's office I hadn't known that New Orleans was my destination until I said it. And even then, I didn't know why.

Now the dream was trying to push through, to tell me something.

All those turns and branchings, all that darkness and disorientation, the search for a wise man, *gathering intelligence* as they say—these were my wayward, blind trip down from Washington.

And knowing that, I suddenly knew, as well, that Gabrielle was the reason I'd made my way, however circuitously and circumspectly, to New Orleans. It had little or nothing to do with Planchat and whatever others were out there. Gabrielle had family here: I remembered now. Somehow intuition had guided me. Somehow I had known, intuited, suspected, that Gabrielle would become important to the end of this affair, that I would need to find her.

I pulled on jeans, T-shirt and boots and walked across Tulane to a pay phone outside the Genghis Khan.

Johnsson himself answered.

"Checking in, sir."

"Ah: David. We thought perhaps you had seen fit to leave us again."

When I said nothing, he went on.

"Things have been peculiarly quiet at this end."

"Here, too."

"Though all the lights, insofar as we're able to ascertain, remain on." He was silent a moment. "You are well?"

"Yes."

Another pause. "And your plans?"

"What I believe you once called 'creative waiting.'"

"Yes, I did say that, didn't I? In another time, one that seems far away now. Is it possible that the world has truly passed us so terribly by, David? That all the things we cared for so passionately, all the things we believed so strongly, have come to be of no more consequence than an old sweater, a stamp collection?"

"I suspect *all* our passions are mere stamp collections to those who don't share them."

"Yes. You're almost certainly right." He turned away, coughed. "May we expect you to check in at regular intervals, then?"

"Yes, sir."

"And if there is anything you need, you will let us know, let *me* know, at once."

"I will."

"I wish there were more I could do. I was not meant for these new games, David."

"None of us were."

"Take care, then."

I was about to hang up when he said: "David."

"Yes."

"One other thing. I had not intended to tell you this, but you will want to know. Blaise is missing."

"Missing?"

"He was last seen during a routine room check two nights ago. When the nursing assistant went in the next morning to get everyone up, he was gone. His bed, seemingly, had not been slept in. His wallet, a small suitcase and select clothing were also missing."

"How much money could he have had squirreled away there?"

"Not much, according to the doctors. Not that it matters. *You* never had much trouble getting money when you needed it. None of you did."

"Any notion at all where he might be?"

"Quite frankly, I can't imagine Blaise going anywhere but right back here. He had no family, no friends or particular place. The agency's *been* his life."

"No sign of violence, I take it."

"None. There does seem to be a car, a Plymouth Reliant belonging to the night orderly, also missing."

"He broke out."

"That is our assumption, yes. Though of course we have a number of men pursuing every possible lead. I'll keep you abreast, naturally."

We listened for a moment to the line sweepers.

"Thank you, sir," I said, and hung up.

I walked back across Tulane to my room, stripped and showered. Then, still wet, I lay on the bed thinking about Blaise, about Gabrielle, about the kid who had died out there on the service road—Adrian?

I decided that I needed, in approximate order: food, people and music.

The first is always easy to take care of in New Orleans, where even rathole cafés and corner groceries are likely to have some of the best food you'll eat. Both the other items on my list, I found at a Cajun-music bar in the ware-house district.

Actually it was more of a dance hall: a vast, long room with picnic tables along the periphery, at one end some sagging flats stacked for a stage, at the other a door to the kitchen with a window alongside through which you could order drinks. But the sign outside said BAR. And that's *all* it said.

The fiddler looked like something carved from hardwood and left out in years of bad weather; his hair was the wavy, peaked kind you see in Forties photos, still jet black. The accordionist was younger, early thirties, with longish hair and a red sport jacket, sleeves pushed up, over a Jazzfest T-shirt and black jeans. The guitarist fronted for the band and sang, working in five or six jokes Hannibal probably told his troops. The bass player picked and slapped at his instrument as though he were somewhere else far away watching all this.

I pushed into BAR through tides of smoke, a gaggle of children and the sound of "*La Porte dans Arriére.*" Most of the audience joined in to shout out the repeating last line of each verse.

A dozen or so older children sat at a corner table, some of them over card or computer games, one reading a Dr. Seuss book in French. Women swept about with plates and bowls of food—*boudin*, red beans, jambalaya and gumbo, fried catfish—or with mugs of thick chicory coffee and hot milk.

I grabbed a beer, an Abita, at the window and sat at one of the tables. Cajun music was what I needed just now. The band threw in something country every third or fourth number, Hank Williams mostly, but these songs came out sounding much like the rest, even the familiar lyrics bent and clipped to strangeness.

A baby crawled beneath my table, pursuing a rattle that rolled away whenever it was touched. A young couple who'd been dancing every song finally quit the floor and went outside, probably to hose themselves down.

With a long warble from the accordion, the band struck into an achingly slow "*J'ai Passé Devant Ta Porte.*"

I walked by your door and cried bye-bye. There was no one to answer; my heart was sick. When I knocked at the door, when they let me in, I saw the bright candles all around your casket.

That's all: two verses. And a waltz. Only Cajuns would make a waltz of something like that.

Having tugged every possible sob from the fiddle, having wrenched from the accordion one final wracking sigh, the band hove without warning into a headlong instrumental before taking its break.

I drank, listened to music and watched dancers through another hour-long set and another break, then left BAR for streets so humid that lights were shelled in hazy rainbows and every window ran with condensation.

Getting into Lee Raincrow's VW on Julia, still amazed the thing was running at all, I glanced up and thought I saw someone pull back into the dark of a doorway.

As I parked on Tulane half a block down from Fountain Bay, I caught a glimpse of a face looking out from a passing car, turning quickly away.

35.

In the dream, largely a new edition of last night's (itself transformed, translated, transmogrified), everything was change. Trees became huge shadowy spiders shouldering towards me through the landscape; or the twisted fingers and arms of old men urging me on towards knowledge and confrontations I didn't care to have. Then, without warning or transition, they were snugly furnished, carpeted rooms where I sat talking with Johnsson, Gabrielle, Planchat, Blaise. Then, like trap doors dropping open, tunnels down which I tumbled to the very center of the earth. Lava rose towards me in the trunk as I fell, fell again, went on falling forever. If only I made it through the lava somehow, at earth's center there'd be no gravity, no air: there I'd be weightless, free; wouldn't need even to breathe.

The phone's ringing woke me, and I foundered, out of breath, still in a panic, on the bed. When I picked the phone up there was no answer.

Then suddenly it was as if I were awakened again—or was this the same time, only seconds later, perhaps? I had thought the phone to be ringing. But the phone was silent. Had I dreamed its earlier ringing? Or had it actually rung then, had I spoken into it? And just now? I tried for a time to remember some telling detail that might assure me—light at the window as I first awoke, sounds from outside my room, the feel of tangled sheets beneath me or my feet on the room's rough carpet—before finally giving up.

Cut to the chase, then, Or more accurately, after coffee and rolls at La Madeleine, to the search.

New Orleans has expansive Irish and Latin populations. They don't live in discrete communities, as they would elsewhere, but scattered about here and there throughout the city's semi-detached neighborhoods.

Gabrielle would have gone to ground near family in one or the other of those populations. I decided to take a chance on the luck of the Irish, and after trying Kelly's Pub out on Airline and Mickey F's Bar downtown, wound up at O'Toole's.

O'Toole's has been IN THE SAME LOCATION (moving one building up Magazine towards Louisiana when the original bar burned out in the fifties, and around the corner, into an old auction house, in the seventies when antique stores moved in along that part of Magazine and property values doubled between Saturday night and Monday morning) FOR 86 YEARS.

Some of the tables and chairs and decorations hung on the wall looked to have been here the whole time. So did a couple sitting at the bar.

I sat beside them and introduced myself, offering to buy them a drink if they'd like.

The man turned his head and looked at me a moment.

"Mary," he said. He tilted his head half an inch back towards his companion. Then, turning away, looking straight ahead again: "Patrick." A pause. "Sheehy. We'd be pleased enough to drink a beer with you, sir."

Actually, they were pleased enough to drink three with me. Possibly four. They also filled me in on the bar's history.

I described Gabrielle and asked if they'd seen her.

They looked briefly at one another.

"She's here in N'Orleans, you say?" the man said.

"I think so. Yes, sir."

"Black hair. Irish, and with a Spanish accent."

"It comes and goes, but yes."

"Well. There couldn't be many like that walking about, even here, could there be?"

"No, sir."

"And would she be wantin' to see *you*, d'you think, young man?"

I told him a version of the truth. That a job had taken me away from her. That she had written she'd be waiting for me. That we were in love.

When I was through, he looked at his wife.

"John Neil?" he said.

She nodded, that same half-inch.

He looked back to me.

"A nephew of ours manages rental properties about town. Owns a fair portion of it himself, oversees the rest for others. He just might be able to help you find your young lady."

He lifted a paper coaster from a stack of them on the bar, turned it over and scribbled an address.

"You'll be wantin' the little house out back, not the one facin' on the street. Go 'round to the right, and there'll be a gate set in just a bit, with a brick path back to the little house. That's where John Neil lives. Rents out the big house."

I thanked him.

"I know things're some different now, young man. But if I were you, when I did find my young lady, I'd be sure to take along a nice bunch of flowers."

He glanced at his wife. She smiled at him.

"Maybe two bunches," he said.

In Louisiana there's an animal called the nutria. Think of a cross between a beaver and a hamster the size of a small dog, and you pretty much have it. John Neil Noel's mother, as they say, had been frightened by one. He stood on hind legs, but the resemblance otherwise, from body shape and the layer of soft dark hair visible on every exposed body part, to fitful, quick movements, was uncanny.

"Mm-hm," Noel said. His pointed face went sharply from left to right, darted towards my own, the window, the floor. "Hmmmm."

On my way there, I'd stopped by a Kwik-Kopy on St. Charles and faxed a coded request to Johnsson at one of the agency's blinds. Within fifteen minutes a clerk had gone electronically calling at the Department of Motor Vehicles, obtained a copy of Gabrielle's driver's license photo, and faxed it back to me.

I showed the photo to Noel now, eliciting another "Hmmmm."

"I think," he said. Looked away. "Pretty sure, really." Looking back. "Yeah. Property down on Camp, just off Melpomene."

"How long has she been there?"

"Week, maybe."

"Alone?"

"You bet. Place's too small for more'n one. Walk in frontways, you gotta back back out when you leave. Hard to rent 'cause of it."

"Lease?"

"Monthly. Six units to the building. Four of 'em, the owner's got long-term tenants, been with him for years. But there's two more tacked onto the back, and those, he lets month to month."

"You're sure it's her?"

"She got a twin? A whatsit. Doppelganger?"

I shook my head.

"Then it's gotta be her."

He opened a drawer of the desk, took out a business card, wrote an address on the back.

"You hold on to this card once you're done with it, now. Be back here someday needing a place to stay, you'll know where to come."

I drove down Prytania to Terpsichore and across to Coliseum, then curved around the knothole-shaped park, turned on to Race and, a block over, hit Camp.

Set close to the street, the disheveled Victorian house had seen many colors over the years; recently it had been oversprayed with a thin coat of white. There was a sidewalk once, and an iron fence, but the roots of a huge oak had heaved up through the latter and shattered it, leaving only some fragments of concrete at the yard's edge, and the remaining couple of feet of fence, driven by those same roots, all but protruded from the ground at a forty-degree angle to it. The oak loomed above the house and stretched one long crooked arm out over the street, but it was dying now.

I followed a narrow path that curved beneath ten-foot banana trees and through thick hedges gone native, to the back of the house. The path's bricks were flush with the ground, many in fact recessed, and streamers of grass and weed grew through them all; those at the edge were worn smooth.

The apartment's door stood ajar. A window, too, was open, and a blue curtain rippled in and out of it, flaglike.

I stood stock still, listening.

Shouts from back in the park. Cars easing their way over pitted streets nearby. The bleat of a house alarm off towards Prytania.

I went slowly up to the door and again stood listening. A radio or TV was on inside, in the back room, volume turned low. Nothing else to be heard. I slipped around the sill and was in.

There were only the two rooms, with a tiny kitchen tucked away at one front corner and an even tinier bathroom at the opposite back corner. Furnished sparsely and simply—a wicker loveseat, a couple of straightback chairs, a low table—the front room was as orderly and unlived-in-looking as a motel room, yet managed, for all that, somehow to feel cozy. Foodstuffs and utensils neatly lined kitchen shelves. Clean dishes lay in a draining rack over the sink.

The back room was another story.

Here, a hurricane touched down.

Sheets and cotton blankets had been torn away from the bed and left in drifts on the floor nearby. Cosmetics, perfumes, mirrors and brushes from atop the bureau lay scattered about. A wooden chair knelt forward onto broken front legs. Capsized at the end of its taut cord, the TV cast its dim searchlight at the ceiling.

My foot nudged a music box lying on its side. Two or three notes came reluctantly out.

Bending, I pushed sheet and blanket away from a corner of something and picked it up.

Its cover showed a young man in glasses, serious as only the young *can* be, something of an intellectual, surely, but with sensuous lips and a far-off, dreamy look to his eyes behind the steel rims. Beyond, sketchy olive trees and open fields stretched to the horizon and what might with equal likelihood be clouds or encroaching city.

Poems of Cesare Pavese.

36.

"I toldja something bad was going on over there." Square in the doorway, she still looked ahead, at me, but clearly her remark was addressed to someone in the room beyond. She wore stretch pants gone baggy at buttock and knee, a matching loose pullover aglitter with metallic threads and sequins. Her hair, crisped by decades of chemicals, was ambiguously mahogany, black, greyish-green.

A younger man stepped up behind her, drink in hand. High cheekbones of an Indian, Latinate bronze skin. His head rolled along her shoulder as he looked me over. He nodded, possibly in greeting, possibly in confirmation of everything he'd suspected, and withdrew.

"Could you tell me what you saw, Ms....?"

"Cohen. And it's Mrs. But everyone just calls me Irene."

I waited, but we seemed to have lost the thread somewhere, the train become derailed.

"What you saw," I prompted. Then: "Irene."

It was as though a switch, a relay, had clicked on.

"I was doing dishes. Quite a stack of 'em since Al ain't been feeling too good and I've been working all the hours I could get at the shop and ain't either of us been able to get around to dishes for a while. Window over the sink looks out on them apartments back there. There's all sorts that come and go back there, have for years. Some days it's as good a show as you're gonna find anywhere in town."

She glanced over my shoulder. At the open door there across the alleyway, the blue curtain waving in the window.

"Two men come to the door. It was open just like it is now. Usually was—no air conditioning, you know? They had on suits, which ain't something you see a lot of 'round here, so naturally I know they got to be law of some kind, right? They knock on the door and when she comes to it the three of them stand there in the doorway talking a little, and then the one doing most of the talking just kind of pushes her on back in the room. The other one looks around him a minute, then he goes in too."

"You see or hear anything else?"

"Not till they come back out I didn't."

"How long was that?"

"Ten, fifteen minutes maybe. I'd finished the dishes by then. Al and I was taking the dog over by the park to do his thing. You know. So we're coming around the corner onto Camp and see these guys in suits coming out from behind the house with the woman."

"This one."

She looked at the photo.

"Could be her, yeah."

"Did she appear to be struggling?"

"Not that you could tell. They was holding onto her arms, though, I'm pretty sure. One on each side. They got in a car, her and the guy who done the talking in back, the other guy in front, and drove off."

"On up Camp? To the bridge ramp?"

She shook her head. "Turned back toward the river." "Do you remember what kind of car they were in, Irene?"

"Couldn't tell you. Never drove one, don't know a Ford from a John Deere."

"Light or dark?"

"Oh, it was dark. Blue, almost black."

"Was it a compact—a small car—or fullsize?"

She thought about it.

"Four doors, or just two?" I prompted.

"Oh, it had four. And it was big, like the law drives."

"Thanks, Irene. You've been a great help."

I had turned to go when she said, "You don't want to know about the other car, then?"

I looked back at her.

"As they were pulling away, a man stepped out from between houses. He got in a car parked down the street a ways and, near as I could tell, took out after them. Turned that same way, anyhow, and by then he was going a fair clip."

"Did you get a good look at him?"

"Afraid not. Too far off for me. Don't think he was a *young* man, though, like those others. Moved more like me or Al, you know?"

"Could you tell how he was dressed?"

"Just pants, what they call slacks, I guess, light-colored. And a golf jacket kind of thing, a windbreaker. Dark shirt under it. One of them athletic shirts, I think."

"And his car?"

"Blue."

"Dark blue, or light?"

"Light."

"Size?"

"Not as big as the other one, but not like those little foreign jobs either. The ones that look like lunchboxes."

"Two doors?"

She shrugged. "I guess."

"Anything else?"

She thought about it. "Unh-unh."

I thanked her and turned again to go.

Al's voice came from the room behind her.

"First car was a Continental, royal blue, '90 or '91. Rear axle's bad on it, and the cylinders are dirty. Other guy had him a Plymouth. Reliant, I think they call it. Nothing wrong with that one. Someone took good care of it. Body's some banged up, but hey, who cares? It's solid. Sound."

I peered around the door. Al raised his drink to me.

"Man's as fine a mechanic as you'll find anywhere," the woman said. "Or used to be anyhow, when he was able to work. Had a true gift. Lots of people said it, and they brought their cars to him from all over. I guess cars is the only thing he ever loved."

She turned briefly away. The smile came back around with her. Her whole face had changed.

"'Cept me, of course."

37

Oversexed and ever-ravenous, nutria are virtually devouring the state's coast-line, while both New Orleans and Louisiana politicians do *their* time-honored best to devour the rest.

Huey Long taught people down here a lot of things: every pot ought to have a chicken in it, every man was a king, no man should wear a crown. Probably the most enduring thing he taught (in those pre-Camelot days) was that a strong man could always go *around*, get things done *his* way. And it's been free-style, catch-as-catch-can politics in Louisiana ever since.

All of it confusing as hell, true—a constant, continuous upheaval for residents, absolutely impenetrable to everyone else—but there's no better place for calling in favors. Favors are understood in a big way down around New Orleans. And Johnsson's fifty-odd years in government added up to a hell of a lot of favors.

Networking, they call it now.

Yeah, I know all about fierce American individualism and independence. Natty Bumpo, mountain men, Thoreau, Huck Finn, cowboys, utopian communities, Chandler's dark knight, Holden Caulfield, hippies. Head out on the highway. Do your own thing. Go west till you've used that up, too. Just say no—like Bartleby. Just do it.

And I revere all that.

Nevertheless, half an hour later I had half a dozen parish and state agencies, the state police and every squad car in New Orleans on my dance card.

The Sikhs, for all their spiritualism, may be right: if you're poor, you're stupid. And if information's the currency of the day and you have access to it and don't use it, then *you're* stupid.

A call to Johnsson was all it took. He rang up a few senators and department heads, a committee chairman or two, and it started trickling down fast. Royal blue Lincolns and Plymouth Reliants were being checked out all over: Algiers, Chalmette, LaPlace, Shreveport, even on into Mississippi and Alabama.

I sat in my hotel room fielding calls. The sixth one from NOPD shut it all down.

A Lincoln answering to my description was known to frequent a strip shopping center on Tchoupitoulas. Area patrols began noticing it after several ticketings for irregular parking; subsequently there'd been a minor collision involving the car, no real damage or injury, the incident dutifully reported by the other car's driver at time of occurrence.

It was like the click Emily Dickinson talked about, when she knew she had a poem. Or like Housman, who'd recite prospective lines while shaving in the morning, and when his beard hairs went on end, then he knew he had it.

That Lincoln felt like the shell my pea was under.

I took St. Charles up to Jefferson, then Jefferson towards the river till it dead-ended into Tchoupitoulas. The Continental was parked around the corner from Alfalfa Video, on a side street, well back from the intersection and from fire hydrants.

I pulled in behind and got out. Squatted for a close look. Both rear tires were worn badly on the inside.

The surrounding houses were shotgun doubles, set a couple of feet off the ground, with roofs that overhung narrow porches—galleries, they call them here. Potted plants crowded the nearest one: that didn't seem likely. Kids played on Big Wheels and plastic bikes before another across the street. An elderly black couple sat in lawn chairs on the gallery adjoining.

But next down, the gallery was bare, floorboards and steps showing little sign of use. Miniblinds lidded both front windows. A band of pink impatiens bordered the brick walkway. Grass in the door-sized front yard had been clipped to a uniform half-inch and carefully edged at flowerbed, sidewalk, walkway.

I knocked, and a face canted out from behind the door as it opened. The face's black chevron of a monobrow tensed at its center.

"Yeah?"

"I apologize for disturbing you in your home," I said.

"Yeah?" Same intonation.

"Mind your manners now," came a voice from within. "Ask our visitor to step in, why don't you?"

Monobrow backed out of the doorway. I took a couple of steps. Behind him were two enforcers—bone-breakers, as they're called. Six foot-two, two-forty or so, thighs and necks like tree trunks. Lots of good home cooking Sicilian style. Mind you, they didn't look too dangerous just now, what with the duct tape holding them in their chairs and the socks stuffed in their mouths.

Blaise sat on a straightback chair with ovals of quilted padding at seat and back. Beside him on a spindly oval-topped table sat a cup and saucer and, as though it were just another common tea utensil, a small pistol, a Glock.

"David," Blaise said. "I had a feeling you might be along shortly. If I'd been certain, I might have saved myself the trip. *Not* that I had anything better to do, you understand."

He glanced at Monobrow, and nodded towards an armchair. Monobrow, who looked like a larval version of the other two, pale and somehow unformed, quickly sat. Vinyl creaked beneath him.

"Thank you," Blaise said. He nodded at the enforcers. "I've never much cared for gagging a man. But these two insisted upon raising such a ruckus when they came around, they left me no choice."

He smiled.

"Good to see you again, David." He sipped tea from the cup beside him and set it precisely back into the saucer's concavity. "Outstanding tea, young man. *Mes compliments.*"

"Name's Donny," Monobrow said. "And fuck you, you old fart."

Blaise sighed. "They never get it, do they? The new generation. Remember when you only ran into professionals out here? Now you got kids who learned their trade from cop shows on TV. I still remember something you once told me. 'In America, each new generation is a new people.'"

"Gertrude Stein: I remember. I also remember that the last time I saw you, you couldn't talk."

"Yes. Well: things change, don't they?"

He glanced again at the two bone-breakers, at Monobrow.

"You have any idea who these jokers are?"

I shook my head. "Seem to be an awful lot of chickens loose in the yard. All of them pecking away at all the others."

"The night I left, I woke up thinking you shouldn't be out here alone. And before I knew it, I'd said it out loud there in the room. Sound of my own voice scared the hell out of me. Also made me realize I was right, and I started packing." He laughed. "Now I see I needn't have worried: you weren't alone at all. All *kinds* of company. These three aren't players, though. Strictly subcontractors, work for hire. We've talked things over, and they assure me they're off the case."

Blaise nodded to a door at his left.

"She's in there. Sleeping. She's fine. *That*'s what I was most concerned about."

38.

Once New Orleans (Blaise told me as I saw Gabrielle and him off to their plane) had been a walled city. In place almost from the beginning, walls and forts endured for over a hundred years, though never in all that time were they of use in repelling attackers.

French maps as early as 1725 show a surrounding wall with small forts. Four years later following the Natchez Massacre, with New Orleanians thinking they might well be the next target of Indian attacks, a palisade flanked by a moat and small block houses with artillery went up. French Governor Luis Billouart de Kerlerec reported his restoration of these fortifications to the king; though when Louisiana passed into Spanish hands in 1762 and Governor Bernardo de Galvez (who would become a hero of the Revolutionary War, driving the British summarily from the state) evaluated the fortifications, he found them laughable.

It was Governor Carondelet who, in 1794, consolidated these walls and forts. His predecessor had been run out of Louisiana by citizens who, though under Spanish rule, still considered themselves Frenchmen *au coeur*, and Carondelet was determined not to let things get out of hand. The fact that heads were rolling back in France, literally, helped support his resolve. That sort of thing might easily spread to the new world.

And so each of Governor Carondelet's days began with a tour of the fifteen-foot wall of mud going up at the city's perimeter, soon to be topped with palisades and fronted by a forty-foot moat. At the river, twenty feet high and studded with cannon, two pentagonal forts were erected: Fort St. Louis (at Canal Street) and Fort St. Charles (at Esplanade). Three additional forts protected the city's rear.

Facing the river, Forts St. Louis and St. Charles were far the most formidable. Yet from the first, walls and forts alike had been built as much to keep the French in, to keep them in every sense contained, as to repel outside forces.

By the time of Louisiana's sale to America in 1803, wall and forts were again crumbling. William Claiborne, the first American Governor, reported that final demolition was made easier when on a dark night one of the rear forts was stolen in its entirety, presumably for use as firewood.

39

"The world has changed more than we can imagine, David," Blaise said.

Outside, a mid-size plane painted white with blue stripes that ran its length, looking like seersucker, breasted into the sky.

"Or perhaps it's only that, having changed ourselves, we can no longer see it as we once did."

We hunched over our coffees. They'd come out of a machine the size of a small refrigerator that promised to deliver everything from espresso and cappuccino to hot chocolate and local *café au lait*. I, for one, had my doubts. I'd seen the counterman emptying in bags of powder as we approached, before he turned to serve us.

To our right, passengers with camera cases and backpacks emerged from International Arrivals. To our left, huge Mardi Gras masks, gold, green and purple, a clown, a witch, a lion, loomed above an exit.

Gabrielle came back from the restroom. I pushed a questionable *au lait* in its styrofoam cup towards her.

"Good luck," I said.

She sniffed at it, looked into the container as though wondering when the goldfish might have died.

"So much for New Orleans' reputation."

"You're in Jefferson Parish now, honey child. Out here on the frontier, it's every man for himself."

"What about the women?"

"They're for himself too."

"Figures." She turned to Blaise. "I overheard what you were just saying, the last part anyhow. You think people ever really change? In any way that matters, that makes a difference?"

"Well.... You come right down to it, I guess I have to, *chère*."

A gaggle of middle-aged Germans came out of the corridor from International Arrivals. The guard at the gate said something to them in German. Keeping faces averted into their own group, they responded, laughing.

"What about those?"

Gabrielle nodded towards a dozen young Latin males in muscle shirts and white slacks. They were seated in a line, matching blue athletic bags at each of their feet.

"You think I should go over and tell them that their women will be making their own decisions from now on?"

"Good point," Blaise said. "But what about him?" nodding towards me.

"Well, true, he's a special case. Always has been."

"*He*'s changed."

"More than I wanted to, originally," I said. "And far *less* than I wanted to ultimately."

Blaise's eyes followed another plane heaving itself into sky. "Life is so very peculiar. So *particular*," he said. "Like a series of snapshots, each one of them slightly, all but imperceptibly, different from the one before. But, still, by the end of the series *everything* is different. You look up and don't know where you are anymore; it might just as well be another world."

"Maybe it *is* another world. Johnsson told me that all the things we cared for so passionately, all the things we believed so strongly, were gone now. That they'd come to be of no more consequence than an old sweater, or a stamp collection."

"Johnsson admitted that?"

I nodded.

"Amazing. And I've known the man, worked with him, over forty years."

I shrugged.

"He is rather a walled city, himself, you know. I suppose we all have been. The nature of the beast, eh, David?"

"Of walls, at least. And Joshua out there now with his trumpet."

"Perhaps so."

"There's a poem by Cavafy, a Greek, that I've been thinking about a lot, Blaise. 'The Barbarians.' In it, this city's always gearing up for imminent attack. People working together, making decisions and passing laws, gathering foodstuffs, building, arming themselves. Because soon the barbarians will be at the gates. And this has been going on for years, for lifetimes. But the barbarians never come, and finally people realize they aren't *going* to come, and then everything begins to fall apart. The poet says he doesn't know what they'll do now without the barbarians. Those people, he writes, were a kind of solution."

Blaise put his empty cup on the table by my own. Gabrielle's remained full.

"It seems there are still barbarians at *your* walls, David."

"Whatever far land they come from, and to whatever purpose: yes. But not a tribe, perhaps. Maybe only a single wild man."

"You know that Gabrielle will be kept safe?"

"Yes. And I thank you."

"Even you won't know where we are. But when it's over—I will know when it's over—I'll bring her to you."

I nodded.

"I don't understand this," he said.

"Nor do I."

"But I don't *have* to understand."

He stood. "Our plane should be about to board." He held out his hand. We shook, then embraced. "What will you do now, my friend?"

"Be still, I suppose, and silent, and trust this may bring them in closer to me."

"You will be wanting a moment alone," he said, and stepped off towards the concourse.

"Blaise."

He stopped. "Yes?"

"You understand why I never came back."

"Ah. But David: you did."

He turned away again, into the concourse, the crowd.

"He's a wonderful man," Gabrielle said.

"He is."

"I only wish I could have known about him before this, known how important he was to you."

"I—"

"No. I'm not asking for explanations, David. *I* don't have to understand, either. But that doesn't mean I don't want to. That I don't hope, in the future, all this might become a part of my life, too."

"How could you want it to?"

"I don't even know what *it* is, not really. But I know who you are. And *it* is part of you. A larger part than you want to admit."

She leaned into me. My arms went around her.

"I love you," she said.

"Yes. You do."

Then she and Blaise were walking away towards the gates.

I hurried to the escalator and stood at a railing high over the concourse watching them make their way together across the polished floor. Line after line of travelers with wrapped bundles and luggage—golf clubs, guitar cases, shopping bags, matched leather—milled at ticket counters right and left. Blaise and Gabrielle walked through them all, down the floor's empty center, into sunlight.

When they were out of sight I retrieved the car from level A-4 (yep, still running, still indomitable) and drove back down Airline, past dozens of makeshift businesses and ramshackle motels advertising free movies and weekly rates, to the hotel. I showered and shaved, and walked across Tulane for breakfast at the Home Plate Inn. It was what used to be called a luncheonette. Huge letters high on the front window announced WE NEVER CLOSE. There was little window space left among a jumble of legends such as *Po-Boys*, *Daily Specials*, *Steaks*, *Breakfast Any Time*, and what space there was, bore a grayish-brown film of forty years' grease, smoke and bad city air, like geological strata. But the eggs, grits and biscuits were first-rate.

So was the coffee, and I walked another large black back to my room. I lay for a while propped on the bed, idly browsing TV—a piece on Japanese gardens, a profile of Anna Akhmatova I'd seen before, a Jerry Lewis movie, various sports events, news updates, cooking shows—thinking about Gabrielle, about Blaise, about Adrian's death there on that service road. Then I discovered an FM-radio channel playing Mahler's First and put the remote down.

Sometime during the second movement's achingly-slow minor-key version of "*Frère Jacques*," I fell asleep.

When I awoke the next morning, Luc Planchat was sitting beside the bed drinking coffee from a plastic cup.

40.

He put another like it on the table beside me. The lamp's round, frosted globe hung above it like a sun gone cold. Morning light held its breath, oddly depthless, oddly indeterminate, in the window.

"*Au lait*," he said. "Fresh. And," retrieving a waxed-paper bag from the floor by his chair, "hot, or at least still warm, I hope, *beignets*."

I pried off the cup's lid and let steam come up around my face. It smelled of nuts and fecund earth and growing things, its depth and richness for a moment preempting the world's glib surface. I took a sip. The taste wasn't as rich as the smell—what actuality ever fulfills anticipation?—but it was close enough.

We sat there. Indistinct voices passed by in the hallway. Sunlight swarmed at the window behind blinds and deadfall drapes, rummaging for entry at some corner, quarter or edge, seeking recognition.

"I know your work, old friend," Planchat said. "I'm a fan. Even have—*had*, I suppose I must say now—two small pieces from some years back, lucite and ebony. Not much like what you're doing now, of course—or what you *were* doing, should I say? But exquisite, truly beautiful objects. Something of a great, cold sadness about them. I'll not forget them. Though I'll never see them again.

"Like your Cendrars, *je suis l'homme qui n'a plus de passé*. I'm the man with no more past."

Or too much of it, I thought.

I scrabbled in the bag for a *beignet*. When I bit into it, tatters of steam escaped, and powdered sugar snowed down onto my chest and legs. Outside, the day turned over, turned again, and finally caught.

"It's not at all of any real importance whatsoever that we survive, you know." Planchat savored the last mouthful of coffee and dropped his cup into the waxed-paper bag. "Either the race itself—or you and I individually."

He looked to the window: that quarrel of light.

His eyes, when he turned them to me, were much like the window.

"One of our preservationists observed how difficult it is to recall to our presence that which we've asked to leave. It's just as hard to rid ourselves of what we've summoned. Perhaps more so. All those stories of monsters, deals with diverse devils, three wishes, Gogol's *Nose*: something in our DNA understands all that. Tools aren't readily converted to other use. Axes make poor cuticle scissors."

He walked to the window.

"Do you mind?" Pulling back drapes, opening blinds. Rivers of light flooded the room.

"There. That's the only speech I have, a short one, and it's done. The story accompanying it will take a bit longer."

He came back across the room and resumed his chair.

"Some months ago I realized I'd come under scrutiny. That I had suddenly become, for some agency or another, whatever its motivation, an object of interest. No single thing I could point up. A half-dozen, then a dozen small, insignificant things. And instinct, of course.

"Once perceived, that interest, that presence, became ever more apparent—finally almost tangible. I couldn't for one moment imagine that it might be other than malignant. And so I fled. Fled *that* life, with its careful, safe architecture, as I'd fled so many others before—and with little more remorse or regret. The quiet years, that interlude, were over. Like Lazarus, I went out into the world again.

"From afar I watched circles of activity around where I'd been, some of it purposeful, much of it puzzling. Eventually I saw that activity withdraw; and what strands I could, I followed. To an electronics lab in Buffalo. To an army base near the Canadian border. Followed the spiraling-down of all these lines, finally, to you.

"Death has sent us a most elaborate invitation, old friend. It occurs to me that we might do well to RSVP that invitation together."

41.

We left the hotel together half an hour later by doors opening onto a narrow alley and canyonlike culvert, wearing gabardine overalls liberated from an unwatched laundry and carrying gray plastic bags we'd stuffed with trash.

Quixote at least had his windmills. We didn't know *what* to attack, or where. None of us did.

There was a certain aesthetic to all this, of course, my own motion drawing along these others, their course in turn circumscribed by Planchat; but it was form only, volumes brought to balance, vectors in momentary equilibrium: beautiful speech without intrinsic meaning.

Over beers in an ancient bar just off Canal, still wearing overalls, two working men among others, we talked through our options. The nameless bar appeared to be illuminated solely by Dixie Beer signs scattered liberally about. Whenever the street door opened, light started in, then remembered its place and, as though nodding to some unspoken agreement, withdrew. We sat at a high hardwood bar polished smooth as elbows.

It seemed best, we decided, simply for me to continue what I'd been doing all along: remain visible, stay in the open, wait for storms to come down. As far as we knew, whoever was out there had no idea of Planchat's presence—and that changed the whole equation.

Circles inside circles.

Later we walked down Canal to the river. It was getting towards noon then, people streaming in from every direction to lodge in clusters by fast-food stands and the mouths of restaurants like leukocytes rushing to infection sites. The river was a shining, keen blade of water.

"You cared for your new life?" Planchat said after a while. We'd been sitting quietly, watching as one of the riverboats filled with tourists for its noontime excursion, listening to the steam calliope of another farther down towards skyline and bridge.

"Yes. I did. I learned to."

"And for someone in it?"

"Yes. That, too."

In mid-water three barges aligned in a perfect eclipse, then began drawing away from one another.

"She's waiting for you?"

I looked into his face and after a moment said that I didn't know.

Neither of us spoke for several minutes.

"When I realized I was being surveyed," Planchat said, "it was with something very much like relief. I'd passed through a number of careers, at length amassed a considerable personal fortune. Women wandered in and out of my life. I couldn't care for them, didn't feel much of anything, really. Two or three in the morning, I'd find myself deserting my own bed, wishing they weren't there, that I could be again alone. Because I *was* alone, I'd always been, and these women's bodies beside me, the anxiety and surrender in their eyes, served only to make that fact unbearably painful to me."

Planchat picked up a loose chunk of asphalt and threw it out over the water. A heron tipped towards the ripples it made, then reconsidered.

"I hated it, David. Eight years, and I hated every month, every week, every day, every last moment of it. Now that's all blessedly done with. I'm awake, and the dream is fading. *This* is what I do. Not the only thing I was ever good at, not at all—but the only thing that ever brought me joy."

I knew then that it was Luc, not myself, who would die.

42.

They came in fast when they came, at four-something the following afternoon, in the tree-shrouded streets just above Tulane, two of them, one in front of me when I turned a corner, the other closing in behind.

No one said anything. I looked from one to the other, instinctively turning sideways. Somehow their concentration wasn't as focused as it should have been, and that didn't make a lot of sense. A little like Doc Holiday stopping off to birdwatch on his way to the O.K. Corral.

Catching an arc of intent that flashed between them, in what amounted to a single motion I looked at A, feinted towards B and came back around in an easy circle to strike at A, who was already moving in to help his partner. The force of my blow, riding on his own momentum, took him down, hard, on his back. And from there it was a simple thing to follow the line of force, feeding it into a body roll that slammed me up against B and dropped him with a loud crack of head against sidewalk.

Frankly, I had no idea that I still had that kind of movement in me.

Education is a wonderful thing.

I looked through their pockets and found the usual half-nothings: faceless keys and a tensor pick, an array of official identification. One wore a suit with Hong Kong's version of an English label and carried British travel papers. The other, in jeans and leather jacket, bore a Polish passport.

That seemed to be all the action. We waited. Finally Planchat stepped out of the cover of trees to join me.

That's life, I was thinking. All the things you wait for, so anticlimactic when they finally happen.

"A disappointing catch, old friend," Planchat said. Then he looked up—maybe intuition took his gaze there, maybe at that moment (I think he did) he somehow *knew*—at the rooftop of a boarded-up Victorian house nearby.

Silently a black-rimmed hole appeared in his forehead.

I dove for the shelter of the nearest parked car.

One eternity went by strutting.

Then another.

Birdsongs had just started up again when a body came over the roof's side, tumbled through the limbs of a huge pecan tree, and fell motionless to earth.

I waited.

Waited some more, then went over to the body. It had been taken down quite expertly. Garotted, most likely, with a silken cord. Most likely with the silken cord now tied in a bow about the man's genitals.

"Garbage," a voice said beside and above me. "Garbage everywhere. Piled up, tottering, ready to fall. Great stinking bags of it, like this one."

She gestured towards the body there at our feet as I stood.

"Now he can have the eternal hard-on he always wanted.

Bastard'll just go on fucking the Void, sticking it in that last dark hole he'll ever sniff at, working away at it forever, while he rots and rots and never comes again."

She smiled.

I remembered a story I'd read in some obscure literary magazine or another. A man is in his psychiatrist's office and the psychiatrist tells him that after exhaustive tests they've found out what's wrong with him. The man awaits this revelation. Well, basically you're crazy as bat shit, the psychiatrist tells him.

I knew her, of course. She was the woman in the vision I'd had in Cross, standing in front of the paintings.

And at our feet was the man with her then, the one whose biography, whose life, I'd acquired afterwards in bits and snatches.

"This really has nothing to do with you," she said. "It was Planchat—Planchat altogether from the start of it. Something from a long time ago, probably now we'll never know what. Not that it could possibly matter."

Her eyes and smile were dark pools where deadly, quiet things lived.

"We all had our borrowed lives. Those careful, makeshift shelters. Then—" She held out, momentarily, a trembling hand. "—the web was shaken."

Like a gate springing open, it dropped into my thoughts: *Michael.* The shipbuilder's son, the man who had turned himself into a wolf. *His inquiries had started all this.*

"It was simple for him," she said, nodding to the man at our feet, "to pull the others in. Inevitable that they'd be attracted—so much water rushing to a drain. Like frog legs. Irretrievably dead. But put them in the pot and they go on kicking."

Her mad eyes nudged one last time at the man's body. Then it was as though the body were no longer there. Perhaps not even the memory of it.

"When Planchat felt the circles closing about him and went to ground, his pursuer turned his attentions to you. Thinking this would draw Planchat back into play. Never suspecting, not at first at any rate, that *you'd* already been called back out to pursue *him*: by fleeing, as it turned out. And certainly with no notion—none of you could have had any such intimation—that I was out here as well."

A car came down the street, slowed almost to a stop alongside us, then hurried on. We started away, just another couple out for an afternoon walk beneath the gentle bower of uptown trees. Soon this place would look like an anthill.

I had been more correct than I knew: circles within circles within circles. Michael's high-minded program to complete his father's gratitude spiraling down to the tight curl of unwarranted killings, to flurries of heedless motion, to young Adrian's senseless death on that service road. Metal shavings falling to the floor.

We walked down Freret and across Broadway to St. Charles, to a streetcar stop on neutral ground by the K&B. Tulane and Loyola students in shorts, T-shirts, chinos, polo shirts. Catholic schoolgirls, Amazonlike, pushing the envelope of womanhood in plaid skirts and unpressed white shirts. There my companion looked off into trees bearded with Spanish moss.

"When the hood's taken off," she said, "the hawk has little choice. He's a kind of soft machine, exists only to breed and to kill. And killing is what he does best. Killing's the very reason he lives."

She looked back at me.

"It's been good to see that none of us has lost the fine edge they gave us. You understand that I had to protect you, of course. Because you're my kind. My *only* kind now, I guess."

So she was indeed one of us, with Planchat and myself. Or just myself. The program's rumored third survivor.

"Wait," I said as she stood to leave. The streetcar lumbered camellike towards us, bucking and swaying. With a shock, with embarrassment, I realized that I still expected, still wanted, it all to *mean* something.

"Johnsson," I said. "Johnsson must have known."

"Yes. Yes, he must have. At some level. If not at first, then surely later on."

It rained all that night in New Orleans. I sat on the balcony of a new hotel in the Quarter picking at scraps of food on my tray, picking at scraps of my life in memory.

Rain obscured the rest of the world and washed over me, and when dawn finally came and I left, it was with a sense that, should I look back, I'd see, abandoned in that chair, my old selves: locust husks clinging to the trees of my childhood.

43.

Six days later I was sitting across the table from Gabrielle in a small restaurant in Washington, D.C. From the outside it looked like a fast-lube shop with an awning tacked on; inside, it was replete with healthy plants, waiters in waistcoats and fiftyish men wearing Rolexes in the company of twentyish women wearing red dresses. It was replete also with an appetizer of quail you'd kill for, and with fine, understated continental cuisine, the impression of which had been but slightly diminished by the *maitre d*'s response to our wine order: "You bet."

Gabrielle was dissecting a spinach salad with infinite care as I attempted to get down two swallows of coffee before having my cup refilled. Blaise sat by her, knife spreading venison paté onto bread as though there would never in the history of this earth be any more. I'm not certain, but I think his eyes rolled back each time he took a bite. Then he would sip at his wine, a Brazilian cabernet, and his eyes would roll back again.

Our conversation had been resolutely superficial, as it often is when huge issues loom, all of us tiptoeing about the rims of various abysses. We spoke of wine and food, music, Cendrars, Pavese. Of weather and the way sudden winds come rolling in over New Mexican plains as doors of colored lightning begin opening in the sky.

Over soup, sorbet and salmon, I filled Gabrielle in on what had happened. Events of these past weeks, my personal history insofar as I knew it, the reasons I'd asked her to leave—much as I've written it here. Letting her graft the facts to whatever frame, whatever understanding, she had already. I told her that when first Planchat, and then his pursuer, died, I had died along with them, locked irrevocably to each by those rushes of *otherness* I'd experienced in the past in times of crisis. That, nailed in place, unable even to think or react, I had felt their lives, felt my own, contract to a single gray point, a point that, pulsing, grew ever smaller, smaller, until it was gone—until there was nothing.

Nothing.

Then I looked into her eyes.

"So which has come back to me?" she asked at length. "Creator or killer?"

"Will it frighten you to hear: both?"

"It would frighten me to hear anything else."

To discover what we know, we have only to decide what we will not see. My memories might well be false, but they would, after all, do as well as any others. Every day we reconstruct ourselves out of the salvage of our yesterdays. And a man who has been, even briefly, other men, one who has gone with these men into the shadow—surely he has brought something valuable back from there, surely he must have things to tell us.

I would return to my studio. There I would live for weeks at a time on coffee and hotplate dinners of stew and soup, and I would produce a stream of sketches, paintings, impressions, life studies, sculptures much like the one long abandoned. Many of these works, these pieces, would be dreamlike. Others would bear into this crowded, wind-torn world an astonishing calm: still places.

Trying to get it right.

Later, all this took on a more reasonable pace, and I emerged from the studio in the evening to music, the smell of a cassoulet I'd put in the oven hours ago, and sometimes friends. And when friends left, when cassoulet, salad and bread were finished, there was always a warm fall night filled with stars and the smell and sounds of life, always a last glass of wine or a final cup of tea, always the moon up there grinning as though it knew the joke. And Gabrielle, always.

POEMS

Temptation of Silence

At the end of the pier where the moon rests
until needed, five posts worry at the water
as though to pull out a single word
of what the garbled sea says, dark fingers.

Light, and these chittering birds, indecision.
Always the sea and earth want you;
you can always go there; they
will take you in. And I have felt for some time

the encroachment of silence at my back,
like a forest. To live as stone, without history,
enduring.... These posts rise like bare, black trees;
soon they will stride off into the water,

tearing land away, leaving only
sky, sea, a thin gray nerve of horizon.
On time also, like these long legs,
my thoughts move, focused in this dark lens.

There would be such comfort in despair,
in knowing. In silence I would hear endlessly
the message of blood, the shush of wind
in my chest, and have no use

for semiologies of sky. As though
this black mirror might shut above me.
A gull quits the moonstruck cloud
it needs no longer, as farther out

fish enter this world in a quick arc
and fail, falling back. Just as well: they might learn
to live on air, but the paperwork, appointments,
permissions would forever elude them.

In that diurnal sea I dwelled a long time,
until the language and disillusion were my own.
I would not go back there now; I would forget
the word for "wind," for "bread," for "pain."

This low murmur, as of crowds whispering.
Semaphore of cloud, telegraphy of star. Yet
the human voice, that and music alone,
consoles us. This resting moon tears at our blood,

this heaving sea pulls us. Our eyes are flowers
endlessly blooming out into the world, endlessly severed
by the spinning blades of the iris. What force must be needed
to keep the world's things separate, to keep them

from collapsing into one another! Then a vast wind.
There is little wind tonight, enough
to barely rumple the sea, while moonlight presses
one doorlike patch flat and bright as a bedsheet.

(cont.)

To watch from afar the storms that
make us human. On your right, ladies and gentlemen,
the dark night of the soul. You will be able to see,
as we pass, the rain of doubt, and high

in the trees, the whipping winds of love. (Please
keep your hands inside the car.) So: with words
we *do* dance over all things, speech *is*
beautiful folly. For we are of language as

the world is of silence. Words slice
through the surface of the mirror, of darkness, like
shark fins, shining under the moon. Into the world, then —
but with speech to hold these things in place.

For the night is still full of wrong,
earthquakes and executions; and unknown ships
gather towards us, towing in their wake
the speechless, unspeakable dead.

Happy Endings

After the party I unsnare each wire
with the tool provided, watch
house driveway car
fall into the sky. It's almost
morning: little dark left
to hold them back.

I think how you steered me
on your arm in there
from friend to friend
for introductions, saying
George Amy Burt Marybeth
I'd like you to meet my husband.

All these things falling
towards stars now. Overcome
with the beauty of it, you appear
at my shoulder, knowing
what I will say: that
you are my wire, I was almost gone.

To a Russian Friend

The morning surprises
a squirrel
in its fall between two trees.

It is Sunday, and in the space
between weeks I sit
on a cold porch wearing the coat
I've worn for twenty years.
It is dark green.

My tea steams in chill morning.
Why do we imagine words
will save us? My uncle had
in his basement workroom, for twelve years,
four chapters of a novel, one page
still in the typewriter.

Andrei: my children, or theirs, vow
they will kill yours. Two poets,
we sit here like old men, muttering,
as terrible engines and agents
go over our heads.

Perhaps we'd both like, most, just
to be safe in history. But the press
of our lives holds us in place.
And there is in me still
such rigor and searching.

Into a room armed
with chairs, windows, walls,
I enter. The rain that began
yesterday continues, and cars collide
like wind chimes on the street
outside—that lightly.

America has no use for its poets
and too many, but there
you are dangerous, or might be.
I think of the pain
our daughters will have from our world.

The razor is sharp, new.
I draw hot water, watch
the space between my self and face
fill with steam....

What is left for us, here
among our families, books and friends,
but to go on as we must.
There will be no more Tolstoys.
There's only the chance to do
what remains:
find beauty, try to understand, survive.

Nine Below Zero

Today a man died on the street. They say
the bullets spread their soft hands
    across his skin like words
and urged it open. Collapsing off the stone
    side of the building
where the loud gun had thrown him,
a corridor appeared in him all at once,
    the size
of a finger. He gave birth to a vacuum,
that sucked his bowels out onto the street
    near Macy's.
The wall behind him slammed by a red fist;
    pebbles, plaster
falling into him. The manager calls the police,
    an ambulance,
and then the workmen. They can come tomorrow.

Today a man died on the street. They say
it was terrible. It makes evening headlines;
    TV coverage
shows him lying inside himself on the sidewalk,
    dead, people
in crowded rings watching. And him, the other
    (they say
he was like that for an hour) standing still
    with the gun
limp in his hand, and smiling.

Today a man died on the street. At Broadway
     and 34th,
3 P.M. on a warm day, the 3rd of December —
but what of it? Why all this bother?

Just that one man is empty
and done with listening to others; and another
finally found a way to speak, to say
all the things he wanted, dumb for years.

New Year

The hands of that clock will not hold you
long. In an upstairs room History tries on various
hats, begins improvising another of its long stories.
Always, when you approach the box, there is mail.

In this land of exile lank women stride out
into sunlight carrying loaves of fresh bread in
baskets. Leaves clutch at the trees. The wind comes
out to explore new paths appearing in the forest.

What can I tell you of the words I use here?
You would not recognize them. They are gloves gone
inside-out with the departing hand.

Poems

Mornings, slim young mothers
watch me emerge
from my half a garage and must wonder
about this forty-year-old
unsmiling, unpublic man.

Evenings, with part of a newspaper
for tablecloth, reading Voltaire
as I finish off last night's curry
and half a cucumber, I watch them
ransom their kids from daycare.

The lizard of inspiration flits suddenly
down the trunk of a tree
outside my window and plunges into sun
on the gravel path: what
will it make of all this?

Memory's Empire

1.

Such abandon! you said when I offered
my back, a thing of little worth,
to bring us closer. On the shelf
by forgotten books where we slept,
you curled about your dreams
of corners and curves.

Snow threw itself into huddles,
like a troubled child, outside our window:
an economy of endings.

Now I have left your bed, taking along
all my names and quiet departures.
You push at the borders of silence,
that shabby suburb. Blood surrounds
air whistling within you: tonight,
because of rain, you cannot breathe.

2.

Slowly night let us know her.
To your body
I came wide-eyed and without words,
as into foreign lands.

In alleys there, red pianos carried on
pursuing their prey,
gobbling down with Mozart and Brahms
the helpless, homeless.

In cramped market stalls not far
from our apartment
we bought two paintings, half a pound
of music, a bag of brightly wrapped stories.

Light here is different, you said. Children
trailed behind us down twisting streets,
their small heads sinking again
and again into blue, yellow, sky.

3.

Had you noticed? you say:
there's more sky. As rain
gathers like a word that finally may explain
what happens down here.

My dear, I have been unfaithful,
the Baron tells his wife. In the pale
yellow gaslight of my laboratory,
out of the loins of my need, from knowledge
and love of knowledge,
I have made a son that is not yours.

4.

Our radios announce again
the old disasters, ancient failures
of language and will.

If only sky might accept us,
would deliver us
from this dull earth rolling like a pig
who will eat them
on the axis of its young.

(cont.)

5.

I was speeding to Conclusions
(just outside Taos) when I came upon you there
on spongy asphalt staring down the sun.

I had packed away all ambition.
Your life was as plain and self-contained
as the cactus it stepped from.

We rolled towards hills like loaves of bread
beneath the sun, a smell
of fresh earth rising from your body.

Heat and light beat about us there
like heavy wings
bearing up, about to become
visible, about to come into being.

6.

The mornings of your life
gather like crows:
you cannot keep them away.

Shuddering with anticipation
in its harbor, the ship keeps count
of bodies walking into it.

Because I can no longer raise
the questions,
because I cannot support
truth or its widower's eyes,

now I will be flame,
the young man says.

7.

Ardent reason, please forgive me.
You must know by now
that I will not be coming back.
Still I care deeply, each night
carry photos of you to bed
where sleep waits
with its luminous scrapbook.

Your face rose over the dark horizon
of a coffee cup. Wet
with a decent happiness, you said,
yes, but mind: what you carry
away from here, you will carry
in bottomless boxes,
ever the lighter for it.

8.

Borne up by my silence
you cross the borders into light.
Sky has become water for you, rain,

and memory's flame at play between us
burns green, bright green,
with the copper of earth and setting suns.

At night by the fire, in your green eyes
I read again this story of ruin:
how hope has moved away
and desire lives alone,

here in this country where
only the past shows in mirrors.

Marxist at 50

For many years
notes for that great book gathered
as he lectured students on the recourse
and inevitability of revolution.

Two wives left him, a daughter died,
with his son he could never agree.

Trees shook their
bare branches over his empty house.

It seemed to him the faces
of his students grew
gentler. The world was huge,
and everything was change, was water.

Once he had understood
so clearly.

The Suicide

I grew so tired of the way
you carried good weather around with you.

Then you left my attic, toting away
(O how I would miss them!)
your startling verbs,
your choice of nouns, in an old suitcase.

Lying beside you in bed
was the only home I had. With your artist's life
of new beginnings, even at the end
you could never understand:

I would have killed for you.
I would have lived for you.

Letter from New World

Dim in the halflight, it's another wound,
the sky split open: this morning that wants to be
full of good cheer when it grows up,
have a career, a fixed address, benefits.
In his studio across town
Karl stands shouting down into stone,
teasing the image out, olly-olly-ox-in-free.
Good morning is our breath leaving,
taking no time to pack, slamming the door.

Years since we spoke. This may have something
to do with the fact that you're dead, but maybe not.
All open to interpretation, right?—you
taught me that. I remember your saying
"The soul's dark pit's a dreary place,
but tents look bright when you pitch them there."
After the revolution, you insisted,
the bodies of the good would hang from posts,
filling the village with light.

I've a small house here at the edge of city and sea
where I sit each morning among gulls
and pigeons, occasional cars,
boats pushing in from the horizon and receding
like memories. Sails feed on the wind
and are never full. There was no revolution,
old friend. Revolution we could have understood.
For that we had precedent, backbone, vocabulary,
place. But not for this withering.

It's all gone now—for me as surely
as for yourself: nights smelling of indigo,
whisper of silk and wind and whirr of wings past
the window, clear streams that ran in our heads.
Here even the sun seems a lesser being.
This morning in early light I write you, in the name
of a world we've lost. We'll never know
how it would have been, the thing we most desired:
to match the sky within and that without.

Manumissions

1.

When I was locked away I thought of you
out there spinning wildly into
the world. I knew little of your affairs really,
but had you, I suppose, at the helm
of some quiet expedition, dispatching chaos, some
tiny corner of it, with wit and disregard
for your safety. The days there were as indistinguishable
as walnuts. It was easy to forget, to believe
that somewhere else worlds opened to take you in
and wisdom sprang up inside you like wildflowers.
But they did not. Our shoulders are still
at that same door, and it will not give.
Our lives bend and twist like old fingers.
Shadows hover and pass on the wall.
The sun falls. There is no redemption.

2.

It is night again because you are here:
we gallop terribly into one another's memory. But then
there is the light coming here too,
those sharp edges, its signals, meanings.
Just as the mind itself comes to light, outward
from its own physical place, in the eyes.
We become what we dispossess, something
of it. But the lines we throw
float out around, return only
the shape of it, a perception. We cannot
contain the sorrow of the wind: it must go forth.
The wind does not know how to stop, to turn itself
away from its pursuit: the wind does not make choices.
And still I hear its feet dragging in the dry grass.
I still hear its mouth that tries to make words in the trees.

3.

Music stands on the shore watching a man drown.
Art and Dance are late and he is just standing here
waiting for them, and watching the man drown.
He throws some more popcorn at the pigeons.
They are all going to a party at Poem's.
When he was young Music could sing
the damndest things, but now he doesn't sleep,
forgets things, gets lost. The man heaves up his arms,
keeping good time. He clutches
at empty cans, balloons and tied-off rubbers
floating in the water around him, knowing
anything can hold you up for a while
if you grab it hard enough, and hold on.
The sun lowers behind him like a bandshell.
Waves clap on the smooth rocks.

4.

Tragedy, too, has its center in language.
Good will not prevail; but we must
pity it, put it down here—its only chance.
And meanwhile bully life into *meaning*.
We're ashamed of ourselves, no doubt of it;
but need in time becomes habit, and my shoulder
will not come away from that door. I move with it,
opening and closing with random winds and intentions.
Symbols pursue us, drag us into the sun, drag
their ivory claws along us; sniff at our heads.
And here we are, with these saucers of milk.

(cont.)

5.

To all clients: Adjustments
must be made in the journey. Countries
have closed; others have filled with refugees;
borders, names have changed. Some of your visas
are no longer valid. Check with Customs:
their officers will direct you to us.

She sits by a nervous river. The balloons of Europe
float behind her, over her left shoulder; rise
one by one into the sky, slowly,
into that rare air, and explode. In her notebook
now, there are glimpses of a blinding light.
Though she speaks several, she knows none of the languages
that drift around her here, bright patches of life.
The telegram tumbles away from her table,
onto that vast windy plain.
In her notebook now there are glimpses of a blinding light.

6.

Falling water pulls down the sky: there
is a ragged edge. On the plane I take
to see you, percentages and real estate
crash into one another, in the clear morning
air, and twirl down with surprised expressions
into still, steaming water. Survivors, a few wild thoughts,
adhere to the wreckage. Someone takes command.
There are debates, alignments, a lack of food.
They eat one another's hands, those
tender palms, saying: For a long time we have fought the sea.
Amidst the rubble of post-war Europe, behind
this shattered fountain, I am at the ragged edge.

7.

Circling Austin, lost
(even on the way in from the airport: we start early),
Tony and I rehearse past years. We follow
streets to their end, or the end of our patience,
then try others. Teddy waits at the apartment,
dressing slowly, urging her contacts into place.
We sit through Albert's full routine and four beers
before descending again to life,
the street outside. The sky above has not changed
for many days now; stale air
hangs there like extinguished promise.

8.

Barter is probably best, the trade
of particular skill (a kind of measured knowledge)
or possession for needs, as: our talent
for poetry. (We would starve.) Music,
nothing else, rescues us
from words. They fly about us everywhere, wanting
to get in. And if we can't have
knowledge, then we'll have the houses
it hides in. So we build elegant traps,
catch and breed them carefully. We will let you go,
we explain, if you will just tell us the truth.
Each morning they tell us eloquent, beautiful lies
then fly away over the rooftops, having pleaded thus,
uncontested, the cause of their freedom.

(cont.)

9.

The war we watched begin on TV in Austin
quickens: bodies, ships sink into it.
Do you remember how far away horizons were, how
we believed the world was shaping itself
around us, *us*, when we met? Languages
we do not know flow around us, through us.
There's such pain to it; far-off snows
fill our eyes. And we pass down the line,
nipping at history's heels, surviving
outside it: look. We are safe here,
even at night, with the smell of this damp earth,
and marching, songs above our heads.

Among Moons

Among the moon
and feathers she was sleeping
and the sound of his feet coming
home up the stairs, home
to her, disturbed her.

Jesus, was what she said
under her pillow after a while
and he was nearly
asleep, Jesus, you could at least
do it with a little imagination.

He sat
on the edge of the bed,
he said, Yes, you're right,
I could. He left. She lay
listening to birds.

(One had said: It's your freedom
makes me do this. And the other:
You contain me.)

Then one day
a noise at the door and there
he was, smiling inside his suit.

He left, was
gone, came back—but
had sensed a flood, could not taste
that pure, clear fall of rain.

Newspapers

You'd bring them to me
Hidden at the bottom of your purse
Like us they were restless there
Their answers brief

I opened them inside mornings
Filled with my fingers

Waking in the afternoons we watched
Heads down they pulled themselves
Across the carpet towards sunlight
Weeping

Art of Biography

At nine you must be in Paris.
Everything is strange
about the man you'll meet there,
doomed as he is to difference
and a life alone. Yet for years he worked
in a room not unlike this one
at the top of narrow stairs,
took coffee like yourself each afternoon
at a café nearby, floated up again
and again, breathless,
from consuming, brief affairs with women.

The Death of Virgil

(for Joe Roppolo)

In the carriage house out back, refurbished
and let for twice its worth,
Virgil packs for departure:
the grips and Gladstones of his mind are full.

What of all this will you miss,
old man? the youth asks, his tender hand
(that could be so wonderfully cruel)
cupped at the poet's brow as though to catch
what might brim over there, ideas, sorrow,
some final redeeming image.

Virgil looks up, at himself, *callow*
coming to mind—such a beautiful word.
Such a beautiful child. And so much
he might have done.

I will miss, most, the world's distractions,
he knows; but says nothing. There is no one
to hear. And that other world waits, the one
beyond speech, that has no use for words
and, like this one, he supposes, little enough
for servants of the word such as himself.

After Noon

The children pick
the shadows
of flowers and bring them to us.

From window ledges we take down
the shadows of vases.

Catching the shadow of water:
that's the hard thing.

PERSONAL ESSAYS

Increments

> "Father, the dark moths Crouch at the sills of earth, waiting."
> — James Wright

On the wall of my study is a poster with a sad little guy holding a no smoking sign. His pear-shaped nose overhangs the sign, his eyes are round and black as wells, a single strand of hair sprouts from his head like a weed. It was drawn by a nineteen-year-old named Debbie who died three years ago. For a long time after her death I sat here and tried to write about her, what she had meant to me, and couldn't. It was all over —the suction canisters burned, the crying done —but I could not get it outside myself. I remember telling my daughter the next day as I took her to school, able to say only: Debbie is dead. Probably there's no one else who thinks of Debbie much now, after these three years.

She had cystic fibrosis, a congenital disease with severe pulmonary replications, and though she was nineteen, the disease's toll was such that she was not much larger than my eight-year-old daughter. Debbie knew she would die from CF, as had so many of the older cystics, all her friends, in the year I knew her, and we often talked about how death would come, whether she would know. Early one evening a few months before her own death she called from the hospital to tell me that Sonya had just died: "I thought you would want to know." I thanked her, and we said no more. Several times she spoke to me of her dread at someday waking and finding her family there with her in the hospital room, knowing only then and by that, that this time she would die.

In the last week of her life the family began gathering. The twenty-year-old aunt and uncle she lived with, her stepfather who had remarried following her mother's death, her father whom she had not seen for many years. She did not speak of her old dread now. And when she called me that Sunday, it was not to talk (for she had little enough breath remaining) but to tell me, without words, that she would not see me again. I said that I would be in the next day. But by nine o'clock it was too late. When I arrived at the hospital in bright sunshine, the room was empty, the trashcans full. She had gone quietly two hours before, slipping over that final sill.

It is altogether fitting that Debbie should have passed so quietly away from us. She was always soft-spoken, shy, carrying with her a strange solitude and inner calm to which but a few of us were admitted. I know that she never spoke to me of her disease with the anger and rage one expected; instead, her delight in life signaled itself constantly. She once described for me in great detail her Christmas shopping—incredibly stressful for her, but that was not the part I heard. When I took her to dinner on pass from the hospital, she ate for perhaps fifteen minutes, excused herself, went into the bathroom to throw up, then came back and resumed eating: she would not let her pleasure be abridged. With the graduation announcement that represented amazing perseverance in the face of her increasing illness, she enclosed a torn-off corner of notebook paper with "Sorry, Jim, I'm too lazy to write" scribbled across it.

But her life, of course, *was* abridged, in ways and to degrees only the chronically ill can understand. It was a slow, painful shrinking: grey formed at the borders of her life and day after day crept ever closer, shutting away more and more, inexorably diminishing her. There was no drama to it—just the relentless procession of days. It was not hubris or divine flaw, not quarreling, capricious gods, but he disease that crushed her: something inside her, part of her. Increasingly towards the end the disease *was* her. And yet she remained concerned about the feelings of her family and those about her, those taking care of her. Debbie wanted so badly not to hurt anyone, *to join*.

She was nineteen: I keep returning to that. And she was excluded from every community but that of her disease, a member of the CF family, of children's hospital regulars. Hospital staff for the most part treated her little differently from cystics who were ten or twelve, as though physical size and maturity were correlative. But even in casual conversation she proved remarkably glib and intelligent, and those of us who chose to look further found at her center a clear sense of self. Chronically ill children, at least in part due to the disproportionate time spent among adults, often evidence a maturity beyond their years, almost as though in such a small room the furniture must be set up right away.

Debbie summoned herself, quite naturally it seemed, towards goals. When I first met her, even with extended hospitalizations, that goal was to graduate from high school, from (as she would say) a *regular* high school. It became difficult then for her to find workable goals, and a kind of gentle fantasy appeared. She spoke of becoming a veterinary assistant, of moving to Dallas and taking a job. She even applied for clerical work at the hospital where she was treated, though the personnel office there refused to take her application seriously and put her off as one would a child, failing to grant her even the dignity of straightforward response. Plans were eventually made that she would come here and live with Sharon, a respiratory therapist, and Kathy, another teenage cystic. Debbie went off to her aunt's for a final visit. Several weeks passed without word from her. Then one night at eleven or twelve my phone rang. She was coming back to the hospital, quite ill. My wife met the plane (I had to work) and after waiting for some time following debarkation, finally inquired about Debbie —who had passed out in flight. The next time my phone rang late at night it was Debbie's aunt I spoke to; Debbie could manage only a few words. This was her last visit, her last flight.

In those final months Debbie continued to resent being treated as a child, and increasingly she voiced her resentment. In the hospital this had as much to do with the habits of the staff as with her size; it was, after all, a children's hospital, and the average age of our patients was probably four or five. Once she had gone to a general hospital but, depressed by "old men with catheters," never returned there. I often recall a time at the airport when Debbie was flying back to Amarillo. The ticket clerk had routinely asked who would be meeting the young lady. The young lady, I responded, is 19 years old and responsible for herself. There was a brief, politic pause while the clerk (probably not much over nineteen herself) looked down at Debbie, then a nod.

A more serious complaint towards the end concerned infringements of privacy. She realized that intimate details of her life were known or readily accessible to anyone about the hospital, a terrible burden for anyone but particularly for a 19-year-old girl, and in her final year grew to resent the continued trespass of well-intentioned staff (social workers, interns or psychiatrists in training) with their biased questions, judgements, advice, curiosity. Debbie felt that she had been subjected to that long enough already and had contributed sufficiently to the education of America's future healthcare pros. Finally she refused to receive any staff aside from the resident attending her case, her regular nurses, and respiratory therapists such as myself who administered her hour-long treatments four times a day. In those habits of thought peculiar to hospitals, where virtually any act of independence or self-assertion is automatically considered symptomatic of psychological illness or (that wonderful nonce word) "maladjustment," Debbie's refusal was discussed widely, taking on ever more baroque avatars and interpretations. But like Bartleby she had said "I would prefer not to," and could not be budged.

We knew that Debbie had come back to us to die. We sensed the motion of those dark moths beyond the sill. Miles had become inches. But we went on talking, when we talked, of the usual things: how her aunt took her Medicaid payments for room and board and was reluctant to give Debbie even a few dollars of it (it was small enough, anyway) for clothes; how she slept on the couch there and didn't even have a place for the machine she used each day for breathing treatments; the taste that always came to her (like an epileptic's aura) three or four days before she became seriously ill.

If there were a photograph here of Debbie — and sadly I have none —it would show long, lustrous black hair; small breasts; smooth, beautiful skin with something of the cystic's translucence to it; soulful brown eyes. It would not show, or would show but slightly, the barreled chest and clubbed fingers she also shared with them, or the ravaged teeth. Debbie would be there; the disease would not be.

Nor would that photograph show the way her skin looked the last time I saw her, grey and dull like smoke, like tarnished silver. *She's so small,* I thought as I hugged her —something I'd never really thought of, never sensed, before that time. She was barely conscious, coming to for brief periods after her treatments, then sinking back into torpor. Her shoulders heaved with the effort of breathing; veins pulsed at her neck. But even with such massive effort she gained little air. A moth, I thought then, would barely tremble from her breath: such a tiny tide.

Of course we all live finally in Zeno's land, proceeding by increments and never arriving, while from the other side of this tissue-thin sky come crashing, with the least tear, the eternal oceans of darkness. Debbie's was simply a far more visible, far less metaphoric form of the ticking death we all play host to, that eats its way out of us, as from a cocoon. I sometimes think of her as the girl in de Chirico's "Melancholy and Mystery of the Street," rolling her hoop towards those brooding enigmas. And I have wanted for three years now to set down here something of Debbie's gentle grace and character, something too of the faltering motions of memory. To retain what I could of her. You have to understand: someone very special has been removed from this world, and the world is diminished because of it. I have to believe that. But of course "the world" (our word for everything we know and don't) is not likely to notice, or care. On another wall of my study there's a drawing of a huge eagle sweeping down from the *sky, filling* the sky, talons black and big as mountains. Before him, beneath him, stands a mouse. The mouse's legs are braced and he has raised his right hand towards that eagle, middle finger extended. The legend reads: Courage in the Face of Adversity.

Gently Into the Land of the Meateaters

They are all listening to a record. Schoenberg. The fiddles take ideas, wrap them in wood, throw them into the air where they strike and grate against others. There is a tremendous energy, and at the same time a certain stolidness, to this music. Outside, the sun hangs on the sky like a boil. They sit facing a long corridor at the end of which they see sometimes, as through a reversed telescope or stereopticon, the faces of people they know bringing them magazines or jigsaw puzzles. They are supposed to relate this music, these people who can fit no two things together anymore, or for whom everything has locked into place with no room left over, to the craft or activity (sewing, potholders, lanyards) in which they are engaged.

I am here because odd seams have sprung open in the sky and will not close.

Emerson tells us that wherever we go, whatever we do, self is the sole object we study and learn. Certainly each of us becomes a metaphor of the world: we figure the world from ourselves. But we may forget this is only metaphor and end trying to balance the whole world on our nose, like a seal with a globe. And when belief in external reality collapses, the mind feeds on itself. Here sundered, sovereign worlds wander through the same closed sky, occasionally (but not often) colliding.

It is Robert Lowell I keep coming back to, his "locked razors" and the description of Murder Incorporated's Czar Lepke:

Flabby, bald, lobotomized
he drifted in a sheepish calm,
where no agonizing reappraisal
jarred his concentration on the electric chair —
hanging like an oasis in his air
of lost connections . . .

Perry sits for hours with his foot on the table, sunk into his chair before the TV, always the same chair, not moving until it is time for meals, for group, for OT, meds, bed. Perry is a chemist, committed by his parents following a suicide attempt. Once as we are walking to the gym for a film about Hawaii, he comes up beside me to say that he is just waiting out his time, that he will kill himself when he is released. I know of no other occasion when he spoke to anyone on the ward.

At night the walls lean towards me. I see in clouds the eyes of whales. I write that shadows perform and stand around me clapping, that the trees grow smaller, the flowers every day more threatening now. Of the purple knife-edge in damaged hands. I write: *I lift the cup, I am burning up.*

Our days proceed like those of Fifties' school-children, dull and featureless as the buildings and walkways through which we move. We march together to the cafeteria, square-dancing lessons with horribly scratched records, ancient travelogue films, a talent show. Three times a day we queue at the nurse's station for medications. At dawn those scheduled for shock are assembled in the dayroom and escorted through trees to a small grey building. They return to us stunned, suspended in an endless present, the clear fluid of their synapses turned to milk.

In the afternoon we are left alone. The long hours stretch out like a barren plain from the TV set where everyone huddles, as about a campfire. Most days I sit alone in a line of chairs at one side of the room with a book of Chekhov's stories. Later I learn that this is duly noted in my chart: I do not participate in ward activities.

An amazing person comes among us, a Cajun who takes over the coffee room, scouring and organizing it down to the last cup and spoon, forever brewing huge pots of coffee into which milk sinks helplessly. Next he attacks the ward floors with a polisher. In such exercise of will, and in this company, he and the knots of muscle in his arms are one: nests of potency, intensity. Like a child he is eager to please. Sometimes at night he strums a guitar and keens old country songs.

Here, as elsewhere and always, I stand apart, watching. This is what an artist does —he looks, he tries to see —and what I had slowly unlearned. In the privacy of my life and art by degrees I had folded in upon myself, a closing hand. Nor did the unfolding begin there in the hospital's close spaces; I had only the sense that soon it would.

Because we are sick we cannot be well. Every action or attitude is interpreted in light of our supposed sickness: Conrad's quite reasonable anger at the patronizing behavior of the nursing staff vanishes into rococo vagaries of analysis; my own solitary ways and disinclination for chatter are surely pathological. We have become self-fulfilling prophecy. One morning I choose not to shave; during the day I am questioned about this by the ward nurse, my assigned social worker and a staff physician.

We are told on the one hand to express ourselves, that we must vent our feelings to survive, yet receive clearly the message that we must not disrupt in any way the effortless, level roll of ward routine — conflicting information not unlike that delivered by the larger society beyond our locked doors. I recall the common history, among schizophrenics, of parents who insist upon truths in direct conflict with what the child actually sees.

It is summer. In sharp contrast to our own lethargies, flies rocket about the rooms and rebound from the walls. One afternoon in the doldrums between lunch and dinner I begin counting them. Fifty-eight.

For so arcane and recondite a body of theory, treatment is astonishingly mechanistic, as though we are simple toys that have broken. Bombed to the ground with chemicals, we are led into groups and encouraged to talk, to "share" our problems, fears, failures. Ambrose Bierce said the only thing anyone could ever do with good advice was to give it to someone else, quickly. Whenever there's a lull the social worker says, And how do you *feel* about that? Four years after all this, a friend who is mending as I mended writes that she rarely gets past the first aisle at the supermarket, stunned by such diversity and choice. I can't decide what deodorant to buy, she tells me, and here I'm supposed to be making life decisions.

And poetry, of course, if it fails to make the world large again, does nothing.

The doctors pass among us at rare intervals, alternately annoyed that we remain ill and demanding of their time; defensive that they are of little help; or simply frightened. For the most part they are residents, putting in their time, paying dues, inclined to accede pro forma to the ward nurse's often questionable clinical observations and suggestions. But while among them I encounter Dr. Ball, who seems very young and speaks to me kindly, intelligently, after shaking my hand, the only one to do so. He asks to read my book, which has just come out. Once when my medication is reduced sharply and I feel the ends of my nerves fraying like ropes about to let go, like evergreens all inside me (I'd not been told of the change), he comes to the ward at 3 a.m., though he is not on call, to reassure me.

Much of our treatment and activity seeks to establish among us a sense of community. In some ways this is successful, though perhaps not as intended. Marx's catechism of oppression, despotism and epochal struggle might commend itself, in this surround, to the most conservative among us. My own inchoate communism, though forever wounded by an unshakable faith in the importance of the individual, flourishes here and returns with me intact to the world outside. At night the glass nurse's station with its pure light seems a great ship pushing its way through the dark, a sentry post, a fortress.

Gene is a burned-out relic of the Sixties who still observes the forms of the time (long hair, sandals, beads, slang) like an emigrant preserving his culture in the new land. He cannot maintain his vegetarianism here; the vegetables are cooked with meat or seasoned with lard, and complementary proteins are infrequent. He tries to fill himself with beans, rice, lettuce and milk, gesturing while in line (generally to no avail) for extra portions, pushing the scraps of meat aside from his cabbage or carrots. He cannot or will not talk, and appears largely out of touch. I am told by an orderly (I do not know if this is true) that he killed his wife and children.

You must understand that this is a place of high intention. This is a city where they mend torn sails, or souls; hammer hearts back into place; make fine adjustments in the eye; replace the mind's printed circuits. Where they roll the projector lens slowly till all the blurred, shapeless forms snap into focus.

But it is also an insupportably mean, petty place, just as the unswept dark corners of our hearts are mean and petty, with hard grey floors, bare walls, windows that will not open. It is every army barracks that ever held recruits, every tough schoolyard or gym, every ghetto, prison, deadend street. Some light must always shine behind our lives; here it is very difficult for that light to get through. The language has a long memory: because we are patients, we bear our pain and trials calmly, without complaint.

The game played on this grey court, as in the world outside, is control —here, though, with little regard for pretense and with the absolute sanction of our illness; recusants simply confirm established debilities. We are the poor through bourgeois eyes: if we are sick, surely it is because we intend to be. Joey is confined to the dayroom, dressed only in pajamas, for failing to get the "phonecard" (a square of cardboard attached to a keychain) before making a call at the pay station in the hall just outside the ward.

One morning a recent arrival comes out of the coffee room with an arm full of cups and begins heaving them into the window. George, he says: Irene, Truth, Love. A week or so later, at 9 p.m., another begins sobbing loudly and weeps for two days without stop.

There is a great evil pushing at the world in each of us, and it needs but a small slipway, an opening. We who cannot keep a tune want to move the stars to pity with our voices. From our mothers' ponderous bellies we pass of a sudden, and then very slowly, into this harsh land. Suns flare and die above us; all is awash with yellow light. The voices of others come to us across the plain. We live on water. We *are* water.

In my final week I finish Chekhov and begin *Notes from the Underground*, which goes with me back into the world.

On the long drive home (like airports, state hospitals are built away from urban centers) I begin to realize again how large the world is, how disorganized, how various. The first lines of Wallace Stevens' "Connoisseur of Chaos" come to me:

A. A violent order is disorder; and

B. A great disorder is an order. These

Two things are one.   (Pages of illustrations.)

Years later I clip from the *Times Herald* a cartoon by P. Kolsti that shows a man cringing under a chair, his own huge brain, his own mind, hovering in the air above. It remains on the wall by my desk.

For several days I sit on my patio, reading sometimes, but mostly watching the procession of people, traffic, animals, light, wind, rain. This is what the artist does, I tell myself. He looks; he tries to see. The weather swings wildly from hot to cold. There are patterns everywhere, but the world remains unreadable as a walnut. In a book on French literature I find this quote from Rilke:

It submerges us. We organize it. It falls to pieces. We organize it again and fall to pieces ourselves.

Somehow, it all seems to end there.

Approaching the Page

Summers I'd spend whole afternoons on the porch and still be there in the evening when locust and cicada began calling, filling the yard, that blurred green universe, with their strumming cries. I'd drag out an old white rocker, stack my books on the floor alongside. It was a screen porch, and the best times were when it rained.

The books were likely to be a strange lot. Biographies of Houdini and Robert-Houdin and Chung Ling Soo, cheap editions of science fiction novels liberated from my brother's shelves, books on Shelley or Oscar Wilde, a copy of The Magazine of Fantasy & Science Fiction with a new story by Fritz Leiber, an issue of Fantastic Universe devoted to Stanley Weinbaum, astronomy and mineralogy texts, the Johnson Smith & Co. novelty catalog, a book promising to teach you to speak twelve languages including Esperanto. At the time I gave little thought to what I might be seeking in those books, just knew there was something in there I needed, something I had to have. When years later, in college, I encountered stories of specific hunger, women peeling wallpaper off the walls and eating it because it had nutrients they needed, I understood.

Across the street stretched an acre or so of close-set shacks, tarpaper and plywood mostly. Thousands of black folk lived there, and all my playmates. Helena had a tire factory, a chemical plant, the river itself: it drew people from all over. Struggling many years later with my first guitar, I'd learn that Robert Johnson had lived a mile or so down the road. Other Delta bluesmen, Johnny Shines, Muddy Waters, Roosevelt Sykes, passed through, on their way up to Memphis, perhaps, stopping off to play at The Blue Moon half a block down from Nick's Café, or over radio station KFFA. Sonny Boy Williamson records still were played on KFFA every day at noon, The King Biscuit Hour. As a young man my father had worked as a policeman. He told me how Sonny Boy's band would turn up on the road crew most Mondays. Sonny Boy'd gone off to London and been revered there, recorded with the Yardbirds. Came back home with a checkered suit and bowler hat and all these stories no one believed.

Meanwhile, from the drive-in restaurant clinging like a boat dock to the edge of my grandfather's property flowed a continuous current of music,

Hank Williams and Hank Snow, Arthur Alexander, lots of Jimmy Reed, often in pitched battle with the Mozart, Shostakovich and Mahler on my turntable. Other kids hummed Brian Hyland songs. I hummed Mozart horn concerti, nurturing the apartness that, even then, moved me towards being a writer.

My brother, now a philosopher, had gone to school with Harold Jenkins, later known as Conway Twitty. In one early poem, in London, I'd write:

My brother John, round
face at the edge of my bed, collaborations
of parental persuasion. Now a man too,
like the bowl of a pipe. A philosopher,
teacher; wife and two daughters
in far-off Pittsburgh.

Everything seemed to be about edges then. And everything, the entire wandering, ancient, ever-new world, seemed far-off. With books and voluminous correspondence, much as my father manipulated his duck call, hand opening and closing about the end the way my own, years later, would cup harmonicas, I brought that world in closer. I wrote to the editors of science fiction and magic magazines, to Willy Ley, to fellow teenagers taken with conjuring. One of my favorite correspondents attended military school and had, stored away in his garage at home, a complete stage illusion once the property of Howard Thurston. The local newspaper published my short stories whenever I sent them in. For a short time I served as editor of *Zombie*, a magic magazine published by and for teenagers, on the cover of which my geekish school picture appeared.

Almost a decade after, taking up again the habit of correspondence, I'd turn out reams of letters as I sat looking across Iowa cornfields listening to Sonny Boy Williamson, Paul Butterfield, Dylan. Some of these letters ran to twenty or thirty pages. It was in them that I taught myself to write. And it was there, RFD 3, that I sold my first stories, three of them all at once in a matter of weeks.

For months, neglecting classes in Modern British Novel and French 201, I had sat in the student union rereading Sturgeon, everything I could find, and writing in longhand these absolutely awful stories, leading to a suspicion I'd later pass along to students: that each of us seems to have a certain amount of garbage aboard, a quota of words we must write out before the good stuff starts coming.

Suddenly, it did start. Walking down the street one day I was startled by a man stepping from a doorway. I hurried along to the student union, sat, and began: *Walking down the street on my way to see the Leech....* I put down

Rilke's *Letter to a Young Poet* halfread to write my own futuristic version. I took the unspoken anger and ever-mounting resentment between my wife and self and forged them into a 6000-word psalm to silence, isolation and withdrawal: "A Few Last Words." The epigraph was from W.S. Merwin:

What is the silence
  a. As though it had a right to more

The first few good poems came in a scatter then, too, but *that* great unfolding still lay ahead, in London, in a bedsitting room just off Portobello Road where often I'd write two or three poems a day and obsessively rewrite others—as with the letters, teaching myself.

But it worked. I'd sneaked into literature through the back door, still the way I prefer to come and go.

The first books I read were science fiction and belonged to my brother, book club editions he'd bought for a dollar. *Puppet Masters*, which laid wide tire tracks across my imagination. Jerry Sohl's *Costigan's Needle*, various Van Vogts, Simak's *Ring Around the Sun* and *Mission of Gravity*, Bester's *The Demolished Man*. At the local library I had exhausted the children's section and, with my brother as spokesman, challenged the librarian, reading for her from a book taken at random off the shelf and receiving my adult card. Somewhere or another, probably on a visit to Memphis, I came across an issue of a magazine dedicated to Stanley Weinbaum which I read over and over, especially the biographical essay, and a British magazine titled Nebula, which listed the twenty top science fiction novels, books I'd for the most part never heard of, like George R. Stewart's *Earth Abides*, *Tiger! Tiger!* and *Children of the Atom*. Soon enough I'd searched down and read them all.

The taste for details of writers' lives by this time had taken hold; I was reading huge books on Shelley, Wilde, Poe, Thomas Wolfe. On a drugstore rack I came across James Ramsey Ullman's novel about Rimbaud, *Day on Fire*. This was the beginning of my fascination with French literature, an interest soon bolstered with a mass-market paperback of Baudelaire translations by Edna St. Vincent Millay and George Dillon, an anthology of French poetry, I think from Random House, containing translations by Merwin among others, and, finally, by Francis Steegmuller's Apollinaire biography. Not surprising that Rimbaud, the eternal adolescent, should become the first French poet with whom I, adolescent myself, should fall in love. Apollinaire became the second, engendering ideals of lyricism and poetic freedom that began to shape my own shabby work. He was also the first poet I translated.

And now the cook's plucking geese.
Ah, fall of snow
falling, no
girl for my arms.

Third, and perhaps the most influential of all, was Blaise Cendrars, in whose *Prose du transsibérien et de la petite Jeanne de France* I locate the beginning and very fount of modern poetry. Of all the world's poems, it is this one—this inexhaustible poem defining both our era and the poet's responsibility as witness—that speaks to me most directly.

Et j'étais déjà si mauvais poète
Que je ne savais pas aller jusqu'au bout

Powerful magic had found its way to me. I was like a child fed sweets for the first time, a primitive shaman given scalpels and bone saws. *Why hadn't anyone told me?* I was dangerous.

But I wasn't, of course.

I was only another writer, just another who found intolerable the notion there wasn't something *more*. Like a truffle-hunting pig I kept digging beneath. Beneath the gray of diurnal life, repetitive labor, the sucking mud of politics, stuccoed walls, tile floors and newspapers, TV newscasts.

Camus' invincible summer was under there somewhere. I'd find it.

Pushing Envelopes

I wonder sometimes, as I stuff yet another perfectly innocent envelope with
return postage, or tear one open to find my manuscript bearing the hoofprint
of the paper clip holding a form rejection to its bosom, whether this is not a
silly thing for a 53-year-old, supposedly professional writer to be doing.

It's been habit, of course, for a long time now. Like Baudelaire's vampire,
whose bones after the metamorphosis go on creaking like a signboard in the
wind. Or, again, as in Apollinaire:

> Their hearts are like their doors
> Always doing business

The doors swing to and fro with distressing regularity. Stories and poems
and essays wrapped up warmly in their best new clothes and sent out the
door—like the boll weevil, jus' lookin' for a home—come back bringing
along unwelcome friends, sad little notes that read Try us again! or invita-
tions to subscribe at special rates.

"Ah, another great Sallis story," a friend said just last year upon seeing
something of mine in a magazine. I pointed out that the story had swum
valiantly upstream 54 times before finally lodging in a bend. My record of
submissions filled both sides of an index card. I'd spent $69.12 on postage
alone, never mind the cost of manila envelopes, photocopies and paper. In
return I received two copies of the magazine.

It doesn't even feel good when you stop, as in the old joke. Every few
years I *do* stop. Tuck little orphan stories away in a shelter somewhere, find
a nice spot for homeless poems under a bridge, and swear never again. But
before long I catch myself sneaking to the corner mailbox with a plain brown
envelope, or get caught slipping out of the house with a stack of submissions
under my coat on a coolish 98-degree July evening.

Now, to secure all that money for postage, manila envelopes, photocopies
and paper, I write books for which I get paid reasonably well, or reviews for
the like of *Book World* and the *L.A. Times*. Those who read my books aren't
likely to come across, even to know about, stories appearing in *Straw Dog
Quarterly* or *Dead Horse Review*, or to care about poems appearing any-

where. Even my book editors have little interest in this other, subterranean life. Questioned by authorities they disavow all knowledge of the "second gentleman" staying with the good Dr. J. Luckily (thus far at least) I've always managed to get home, drink the antidote and change back in time.

So just why *is* it that I go on shoveling good money and fair-to-middling effort into such enterprise, sending out stories and poems to publications likely to be seen only by other contributors? (Note that I do not say *read* by other contributors.) Reputation? I've had mine, such as it is, for years now, like a pair of old jeans; it's unlikely to be much affected by a poem buried among dozens of others in *Driftword* or *Wormturn*, or by a two-page story in *Elephant Hump* stating that its author needs no introduction. But I *do* go on, like some out-of-control, perpetual-motion existentialist making his leap into faith, nostrils pinched shut with finger and thumb, again and again. When recently a friend offered his definition of *crazy* as "doing the same thing over and over expecting different results," I cringed.

Maybe more than anything (this just occurred to me, go with me on it for a moment) it has to do with getting the little buggers out of house and mind for a while. Ghosts, once-beloved pets gone blind and incontinent with age, bunions or heel blisters: choose your metaphor. They're always there; they don't go away. But if you work at it, you can get temporary relief. Hand the kids a few dollars and tell them to go take in a matinee, buying your ticket to a little peace.

Truth to tell (though I have to confess that my favorite title for a book about writing is *Telling Lies for Fun and Profit*), I don't even know what to call the things anymore. Little magazines? Well, lots of them make pretty good door stops these days. Literary magazines? Sure...if you're in the habit of calling your pants trousers and got reared instead of raised—in which case the word is pronounced *lit'ry*. Increasingly, even among book readers and interviewers, I find myself having to describe these publications. Your basic show and tell situation. Remembering all the time Louis Armstrong saying of jazz that if you had to ask, you weren't going to understand the answer.

Not only don't I know what to call these publications, I have no idea where they fit in anymore, what function they might serve. Where on the bus of a nation whose conversation and very mythology come from last night's sitcoms and movies, does a magazine filled with knickknacks of poetry, essays and short fiction find a seat? Most nowadays seem vaguely proprietary, attached in one way or another to university writing programs, the intellectual-property equivalent of corporate newsletters. There's a sameness to them, never stronger than in those most adamantly transgressive, a flattening-out that admittedly may have as much to do with my own age as with intrinsic quality.

We thought we were doing important work. I remember. We thought literature was important and would always be, that it offered us maps to find our way to new worlds. Now we just go on overbuilding the world we have, and the maps lie in shreds around us. Publishing has become a kind of demi-intellectual garment district, with runners pushing racks of clothes everywhere in the street, obstructing traffic and getting in good people's ways.

And literature?

Years ago I wrote a piece for *American Pen* suggesting that, abandoned by mainstream publishing, our literature—even then we'd begun to miss it, you see, and to go looking—had fled to these magazines. Like those remote islands in science fiction upon which prehistoric life has survived into the present. Now I don't know *where* it's gone. I've looked. I can't find it. If anyone's seen it recently, please call. I'll pay for information, photos, confirmed sightings.

Always we believed, those historical magazines and historical me, in literature's adversary intent: that literature necessarily sets itself against prevailing currents—the received wisdom and assumptions of our time. Frost might be right that "We can't appraise the time in which we act," but by God we were gonna try. We were meant, as writers, to be outlaws, hired guns, eternal outsiders, long riders. We didn't light out for the territory, we planned on hauling the territory behind us, right back to civilization.

Maybe these days when I slip these manuscripts, these stories and poems and essays, into envelopes, maybe, more than anything else I'm doing, I'm reminding myself of all that. What it felt like to believe that literature and the people who create it are important. That we might change things. Maybe it helps this one over-civilized, over- comfortable, housebroken writer sustain the illusion that he's still out there with dust and starlight in his face, far away from all the Aunt Sallies and all the compromises, out there where there are no fences and anything, *anything*, can happen.

Temporary Life

This happened some years ago: on March 6, a few days after her thirtieth birthday, my wife took a massive overdose of the medication given her for depression.

We had been married less than a year then, since May. The last months had been difficult ones as I pressed her to seek help and she denied needing it. There were sudden rages, long periods of withdrawal, a bottomless sorrow.

Kim was brought to the hospital where I served as chief respiratory therapist. For almost three hours we pumped her stomach, flushed her full of charcoal and Ipecac, resuscitated her. She was having terrible seizures and required huge doses of Dilantin. She had almost stopped breathing. The medication she took, we all knew, often leads to brain damage, kidney shutdown, cardiac dysfunction.

I held the mask over her face, leaned close and spoke to her the whole time as I breathed for her. She remembers none of this. I will never forget it.

At last she was stable and we rolled her along the corridor, out into bright, bright sunshine to the waiting helicopter. Kim rose with a mighty heave into the sky. It was a three-hour drive and I didn't know if she'd be alive when I got there. I had to clean up, see to the girls, pack Kirn's things. I looked down and saw charcoal all over my tie, shirt, pants. Then[1] was blood, too, not a lot of it, but it was Kirn's blood. The director of nurses made me drink a cup of coffee. It kept spilling into the saucer.

The first time I wrote about her was in an essay on death published in the *Star-Telegram* not long after we met. There would be others later on — "Standing by Death" as the gulfs between us grew, and finally, when Kim was gone, gone at last after many rehearsals, "Old Story at Airport" — but much about that first essay now seems prophetic.

I watched three people die today, it began. Then went on: It is something I have been doing for a long time now, something one does not want to become good at, but does. One signs off the chart, gathers up equipment, walks away.

On my thirtieth birthday a fist closed inside my father's chest and he fell to the floor. Almost without thought I started CPR, and the world came slowly back to his eyes. But it was a much smaller world than the one he'd left. For almost a year we watched him hunt empty fields, sniffing at the stillness, disability, pills, his days like birds forever suspended in mid-flight against the morning sky. After several practice runs, at the end of an afternoon spent in a lawnchair in the sun watching me mow the yard, he at last left us.

Tonight, as the moon buoys in and out of clouds, I have lain awake thinking of all the others. The first I remember is Mr. Sheldon, dying of emphysema. For almost thirty years he had carried in his wallet a tattered pay stub from the week he'd made over a thousand dollars operating heavy equipment, and showed it to me late one night in his room.

Mr. Petrie, a bus driver whose lungs blew up like stiff balloons and burst. The newborns I've worked with for so long now. Debbie. And the other kids —cystics, surgery patients gone sour, Siamese twins, chronic hearts — each with his own private battle pitched, and going on invisibly, above the bed.

An hour or so ago, unable to sleep, I walked to the corner store for a paper. A nearby house stood burned out in the moonlight, car after car reversing or slowing to look at it. For months, walking by, I had watched the woman and the children who lived there, wondering about them, what their lives were like, what things might be important to them.

Lately, they'd not been around very often. I'd see the car in the driveway some days, and once or twice a week old newspapers got collected from the front yard. I supposed that some great change had occurred in their lives.

So many things crowded into my mind as I walked. I remembered a poem of Edna St. Vincent Millay's: "I shall die, but that is all that I shall do for death." I thought of the knight's wife in *The Seventh Seal* saying to Death: "You are welcome in this house, Sir." Of Dylan Thomas' "Do Not Go Gentle" and "If My Head Hurt a Hair's Foot," a dialogue between mother and fetus. Of Camus, that there is only one imperative: to come to terms with death, after which all things are possible.

Back home, I lay staring at the moon's pale, round face. Clouds the shape of a piano, of Brazil, of a fig, crossed it. Winds nudged at the side of the house. I fell asleep, death's first degree, that daily rehearsal.

Six weeks have passed (*I wrote*) since the above words were put down. As often occurs, there was a space between the beginnings of a piece and its end; these words waited in a file until I came back to them. I always do come back, sometimes after moments, sometimes years.

There have been other deaths in these weeks. As I write, a twenty-two-year-old woman daily loses ground in ICU. In the other ICU, for newborns, a twenty-five week baby struggles for life. I stand over him thinking what a sense of loss these children must have, obtaining the world.

Almost daily I walk by the burned-out house.

On the day I watched three people die, I went out for the first time with a woman I had watched across many rooms. She told me of a man she had loved who killed himself. I had no idea, writing of death later that night, how important she would become to me, how in later weeks my days would gather around her troubled face or smile.

It's a warm, windy afternoon and she'll be over soon, after work. I have been defrosting my refrigerator, and something about that — the slaking of ice, unfolding the ice's lie, its whiteness — seems appropriate.

As a child, I fell from a fig tree. The world went away, and I could not breathe. For what seemed a long time I existed in a kind of limbo, not breathing (and so not quite fully alive), senses poised but blank. Like moonlight, like ice, I was white, I was pure, in that moment before the world reclaimed me. I had then, I think, my first sense of how terrible and difficult endings are.

When I wrote that, I was living in a garage apartment in Arlington, Texas, not far from the hospital where Kim and I worked; many days I'd walk over. I spent hours walking all *over* Arlington, hours more watching squirrels out the window, the remainder of my free time writing. I was writing at a fairly speedy clip: a novel in a little over a month, a dozen or so stories and articles, new poems. I'd no expectations of ever being other than alone and had given up dating. I'd just go on writing, working, listening to Mozart and Mahler, walking, running. Martinis at night as I read.

Then Kim came into my life, like a nail into cork.

Everything had always been difficult for her— childhood, previous marriages, parental relations — and as I got to know her (or thought I did), I thought I would be able to make it all easier, I began to want to.

We just met incidentally at work, at first. In the halls or cafeteria line, at various nurse's stations, in ICU when we were both assigned there. We began to talk, a little more each time, coming to recognize our common attraction. Then one day I asked her to have lunch with me and, after lunch, walking back to the unit, dinner the next evening. *Yes.* For hours that afternoon, gravity lost any claim it had on me.

I was forty, Kim twenty-nine.

When I picked her up that first evening I was stunned, stunned as I have been ever since, by her beauty, by the life in her eyes, the gentle ease of her body, by the way her mouth shapes itself around words. As we swung out onto 1-30 for the drive to Dallas, everything about me — my writing, my books, age, prior marriage, study of French and Russian, longtime work as a musician — came out in a sudden rush. Kim was quiet for a while then. She crossed her legs, tucking her feel under her, and looked off towards Dallas, towards Reunion Tower. "There's nothing to tell you about *me,*" she said.

I looked at her and felt something changing inside me: borders or walls going down.

There turned out to be, once we settled in at The Wok, quite a lot to tell me. For almost two hours Kim talked about her life. The man she'd loved nurse and parent, to movies at two in the morning and morning drinking. We had been so proud, right up to the end, of our sexuality together; and when that went, when you could focus only on your need, I knew it was over.

I've also been thinking of your seizures in ER, those great shudders as though death were already violating you horribly. About the scars and bruises that riddled your body for weeks afterwards.

But finally there's no moral to a near-death, Kim, just as there's none to this rain, to a morning walk along *A* spring, or to terrible, difficult endings. They happen and we survive them, finally. We go on.

Gradually you stopped caring. Clothes were removed and thrown on the floor where they stayed. The bed remained unmade. I cooked all meals, did all cleaning. You put makeup on only when we went out, and instead of brushing your teeth, ate toothpaste. Then you lost all taste for food and for days ate nothing. I found lipstick on the gin bottle's mouth. When I came home you were always on the couch face down, half-nude.

Now you are elsewhere, in some other house, one not burned-out perhaps, and I have my own pain and terrible anger to deal with, to survive.

Your first weekend out of ICUI visited, sitting with you for hours on plastic chairs beside heaped

ashtrays at the end of the hall, pigeons looking in at us from beyond locked windows. The following weekend they gave you an overnight pass and we spent it in restaurants, bars, a cheap motel room, holding one another mostly, looking into one another's eyes and talking, trying to rekindle kindness, concern, love.

I think about how we felt that weekend, Kim, how you could hardly speak from having had the tube in your throat, about the way your back hurt and the sadness and surrender that's never since left your eyes. Maybe it was always there.

It goes on raining.

Returning to the house after it was all over, that first part of it, ER, court, telling the girls, to hurriedly pack things for you, hoping you'd need them.

Breakfast dishes were piled on the counter, drawers and cabinets stood open. A saucer with the birthday cake Melba brought you was on the table. A few bites had been eaten; much of the rest was smeared across the table's surface and edge. A fork lay on the floor alongside, encrusted with icing. There were pill wrappers everywhere.

With even greater dread I walked to the bedroom. Peaceful and orderly here, just a blanket pulled onto the floor, phone on the bed, your clothes spread about on bureau and chair. It doesn't look at all like a place someone's life almost ended. There's no real sign of the pressures, of the crushing pain and turmoil you went through just hours ago here.

How could anything so terrible, so devastating, I think, leave so little wreckage in its wake?

Damaged though she was, you have to understand this, Kim made me part of humanity again. Taught me to feel, to care deeply, to turn loose and give up myself. And so in her months of need I flooded her with letters, poems, stories, notes. I thought words could fix her, words could repair the damage, bridge the gulfs opening between us. I've always believed too much in words.

And much as I did, *just* as I did, all of you are waiting for the expository lump, for the part of the movie where some eccentric genius comes on to explain it all away: to tell us why things have got to be the way they are, and how, with the employ of his rare understanding and arcane science, they will be set back in order by movie's end.

As we went from facility to facility, from crisis to crisis, each one more bleak and damning than the last, I waited for explanations, for magic pills or words, for some god (wearing a white labcoat, of course) to descend from the cyclorama and tell us what to do. I knew better, of course. But I *loved* her, you see: that's what this is all about.

So you won't find explanations and a tidy case history here, because I don't know; no one knows. All you can expect from this accounting is a scrapbook, a collage, bits and pieces — because that is what our life together was.

Somehow Kim never learned to act, only to react. Her entire life was a passing parade of improvisations, of momentary coping in which truth, often in the same conversation, took on quite different masks. Speech and action grew ever more dichotomous, and her focus, her attention, was tugged a hundred ways at once. I managed to keep her up, keep her afloat, for a while, but when *my* energies were expended, we both almost went under.

Sartre tells us that life is the reworking of a destiny by a freedom. For Kim, all her life, there was only a destiny. She couldn't break through to the freedom, couldn't find it, couldn't believe in it.

It's four in the morning and the untidy pile of manuscript beside me is almost done now. Beer cans litter the apartment. I am playing country music because that, too, is part of Kim, part of our life together. A thick folder of her letters and notes, of mine to her, of souvenirs retrieved from unlikely places, cardboard boxes and the back corners of drawers, lies on the floor beside me. There's no desk or table in the new apartment and I'm sitting on the foot of the bed with an end table pulled up to me, typewriter and dim lamp on that. This is how I've lived my life: with these departures and partial retrievals, alone with words in new apartments in many early mornings.

This all happened years ago.

In *this* early morning, in my bare apartment, in Texas half-light with the smell of magnolia and tomorrow's rain lofting in from outside, I take out an old manuscript and read it through, making changes as I go, adding words or phrases, deleting whole paragraphs: *this* manuscript.

I have gone on to another life, and from these calmer ports am trying again, as I tried then through storms of sentiment and anger, to understand.

Day puts itself together outside my window, finding me not at all surprised that I don't understand much better than before. And while anger and pain remain, sadly I can recall now little of the joy or good times, little of that love I felt so strongly, save what I've put down here —reason enough, surely, to send this story, after all this time, into the world.

NOVEL

Renderings

To Michael Moorcock

Who are the compatriots
a. They make the stars of bone
—W.S. Merwin

I.

They come in the dark and do terrible things to me. They go away.

In the morning there are bruises, memories. Eva traces them across my chest, down my arms. She asks no questions.

Their heads are like foxes. (I have seen, in the old books, pictures of foxes.) Their feet are hooves. They leave prints of bloody paws on the door, the sheets.

I do not know what country I am in. A strange sky streaked with blue clouds, yellowish hills far off, always the smell of damp clay and dust, and twilight hovering over our heads like a moth. I do not know the name of the language I speak, though I speak it, I'm told again and again, quite well.

Eva does not speak the language.

Eva paints.

Her latest: myself, dying. There is a smile (I think it a smile) on my lips, the smile of a man who has achieved his life's ambition. For some time I envy the man trapped there, this circle closing itself.

What, in the drudge and dazzle of days, I keep forgetting: I am here for a purpose. The expedition is well financed; they will expect results. This journal? Eva's paintings? Neither will be enough. They expect nothing less than *une petite cosmogonie complète*. While my own book lies dormant as the Kraken, as Kansas corn, others continue, miraculously, to find their way to me—they simply appear in my room—for jacket blurbs, review, consolation, criticism. And in the meanwhile my poems wander among the baffles of their words, looking for salvation, redeeming wisdom, gnosis, wherever seams and corners come imperfectly together.

I visited the grave today.

It rests in a tiny valley between two hills. Atop the hills are fig trees, down their sides, kudzu. There is a small stone.

A woman was there before me and stood looking down at the grave. From behind I could see that her shoulders were wide, waist narrow, legs muscular and long. She wore a leiderhosen sort of thing, of old leather or something much like it, over a long-sleeved white shirt. On her feet were ankle-length oxblood boots with low, narrow heels.

Strangers rarely came to us here, and I was startled to encounter one so casually, still more startled at her hair, of a forbidden black. My own had been bleached to a pale bluish white before I came.

When she turned I could see her breasts, but partly contained by clothing, small, upturned. I thought of the snouts of small animals in the old books.

—I came too late, she said. On her face a mask, beneath it (I sensed) a smile. —I tried to come earlier. Everything has become so difficult. Why do they always leave me?

I sensed, could almost feel, her own features sliding inside those of the mask, rearranging themselves.

—They always go away. They flee to foreign lands, the back rooms of libraries, they have families, become editors, forget me. I ask so little of them, only love. Am I so hard a woman to love?

The features of the mask changed perceptibly.

—Look at me. I am beautiful, *spa?* And young, always young. Anything a man wants, I can be. I become the hollow only he can fill, I empty myself into him, nourish, protect. And still he will not stay with me. My hands close on air, my legs clasp empty space.

The mask was now that of Greek comedy. *Inappropriate affect,* I thought, remembering words read long ago, when I still thought it possible to understand, to *know.*

The sun shrugged to its zenith overhead as shadows flowed back to their sources, this woman's mask *blanc* now. A hand moved, palm open, towards the gravesite.

—The last spoke of killing me. He put his fist against my throat. Another time, a knife between my legs. I saw the world spinning about—a *désordre* I had never known. The walls of the room collapsed. I saw at the window the eye of a whale.

A shrug, or shiver, passed over her. For a moment the mask was silver, a mirror in which I swam watching.

—Some of the things *he* saw: I do not doubt it. But I don't know how he bore them. How any of you do.

She turned away towards the grave again.

—I have been in a hospital, she said.

—Yes.

Features flared on the mask, faded. —You knew?

I told her my name.

—You have changed, she said finally.

I nodded. —It's been a long time. Many years, many poems, many abandoned books and stories.

—And women?

—Abandoned?

—Or otherwise.

—A few. One in particular, a painter named Eva. She is here with me.

—But you will send her away, now that I have come.

—No.

Her silver mask tilted upwards and swept slowly across the sky, a tiny observatory dome.

—You cannot go on without me.

—Perhaps.

—You will encounter deserts and thirsty rivers. The ground itself will tremble as you pass across it.

Taking a step towards her, I lifted a hand to the mask.

—That is not allowed, she said.

—In art, I said, all is allowed, and pulled it down. It hung, ineffective, pitiful noose, about her throat. While above it like a moon rose Eva's face, impossibly old.

And so I walked away from that grave, from that place and time,

And I came at last onto a green field beyond which I could see the small settlement,

Like (I saw for the first time) a natural thing, a growing thing, alive,

And the vast empty spaces around.

They come no more at night.

I watch Eva's face in the moonlight.

The book is almost finished.

Metonymies of Europe and its civilization: tea, excellent manners, trains. I had my taste of the first two while waiting for the third.

The tea shop nearest my gate at New Paddington Station was a small one with perhaps eight tables, all of them empty so early in the morning. I shrugged out of my wet mac and was served by a middle-aged woman intent upon making, of my tea and toast, a deferential ceremony. She wore a rather tight brown uniform and, over it, a navy blue cardigan stretched long in front from many years' pocketed tips.

My train sat idly steaming in its slot. A few passengers made their way aboard, most of them burdened with various bundles and unwieldy bags, as I sat over breakfast. At last taking up my own single parcel, I walked the train's length searching for empty compartments, finally settling on one encamped by (as I soon learned) a young seminary student. Moments before departure we were joined by a breathless woman of about the same age.

"I assume you're not a believer, of course," the student said as we pulled away from New Paddington, looking up from his Greek bible first at the woman, then, getting no response, at me.

I simply looked back at him. The woman took out a paperback *The Brothers Karamazov* and began reading (though there was no marker) somewhere near the middle of the book.

"You don't have to believe, of course: that's the message of our modern world," he told us. "Only faith matters. And if you can only have faith—in beauty, in the world, yourself—those also are among the names of Yahweh."

Having got all that on record, he took refuge again in the orderly decline of Greek. I thought of Tillich as apologist, the history of religion a graveyard of dead symbols. This gentle young man with his dead language and dead mythologies. This city illimitably, yet with great civility, dying also. I watched, silent witness, as station after station went past. At first these were frequent, active; then the intervals between increased, their platforms ever more sparsely populous, until the last hove into view overgrown with honeysuckle and kudzu, colonized by rats the size of beaver.

Soon then, our train broke into a blasted, scabrous landscape. Stark and sere, trees stood, jagged dark teeth, on the horizon. We thundered past collapsing structures once buildings, past steel and cement, water towers like downed Goliaths, the plundered remains of bridges, signs gone grey and featureless as stone.

The morning's rain had given way to sun. Soon, too, our tracks gave onto bare earth and, both my companions being occupied with books, there being little landscape to observe now, I elected to join them.

Untying its thong from around a sort of button, I opened the cardboard satchel I always carried with me and took from it a manila folder. I read over the most recent pages—it had become my habit to type up the manuscript page by page as it progressed, and the newer pages were uppermost—then replaced the folder, removing in its stead a pad of cheap yellow paper and a pen.

Far off beyond the hills, I wrote, *I hear the rumbling discourse of their dynamite, and wait for the winds that will roll down towards us.*

In her letters Violet writes of ordinary things that seem to be receding ever further from me: walking to the store for milk, a new coat, newspapers. The sky looms overhead like promises one should live up to. I read Dostoevski and wait for meals.

Today, walking in the hills, I came across a gravesite.

Towards noon, hand wrapped about a teacup that would do most others for a soup bowl, the train's engineer joined us. I took note of a limp, the left leg, if I remember correctly, and mused that his face resembled some wooden implement left outdoors for weeks and finally retrieved.

"First time?" he asked my female companion, who went on reading.

"How about you?" he said to me then. "Been to the settlement before?"

I said that I had not.

He drank. I noticed that his left hand, whenever he removed it from the cup, shook.

He took in the land outside our windows with a quick glance.

"'S the future," he said. "You don't doubt it, do you? I been a railroadman a long time." Another mouthful of tea. "Pushed down some borders myself in my day. Lasted longer than most, too. My kids come home from school and they don't know what any of it was all about, what it was *for.* Don't have enough history to cover a shirtsleeve."

He drank what seemed to be the last of his tea.

"That's what'll save us, the settlement up there. I hope you folks have a nice stay. Do it myself in a minute, if I could."

He trudged along the aisle and out the compartment's doors.

The woman had exchanged *Karamazov* for Balzac, the student his Attic scripture for a Talmud. Miles to go, one supposed.

"The captain strolls on the deck in moonlight," the woman beside me said after a while.

I nodded. "Quite."

The student looked up, a little befuddled: our scriptures were apart from his. I became acutely aware of the woman there with me, of legs tight against the coarse fabric of pants, the lift of breast and bare arm, more than anything else, perhaps, a familiar, fugitive sense of promise, of possibilities.

"You are traveling alone?" she asked.

I said that I was and she returned to her book. I watched out the window for a moment—a few low clouds, an abandoned machine or two—before returning to my own.

I remember, as I entered the settlement for the first time, thinking that I was aware, not in some remote, faintly acknowledged manner, but physically aware, with a rise along my spine, that simultaneously we all inhabit two worlds, the one we carry within our minds and the external (or projected) one, and that these two meet, the "real" and "shadow," only selectively, like the scant overlapping lips of Venn diagrams.

With some surprise I realized that both my chapter and journey had come to an end. The train was at a standstill. Clusters of simple buildings loomed in a curious twilight.

Both companions already stood. Leaning close as I closed my satchel, the woman said: "My name is Eva. We'll see one another often."

I'm so tired of it, the women with trees
Between their legs, the forest of possible eductions.
And the stork riding his ridiculous red roses
Towards us across the desert
Again.

    the tracks progressing well
    cable, Ready soon, rails laid on time
    the locomotive will

Red needles swing across the face of our days, leaving red
Behind. Mensurate, commiserate. Anacoluthon—hearing
Delicious lips open inside a morning. The giraffes' snakelike
Heads silent above the trees.

    commensurate, comminution, commissure

And the silver threads dashing along the cobalt seams,
Day. The comity of nations continues, allows us to remain
Here. Horizons appear at intervals. Then the work stops;
An ostrich comes to borrow water from our tanks.

    and other manifestations of length, duration
    the absence of ants, flies, inchworms
    the moths crouched waiting

Insects desert the sun in a line from the horizon, in single
File. Gracchus laughs and watches each queue and wait
Its turn. He names them. Another cable, Rails almost done
Trees down No more Please cable return Further
Instructions

    the horizons vanish

Feet among ties, even the giraffes are waiting. We release
The construction into the landscape. It scatters,
Correcting the sand's pronunciation; it lies under the sun
In articulate fragments, random as facts. Someone applauds.

"there was no other choice"
"but within it lie other choices"
the cable unanswered

The insects pause, then march one by one into the aardvark's
Dead mouth—and tumble
In knots from the eyes. We wait, and watch.

David,
Increasingly I come to a sense of life as a series of departures which we, as
artists of a sort, document. So you'll have to forgive my being so long out of
touch, you see. And in fact I have no way of knowing if *this* will reach you.
There are mailboxes here, but I've yet to see one used.

Bleached by this southern sun, days pass bone-white and uneventful. I've
tunneled my way well into Proust. Morning and late afternoon I walk for
miles, often until the settlement is out of sight. Tea with the ladies, whisky-
and-water with the gentlemen at night.

I have been trying to recall when we were last together and think (astonishing fact) that it must have been over two years past. I was living alone in that
tiny apartment near the university. We sat outside watching squirrels. Neither
of us spoke of the women who'd just fallen away from us, though they were
there too. After work Kim came over. We drank beer a while and you left. I
gave you some early versions of the revolutionary poems to take with you.

Then things began to happen fast in our lives. Like that line of MacLeish's:
Saw it start to, saw it had to, saw it happen. I remember a string of brief notes
from you as your second marriage crumbled—bits of your land slaking into
the sea, as you put it in an old poem. I didn't know about Tony until I saw
your essay on suicide in *Chariton*. I still remember him with his quarter-size
fiddle.

And here *I* am, cast up on *this* strange shore. (But alive, at least. Still alive.)
Our voyage is half done, my friend: maybe we should take consolation from
that.

I am working perfunctorily at the book, which begins to take on the heft,
the weight, of a novel, if not its volume. Real progress has been difficult.
Everything reminds me of something else, everything seems to fit. For respite
I turn to my notebook and to poems, but these always lead me back to the

book. What began as *The Collected Love Poems of Adolf Hitler* and as a light comic romance, has become *Krafft-Ebing, I Love You* and, more recently, untitled, and no more a romance than it is light or comic.

(I notice that the words *begin* and *become* appear increasingly in everything I write now.)

Walking in the hills today I thought how surprised our old professors would be at the way I write. Suckled on New Critics, they believed the writer a master manipulator, a kind of conjurer, every word and motion bent inexorably to the final effect. I believed it too, but when I began to write, from *this* side of the door, that all collapsed. The only way I could do it was by winging it; if I knew things ahead of time, I simply couldn't make myself write. From page to page, word to word, I never knew what would happen. I still don't.

Stumps of memory like Cendrars' hand.

And look how long it's taken me to get back around to what started this letter into being. Which was to tell you that I'm seeing, more or less regularly, quite an extraordinary woman, a painter enamoured of Dostoevski and a journal-keeper like myself. I am, I guess, more or less in love. And I feel like a fool for it, at my age. But I don't think we ever recover from this terrible ache, David, from these words wanting eternally to be born in us; I think we'll know all our lives this wanting, these hollows.

Yes, my friend: the air at world's edge is thin. Perhaps we will never again be loved as we have been.

The old songs die within us. I see them tumbling over horizons, all those future poets thin as cypress, their saucer-big eyes turning in air, casting about in the fall for good advice, help, hard words, the hopeful shores of women.

He has known: moments of terrible sobriety, encompassing dreams, desire that leapt like a tearing along his body, the suffocation of memory, airless mornings, malignant nights.

Sometimes he watches her straining upwards above him and it's as though he is not there, as though she is alone in this damp becoming. Only afterwards, lying alongside her, does he feel something like the conjunction, the blurring of borders, he always hopes for. Then she is gone and there is nothing but a life to be put back on, and worn.

Always the past events of his life elude him. A face, dragged out of memory, will float away in the sift of present sensations. This woman he is with becomes *every* woman he's been with. And for the future he holds no great expectations. Things will go on happening, and will be largely like the things that have already happened.

In a woman he once loved there came to live a terrible, swelling sadness. Waking in the morning he would find her already at the window looking out, coffee cup in hand. Nights, at one or two, she would quit his bed for the dark kitchen or bathroom. And gradually, without words, this sadness, that had no name, that she could never define and he knew all too well, bore her from him.

You are alone again, a friend said when he learned she was gone, *or still.*
Yes.

He had become once again, as in his youth, a great letter-writer. Page upon page flowed from his garage apartment to friends, old teachers, past loves. Behind the glass wall out of which he watched squirrels, milkmen and young mothers, as spring gave bent to summer and fall hung heavily on the trees, he went on inventing a life without her.

He thinks of Merwin: When you are gone the knives come out of the mirror like sharks.

He thinks of Cendrars: *Je suis l'homme qui n'a plus de passé.* I am the man with no more past.

A newspaper litters my table.
I work in my empty room, behind a blind window,
Bare feet on red tile, and play with balloons,
        a child's trumpet.
I am working at THE END OF THE WORLD.

Newspapers (even before coming here, where there are none) he could never abide and would not allow in his flat. There was altogether too much information abroad in the world already. Minds were unnecessarily littered with facts, with inconsequentialities. In the end all one could know was oneself, and all else was distraction. The settlement itself echoed this, its tonsure of hillocky trees yielding to the illimitable grey plane of desert, that eternal present.

Here, indeed, he pursues a monklike life, circling forever in towards himself. Time draws back from him, uncertain, watchful. He wakes to the sound of birds in the trees outside his window, passes the morning over books and tea alone, in the afternoon walks, alone still, in the hills. There are no more letters. Nights he takes a simple dinner (bread, cheese, leftovers, fruit) and waits for her to come to him.

Everything he is, is contained in that waiting.

At this still center of a turning world, at this place that *will* hold, behind the shoal of hillocky trees, he reclaims himself and retrieves his life. Everything moves slowly into focus on the pages, in his mind.

After she has fallen asleep against him he rises, goes to the table and, finding an abandoned scrap of paper (the front of it bears a few lines of poetry), writes in telegraphic fashion what, tomorrow, will become a new chapter, now only words.

One measures a circle beginning anywhere, he thinks, standing at the window. Finally it doesn't matter which moment of a man's life we choose to examine, because the whole life is within each moment. And it doesn't matter what one studies—a leaf, a stone, a door, oneself—since everything is there.

Everything resounds with meaning, everything depends on our interpretation of the silence around us.

For a long time he stands looking out into darkness.

Against the window she undresses as he wonders why he bothers. Not with her, of course, for she, her visits, are closer to sacred than anything else in his life, but with all the rest. All this scribbling at innocent paper, this endless scrimmage after truth, these words rising over his head like balloons, *larger* than his head, more substantial.

Sometimes her body, there beside him, for a moment seems enough: the heft of her breast, the swell of flat back into buttock and thigh. In certain music— Shostakovich, Mahler's First and Ninth, Willie McTell, Robert Johnson, Cajun minuets, Mozart always—he finds the same abandon. And in literature, of course, though decreasingly so.

Yet this body by which, almost daily, he finds his way back to the world, this solitary bridge joining him with others of his kind (and even that bridge, perhaps, failing), remains to its owner a source of gentle shame: she is uncomfortable with it. As he lies holding one breast in cupped hand, thinking how he could not, *would* not, live without these times, these bright, quick moments, he holds also the skein of scar tissue where one night long ago she attacked that breast with the shards of a dinner plate thrown against the wall moments earlier by a man she had lived with and did not see again. Another time she waked on a ventilator in ICU, furious to be alive, raging at her failure. Each man in her life encircles some catastrophe, and he sees no reason to believe that he will be any different. Sometimes a face drifts towards him in dreams, and it is familiar, but he cannot make out its features. He supposes there is something it wants to tell him.

In the plaster ceiling above them a pattern of cracks echoes the scars on her breast. Similarly, their dialogue spiderwebs out from some central collision, a momentary, imperfect penetration.

He remembers old apartments and houses of friends chock-full, in that long-past life, with *things*, as though to counterbalance the emptiness of the occupants' lives, and looks about him at the spareness here, the simple bed, table and chair, the Mexican pitcher, simplicity of this place and landscape.

Her gentleness amazes him. Once he tied her arms and legs, spread apart, to the bed, and toyed with her, teased her, then (with kindness, yes, and with love) raped her. Watching tears course down her face below him, bearing tiny stones of mascara.

Another year, and the ground pulls harder.

He enters her from behind, as she wants him to, breasts tumbled into his hands, that long slope of her back and her faceless, hips working into him, the deep rumble of her pleading, her breath tearing at sky, and when she comes, he is shipwrecked, heaving.

It is not necessary to understand, he thinks. It is not even possible. Her visits are closer to sacred than anything else in his life.

Morning opens around them as she has opened for him. Her eyes empty into blue rivers, into sky. He cannot hold her back. He will not live without her.

You have gone when I get up, something I have come to accept. And no longer try to read what the child has scrawled on the wall with his crayons, or the map on the ceiling above the bed. Or to move the mask aside, touch you.

Last night others came and nailed mosquito netting to the ceiling, all around the bed. I woke as they entered the room. Watched white shoes move beneath the edge. There was silence and the sound of doors closing. The head of each nail a different color.

I pick it up from the floor where it lies by the mail slot: If you go out today you'll come home with a bullet between your eyes. He comes about this time each day. The last one said: I love you. There were fifteen signatures.

Somewhere out there you are working. It's autumn and you rake leaves towards you. Put them in little jars labeled oregano, basil, bay, thyme.

Below, classes were letting out, and students came pushing past to throw themselves onto the tracks down by the library. Well, that's one solution, you said. The river's another. The last of the records falls onto the turntable. The arm is so high it looks like a tiny crane. Mahler's First.

Cold here, and I wonder. Was I happier when I lived in the old furnace downstairs, before you found me.

I ignore the knocking at the door. It stops, something is set down, it starts again, with two hands now. I know you're there, he says, and the pounding starts again, stops again. I know you're in there, damn it. Silence for several moments. Are you listening to me. Listen to me, there's still hope, you have to know that. He beats at the door again. You've got to believe that. He is quiet for a while and goes away. At the window I wait, watch him walk down the street with books under his arm. He has stopped off to see the girl who lives below me, and she stands by the house now crying. She throws herself under the first car that passes. I know you have sent him because you could not come yourself.

Perhaps like Ionesco I've never succeeded in becoming completely used to existence, neither to that of the world, nor to that of others, nor above all to my own. I refuse to believe the fault is mine. I've tried. Perhaps the evidence you send me is not enough. At night I hear the projectors whirring like insects in the dark. And you lie awake beside me struggling to decide what will be sent tomorrow, what I will hold onto.

I have the sense there is something under your skin that, if I touch it, disturb it, will come forth, rise as though from beneath broken water. Then once you say: In three days' time, darkness will ask me to dance. I will make other arrangements. The next night this girl, this woman, was beside me.

But also this. One night, very tired, when I went to sleep. Saw the door open and someone like myself come in, but he had a fox's head. Walked to my desk and put a paw on the papers there. Left a bloody mark. Then came over to the bed and looked down. Said: You're killing us. And went out the door.

I know it's autumn, for the child has brought from outside colorful leaves to press and paste into books.

Taking down the revolver from the wall now, opening one chamber to remove the pink capsule it contains. I am very old today, the sky is grey, I am not very well. Nothing can prevent madness. As an honorable man who abhors exaggeration, I do not know what to do.

Where I touch her, there are bruises. The print of lips on one breast moves as I speak. I am silent. She hands me pens, crayons, ink, paint. Says: You must finish the mask, give it features. The face beneath, she says, is plain, it waits for you. Sometimes I feel I know her voice. Anticipation has created a language by whose aid we can in principle examine everything, I say, looking up at her. Her features move, there, beneath the mask. She throws her hair back and moves faster upon me. And I flower, flowing upwards into her.

Perhaps tonight the others will return, with oars, or a helmet. Perhaps the child will stand by the bed again, beside us, crying: Stroke, stroke. Perhaps we will play again the game in which he smears himself with ketchup and screams.

At night you bring home dead letters from the post office where you work and we answer them.

There is not much light left in the lamp.

Each day the child comes home from school with a new coat. He hangs it in his closet and the next day brings another. Coming out of his room he holds up the hand I've left there, gaily wrapped, on the bed.

All the leaves are turning color, from the tip or edge inward, like a fungus advancing, some of them looking now, as I watch out the window, like tiny tiger masks, and one clump of them, bustled together (I just noticed), like a huge yellow orchid.

Everything would be dark except for this room, and quiet, but for the rain.

When the girl from downstairs comes each day to the door, I don't know if this is because you have sent her, or because she believes I know the man who comes with his books to tell me there is still hope. There may be other reasons. At night she stands under a light in the street below, looking up. Cars pass with a ripping hiss in the rain.

One day he doesn't come and looking down I see them tangled together in the grass below my window. His arms are out beside her, buried in garden soil to the wrists. And each time he rises I can see her mouth opening like a fish's. Small things seem to run out from under her body, into the grass and leaves to hide, each time his weight is taken off her; then she turns, hips up like a tent or caret, and with her face against the ground takes mouthfuls of dirt.

A single capsule remains in the revolver. Goldfish float at the top of the bowl and snails make their way up the glass sides towards them. (Those were the child's, or yours.) At the first chill of fall other snails will go straight to the earth, close the openings of their shells with lime, wait for spring. It's those small doors that sing when they're boiled.

The next day there are two voices at the door. There is still hope the voices said. Yes, I suppose there is. But thought of nothing, only hands turning, hands falling always towards the center of the earth, doors, voices, you. At the hospital you tried to walk through every door you saw. You'd start to say something, stop, and bang your hand on your leg. Turn away, shake your head, the words weren't there anymore. Your eyes were vacant rooms, pools of still water, soft stone, blue. I'll make other arrangements you finally said.

When you lean over and listen in the night now this is what you hear.

England's intellectual camels
Are going on safari; they will be accompanied
By two violinists, a turkey (because he speaks
The language), and a gang of nun assassins
From the West End...

"Also: Baron Someday, who prays for them.
And Quasimodo, one of their own kind,"

He says.

—To the desert, and they build a railway.
Or a tower. Haul in civilization on their backs.
They hang some effigy

Of a man outside
And sit in the sun playing cards. For them
The afternoon is precisely defined
By the sound of flies in the sun.

That first afternoon it reminds him of Peking,
The last time
He was there, it was autumn.

—Those accents over dust and change
(and his hand in the sun)
   They're all that's left.
—But it's sand.

Explosions on the hill: construction: a wind in the tents
At 30 miles an hour. One morning the third month,
Sanders sits there saying *Testing, Testing.*
The generator is dead: no repair, no petrol.
And the water almost gone.

(Till one day you find yourself
beyond the fields of ice,
too late. With hands
that make mistakes.)

5.32.9-.
Nothing continues to happen.

Your wife is a thousand miles away.
But there were times she lay alongside you in bed
And was farther. In their brown envelopes
Your letters pile up on the window ledge, unmailed.

There are no remains of the first expedition.
When I am dead, Pamela says. She is filing down
A leaf spring. Will you fasten
A goose to my grave
With a silver chain and feed it well.

Say yes. For all she's done and left undone, for you.
For the nights she came to your sorrowful bed,
For the way you became yourself inside her, at last.

The thing that's eating away her stomach and sex now.
Mornings she rose from the bed
And your own weight went with her.

Some mornings the Bedouins come to the top of the hill
On their camels and sit watching.

—Do you think they're all dead?
—Does it matter?

Today Ahmed and I sit by the tent alone
To watch the sun rise.
Ahmed refuses to speak English.
We are naked.
The sun does not rise.

I can tell you in a few words who I am: lover of woman and language, in terror of the history whose responsibility I bear, a man awake at night and alone.

Often, holding her against me and knowing what will happen, what *has* to, knowing her pain and destruction in ways she cannot, I wonder how two lives could ever come to this, how, having passed through so much, we come to find ourselves together here, on this improbable beach, wreckage of our separate ships, and the world, floating in the water around us.

There is at the same time a knowledge we move towards as plants do light, a knowledge we strive for (if we strive at all) all our lives, and yet another knowledge we do *not* want, which, given the barest chance, we will push away from us.

I do not question her absences, those days she is suddenly gone then, just as suddenly, returned. I make no mention of this new weight settling upon her. And when she sits the full morning at the window without speaking, I am quietly there with her, or working at the table nearby.

Do I still believe that I can make sense, or at least a pleasing pattern, an esthetic, out of all this? Sometimes it seems that I do; others, that I am able scarcely to keep madness at bay, that only these pages and her body (if anything at all) can save me.

For almost a week I have not seen her. There is a problem with the power station, electricity is rationed, and I am able to work only during daylight hours. I've spent the nights reconstructing my college philosophy courses down to the meanest detail: smell of the classroom, perfume of the girl beside me, color shirt I wore, weather beyond the windows. Perhaps (my intention seems to run) it is abstraction that confounds us, and only experience in its totality will give up whatever meaning, whatever lesson, it has.

All of this, of course—faith without belief, ethics and the moral good, symbolic logic, epistemology—existed in that other country where such things worked. But if ever philosophy was necessary, was of any use whatsoever, it should be necessary and useful now, in this too solid Republic.

Pilloried on his *shoulds*—that's man.

And Eva is woman. "I could be anyone to you," she told me one night when I woke and found her gone from my bed, standing outside in moonlight, "any woman at all, the thing itself, the quality," and certainly in a sense she was right. There *is* something elemental in her presence, just as there is to her despair, her refulgent anger, her self-destruction, something unreachable and abiding—like

Guillevic's dead, done with their dreaming at the bottom of lakes.

And yet I've seen her sit crying quietly at the beauty of sunsets, heard her beside me cry out again and again in terror of her dreams.

One of those dreams comes back to me now. I had to get inside the shell of a shark, she told me, and I was put into this tank where I had to learn to swim, to live, like a shark. There were at least thirty real sharks in there with me and they'd know at once if I didn't swim, didn't act, correctly.

Another time she said to me: All my life I have been at war with the world, a war largely undeclared and almost certainly hopeless, one carried on in brief, sudden skirmishes, guerrilla warfare really, an ongoing, gradually beaten retreat. She looked across the room as Mahler—tympani, cymbals, horns—broke about us. I can't retreat much farther, she said. Daylight pecked at the windows.

And Eva comes to me, putting her worn copies of *The Brothers, The Idiot, Crime and Punishment, The Possessed* on the table by the door as she enters. Sometimes when we are making love I reach up to her face and find tears there. Conversation about the past, our own or the world's, has become for us a kind of catechism to be touched upon daily, reaffirming, hollow.

I am done, and undone, she says, by the past.

I answer: Yes.

What has happened, is the world.

I respond: A part of it.

There is nothing I believe in, you know.

I know.

Nothing.

Yes.

Life as the reworking of a destiny by a freedom.

She senses that freedom not at all, and knows all *too* well the pull, the sluggish gravity, of the first.

And yet, through dreams—by way of art, of illusion, of fiction—we do, or can, reinvent ourselves.

He had hoped they would become to one another not substantial, but transparent, subjective life offered up completely, completely given, alongside the objective one they shared. That was one of his dreams.

To change someone, he knew from the first, you must love that person very much.

Perhaps the reverse is true as well, he thinks now.

Walking in the hills at evening.

To survive, to go on and to give birth to civilization, cities and civil suits, we learned to communicate, and now we've become compulsive communicators, unable to stop even when there's no more to say, unable to acknowledge silence.

And perhaps that, communication, is finally but another avatar of our compulsive pattern-making—of the art, music, literature and philosophy through which we impose temporizing form on the chaos we see all about us, because we cannot do otherwise.

It is the silence here that he loves and fears most.

From his wallet (why does he still carry a wallet?) he removes the only photograph he has of her. Poorly focused and fading with wear, it is a small one, half the size of an index card. In one corner he can see the edge of the table he uses for a desk, some papers stacked there. The bed is unmade. She lies facedown on it, nude and sleeping. He has no word for what he feels, looking at this.

Once, he understood so clearly.

And once, in stories and poems, perhaps most of all in the letters which preceded them, his vision of the world, what he saw, *entered* the world. But that vision did not change it, only made it a little more crowded, a little more choked with communication. Now unmailed letters stack up like newspapers, and in Rilke he encounters this passage:

> I mean to write no more letters. What's the use of telling anyone that I'm changing? If I am changing, then surely I am no longer the person I was, and if I am something else than heretofore, then it's clear that I have no acquaintances. And, to strange people, to people who do not know me, I cannot possibly write.

Change. Revolution. He cannot remember what that earlier man, that earlier world, was like. He tries to recapture waking beside her, the sound of birds in the morning, and cannot. He tries to recall the hopes or beliefs that led him to write the revolutionary poems, and those that let him go on living when she was away from him. He sees her face in the darkness above him; he does not see his own, but a stranger's, a younger man's.

He loved her, and she is gone. A copy of *Notes from the Underground* left behind on the table. It's the silence within the word that he burrows after now.

Each time she returned, there were new bruises, scars: her body's history. Towards the end she barely spoke at all, only watched his face as he came to her and went away, like a small, pale sun.

There will be nothing else like her in his life, nothing so central to it.

He looks down at the settlement, and other words of Rilke return to him:

> It submerges us. We organize it.
> It falls to pieces. We organize it
> again and fall to pieces ourselves.

At three that morning he gets out of bed and stands looking at the book she has left behind. I am very old today, the sky is grey, I am not very well. Nothing can prevent madness. As an honorable man who abhors exaggeration, I do not know what to do.

I do not know what to do, he says to the darkness. I do not know what to do without you, Judith, how to go on. I will have to make other arrangements.

For a long time he stands as though listening.

Then, sitting finally at the table, he begins searching for the right words to surround this silence, words that will take on the shape of her absence, of his loss.

II.

That summer strange fish, or I called them fish, were coming up out of the sea, and in the afternoons I'd leave the cabin and go down to the beach to look for them. That's where I found the girl.

She was kneeling at the water's edge with her back to me, her body bare and white as the sand, buttocks two perfect eggs balanced atop her heels. There were old cuts and bruises on the soles of both feet, brown hair cut straight across just above her waist. A few yards up the beach her clothes had been neatly folded, abandoned, like a patch of flowers on the sand. She was holding a fish out in her hands, the length of it lying inside her palms, where it fit precisely. It was amazingly bright, one of the most brilliant I'd seen: crimsons, gold. Fins ran along its body on either side, set low, and it had no mouth. She was staring into its eyes.

—It's a fish, I said. Dead.

She turned her head very suddenly to watch me. Her hands didn't move. A strong face, full of life but expressionless: Jewish? Slavic? Brown eyes.

A long quiet as the sea spoke on the beach and fell back into itself. Then she looked again at the fish. It was very still. Hair tumbled slowly off one shoulder, moved across her back.

—It's not dead. It's trying to breathe.

—Yes, I said. They all do. But look under the fins, near the front. You'll find a small pattern of purplish veins, like on a leaf. That kind never lives more than twenty minutes out here.

—Others do?

—One I saw, almost an hour.

She lifted a fin gently with the tip of her index finger. She was left-handed and wore a square plastic ring, transparent, blue.

—Then I could put it back, she said.

—It would only come out again.

Her back moved, and I think she was crying. I tried to recall how it had felt for me at first. Sometime it must have been more than the cages, nomenclature, symbology. But there had been so very many.

—Always?

I nodded.

She stood and walked to the water, buttocks swaying, no longer perfect. I caught a flash of scarlet and scales as she threw the fish out into the water. She stood there for several moments watching, then turned towards me. Her breasts were small and upturned, with a dark smudge near the nipple of the left one. She raised a hand to her eyes against the sun. Edges of sky and sea met inside the ring. There was a thin line of bluish fluid on her palm.

—Do you live here?

I nodded. —In one of the cabins, I don't know whose it is. It's quite small, though.

—And you are alone?

—Alone? Yes. For a long time now.

Halfheartedly she covered herself. —Any chance I might stay with you just for the night?

—If you'd like.

—Just for a while. You're sure?

I nodded yes. A jet broke suddenly above our heads and hurtled out to sea, leaving behind a heavy silence.

(I heard....

I think it was a bird.

I think it was singing.)

—Shall I get your clothes? I said.

As we walked away, the fish was dragging itself back onto the sand. There were some others following it.

Often I am certain that the sea repeats over and over, very distinctly, a secret I can almost (but never quite) make out. And yet its urgent, patient murmur continues, after all these years, after all we've done to it and to ourselves.

Our bodies repeat the landscape: the rise and fall of ground, of stone, the forms of our habitats, seasons, trees—what, then, when we come to the sea? The sea has no face. The sea is change, flow. The sea is a great level.

I lie awake at night in this odd pink light listening to crabs as they clatter at the pylons below and trying to find—in the sea, these ravaged fish, a pink sky—some form for my life. A habit I'd thought long abandoned.

Once everything was all *too* fraught with shape, with significance. Epiphanies flew from the points of our pens, insights leapt upon us in our dark rooms; we shuddered with understanding. And so much, everything, seemed possible. But the world shrank, or our own lives, like fears long shut away, grew huge, disabling.

So: everything leads to art, to the ceaseless clatter of these words. For how else will the legless man walk?

I turned in time to see her pull the shirt closed, button it. She took the cup in both hands and blew into it, sipped.

—You didn't know about the fish.

She said nothing.

—You seemed surprised, so sad, when I found you out there, I said.

—I'd heard about them, of course. She looked up, paused. —How long has it been like this?

—I don't know. I've been here a year; it hasn't changed much in that time.

She looked around. The cabin has only one room, and the wall nearest the sea is completely taken up with shelves. Earlier she had stood in front of those shelves for some time, staring into the still cages. Now she walked to the table I use as a desk, the wall above it bare except for a crude drawing in pencil: a fish with a noose around its body just under, or in, the gills. *Jane* was scrawled underneath, either as title or signature, impossible to say. At the point on the paper where the rope ended, a nail seemed to support both noose and drawing. A gold band hung on the nail.

—Why are *you* here? she asked.

I shrugged. —*The world is the case,* maybe. I don't know. I never seemed to have much reason for doing what I did; it was all just what happened.

I went back to the counter and started rinsing cups, pot and spoon with sea water from an orange and yellow Mexican pitcher.

—I came here with my family, a short vacation. And I couldn't go back. I was going to stay on a week; then another week. After three months I sent my wife a telegram: I can't. The drawing's hers—her reply.

I turned to her and smiled, then back to the counter with its camp stove and stacks of tinned or dried food. A preponderance of beans, a galvanized pail of rice.

—I watch the sea. I couldn't bear, any longer, watching the rest.

The room was quiet. Out the window I could see water heaving itself up onto the beach then giving up, lugging back. Either it made no sound or I had grown so used to it that I couldn't hear it without listening. A solitary gull skipped from place to place, the same places again and again, ten or twelve of them, as though it had hidden something, something very important, and forgotten where. The gull was silent too. Was it snowing?

—*For I don't know how to go to the end and I'm afraid,* she read from one of the papers on the desk. —You're a writer?

—At one time, yes. But that's Blaise Cendrars, something I've been trying to translate, I'm not sure why. *My eyes lighting old paths....*

She walked back to the cages and stood there.

—Do you know why I was on the beach?

—I know.

She nodded without turning.

—I've been here a year, I said. There have been many; the sea broadcasts some ancient call. The government can't stop them, and it doesn't try anymore. There are too many.

I waited, then said, —Crews come out every few weeks and haul away what bodies they can. Great tangles of human flesh, dead birds, fish, vegetation, industrial waste, oil slick.

I wondered again, as I used to do so often, how we'd ever conceived that we were something apart from the rest of the world we live in.

—Most of them are young, I said. The crews bring provisions when they come. I tell them where the densest clots have lodged.

I heard the gull cry once, a single stab of pain out there somewhere on the beach, in the afternoon. She turned at the sound and looked out the window.

—That's such a lonely, desolate sound. Somehow it's always made me think of aborted children. Do you have children—I don't even know your name, do I?

—Henry. And yours?

—Judith.

—Yes, I have a daughter somewhere in the world. And a son somewhere even farther away.

—You don't see them?

—I don't see anyone.

—Do you see me?

I nodded.

—And are you ever lonely, Henry?

—Only alone. There are too many people inside me for one of us ever to be lonely.

The gull shot out over the water. She smiled. The gull came back.

—And I can't remember a time I *wasn't* lonely.

—That's youth, in part. With age you learn to live in the past: so much happens to a person, and there's so little else to sustain one. You become all the people you've loved; what you have done.

—I almost had a child. I don't think I've ever been in love.

—Parents?

—My father is a vice president at Texaco. My mother is the coat by which he crosses every social puddle.

She walked around the room, touching the walls lightly with her hand, and stopped again by the shelves. The cages are about the size of shoe boxes, made of thin bamboo. There are perhaps a hundred of them. They contain the skeletons of fish.

—They're perfect, aren't they? So fine and delicate.

—Yes, I said. They are.

Outside, the gull was above the sun now, the sea still and red. Another log collapsed into fire. Embers shifted on the slope. There was a long silence: only the sea's churning.

—Will you stay with me? I said.

—For a while, yes, she said.

When did we first meet?

It was in Brownsville. A friend of yours was playing at the college and you'd come along for the ride. I came to pick him up the morning before he played. It was eleven in the morning. You were sitting outside the motel room with *To the Lighthouse* and a martini in a plastic cup, looking out over the lake. A snake stuck its head up out of the water nearby. You like Virginia Woolf? you asked me. I said I didn't know. Are you a feminist? you said. I told you I didn't know that either.

I remember how young you looked.

I *was* young. Twenty-one, a senior.

Studying English literature. "Reading" it, as the British say. I was thirty-nine, living in a garage and chiefly off the charity of friends, I had just finished a novel. The *Revolutionary Poems* were being published.

You said you wanted to touch the world with as few words as possible, to remain apart from it always just a little. You were publishing all those very short stories, three or four pages long.

So then I vanished into my garage and came out with a six-hundred-page novel.

Set in historical Poland, yes. It's still my favorite. And then, a couple of years after that, *Laying Waste*.

And after *that*, not much of anything. In the evenings you'd come over after work, at eleven or a little after. We'd drink and listen to music—Ravel, Bessie Smith, balalaikas. That was what I loved most, I always looked forward to it. Even after you were gone I went on trying to recreate it.

Yes. You could never live in the simple present, in what *is*. There always had to be memory. What you came to call *history* in the book.

Yes—and anticipation. The present always double diluted.

You were fascinated for a long time, I remember, by the Hopi.

And by the fact that *I* in every language is a short word.

You once said, Imagine a language in which the word for self is terribly long and difficult, while the words for you, he or she are monosyllabic, mellifluous.

I had forgotten that.

Have you forgotten the first time we went to New Orleans?

I spent a whole day in a barbershop there.

Soaking it up, you said, for an essay on Buddy Bolden you never wrote. Then driving back, somewhere in Mississippi you said, This could be where Bessie bought it. We passed a tiny hospital in Tupelo or someplace and you said that was where Skip James died. You hummed Robert Johnson songs the whole way.

And is memory all we have—myself here on this dying beach, you in dead London?

We have the past and what is left of the present. What more could there be?

Only the ceaseless clatter of these words, I suppose.

Every morning he puts on water to boil in the pan he uses for everything. He has also a skillet, two forks, two spoons and a sharp knife, a teapot and cups, an orange and yellow pitcher. He takes that first cup of tea outside and sits on what is left of a low stone wall. Sometimes he reads as he drinks and other times just stares out into the sky or sea. Afterwards he goes down to the beach to look for the fish who have made their way onto the shore and died there.

He spends weeks without the need to speak, and when he must do so finally, his voice sounds to him hoarse and alien; it is almost painful. Even in his head the words come to a stop. He can watch a sunset and have no name for it, never think: *red, beauty, night.*

Returning to words he always feels that he becomes another person. Returning to words he feels a quiet sadness unwinding within him. There is no word for that sadness.

Her breasts fit his hand, his long fingers, precisely. Her hips rise to him like the earth itself, reclaiming him. Waking in the night (for the insomnia does not leave him) curled about her and unwilling to wake her, the long line of her legs against his own, he wonders at things still unflattened. Not more than once each hour will he let himself move. And in the dark that shudders or clatters towards morning he improvises a catalog of heroes: Gandhi, Thoreau, Woody Guthrie, Che, Goethe, Voltaire, Clarence Darrow, Beethoven, Rosa Parks, the Rosenbergs, Rudolf Serkin, Esenin. Each night the catalog is different. Each day at dawn it stops: history coiled, waiting.

When he first met her (for *her* name, too, was Judith: lying awake beside her he recalls other women he has loved) she lived with two men already, alongside one in her own apartment and close to another across town in whose apartment (with its tiny Bonnard and Inness) she had her studio, and she'd had little difficulty accommodating a third. At one or two in the morning she'd get up to go back to one or the other of them. Always he would ask her to stay and she would say, I can't. He'd walk her to a cab and say goodbye.

At any hour she might show up at his place and ring the bell from the street below, bringing him cheese or apple juice, a red towel, a tea strainer like a silver witch's hat, many kinds of tea, *A Passage to India*, Barthes, the Brontes. You don't take care of yourself, she said. She was right. He ate whatever was at hand, drank endless pots of tea laced with sugar and milk, slept irregularly, read in bed half the day and wrote the rest. I heard you were sick, she said the first time after he'd looked down and seen her standing there by the door. Minutes later they were in bed, peeling dark tights away from her legs. She sat up and crossed her arms; under the sweater her breasts tugged upwards, paused, and fell into his hands. Towards the end she turned her face to the wall and opened her mouth soundlessly.

When he first met her she was with a friend, a writer, and seemed to him impossibly young, almost schoolgirlish. A week or so later she called him. His wife relayed the call to the upstairs study and asked no questions. I'm coming into New York this weekend, he said, and on that friend's floor a few nights later came into her bowled hips, and came, as she chattered on about the men in her life. His friend ground coffee for them the next morning. After that, whenever he was in town he would call her and she would always come to his hotel. Each time he saw her she was using a different name: Chris, Renée, Cathy, Suze.

His own fever, the room's coil heater, the smell of her sex—all these came together for him then. Years later he would look up from others' bodies and expect to see that same dull red glow in the room, those quick motions at the corner of his eye, to have again the sense that he himself glowed with his body's heat.

Once her mother had answered the phone (Christina is ill, she said) and told him that he should be ashamed of himself. You're absolutely right, he had said, but surely you *must* realize how very attractive your daughter is. Yes, I only wish she'd got something besides *that* from me, her mother said; it's so difficult rearing a child all alone. And from that day Dianne, a cellist who often practiced stark naked in her living room, pale flesh against the instrument's ancient dark gleam, took the place in his life formerly occupied by her daughter.

The sight of women, their smiles or downturned eyes, apparitions of arms emerging from sleeves, could so excite him then. Unaccountably, Chris's pelvis had failed to cant forward, remaining aligned on its prepubescent vertical axis; it was this which had caused her to appear at first so girlish, and the memory of it still filled him with longing, with desire. As did thoughts of Dianne, bow arm brushing against her breast (the Amazons' sacrifice), legs spread for the cello as she leaned forward into it and the music it gave her. Or Elizabeth's lisp (Elithabeth'th lithp?) on the phone at night.

She burned candles as she wrote strange and unsettling poems in which few sentences had subjects, her shelves full of Isak Dinesen, Doris Lessing, Virginia Woolf. Slept with all her husband's friends. Read to large groups at St. Mark's while their baby snuffed and suckled at breasts the size and shape of figs. Vanished one day, baby strapped to her back, shoulder bag full of notebooks and Dostoevski, in the general direction of Latin America. Three books published since. Answered no one's letters.

Or Nora: always so quiet, able to talk to him (and in that low, private voice always) only on the phone, turning her head to one side and downwards at night as though to hear the very sound of him moving inside her. And every morning there would be tears, slow, unoccasioned tears that never tasted of salt.

From the window of my garage apartment I watched women in their slit skirts and tight sweaters deliver children to daycare.

Your daddy feels like a broke-down engine, and the blonde with twins pulled in across the street. *Low-down, broke and lonesome:* the tiny, beautiful Vietnamese. I had discovered a cache of rare blues recordings at the university library and was working my way through them. *At a distance all women are erotic,* I wrote in a story begun then and completed many years later.

In the evening I composed long letters to old friends, wordage rising as the level of gin in the bottle fell, Robert Johnson's hellhound, his Terraplane, his crossroads, around me.

In the morning, most mornings, I tried to write.

Not much was finished. A piece on squirrels (because they ran up and down and leapt between the trees outside my window), another about crickets (who secreted themselves in kitchen cabinets and chirped all night long), a few poems.

I read two, sometimes three, books a day. *Frankenstein, Moby Dick, Lord Jim, The Master and Margarita, Man's Fate. L'Etranger* again and again while wind snapped and rattled in the trees just outside.

On most of one wall I stapled news photos of torture victims and mass murders in Latin America. In the overheated room these pictures yellowed and dried quickly, crumbling away from the staples so that there was forever a deposit of them, like fallen leaves, on the floor beneath. Though never lack of a fresh supply.

The wall opposite was hung with color reproductions of surrealist paintings, these affixed with map pins, many of them De Chirico. ("You *would* like surrealism," my wife had told me. "It's so *literary*.") Something about these brooding contradictions, contractions of reason, these frozen, timeless eras, fatally intrigued me, it's true.

To live, I think, we must forget, forget our own desolation and others' pain. And from my thirtieth year, suddenly, I could not. Sunsets ran with the blood of Salvadorans, shaded quiet pools gave back visions of Vietnam, Ethiopians died of famine as I wrapped *injira* about stewed lentils and greens.

Above all we scheme, not to survive, but to love and so betray ourselves into *choosing* survival.

Surely we dream the world, and ourselves into it. But to say that the world is illusion is not to say that it is not real, only that it is not what it seems (and who ever believed that it was?), that it is constantly becoming, constantly being made.

Even our nightmares, in their strange, forbidding beauty, hold forth wonderfully unattainable ideals.

"The final belief," Wallace Stevens wrote, "is to believe in a fiction, which you know to be a fiction, there being nothing else. The exquisite truth is to know that it is a fiction and that you believe in it willingly."

—The fiction of these pages, these scenes, these renderings? Half memory, half improvisation. Or the fiction of art itself, for it will not save us. Hoping to lure into the net of these deft metaphors something besides (for this part is true) dying fish, dead loves, defalcations.

Along the shadow of his roof on the ground outside he watches the smaller shadow of a squirrel move. A moment later the squirrel pokes its head over the edge, watching him at his work, the table, the typewriter. He does not move because he does not wish to frighten the squirrel. For several minutes, it seems, they regard one another, each motionless; then with a bound the squirrel is gone.

Cendrars sought salvation between the legs of women, certainly the only place (besides art) *I* ever bothered to look for it.

Moving into my garage apartment, I left wife and daughter behind. But some ties would not let go: Carol left bags of groceries on the porch for me, called (once I got a phone) almost every night, asked me out to eat at the Indian, Chinese and Ethiopian restaurants I adored. Paid bills and gave me money. Pot after pot of soup (vegetable, lentil, black bean, chick pea) steeped on the stove as I tried to deal with a difficult stew of remorse and abandon.

I saw other women, at first *many* other women and later on, chiefly, two.

One, burr-tongued, fair-skinned and slight, at thirty-five never married, was a Scot for whom Paris had long been home. The other retained her former husband's Indian surname, wore wonderful jewelry and read (unlike myself) one book at a time and deeply. I always had five or six, sometimes as many as ten, in various stages of use, a kind of literary peristalsis, places likely as not marked with folded squares of toilet paper; it was a standing joke. In earlier days I had not needed the place-markers. Now I did. In earlier days I had a family. Now I was alone, or nearly so.

There occurs a period of abnegations.

At first, unintentionally: the hot-water heater stops working, the landlord is slow to make repairs, and he discovers that in fact he rather likes the morning and evening ritual of heating water in large pots. Soon he is reading by the light of candles. He has for utensils a skillet, two forks, two spoons and a sharp knife, a teapot, cups, a pitcher. He has a few books; all else is put away. Until at last he has not spoken for weeks and has no idea of the date, the month, has almost forgotten the year. He sits looking out at this southwestern sky, his life now made up of small rituals and repetitions, yesterday's indistinguishable from today's, today's preparing tomorrow's.

Kucha nuptu, he says to himself at first dawn: the white is arising. Or later, *tala vaiyi:* the sky is painted with light. And at sunset, *tawa paki:* the sun has gone in.

He is very close now, he thinks, certainly as close as he will ever come, to being a Hopi.

From each room you can hear the work going on. Like Fouré cultists and Anabaptists of the late nineteenth century we had fled a shattered, confounding world for the sequester of communal life and (we so desperately hoped) Vanzetti's serene white light of a reasonable world. Yet still our lives looked back, to what was lost, not gained; and painfully we tried to understand, each of us in his or her own way, in stories or poems, in paintings, in music, there at that rag end of a raveling (not reasonable) world, what had become of the one we knew, of its reason, its clarity. Dimness everywhere now: in that

cobalt sky, our own intentions, the corners of drawers. And so you sit listening while in the kitchen Laura's typewriter clatters rhythmically, regularly,
setting down sentences and paragraphs completed already in her mind while
doing dishes and other chores or walking, and while Robert's in the library
stutters (a word or two at a time, a pause, a rapid deletion, another sputter
of thought) towards whatever difficult end or meaning it may contrive, that
curious old Remington, for him, in him, to him.

In the bedroom Marie wonders about her daughter.

Somehow we always knew that the choice was annihilation or withdrawal,
and this, the house, our art, became the first of many retreats, our lives a
series of anacoluthons. The lyrical gift, you argued one evening before our
communal fire (as others sat reading, over chessboards, back to back playing
flute, or was it recorder, duets), consists in a suspension of time; the more
time is allowed its motion, the more narrative a work must become. We
looked out on that cobalt sky, into the corners of memories, the expectation
of pink mornings. (Apparitions of arms emerging from sleeves?) Everything
accumulates, you said. Everything accumulates, but all we ever have is the
present, this endless goddamn present. *Wer, wenn ich schriee, hörte mich
denn aus der Engel ordnungen?* you asked. And now (for, as I write this, you
are at least as real as crabs clattering at the pylons below) you are at the same
time there listening and beside me, as you were then, in the tottering dawn,
and you go on with Rilke:

> Yes, the Springs had need of you. Many a star
> was waiting for you to espy it. Many a wave
> would rise on the past towards you; or else, perhaps,
> as you went by an open window, a violin
> would be giving itself to someone. All this was a trust.
> But were you equal to it? Were you not always
> distracted by expectation, as though all this
> were announcing someone to love?

Yes, I was, always, again and again. Yet I remember all of you: the way
your skin felt against my own, the smell of your hair, the exact weight of your
breast, my sad face turning towards you like a planet.

I lay against your cold body for a long time that morning. I didn't know
what else to do. So little to remember of you, so much dimness. At last I rose
to make the necessary calls. I should have known you could not leave this
world, that it could not go on without you.

For many years Robert lived in the basement of an apartment house in Boston. His possessions were trunks of clothes long outgrown and out-moded, boxes of books and records put in storage by former tenants and left, forgotten. Each morning he removed a single newspaper from the stacks and read dutifully of the assassination of Kennedy, a demand for equal rights in Montgomery, Czechoslovakia's occupation by Russian troops, Senator McCarthy's capers, a new college or mental hospital dedicated by Governor Earl Long. He cooked kebabs in the furnace on long skewers made of un-wound hangers. He was happy there with his newspapers and books (many of these, schoolbooks; he had, for instance, eight copies of *Walden,* all of them in mint condition) and rarely left the basement. He thought of moles, Morlocks, Emily Dickinson's "Before I had my eye put out," Plato. When, rarely, tenants came downstairs to deposit new boxes or for another reason (one man descended almost weekly to rummage through an assortment of men's magazines in a box of his there and to masturbate in one corner before returning to his wife on the third floor rear), he hid.

On one of these rare outings, though, near the ranked mailboxes in the entryway, a girl smiled at him, a girl not at all special, in fact rather plain (though *he* soon made her special), dressed in old jeans and yellow T-shirt with the pocket torn off, and with bare, dirty feet. Before long she started coming down to see him at night. They'd sit by the fire and read *Bleak House* or *The Magic Mountain* together, taking alternate paragraphs. Then she started staying. That was fine for a while, but he was embarrassed when the tenant from third floor came down (she hid with him, and loved it), and he realized that he missed being alone, missed his old solitude (though sex after they watched was great), and that he *changed* when around others, something he began to think of as a kind of reverse alchemy. But then he recognized that it was not alchemy, not magic of any sort, only that limitless Jeffersonian leveling, only Tocqueville's "great beast," the lowest common denominator, water seeking its level, democracy.

He moved into an apartment some miles away where he lived off coffee and stale bread, listened endlessly to Mahler, and wrote four novels (the first of them mawkish, the last excellent) about Patricia.

It was always arcane knowledge that we pursued; you know that now. Early fascination with science had given way to passions for magic and conjuring, astrology, religion, contemporary poetry in several languages, quantum theory, the New Novel, Buddhism, obscure musics, obscure heroes.

Now he lies in this pink light alone and can think of nothing more arcane, finally, nothing more secret and recondite, than the attractions of a female body; of no knowledge more mysterious than this heaving, deadly sea, this raveling, universal end.

First I must tell you that I do not know what to tell you. I am as uneasy here as yourself, as uncertain; only I've had more time to become accustomed. It is a strange place.

I have watched you walk along the beach in the half-light of morning, looking out into the sea's reaches, and I remember.

Tonight there is only sea, sky, a thin grey nerve of horizon. All day I have tried to write, to read, to understand something of this moment I'm suspended in. Where once there was history, there are only events, days, the endless accumulation of this present.

In your brown shirt and green shorts you could be a bit of woodland come to homestead the beach. A latter-day Daphne in the first stage of transformation, maybe: any moment you will be nothing but a laurel tree. I look at your footprints as though hoping that some message or meaning might emerge from them, learning only, finally, that my island is inhabited. (Had I doubted this?)

How many days have I watched you? Then when you are gone, editing the film in my mind: advancing past frames, slowing your motion, freezing this frame of partially bare breast as you lean over to pick up a shell, splicing in shots of pink and grey sunset, considering subtitles, dubbing. I have the very stuff of time here.

Like art and totalitarianism, memory bends the world to its own designs.

Something must happen—and that explains most human commitments, Camus wrote.

Perhaps soon we will meet.

Sifting lentils (tiny, perfect stones) into orange turmeric and mossy coriander. Saffron set out in one of the cups half full of hot water. Rice coming to a boil.

—What did you do? for a living?

—I taught.

He turns to look at her.

—History and French. Music sometimes, just to fill in.

—You play...?

—Cello. You?

He shakes his head and turns back to the stove, thinking about Emerson's correspondences.

—I've not had Indian food before, she says after a while. Where did you learn to cook it?

—I lived in London years ago. I didn't have much money and could eat well at Indian restaurants. I loved it when I first tasted it and grew to love it more. Finally I bought some books and began learning more about it. The whole thing's improvisation, like their music.

—What were you doing in London?

—In approximate order, editing a magazine, trying to stay alive, recanting the U.S., and falling in love.

—With someone in particular, or just generally?

—With a lot of things. With being alone, with living in an alien society, with the perspective that gave me on my own. With a girl named Pamela. With tea and the food you're about to eat.

—Pamela was British, then?

—Oddly enough, no: she was American, though I didn't realize that at first. She'd been in London a long time.

—What happened?

—Happened?

—With Pamela.

—I'm not really sure. I loved her, though. I couldn't call her and would wait all day hoping she'd come by. I'd walk her to a cab stand early in the morning, felt boots slapping through London slush, then return to the electric heater's red glow and, hours later, the jangle of milk bottles with their red and gold caps. She was more or less living with two other guys. I guess I kind of backed out of her life without intending to; I've done that before, and since as well. I guess she probably settled in with one of those other men; I don't know.

—She was a writer too?

—A teacher and hopeful painter.

—How did you meet?

—We happened to leave a dull party in Kensington at the same time and shared a cab. At last I gathered courage to ask for a phone number and was given three. I reached her, at the first I dialed, the next afternoon. We met at the British Museum beside William Blake's *Ghost of a Flea*.

—And you made love that night?

—As a matter of fact, not for some time afterwards. We walked through the museum, out into London streets, out of and into tea shops. She brought me cheese and apple juice. I boiled too much water on the stove, raising the level of entropy in the world. Ate chocolate-covered "biscuits." Read Dickens, Sylvia Plath, Tom Disch.

He listens. There is a crash of sea onto beach. The caw of a gull. Wind rises.

They sit for a long time over rice as yellow as sun and dark curry, talking of London and the boat across, languages, weather, Pamela. When he left, there was a flurry of letters, often two or three a day, letters he somehow never answered (he meant to) yet has kept with him, through all the disjunctions of his life, to this day. He recalls lines from a friend's poem: I loved her more than any/but with the same disabilities.

Eventually they make love. In the dark he looks up, expects the glow of the heater's coil, hears only whispering sea. In her sleep, afterwards, she murmurs beside him, *like* the sea.

When Buddy Bolden played, you could hear him miles away, all across New Orleans, and what he played (his band's horns pawnshop-cheap, relics of Civil War military bands) was a new music, a new tradition at odds with the classical, European one, music coming in a jumble from popular tunes of the day, brass-band numbers, ragtime and blues, the call-and-response of African song, African instruments, and free in a way its players could never be, dissembling, pure improvisation, the very squeezings of a moment in time: this is how our century began.

In embracing aleatory music, the *late* twentieth century, by contrast, underscored principles of chance and randomness, of the arbitrary, then perceived as controlling. For chance was certainly to be preferred over its Manichean alternates, and within *them* lay paranoia, madness, or worse.

Madness found Buddy Bolden there in those New Orleans streets as it had, years before, in other streets, similar streets, found Nietzsche. And madness sang Buddy Bolden a new song: his world was transfigured, his heavens were full of joy.

I hear your tears in the dark, their slow gathering. The disjunctures of film-time become our own. Days and nights break around us. You had hoped this would be different, yet never could believe it. The beauty of rain, the beauty of stone. Should I touch you now, or wait.

The disjunctures of film-time became their own, past, present and future running together in a kind of temporal plaid. Events were prefigured; memories eclipsed into fanciful flashbacks. Everything was design and converging lines. The last few minutes would explain it all.

Just so, they had come somehow in those final years to believe that a good and just world would at last come into being if only they could bring about the overthrow of certain evil powers and institutions. It made them (I must tell you) a little crazy.

Leaves fall from calendars. The city grows, with time-lapse photography, huge in three minutes, its long fingers moving against the sky. Flowers appear and vanish. Suns arc above in a succession of bright Venn diagrams. Snow falls, and corn comes out of the snow wrapped in green corduroy. Pans on the stove boil too much water.

Yes, it all seemed clear, Lamia fled, but a few frames left before the credits. Leda's sex withered and sere.

And so it is evening all day. They watch the sea grow quiet, the glow of fires further inland, tasting ash and sand, desire but another part of their history now. Even an audience must know the end; it cannot end well.

We understand, and burn.

I sit remembering the gull cries in Harry Partch's *Daphne of the Dunes* because you are gone; thinking of the glow of heaters, Hopi verbs, daily crimes, the Crimea. I read a book given me almost thirty years ago, a copy of the collected T.S. Eliot inside which my brother inscribed: *dichterisch wohnet/Der Mensch auf dieser Erde.* Holderlin, who withdrew from *this* world into his own imagination and a carpenter's quiet house.

That summer you came to inhabit, there in the copse of forest and cinder block, your own island, ballooning above the silent lives of orderlies, nurses, attendants, your mind ablaze with understanding, ever hot on Friday's tracks. You were alone. In the afternoons (you told me this later) you wrote dense and intricate letters to me, letters never sent, typing them up just as though they were manuscripts, name and return address, word count, broad margins. Once as you sat by a window in the day room typing, a cricket emerged from within your typewriter, as though given birth there.

As though, yes—because you were lost in thickets of symmetry, marooned in a world where everything connected, everything *meant,* and you *had* to get its meaning.

You told me that you could feel your body turning to something insubstantial, something like dew, like ash or sand.

You saw in the window the eye of a whale, apparitions of arms emerging from sleeves, trees bereft of birds, the ravage of morning, your own terrible face.

What pure improvisation: the remaking of a world. And then you came back to me, for a while.

I lay against your cold body for a long time. As though if I did not move, it would not be true. Slowly dawn shaped itself around us. I listened to birds, the far-off drone of a plane, voices. And knew instantly the rest of it: this beach and pink sky, crabs clattering at the pylons, these cages, the gull's cry. As though remembering it. As though the future were already past.

They found me early the next day. Tides had swept me back in and I was lying on the beach staring up at the sun with my mouth gaping open and shut, body not moving at all.

This year the fish are all grey. Or white, like the ice. I still call them fish; I don't think they are. They come to the surface and float with their bellies up and they're dead, all of them, I think. The sun is bright, orange, maroon, and the sea's an impossible blue, like her ring. But I don't go down to the beach anymore.

It's summer again. Again. We watch crabs emerge from the sea (ignoring its babble) and make for the trees. They seldom make it and when they do, rot on the limbs like fruit. Beside me on dry earth scattered with sand sit the Mexican pitcher, an untouched pot of tea, inviolate stack of paperback books. Yellow moon in the sky.

—What are we waiting for? she says. She is lying on the ground beside me; she lifts her head and turns her face, two separate motions, turtlelike, to watch me. Pain waits in her eyes. —Please talk to me, she says. I have sat all morning without moving, here in this deck chair by the cabin.

—We are waiting, I say, for the end of the world.

I can see it far off over the water, moving towards us.

about the author

JAMES SALLIS has published over two dozen books including ten novels, multiple collections of stories, poems and essays, three volumes of musicology, a biography of Chester Himes, and a translation of Raymond Queneau's novel *Saint Glinglin*. His work appears frequently in such publications as the Washington Post, L.A. Times, Alfred Hitchcock's and the Georgia Review. He contributes quarterly columns to *The Magazine of Fantasy & Science Fiction* and literary website Web Del Sol, and a monthly column to the *Boston Globe*; plays with a number of bands; and in his spare time teaches at Phoenix College and at Otis College in L.A.